PARALYSIS

A NOVEL

JEFF D. COPELAND

C&C BOOKS

PARALYSIS
A C&C Books Edition

Copyright © 2003 Jeff D. Copeland
Cover Art by JD Copeland
Typographic styling by JD Copeland

ISBN: 0-9741617-0-5
Library of Congress Control Number: 2003096651

C&C Books®
www.CC2Books.com
Richland, Washington
First Printing, November 2003

PRINTED IN THE UNITED STATES OF AMERICA
10 9 8 7 6 5 4 3 2 1

ACKNOWLEDGMENTS

A novel has a life that is not always understood, often taking the writer down unexplored and mysterious avenues. The one literary constant is that there are no constants, only challenges, mountains to be climbed. I would like to believe that during this adventure, I have expanded as a person as well as a writer. I have been stretched to my mental limit, and have seen and experienced more than I thought possible. For these reasons, I owe so many. How do you thank those who have helped you achieve a dream; you immortalize them in print.

My wife Lisa has lived the highs and lows, has inspired when direction and hope were lost. To her, I owe my love and life. My children, Adrienne and Allyx are the architects of my heart, the windows to my emotional strength and weakness. To them, I owe what I am today.

On a less philosophical note, a special thanks to Carol Lake. My editor, agent, friend, and New York travel buddy, you were the first to believe when there was so little there. Steve Wallenfells, screenwriter extraordinaire, your suggestions gave PARALYSIS (including the title) a push toward greatness. Jerry Gross, you lifted me to the next level. Michael Seidman, your advice during our meetings in San Diego and on the internet (beware of those who have no eye for talent) inspired me to chase a literary moon. Elizabeth Engstrom, with a backdrop like Maui, how could you be anything but fantastic? The retreat, and its amazing people, gave me focus and a will to survive. Torena O'Rorke, you have the empathy of a writer and the heart of a lion, and I look forward to your next novel. Debbie Takata, you challenged me, pushed me, and opened doors that I might not have otherwise ever passed through.

There are so many others, it would take another book to thank them all. But there is one more, LaVonda Kellogg. Your energy and love for PARALYSIS will help bring it to the world.

Strange that science, which in the old days seemed harmless, should have evolved into a nightmare that causes everyone to tremble. One should always question.
—Albert Einstein (1879 - 1955)

October 20, 1933 — *The Nobel Prize for Medicine was awarded to Dr. Thomas Morgan for his discovery of the chromosome's function in determining heredity.*

April 20, 1940 — *Radio Corporation of America's laboratory in Camden, New Jersey, publicly tested the first electron microscope. It magnified images up to 100,000 diameters.*

October 18, 1962 — *The Nobel Prize for Physiology was awarded to Dr. James Watson of Harvard University, Dr. Maurice Wilkins of King's College of London, and Dr. Francis Crick of Cambridge, England for their discovery of the molecular structure of deoxyribonucleic acid (DNA).*

August 28, 1976 — *A scientific team from the Massachusetts Institute of Technology synthesized the first bacterial gene and successfully implanted it into a living cell.*

June 16, 1980 — *The Supreme Court ruled that organisms genetically created in the laboratory could be patented.*

October 14, 1980 — *The Nobel Prize for Chemistry was awarded to Dr. Paul Berg of Stanford University for his work with gene manipulation and recombinant DNA.*

June 4, 1984 — *A scientific team from the University of California at San Francisco cloned the cells of an extinct animal.*

October 9, 1989 — *The Nobel Prize for Physiology was awarded to Dr. Michael Bishop and Dr. Harold Varmus of the University of California at San Francisco for their work with retroviral genes.*

May 5, 1995 — *Congress held hearings to establish whether scientists had the capability to genetically engineer a retrovirus that could attack the human immune system.*

March 4, 1997 — *President Clinton restricted federal funding for genetic experimentation. He urged private-sector scientists to enact a similar moratorium voluntarily, while government advisers reviewed this ethically troublesome issue.*

November 28, 1998 — *United Nations inspectors discovered documents that detailed Iraq's experiments with genetically altered viral ribonucleic acid (RNA). They accused the Iraqi government of testing the altered viruses on unsuspecting nomads living along the northern Kuwaiti border. Iraq expelled the UN inspectors and their findings were withheld from the public.*

December 21, 1999 — *In a joint session with British Prime Minister Tony Blair, President Clinton ordered increased military action against Iraq, accusing them of developing biologic weapons of mass destruction.*

June 26, 2000 — *President Clinton announced to the world that the human genome had been successfully mapped, opening new doors to future genetic achievement.*

October 12, 2001 — *A letter containing genetically purified, military grade anthrax was opened in Senate Majority Leader Tom Daschle's office. Thirty-one people were exposed to the deadly virus.*

March 17, 2003 — *World Health Organization issues a global alert for an unidentified infectious virus with deadly pneumonia-like characteristics that has caused serious worldwide fatalities.*

June 13, 2003 — *An expedition deep into the heart of the Amazon Lowlands discovered a lost tribe, suspected to be descendants of Mesoamerican Indians.*

October 3

11:18 a.m.—Amazon Lowlands, Brazil

Tealoc held his fists against his temples as he fought another headache. Pain blurred his vision while his bare feet slipped along the muddy trail. The green world around him began to spin and he struggled to keep his balance, but was too weak.

For the third time in the last hundred paces, Tealoc's knees buckled. He stumbled and fell to the ground, where he lay motionless, tangled in a web of wet leaves and vines. A steamy haze settled over him, engulfing him, deepening his isolation. His heart thumped inside his bare chest and his lungs labored with short erratic wheezes—the time was near.

On his pilgrimage to die amongst the gods, each tormented step had taken him farther from his village, his home, and his family; he had done this in accordance with the Ritual of Passing. At the first light of dawn, Tealoc had entered the jungle to purge himself of his earthly desires. Becoming part of the jungle after death was his duty, the destiny of all humanity, and there was no greater honor. The gods had selected this path to show him and his people their beginning and to help them reach enlightenment.

He sought divine acceptance and had obeyed the custom without question. Yet at thirty calendar cycles, Tealoc, Watcher of the Night, heir to the Keeper of the Record, was not ready to die, not like this. Why had Fate brought this degradation upon him? A fearless and proud warrior should lose his life spirit at the hand of an enemy, another warrior, not some merciless disease. If only the medicine given him by the village elder had worked, maybe then, he would have stood a chance. It was not meant to be. The disease invading his body must have come from another world; an omen. What had he done to shame himself before the gods?

Sunlight splintered through the forest canopy, slicing the bluish mist thickening above the jungle floor into ghostly apparitions. All around him, Tealoc sensed the mystical presence of his ancestors. They were there to guide him on his last journey, his Vision Quest.

Voices echoed through his misery. "This is your domain, your destiny," they whispered in the ancient tongue. "You must not be afraid." Their words comforted him, sending a soothing warmth through his body.

Tealoc reached out from where he had fallen and forced his fingertips down the center stem of a large fan-shaped leaf. Just beyond his touch, a small yellow orquídea gave off an iridescent glow. The sight reminded him that he had not enjoyed the sweet scent of the jungle for more than two moon cycles. How he missed the smell of the animals, flowers, and rain, even the cool earthy aroma of the ground on which he lay. Could the paradise the gods offered be more beautiful?

Something rustled in the mossy trees towering above his head. Tealoc looked up and tensed for the attack. It didn't come. Before long, he heard the excited shriek of a troupe of spider monkeys, then he saw their fleeting shadows dance among the snarled branches. He sighed, safe for a moment, but soon, scavengers would prey upon his helpless body.

His eyes barely open, he scanned the undergrowth. Pain and death were familiar to him, for the jungle contained countless forms of each. The bite of the acoralado snake, the sting of the venenosa plant's spiny bristles, and the unpredictable swarm of the killer abeja: danger had surrounded him his entire life; it was all he knew.

Unable to move, Tealoc's throat constricted and he choked, coughing up blood and gasping. He filled his lungs with every ounce of air that he could take and focused on the tribal teachings, freeing his terrified mind from the torture he endured and the fear he faced.

The Burbános people believed their essence ascended from the jungle's humid moisture and they lived to pay homage to the gods. As heir to the Keeper of the Record, Tealoc recalled the fables told by the elders, the chosen storytellers. Those written chronicles detailed his people's past and provided guidance for their future. A specific passage held his thoughts: "Beware of the bearded White Devil of Death, and take heed, for a tormented end will befall those who meet him."

The legends of the mythical being had been handed down for more than four-hundred calendar cycles, and until now, Tealoc had assumed they were tales of a lost past. Nothing made sense to him anymore. Had the White Devil caused this sickness? His body sank deeper into the decomposing vegetation littering the jungle floor. Sweat soaked his matted black hair, and rain pelted the ground, intensifying the pounding in his head. He had never been so confused, so frightened.

Leaves covered his face, and he prayed for the gods to end his agony. His eyelids fluttered; he had seen his Vision Quest. Humanity's trials were to be experienced to achieve spiritual immortality. Though his pain had become unbearable, he drew courage from his ancestors and through cracked lips recited the sacred beliefs.

His eyes slowly closed and he visualized his children playing, running through the village. He saw their innocent faces, heard their laughter. Next to his hut, his wife and eldest son stood silently, watching while Tealoc waved good-bye for the last time. The memories eased his anguish. They had accepted his decision and understood his fate; it was best for all.

Blood seeped from his nose and ears. He beckoned the stillness of the jungle to take him, but within the darkness came a sound foreign to his surroundings. Something was wrong and he fought to open his eyes. His strength failed him and his spirit edged closer to the Afterworld.

As the vacant shadow of death stole his soul, Tealoc's last mental image was the noble face of his firstborn son, shimmering white above him.

8:25 a.m.—Central Coast, California

Matt Wells watched a living, breathing, academic legend move among the students. "Good morning, class," Dr. Christopher Ruhpor said as he set his notes on a small metal desk. "This is Soil Microbiology 432, and for those of you who want to escape, now's the time."

Although a petite Asian girl in the front row squirmed, no one raced for the door. Not knowing what to expect, Matt considered that a reassuring sign. Dr. Ruhpor had a reputation for eccentricity and for causing academic burnout. The many undergrads who had suffered through his tests compared the experience to a Machiavellian disaster, and the homework load ensured his surviving students led a life of personal purity. Then there were the Doc's lectures, which carried the dynamic resonance of a great orator. His gestures were animated and fluid. The tempo of his voice rose and fell in a hypnotic rhythm while he captivated his audience with wit and wisdom. Information flowed from him like water falling from clouds during a gentle spring rain.

According to the hallway gossip, the Doc's lectures

were an experience worth the anguish of a test or two from hell. Matt just hoped the rumors were true and that he hadn't made a mistake by leaving San Diego and coming here.

"Since you've decided to stay," the professor continued, "let's get started." He went to the whiteboard and wrote, VIRUS. "An unknown fact to many people, viruses are amorphously ubiquitous micro-creatures, which mostly originate in soil. Many are dormant in their native habitat, waiting until they encounter the right host. Can anyone give me a list of typical viral entrance pathways for a human host?"

A demure looking girl seated near Matt raised her hand. She glanced his way. Obviously hoping to go unchallenged, her expression gave him the feeling that she would faint at hearing even the slightest impolite word. His heart went out to her. He was surprised that she had volunteered.

"Uh . . . well . . ."

"Yes, Leila." The Doc gave her a paternal smile. His sun-dried facial features seemed to soften, and he drew answers from her with a guiding tone. "Take your time." With the calmness of an ancient Tibetan mediator, he raised her confidence using simple body gestures, a nod and an occasional smile, until she was more comfortable expressing herself before the class. Matt was impressed.

After a deep breath, she began. "Viruses enter a host by, uh . . . ingestion, inhalation, or by coming in contact with a fresh wound, while some can even penetrate healthy skin." The hair on Matt's arms tingled.

"Very good." He gave her a respectful nod. "Thank you, Leila. Keep in mind, sensitive membranes associated with the eyes and genitals are also vulnerable."

Matt crossed his legs.

"Once inside the body viruses flourish with the hunger of a ravenous animal. They invade and consume. Their victims are never the same." The Doc's eyes widened and his mouth contorted, transforming him into the embodiment of an insane Mr. Ruhpor. The visual metaphor reached home with the students. "In essence, a virus mutates within the host, sometimes even taking control." He twirled a whiteboard eraser, his gaze fixated on the spinning object. "Picture it. A living organism now resides in your body, reproducing at will . . . and there's nothing anyone can do. Your only salvation may be death."

Matt whispered under his breath, "An optimist."

Wandering through the room, the Doc stopped at the window, where he set the eraser down and leaned on the sill, gazing toward the university clock tower. At first, he said nothing, and then, without turning around, he spoke softly. "A virus is nature's most efficient predator. Its entire genetic structure has one goal: find a host and feed. What's the disadvantage for an entity with this parasitic future?" He turned quickly and tossed the eraser to a guy seated on the far side of the classroom.

"Paul, heads up."

Apparently, no one slept during this class without a certain level of personal risk. Paul snagged the eraser out of the air with one hand and pitched it back. The professor caught it easily.

"Your views on the subject?" The professor bowed, relinquishing the floor.

"The way I see it, the host could die, and so could the virus."

"Good answer." He beamed. "However, when the host doesn't die, the virus can grow even deadlier. As it is now feeding and spreading within a living carrier."

"What about genetically derived medications?" another student asked.

The Doc went to the board and wrote DRUGS next to VIRUS. "Why not take a pill? Granted, we have made significant strides in treating viruses, even have a few vaccines, but it's not easy. The tenacity and mutating ability of many viruses have shown the frailty and limitations of modern medicine." The Doc paused, and dipped his head. "I predict, anyone who finds a way to effectively combat viruses will retire wealthier than Bill Gates."

A chuckle moved through the classroom. The professor had piqued their interest. They hung on every word, anticipating more academic morsels.

"Because of their resilience to standard medical treatments, viruses have created an economic boon for many medical researchers. Commercially, hundreds of different viral strains are studied worldwide. To date, the only real defenses mankind has had are the human immune system and natural geographic barriers."

"Dr. Ruhpor." A female student, seated to Matt's right, raised her hand. "Sweet looking." Matt smiled. She ignored him.

"Allyx." The Doc gave her his full attention, as if everyone else in the room had disappeared. His eyes held her movements, read her lips. The Doc and this girl had a connection. Matt wondered what it was.

"Would you agree that natural barriers don't really exist anymore?" She had a pleasant voice, clear and low-pitched. The Doc gave her a nod and she continued. "Airplanes and other forms of intercontinental transportation have mobilized many geographically restricted viruses."

"Your assessment is quite accurate, and that's where the difficulty lies. The day when mountains were too cold and deserts too hot has ended. We kindly provide viruses with protected passage over the mountains and across the deserts." He refocused his attention on the rest of the class. "Not only can a virus move more freely with our help, but we're also unlocking new regions in the world where strange and deadly viruses have remained dormant for eons."

The Doc checked the wall clock. "I'm sorry to leave you hanging, but that will be all for today. Please grab a copy of the handout before you leave." He waved Matt over. "Could you stop by my office tomorrow morning around eight-thirty?"

"Uh, sure thing, professor."

9:25 a.m.—San Francisco, California

Ben Singular entered the boardroom of Janstone Pharmaceuticals' cobalt-gray high-rise. He checked his watch and swiftly made his way to the conference table. The burgundy carpet rebounded under his black wing tips. He set his briefcase on the tabletop, unlatched the locks, and wondered.

Only once before had they met in the boardroom. Steele had a reason for everything he did. The man never left anything to chance. So why had his client picked this particular location? Ben tapped his knuckles on the table's dark mahogany surface, contemplating their meeting and the room.

The massive conference table commanded the boardroom's center stage. Hand cut from the Peruvian rain forest, the wood's swirling grain pattern continued unbroken for its full length. Dim white light cast down from inset ceiling lamps reflected off its glossy surface. Two dozen high-backed leather executive chairs bounded its perimeter, each with a brass desk lamp and tan suede, writing pad.

Ben rolled his shoulders, releasing the stress while his eyes scanned the accouterments. The room provided for distraction. Leading figures in the fields of politics and medicine gazed down from photographic portraits on the cherry wood wall to his right. Presidents Truman through Bush were aligned in a row to the west, and Surgeons General Burney through Carmona trailed to the east. Personal inscriptions on many of the photographs commemorated the pharmaceutical company's dedicated service in advancing modern medicine for over four decades.

A fully stocked wet bar, flanked by six double-pane windows and a panoramic view of the San Francisco skyline, occupied the boardroom's northwest corner. When the heavy burgundy curtains were pulled back, Ben knew the city's Fortune 500 companies and their imposing skyscrapers dominated the horizon like a forest of ancient redwoods. Today the curtains were drawn, cloaking the bar and the boardroom behind a veil of subdued darkness.

The door on the opposite side of the room opened. A moment later Jolon Steele strolled in, carrying a small gift-wrapped box and his signature Cuban cigar. He made his way along the conference table, stopping in front of Ben.

Steele set the package on the conference table. No amenities passed between them. Their meetings always started like a sparring match, forcing Ben to remain cautious of Steele and his motives, never willing or able to trust him. It was not like that in the beginning. No, they had evolved into adversaries, a relationship of need, nothing more.

A few feet away, at the limit of the reflected light, Steele stood, eyeing Ben the way a pit bull probes for weakness. Ben waited, lingering within the perceived safety of the boardroom's empty shadows. As the unbearable silence continued, tension crept back into Ben's shoulders, contorting his neck muscles with wrenching spasms. He hated these premeditated face-offs, but what else could he do? Their project had already altered the direction of modern genetics, and any error in judgment would ruin all they had accomplished.

Jolon Steele's powerful presence never ceased to amaze Ben. Steele was an impressive figure dressed in his pinstriped charcoal Armani suit. A touch of gray accented his jet-black hair, offsetting the hard-cut wrinkles framing his yellowish gray eyes. Starting with his tailored suit and ending with his expertly groomed hair, no detail was ever overlooked. Even his substantial stature, over six-foot-three and two hundred and ten pounds, added to his aura of ultimate control. Except for a few minor scars on the palm of his left hand, Steele was the persona of physical perfection. Ben suspected that down to the smallest detail, Steele knew how to get what he wanted and would sacrifice anyone who got in his way.

"Status report," Steele ordered. A wisp of bluish smoke escaped from between his lips.

Patience and compassion were not virtues Steele valued. Ben shuddered, afraid to speak his mind. To Jolon Steele, performance and profit were all that counted. That attitude had helped him rise before the age of fifty to the presidency of a Fortune 100 pharmaceutical company.

"Yes, sir. Subject 29-b3 entered the jungle at two-twenty-six our time this morning. We dispatched a recovery team and our surveillance cameras are recording the collection." Ben opened his briefcase and removed his notes, twisting a pencil between his thumb and index finger. A compulsive urge to pace burned inside him. He gritted his teeth and met Steele's cold stare.

Ben was a geneticist, unaccustomed to this cloak-and-dagger stuff. Principally an academic, he was a gifted researcher, seeking cures to the illnesses that plagued humanity, and at thirty-four, he was unprepared for the tension of backdoor negotiations. Even his wife had commented on his deteriorating health: the blackened circles growing below his brown eyes, the new white streaks that had made their way to the surface of his wavy brown hair, and the extra fifteen pounds he carried. He swore she had an electronic spreadsheet documenting his sagging health. Truth was, Ben Singular had aged even more than his appearance suggested. He assumed that was the cost of success.

How did Steele do it? He looked to be in his late thirties, not his mid-fifties. The man thrived on stress, the type of individual who lived his job. Even so, it must take its toll. Ben's stomach knotted as the digestive acids churned.

Steele's eyes never wavered. "What was the location's Effective Contraction Rate?" Standing half a head taller than Ben, Steele scowled at him, shooting questions as though he were interrogating a junior accountant over a budget error.

Words stuck in Ben's throat. His pencil snapped in two. "Uh, yes . . . the ECR . . . uh, well uh . . . it increased forty-three percentage points compared to the last run. Two additional subjects contracted the test virus after the initial exposure."

It was not the answer Steele wanted. Lowering his head, Ben hid his contempt for the man. How could Steele speak that callously about living beings? Did he not care for anyone? They were statistics to him, a convenient tool to a profitable end and nothing more. Ben wedged two fingers under his paper-thin, red virgin-silk tie. He couldn't breathe.

"The dormancy was less than sixty-three days, and the most recent subject showed no outward signs of infection."

"Unacceptable!" Steele's eyes narrowed—darkened. "The ECR has to be above the 90th percentile by the end of our fiscal quarter. Does your team grasp this concept?"

"Yes we do, but you have—"

"But, nothing!" Steele slammed his fist on the conference table. "Do not give me excuses! Timing is everything. I bought results, not excuses. You have two weeks to push the ECR up another seventeen percentage points." He stroked his cigar with his fingertips. "I expect you to achieve our goal on schedule."

"Yes, sir. We will." Ben's knees trembled. He hated himself for his show of cowardice. Men like Steele did not fail, nor did they tolerate those who did. Failure on this project meant Ben's professional death sentence.

At that instant the realization hit him. Steele's financial enticement had been a monetary lure. Ben was trapped. He had been living a delusion, seeing only the need to save his company. Stunned by the implication, his eyes traced the woodgrain pattern of the conference table. Somehow, there had to be a way to protect himself and his employees, his people. The brightest biogenetics team in the world worked for him at BenaTex, and this project guaranteed their economic salvation. What other choice did he have, but to see it through?

"Oh, and Dr. Singular."

"Yes?"

"You might want to keep a close eye on that son of yours. The beaches of southern Baja have seen their share of crime. I would hate for anything to happen to such an aspiring young mind. And before I forget." Steele handed Singular the gift. "Tell your son, happy birthday, the next time you see him."

"But . . . how did you—"

*　　*　　*

Jolon Steele directed the distraught Dr. Singular out of the boardroom and returned to his office. A satisfied smirk crossed his face as he closed the door and approached his desk. Toying with Singular's mind had been a pleasurable distraction, although manipulating him had taken longer than Steele had anticipated. Regardless, he now had Dr. Singular right where he wanted.

Singular's Achilles heel had been his precious company, or maybe the people he employed. Either way, it did not matter. Steele had simply cast a brighter financial light on BenaTex's future, and that was all it had taken to master the brilliant geneticist, Dr. Ben Singular. Snared by his own naiveté, the man had no clue of what he had done. That was business. Some succeeded, while others were buried alive. And if Singular ever strayed too far, a little applied leverage on his son would correct the doctor's attitude.

Steele crossed the room and one of his trusted vice presidents rose from a chair.

"How did the meeting go, sir?"

"As expected, Mr. Garver." Steele rounded the corner of the desk. "Did you make contact with the Ambassador?"

"Yes, sir, but I don't like it. He's a disgusting human being. And if the White House gets wind of what's going down, they're gonna be—"

Steele's stare stopped him.

"It's . . . it's just during the hearings we informed the President and Congress that genetics technology wasn't far enough along to reengineer a retrovirus. Though we admitted having the capability of exploiting a few general viral characteristics, we stated wholesale adjustments were still beyond our grasp. Five to ten years was the forecast. If the oversight committee ever discovers otherwise, there'll be serious repercussions."

"If they do, and I emphasize if, it will be too late. The project has been put into motion. We will have our retrovirus." Steele noticed hesitation in the man's posture. "The current administration is too preoccupied to challenge us. They need our support for the success of their futile Global Economy program."

Again, Steele mused, even governments had their price. It had been easy to hook the President with his sagging foreign policy. He wanted a legacy, and Steele's international contacts provided the appropriate motivation, swaying political opinion in all the right places. The peon had no idea who really determined the attitude of the world. Large corporations had been deciding the fate of countries since 1599 when England's East India Company bartered for their first slave along the Ivory Coast. All governments had their internal vulnerabilities. Exploiting that simple fact was part of the game.

Politicians were full of themselves, and so easily manipulated.

Yet, Steele's political and financial successes never seemed to be enough. He remained tormented, unable to affect the inhuman treatment his race had endured under western colonialism: their society destroyed, religious beliefs blotted from history, and people thrown into slavery. The once great Maya empire had been reduced to a tourist sideshow.

Christianity had brought this plague upon his people, and soon, the tide of human suffering would shift. From the lands of the Yucatán to southern Guatemala, voices haunted him to lead his people to glory. Steele had a destiny to fulfill.

Few knew of his Maya lineage. The planning had spanned three generations. His corporate pedigree had been carefully constructed, and his rise within Janstone Pharmaceuticals professionally orchestrated. Who would suspect Jolon Steele had a hidden agenda: resurrection of the Maya empire?

Since the first Spanish rapist set foot on Maya land, there had been war. Even now, the hunger for freedom burned deep within the hearts of his people. A mere two thousand Zapatista peasants took over San Cristóbal de Las Casas and five other regional towns in 1994, shocking Mexico and the international community with their boldness. Sadly, their uprising fell short and their voices were never heard.

Contrary to the lies spawned by the western news media, the taking of Japan's Peruvian embassy in 1997 by MRTA guerrillas had gained the Maya nothing except more martyrs. No, it was obvious to Steele; the elite ruling class of the western world must be driven to their knees. He swore to unite the Maya and finish what his Zapatistas had started. There would be no peace. The revolution would be won. Mexico, Portugal, Spain, United States: all who had enslaved the Maya would atone in terror for their crimes.

However, no victory ever came without some losses. And although death was an enviable path predetermined by the gods, the course Steele followed called upon even more Maya to lay down their lives. No individual was greater than the common goal of unconditional conquest. Though pain purified the soul, the pending loss of so many believers cast a darkness upon his conscience. Steele recited a silent vow to remember their offering. Their sacrifice would also be their salvation.

It was almost within his grasp to upset the balance of world power. The political connections and the growing financial influence were his to command, but the retrovirus gave him the physical muscle. Once unleashed, nothing could stop his lethal creation, not even the awesome power of the United States. His genetically engineered bug was deadlier than the most modern army; a silent killer, programmed to infiltrate and destroy all in its path. Steele suppressed a satisfied smile. Before long, the North American landscape would be changed forever.

Leaders of the world would taste what his people had endured for centuries; the demoralizing anguish of subjugation and persecution. Those who did not readily adopt his vision of a new world order would be consumed. Jolon Steele would not be denied his place in history. The blood of his enemies would flow as an infected river across a barren plain.

The prophecies were quite specific: a leader of the Maya would show himself and open the gates to Earth. Then in the year 2012 of the Gregorian calendar, Quetzalcóatl, the Feather Serpent man-god, would cast out the unbelievers, the Christians. This time Steele allowed himself a small smile. Through the strength of his gods, he held the future of the world. Nothing could stop the second coming.

He looked into the eyes of his vice president. The

fool had no idea who he dealt with.

"But, sir. The Ambassador represents a rogue terrorist group. If the White House discovers our—"

"It will all go as planned, Mr. Garver. I assure you."

Steele waited, watching. The continued silence ate away at Garver's resolve. Profit, that is all this idiot understood—predictable and manageable. He saw the perspiration bead on Garver's forehead, another underling whose usefulness had neared his end.

"I control the Ambassador and his puppet revolutionaries, just as I do those contemptible Washington politicians."

"We're taking a big risk, sir. These people are extremely dangerous."

"Wrong again, Mr. Garver." Steele lit a wooden match and watched it burn. "Like the fire I hold, they exist only for as long as they are useful." He pinched the flame between his fingers. "Do I make myself clear?"

"Perfectly, Mr. Steele."

"And Mr. Garver, before you leave, what is the status of the other gentleman?"

"He will be here tomorrow by 11:30 a.m."

"Then that will be all."

9:36 a.m.—Golden Gate Bridge, San Francisco, California

Traffic on the Golden Gate snarled itself to a complete stop and Ben Singular impatiently tapped the leather steering wheel of his loaner BMW 532e. He wished his own car was not tied up with maintenance. Lately, nothing seemed to be going right. The confrontation with Steele. His son.

What the hell did Steele mean? How did he know? Only three people in the world knew Ben had a son. Not even Matt Wells knew Ben Singular was his father; a secret kept buried for over two decades. That was Steele—always prying, even during their brief initial meeting, he had probed.

Almost nineteen months earlier at the BIO-Europe Conference in Cologne, Germany, Ben had a feeling that Steele had checked him out, looking for hidden skeletons. A month after the conference Steele surprised Ben even further by pitching him the retrovirus project, packaging it with an irresistible financial offer. Within two days, they had sealed the multimillion-dollar agreement with a simple phone call, changing the future of BenaTex forever.

The thought of saying "no" to Steele had never crossed Ben's mind. Why would it have? Steele had an industry-wide reputation for identifying talented people and promoting alternative technology. Most companies would have given anything to work with the man. He was recognized as a genius in the field of viral pharmaceuticals and a Twenty-first Century innovator of genetic medicines. His charismatic appearance before Congress in the early 1990s saved the Human Genome Project, setting the stage for embryo cloning and a new generation of medical miracles.

Looking back, Ben wondered if he had moved too quickly. Had it all come together too easily? The retrovirus project started like any other, and then the demands began. At first they were small, a tweak here, another there, eventually Steele's influence grew and so did his domineering behavior: additional secrecy requirements, subtle changes in the retrovirus' design characteristics, and more input into the decision making process. It took only a few months before control slipped away from Ben.

And now it appeared that Steele's interest had extended beyond BenaTex and the retrovirus project.

What did he want with Matt? Steele had to have an ulterior motive. Ben glanced over at the wrapped box resting on the passenger seat. Steele knew Ben could not give Matt the present.

Sure he did. Steele was too thorough. Everything was calculated, predetermined. What could Matt be worth? Could he be used as a blackmail source? How did Steele find Matt? With all the complications in his own affairs, Ben could hardly keep tabs on his son. "My son . . . oh, damn. Not now."

Steele's intervention might prematurely force Ben to do what he should have done a long time ago. . . .

It wasn't even two months into his freshman year at Yale when Ben met the girl. He remembered the wave in her hair, the curve in her smile. Lorie was young, and so was he. They dated and became intimate. Things happened—an unplanned pregnancy. Ben could not raise a child, not if he wanted to continue his studies and go on to graduate school. The cost, the time: they were too great a commitment. He had a vision, and a child would have changed everything. Lorie would have nothing to do with an abortion or adoption.

Without warning, she disappeared; quit school, and moved away. Everyone had been caught by surprise. Ben was left alone, stunned.

He regretted his decision, forcing her to flee, to handle the future on her own. Counseling might have helped them. His words were too harsh, and she took their meaning wrong—too many complications. How could he have been expected to see clearly?

At only nineteen and just starting college, he was afraid his dream of becoming a top geneticist was about to crash. It wasn't right for her to leave. They could have found a way.

Those were lean times and Ben did not have the financial resources to search for Lorie or his child. He had to wait and focus on his own needs. Fifteen years would pass before he found them; and a lot had happened during those fifteen years.

Was Steele forcing him to deal with the past, or

was this another veiled business manipulation? Ben set his hand on the gift, rolling the red ribbon between his fingers. "What a mess."

He tugged on the ribbon and peeled back the blue wrapping paper. What would he find? Should he even look? His heart migrated into his throat as the package fell open.

Inside of the plain box was a polished black steel picture frame. The traffic began to inch along, covering about a hundred feet before stopping once again. Apprehensive, he removed the frame and viewed the photograph, studying the image as the car ahead of him crept forward. It was a grainy eight-by-ten, black-and-white glossy of a handsome young man and a beautiful blonde kissing on a beach somewhere. "Matt . . ."

12:48 p.m.—Amazon Lowlands, Brazil

The torrential rain dissipated and all movement ceased beneath the forest's lower canopy. An eerie quiet had taken hold. Not even a breeze passed through. Only the thump of water droplets falling from leaf-to-leaf eventually impacting the muddy ground filled the soundless void. The heavy damp atmosphere seemed to conspire against Commander Bill Stripes as he and his two men moved along the overgrown trail. They had fallen behind schedule. Nothing had gone as smoothly as the desk-soldiers had planned.

Another branch on a hidden bush snagged his pant leg, and Stripes grumbled. Frustrated with their slow progress, and contrary to his own orders to keep the noise down, he ripped himself free. His entire team was having difficulties. Their bulky antibiological clothing and equipment kept getting in the way. They had been lucky to make two hundred yards in an hour. Even so, his men did their jobs well, silently suppressing their physical discomfort.

They needed to reach the fallen body before decomposition started, and in the heat and humidity of the Amazon that meant minutes. The efficiency of the jungle to digest dead organic material boggled his mind. This place was a massive composting bin, and what didn't disintegrate on its own was either picked apart by insects or devoured by carnivorous animals. Stripes surveyed the trail ahead. Maybe they could cover some territory now that the rains had ended, but he worried, knowing this giant mulcher would soon kick back into high gear.

Stripes verified their Grid Four map position, then took a GPS reading. He compared the map coordinates with the data shown on his hand-held global positioning system computer. Out of habit, he used a compass to confirm the result. The distance from their current position to the downed Indian was forty-five yards east. They'd get there soon enough, and he knew what to expect.

Telemetrically operated minicams concealed within the Grid had shown the body going down in a small clearing. The cams, powered by miniature solar-electric motors, had monitored the Indian's movements since he started his fateful journey. Their electronic downloads streamed by way of a line-of-sight transmission above the emergent layer, the uppermost canopy, to a processing station located a thousand yards north of the Indian's village. Passing through the station, the video images bounced off a privately owned communications satellite to a remote location in North America. The entire process took less than ten microseconds. In essence, Northern Eyes observed the Amazon events in real time, and those same devices would record the recovery of the corpse by Stripes and his team.

Though Stripes valued the accurate intel, he had to admit, the thought of someone peering over his shoulder unsettled him. They were always there, critiquing his actions. If he had a choice, they'd be gone. Stripes did his best work alone, in the shadows, on his own terms, not at the pleasure of some techno-nerd sitting at the dumb end of a video screen. He was an old-school mud-slugger who distrusted anyone who hadn't gotten wet. But that wasn't how things worked in the modern world.

As Stripes blocked the mental distraction, he caught the subtle hesitation of his team's point man eight yards ahead. Stripes stopped moving, checked the perimeter, closed the distance, then crouched down and waited. His man also remained low to the ground, barely visible among the native vegetation. He probed the terrain, one-step, then another. Raising an open hand, he gave the "all clear sign." Stripes acknowledged the signal with a thumbs-up okay and pointed to his own eye, instructing him to stay on watch.

They had found the location, time for the team to get ready. Stripes held his neoprene gas mask in place and yanked the straps tightly behind his head. He hated the damn thing. The constantly fogged glass plate added yet another inconvenient level of difficulty to their mission.

A final adjustment to the mask's placement and he pulled the biosuit hood over his head, sealing the edges with duct tape. He tapped his number two man on the shoulder, receiving a comprehending nod. They moved together into the clearing while their point man swung left behind a branchy rubber tree, guarding their backs.

This was the fourth subject to go down in the last two weeks and Stripes had no reason to suspect anything unusual. Still, as they closed in on the body, he and his number two man remained cautious. Training always overrode complacency.

They knelt next to the dead Indian. His black eyes remained open and unresponsive, just lifeless sockets staring at them while they removed their rucksacks. Stripes unbuckled a side pocket and extracted a vibration sensor. He guided the device's rounded tip down and along the Indian's throat, and as expected, found no sign of a pulse. With a nod, he signaled Number Two to begin the transport procedure.

After hacking away the shrubs and readying the site, the men went to work with practiced precision. They lifted the Indian and placed him on a sterile rubber-like tarp, which also served as a work pad. Removing the victim's loincloth and feathered necklace, they examined the exposed flesh for insects and other foreign matter. Although none were found, his number two man treated the corpse with an insecticide and a bactericide to eliminate a possible infestation during transport. Each procedure was executed with extreme caution. One mistake and the ground team would suffer the same agonizing death as the Indian.

Stripes wrapped the naked body with three layers of transparent Mylar film, a by-product of recent advances in aerospace technology. The material was thin, about three millimeters, yet it had the strength of a fiber-reinforced polymer. The film clung to itself, forming a pseudoskin covering that would contain the Indian's deadly bodily fluids and prevent oxidization of the remains.

The wrapped corpse was rolled inside a black bag lined with two inner layers of PVC plastic and an outer protective layer of Gore-Tex®. Stripes helped Number Two stuff a dozen small field-maintained ice pouches beside the body and hermetically seal the bag. After inspecting their work, Stripes connected a small hand pump to a polypropylene tube and vacuumed out the air. He replaced a third of the original volume with nitrogen contained in a small, pressurized bottle, then sealed the tube. Stripes stepped back and inspected their workmanship. He gave Number Two a satisfactory nod.

Their mission had gone well. His ground team was very proficient.

10:50 a.m.—Arabela, New Mexico

Five miles southwest of Arabela, located within the eastern rain shadow of New Mexico's Sacramento Mountains, the observation post for the White Sands Missile Range had not served anyone, except snakes and rabbits, since the late 1970s. A weathered chain-link fence encircled the compound. The main gate angled to one side, teetering on its last surviving hinge. Next to the road, a wooden one-person guard shack stood abandoned. Targeted just inside the doorway, a laser motion sensor projected its narrow red beam across the compound's entrance—just one of many passive security devices strategically hidden throughout the abandoned facility.

A hundred and fifty feet past the main gate, up a dirt road and surrounded by three corrugated metal buildings, stood the deserted listening tower. Enveloping its northern leg, a dust devil swirled into the air, snatching tumbleweeds and launching sand at the three cars parked in front of the easternmost Quonset hut.

Margaret Hines turned her eyes away from the window overlooking the desolate view and glanced at her watch. It was time to make the call.

"Dan, this is Meg." She spoke calmly into the receiver, confident in her ability to handle things. "Sorry to disturb you, but Rick and the techs are gone for a few minutes, and we're ready for a pickup. . . . Yes, that's right. Minicams recorded everything. Subject 29-b3 is being prepped. . . . I'll take care of it. Thanks, you too." Dan Noble was the North American team's project head and one of the sharpest men she had ever met. He was decisive while always willing to listen, an unusual combination for someone who wielded such power.

Meg activated a satellite-linked transmitter. "Glow Bird, this is Northern Eyes." She waited for half a minute. "Glow Bird, this is Northern Eyes."

A speaker above Meg's head crackled, followed by, "Northern Eyes, this is Glow Bird." She keyed her transmitter. "Glow Bird, we have a package ready in Grid Four. What's your ETA?"

"Northern Eyes, twenty-six minutes."

"Sounds fine, Glow Bird. Go to station 42-3 and hold until the ground team signals you. Please repeat."

"Bird, copied. Will hold on station 42-3 until signaled at Grid Four. Hey, babe, how're things in computer land?"

The attention brought a grin to Meg's face. Damn 'copter jocks, they're all the same immature kids flying big metal vibrators. "Stick to radio protocols if you don't want to lose your toy."

"You're a dud, Meg. Bird, clear."

She smirked. "Northern Eyes, clear."

Flirting with the boys was okay, but what Meg loved most was having state-of-the-art electronics at her fingertips. She could touch anyone, anywhere, within milliseconds. Computers, satellite systems, and electronic encryption devices: the latest technology filled the room, and it was all hers. Meg experienced a sense of power when using her high-tech toys to direct the movements of an elite group of mercenaries. The men on the ground and in the air were her very own lethal weapons. Meg had heard some say that she was the Company's cerebral cortex; nothing happened without her.

At twenty-six, she had freelanced her computer skills into the Federal Government's Black Ops programs. These were the covert espionage actions that no one discussed publicly. Her reputation as a crack computer programmer had quickly circulated through Washington, DC's inner circle, and a secretive group that operated on the legal fringe recruited her. They had few requirements and a simple code: "Our allegiance is to those who lead from the front."

Proud of her accomplishments, she tipped her chair

back and laced her fingers together behind her head. Compared to her other assignments, this one was the easiest. The location assessment indicated a low threat potential to her team, and the pay was excellent. Within a couple of weeks, they would close shop and move on. Ah, but first there would be a brief side trip to Tahiti for a sordid vacation.

Meg laughed. If her college buddies could see her now. She was the only female within three hundred miles who had more than two dozen, studly men at her beck-and-call, and had billions of dollars worth of the world's most advanced electronic gadgets to tinker with. All this and she still found time to direct a team of proficient killers marauding on another continent. What more could a girl want? Meg smiled, not bad for a dark-brown-haired mousy daughter of a corn farmer. The plains of Iowa were definitely a long way from the desert sands of New Mexico.

On those rare occasions when Meg recalled her past, especially her reclusive college experience, she accepted the years had hardened her. Meg had evolved into a loner, which must be why she gravitated to this special kind of employment. Hers was a disconnected friendless line of work. Oftentimes, there was no one else around; it was simply Meg and the field teams linked via satellite communications.

Northern Eyes' electronic devices enabled her to examine events and coordinate the action without knowing how it felt to be in-country. Meg had often wondered what it was like to be in the middle of a ground-op, where decisions had immediate consequences. A gloomy sense of detachment began to bother her. She shook it off. No worries, stay centered, all she needed was a vacation, nothing more.

Meg spun her chair to the right and faced the computer console. She punched in an authorization code and initiated a systems diagnostic, having no reason to deviate from standard maintenance procedures.

Lights flashed along the console as each subsystem responded. Meg watched the electronic kaleidoscope with satisfaction. She folded her arms across her chest, pleased with the system's performance. Her software design had given Northern Eyes the real-time visual capability they were now using. That stroke of computerized genius had earned her a fat bonus and a stronger voice in how things were done. Whoever said a mercenary had to weigh more than two hundred pounds and slog through snake-ridden swamps? This was the age of high speed optical processors and Quantum Physics after all.

Meg kicked her feet up on the counter next to the communications interface computer and sipped her coffee. It wasn't always fun and games. Some sacrifice went with the seclusion and long hours. Her personal lifestyle ranked a negative two. Relationships were held to a handful of trashy one-night stands. Then there was Rick, her boss. Now, he had a nice physique. She laughed, and a beautiful mind of course.

Closing her eyes, Meg visualized him lying naked on her bed. Six feet tall, medium length sandy blond hair and icy blue eyes: her definition of a real man. Meg had stumbled into an affair with him, but even that stopped before it had become too serious. Rick had ended it, which was too bad—for him.

1:12 p.m.—Amazon Lowlands, Brazil

The field team consisted of three men on location while another two hovered in a helicopter two hundred feet above them. Each man on the ground was a specialist in jungle tactics and surveillance. All were expert mercenaries, able and willing to kill without hesitation; that knowledge comforted Bill Stripes.

He pulled a small radio transmitter from his rucksack and switched the homing beacon to on, then clicked his FM band throat microphone. "Glow Bird, this is Ground Team One. Do you copy?" While waiting for a response, Stripes reached down and touched the body bag. Even through the multiple layers of protective plastic, he felt the emptiness of a meaningless end, and it made his skin crawl. He was accustomed to death, but mercenaries were hunters, not scavengers, and collecting bodies after they dropped grated against his personal code. Everyone had the right to fight for life; these poor bastards hadn't even known what hit them. What a pathetic way to go.

"On location, Team One," responded the hollow sounding voice of the approaching helicopter pilot.

"Glow Bird, package is ready for pickup."

"Ground Team One, hold your position. We're lowering the cage on your mark in forty-five seconds."

"Team One, clear." Stripes hustled back a couple of yards, blending in with the thick jungle greenery. His number three man remained hidden in the bushes; Number Two crouched down six yards to his right. He didn't have to see them to know they were in position; training dictated their actions.

Stripes and his team had been together many times before, the last in Angola, where there had been a trained adversary. Angola . . . a whole world away. This godforsaken place had no trained fighters, only victims. How did he get into this mess anyway? Shit, never question a field op, especially not during one. What was he thinking? The mission had eaten its way under his skin, that's what. How would he die when the time came? Bad thoughts, wrong thoughts; Stripes needed to get his head on straight, get focused.

An aluminum cage broke through the trees, eighteen feet above Stripe's head. He moved to one side and watched. The cage swung left, suspended by a cable attached to a noise-suppressed AH-6 helicopter holding above the jungle's uppermost canopy. Signaling Number Two with a thumbs up, Stripes stepped forward.

"Glow Bird, this is Ground Team One. How do you read?"

"Loud and clear," the pilot said.

"Lower the cage three more feet." Stripes mentally diagramed the pilot's routine. He'd make minor corrections to the helicopter's stick and collective. Holding his bird level in unstable air, roughly four feet above the rugged treetops, took extreme concentration and a bit of luck. Helicopters were as aerodynamic as rocks, and dangling a weighted umbilical cord compounded their stability problems. Every few minutes the pilot's eyes would skim the wind speed indicator, the skies in the immediate vicinity, and the horizon. Most of all, he would use his skills to anticipate anything that could affect his vertical clearance. The sky was his friend, the trees were not.

An intimate understanding of everyone's job and ability was basic information to Stripes; a narrow-minded, ex-Navy SEAL Chief had hammered him on that little necessity. The success of a mission often depended on the details, and although Stripes would never admit it to anyone, that one bit of discipline had probably saved him, and his men, more times than he cared to count.

"Glow Bird, cage is down. Maintain position. We're loading." He gave his number two man another thumbs-up signal, indicating the helicopter was waiting on station. "Team One, clear."

"In position." The pilot's voice crackled. "Make it quick gentlemen. Bird, clear."

This was the trickiest and most dangerous part of the procedure. If a wind gust caused the helicopter to shift, the encapsulated body or its protective covering could be damaged. To prevent such an accident,

Stripes and his partner tied the cage with black nylon ropes between two sturdy mahogany trees growing along the clearing's margin. Like everything else on this mission, the process was tedious, but necessary for their success and safety.

Encased in his protective rubberized biosuit, Stripes dripped wet with sweat, each movement chafed his soggy skin. He ignored his misery and glanced across the cage at Kevin MacIntyer. Over the last decade Stripes had redecorated a few bars with MacIntyer, a crazy kid from Queens, and considered him a friend, or the closest thing to a friend his career choice allowed. Their bond had evolved over countless adventures, and on many occasions, they had depended on each other for survival.

MacIntyer had just finished strapping the body into the cage when Stripes instinctively crouched down, raised his silenced machine gun, and swung it to the right. Someone was there, beyond his view. He couldn't explain it; the same intuitive awareness had saved his ass before. Stripes sifted the shadows along the clearing's perimeter, searching for danger signs. Maybe this time his sixth sense was wrong—doubtful. With effort, he ignored the apocalyptic sensation, focusing on the current task. He locked the aluminum cage and signaled MacIntyer to untie the ropes.

"Glow Bird, this is Team One." Stripes whispered into his throat mike while monitoring the jungle for intruders. "Our package is ready to fly."

"I copy," the pilot said. "Package away. Bird, clear."

"Team One, clear."

A second later, the cage and its dead occupant ascended into the humid insect-filled air, where it quietly disappeared behind the tangled canopy. The entire procedure was completed in less than four minutes.

Relieved to be finished, Stripes blinked away a bead of sweat on his eyelid and gave MacIntyer the "all clear" sign.

No return verification. MacIntyer was out of position. Stripes moved a foot to the left, then motioned again. Still, no recognition. "I hate these damn biological masks," Stripes grumbled. "You can't see a friggin' thing."

He keyed his throat mike and realigned his earpiece, irritated for having to break his own order to keep the radio chatter to a minimum. "MacIntyer, let's move."

As before, no response. Something had gone wrong.

"These damn suits." Stripes ripped off his rubberized glove and raised his machine gun. He crouched down and gripped the weapon's steel handle with his sweaty palm. "MacIntyer, Kevin, acknowledge!"

10:27 a.m.—Central Coast, California

Dr. Ruhpor adjusted the brightness on his computer monitor, cutting the intensity. His eyes were tired and there was still a lot to be done. He heard footsteps and peered above his black horn-rimmed glasses at the Dean of the Natural Sciences Department.

"How's the research coming?" Dr. Theim asked.

"As well as could be expected, I suppose." Dr. Ruhpor dipped his head, glancing back at the computer monitor. The professor was not fond of bureaucrats, and was free with his opinions. Sure, Dr. Theim had once been an instructor, but that was years ago. Nowadays, the Dean's consuming passions were budgets, enrollment quotas, and lab supplies. This bureaucratic bottom-line mentality conflicted with Dr. Ruhpor's priorities, which began and ended with his students and research. He was a man of conviction, who often found himself defending his students before numerous department and administrative committees. To say the least, the school's administrators did not appreciate his outspoken nature, which only added another thorn to the recent tension growing between the Dean and him.

Ruhpor noticed the Dean eyeing the inscribed plaque mounted above his door: "We're here for the students, not for ourselves!" His motto brought terror to the bureaucratic heart.

Affected by Ruhpor's weak attempt to disguise his disdain, Dean Theim shuffled nervously, then straightened his tie and cleared his throat. "BenaTex is our largest and longest standing grant. I'm sure things are going just fine, but if the department can help in any way, don't hesitate to ask."

"Thank you. I won't."

"Before I go," the Dean moved a step closer to the door, "how was your guest lecture at SDSU?"

The professor was anxious to continue his work, but something was on the Dean's mind. Ruhpor took off his reading glasses and rubbed his bloodshot eyes. He had been at the computer for more than five hours and exhaustion was taking its toll. A rapid eye blink purged the blurriness. That's when he noticed, Theim wore a new, light gray Adolfo suit—a little rich for a university dean's income. Besides, the man's fat stomach did nothing to complement the outfit's finely tailored lines.

"Yes, the SDSU lecture. It went well. They have a strong program and good kids. One of them, Matt Wells, wanted a new challenge and had his first class here with me this morning."

"Excellent. We want the best of course. Have you okayed the new student acquisition with the BenaTex rep?"

"He's stopping by the day after tomorrow. I thought it best to review the details then." Ruhpor stared at the Dean. "We discussed Wells before I left town. Remember? You were the one who suggested I talk with him."

"So I was. The conversation must have slipped my mind." The Dean's eyes flitted from one end of the room to the other, to his watch and the door. "Have to run." He fidgeted with coins in his pocket and left Dr. Ruhpor's office.

Tilting his head to one side, a confused expression creased Ruhpor's brow as he watched the Dean scurry through the doorway. The spectacle reminded him of a pudgy gray rabbit stuffed into an overpriced suit. Admittedly, in a morbid sort of way, he took pleasure in making the Dean uncomfortable. Though, for some reason, this had not been one of those occasions. Dr. Theim's clipped conversation and sudden departure were uncharacteristic; something Ruhpor might not have caught if it had not been for the strain evident on the Dean's face.

The professor set his glasses on a physics textbook next to the computer. He crossed his arms, reclined in his chair, and reevaluated their meeting. The Dean's abruptness troubled him, and the professor made a mental note to look into it further.

1:28 p.m.—Amazon Lowlands, Brazil

"Damn humidity has sent this radio mike on the fritz," Bill Stripes complained. "Nothing lasts in this asshole place for long." When MacIntyer had not answered, Stripes moved his finger to the trigger of his machine gun. Something had gone wrong. Danger was near. He wished they weren't handicapped by their biosuits. Again, he gave the signal to evacuate using his throat mike, with no reply. MacIntyer had not budged, remaining hunched down a few yards away.

With his number two man's face hidden behind his biological mask, Stripes could not tell what had happened. His first thought was the virus, but he ruled it out as too sudden. He raised his right hand while watching the bushes to his left and signaled Number Three. Swirling his clenched fist in a tight circle, he pumped it up above his head. . . .

The thin shaft sailed through the air and struck with astonishing precision. Its razor point punctured the rubberized clothing and plunged deep into his flesh with a subtle thump. Stripes groaned when his oblique muscle contracted. He fell to one knee, grasping at the arrow protruding below his right armpit. The primitive shape of the wooden rod astonished him. With his left hand, he grabbed hold and pulled, twisting his torn flesh. He shuddered and bit his lower lip to quench his screams. The shaft broke in half. A second arrow pierced his chest and toppled him backwards.

Rolling on the muddy ground, Stripes tried to get up, but could not. His chest heaved in short, wet breaths. The second arrow had punctured a lung and he had already lost sensation in his hands, then came his feet. His vision swirled behind the fogged faceplate. He took the symptoms for shock, that was before the muscle spasms began. "Son-of-a . . . , poison!"

As Stripes realized he was going to die, he experienced a moment of complete mental clarity. The arrow's tip had most likely been dipped in curare or some other local alkaloid concoction. With his shitty luck, the stuff was probably made from a frog. Stripes hated frogs. The muscle spasms worsened, and he grimaced. Either way, it didn't matter; all would end soon.

Bile rose in his throat and Stripes swallowed hard. He laughed, even with all the pain, arrow wounds don't bleed much. His body convulsed and he clenched his teeth, fighting to hold on. Slim or not, a chance remained the other ground team might . . .

11:32 a.m.—Arabela, New Mexico

Meg watched the forty-eight-inch video screen, paralyzed in horror, captivated by the gruesome vision. Her

Amazon comrades were dying. Her men were dying.

Rick Jansen kicked the leg of the communications console. Meg jumped. "What good's all this electronic crap?" He asked. "Stripes and his men are isolated, and we might as well be jerking off! I wish we had at least a split A Team. That would have given us six shooters on the ground. Three's not enough. I knew it wasn't enough. This was supposed to be a walkover, God damn it!"

Meg stared at the screen as the first two men, one on the perimeter and one in the open, doubled over dead. The Team's commander, Bill Stripes, was unaware that his men had been killed and he was next. An arrow launched out of the dense foliage struck Stripes in the side. Seconds later, another struck him in the chest. It all happened too fast.

"Quick, Meg." Rick flailed his arms and screamed orders. "We can't contact Stripes, but we can sure as hell tell Ground Watch to emergency evac. Do it now! Get that fucking helicopter moving!" He pounded his palm on the console's counter. "Tell them Ground Team One is down!"

With unsteady hands, Meg flipped on the transmitter switch while her eyes remained glued to the viewing screen. "G—Ground Watch, th—th—this is Northern Eyes."

"Meg, get your shit together," Rick commanded. "Don't lose it on me."

Her eyes welled up. "Evac code 86. Evac code 86. Do you copy?" She waited for an answer, gritting her teeth and fighting the tears. Her white knuckles strained above the communications' keyboard. She repeated the command, "Ground Watch this is Northern Eyes. Evac code 86. Evac code 86. Do you copy? There's no reply, Rick! What should I do?" Her eyes pleaded with him to save their people. She had never seen field agents die before. In a way, she had believed they were immortal. Moisture had accumulated along the sides and back of Rick's shirt. But he never sweats. Her resolve weakened. Meg wanted to scream.

Crackle . . . "Control . . . repeat evac . . . you're . . . breaking." The garbled message reverberated off the tin walls of the control room.

Averting her attention from Rick, Meg hit the switch; thanking God that they responded. "Ground Watch, this is Northern Eyes. Evac code 86. Ground Team One is down. Do you copy?"

"We copy, code 86. Ground Team One, down. Will evac site and send Chism to recover Team One. Update within 24-hours. Ground Watch, clear."

"Northern Eyes, clear."

No one dared to speak. Meg heard the hum of electronic equipment. Rick rested against the side of a floor-mounted computer stand; his defeated stare trailed up to the ceiling.

"I'll contact our employer and tell him what's happened. Meg, you call Noble. He's gonna shit."

Meg saw Rick's jaw muscles flex as he looked back at the screen, solemnly watching the surveillance camera record the last agonizing contortions of Bill Stripes and his men. She knew Rick hated this part of the business. Inaction was not something he understood.

Rick faced the jungle scene while he spoke to no one in particular. "Darkness will hit the location before Team Two can get to them. There will be no rescue until morning."

His words were quiet, calm, and prophetical. The tone unsettled Meg. She just wanted to curl up and hide.

"The attack on Stripes was a synchronized assault. The rest of our men are in trouble, and there's not a damn thing we can do. These Indians deal death with a vengeance, and they now know we're there."

The video monitor flickered and they lost the link.

5:23 p.m.—Amazon Lowlands, Brazil

Bill Stripes discerned fuzzy outlines of giant trees and thick shrubs dangling above his head. The pain in his chest was excruciating; each breath became more difficult. His thoughts remained clouded, although lucid enough to know he was lying in the clearing. How long had he been there? The limited daylight illuminating the jungle floor was fading quickly—sun must be setting. He remembered the arrows, collapsing, and a prickling sensation radiating throughout his body just before the convulsions. The pain was gone, replaced instead with a tingling numbness in all but his chest.

Stripes strained to get up. His muscles did not respond. The poison must have paralyzed his motor nerves. Helpless, he forced his mind to suppress his growing terror. He caught movement on the right, at the limit of his peripheral vision.

"Yes! Yes! MacIntyer!" His cries went unheard, soundless gasps. Stripes shouted with all his strength, "What's happening to me? Help! Kevin, help!" His voice remained mute. MacIntyer landed on the ground next to him, remaining strangely motionless.

They lay together, half-buried beneath the jungle's clinging undergrowth and decaying leaves. Stripes felt the weight of his friend's body. He was so still. Their protective biosuits had been torn away, exposing bare chests. Biting insects swarmed, choking the air above them. Things crawled across Stripes' skin and he wanted to call out, but knew the effort was futile.

When the silhouette of a man moved between the bushes, Stripes felt a tinge of hope. Was it Team Two? A shadow passed over his face. A Burbános Indian? It couldn't be. "Kevin, get up!" Panic gripped him. His silent screams echoed through his mind.

The Indian lingered above their immobile bodies. MacIntyer's weight shifted and his head drooped to the side. Stripes saw the vacant stare of pale blue eyes frozen on a chalk white face. He heard fabric tear. What was going on?

"No! Not, Kevin! He's still alive. His eyes. Stop! What are you doing? No . . . !"

October 4

3:42 a.m.—Central Coast, California

Matt raised his head and squinted at Cindi DeLong as she sat next to him on the bungalow's beach towel, brushing away sand clinging to her golden-brown legs. Sunlight backlighting her blonde hair created a surreal halo. He held the vision, closed his eyes, and floundered facedown.

"Hey, you." Cindi nudged his limp body with her knee. He responded by slowly rolling onto his side. "A birthday trip to Cabo San Lucas was supposed to put you in a better mood. We've been here four days and you've been a slug. Look at this place." She made a sweeping hand gesture. "Great beaches. Fantastic blue skies. Excellent surf. And of course, the hot nights."

"Sorry." Matt remained on his side, choosing to prop himself up on his elbow. "I hadn't intended on being a drag. My mind's in the wrong place. Summer classes were a joke—a bad idea that made the school year too long. I'm digging myself an academic grave."

Cindi returned the tangerine-colored drink she had been sipping to their ice bucket and ran her other hand along his forearm. As the heat of her tender touch penetrated his skin, Matt worked his free hand beneath the surface of the beach into the cool Cabo sand. Quartz grains crunched between his fingers. Cindi was too beautiful, too enticing. He restrained his carnal desires, try-ing to organize his feelings and guard his deepest thoughts.

Along the shore, a translucent wave formed a cas-cading curl. Inland, to the north, a mosaic of wind-carved hills and volcanic rocks were backdropped against the buff-colored sandy beach. Wooden shacks dotting the dry hillsides contrasted with the ultramodern hotels erected by the waterfront. Drifting outside the aquama-rine surf, a cruise ship made a careful turn within the confines of the protected harbor. A rocky spit thwarted the fury of the Pacific Ocean six hundred yards to the west. Baja's Cabo San Lucas, with its quiet harbor, warm cli-mate, and relaxed atmosphere, was supposed to be a place where Matt could let go of his worries. Why hadn't it worked? He met Cindi's probing stare. What could he say to her? How could he explain?

"Okay, Matt, what's really bothering you? Did you meet with your department advisor before we left San Diego?"

"Yeah, I saw my advisor, and what a waste. When you're in the system, they don't ever want to let you go. I'm just rotting academic meat hyping a grant request so the department can grab their share of loose fund-ing."

"Whoa. You're a bit negative." Cindi shook her head. "Matt, you're becoming such a cynic. There are some good Profs out there, and I'm sure a few of them care about us." She reached over and stroked back a black curl above his left eyebrow. Cindi never could resist his helpless moods.

He rested on his left elbow, watching her expression, mesmerized by her full red lips and high cheekbones. In-haling a deep cleansing breath, Matt emptied his mind, which, after all the Coronas, wasn't too difficult. "I have to make an adjustment."

"You're not going to quit school, are you?" Cindi leaned over, narrowing the distance between them.

How could he tell her? Without answering, Matt tilted his head toward the sky, shut his eyes, and listened to waves crash along the shoreline. The roar of the ocean took him back to when he was a kid living in northern San Diego County; the hurt he had experienced when his dad banged his half-brother James around because he hadn't lived up to some impossible standard. He harbored the confusion and sadness that had overtaken him when his parents divorced, the nights listening to his mom in an adjacent room, embroiled in another drunken argument with a new boyfriend. Matt was supposed to be a man, be tough, but the unshared pain had eaten away at him. His only escape had been sneaking down to the beach and listening to the sea expend its energy along the shore.

Matt rolled onto his opposite side, reached into the ice bucket and grabbed another cold Corona. "Cindi, how long have you been working on your bachelors'?"

"Over three years. Why?" She studied the pounding surf, then him. He caught the mischievous gleam in her eyes.

Cindi DeLong was both beautiful and intelligent. Virtually every male in the Business Department at San Diego State lusted over her. And why not? At five-foot-eight, she was mostly legs. Her shoulder length, silky blonde hair framed a model's face, and the sparkle in her grayish blue eyes melted even the coldest heart. She had a lot to offer a man. Too bad Matt was not ready for a commitment, but then . . .

He moved closer. The sensual scent of her Navy perfume aroused his desires. "Uh, well did you always plan on being a business major?"

"I guess so." She frowned, scrunching her eyebrows down. "What are you scheming, Mr. Wells?"

"Nothing."

"If you say so."

"Honest. Nothing." Inspecting her sensual curves, Matt grinned. He knew Cindi didn't believe him.

Stretched out on her towel, the cut of her purple thong bathing suit accented her firm body. Her tan skin glistened in the warm Mexican sun. The image was worthy of a Sports Illustrated cover. Damn, she made it difficult for him to think straight.

"Unlike you, Cindi, I was guided, no, guilted into mechanical engineering. My dad wanted engineers in the family. That's all my brother and I heard since we were kids." Matt twisted the top off his frosted beer and stuffed a sliced lime inside the neck of the bottle.

"So what's bothering you?" Cindi rolled onto her side, giving him her undivided attention. "This preoccupation with school's unusual."

"Dad pushed hard, especially when my brother went into the archaeological sciences. That one nearly killed the old guy." Matt smirked. "James pioneered his own way. He said that when compared to engineering, collecting bones and unearthing the dead were socially more responsible. I figured he just liked the solitude. Maybe he was right."

Taking a drink of his beer, Matt's mind wandered. The only movement within view was on the water, where, a couple hundred feet away more than a dozen sailboats and at least that many powerboats rocked on their moorings. He pivoted to the west when noises coming from the Las Margaritas Bar and Grill caught his attention. An aroma of spicy chorizo and other Mexican breakfast delicacies filtered down from the kitchen. For the cooks, at least, the day was going to be busy. He smiled, took another sip of his beer, and read his diver's watch, almost ten o'clock. His morning privacy would soon end.

"My old man meant well by pushing us." Matt sighed. "In his mind, mechanical engineers had career flexibility. Dad stressed a lot over our financial futures. All those years as a corporate accountant had jaded his perspective. He had witnessed too many good people get laid off or fired. Regardless, mechanical engineering's not for me."

"Is it that serious?" Cindi removed the pear-shaped glass containing her Tequila Sunrise from the ice and took a drink.

"I don't like engineering," he said. "Everything always has to add up to a hundred. They have too many rules and rarely use creativity or intuition to get an answer. I want more."

"A little entrepreneurial of you, Matt. Why not switch your major to a science or something else?"

"Yeah, possibly. I want to make a difference, not just collect check stubs on someone's payroll roster."

She played her fingers through his hair. "So what's the problem? Just go for it. You've never hesitated before."

"The problem is, if I dump engineering now, I'd have to throw the majority of the last two years out and start over. I'd also lose my scholarship. Besides, aren't scientists kind of nerdy?" He chuckled. "Except for my brother of course."

"Of course." Cindi shook her head. "Matt, everyone experiences the college blues. Trust me, it's not such a big deal. When you're in the middle it's difficult to see the end. Here, roll over." Cindi pushed him onto his stomach and navigated her way along his back. Her hands outlined each muscle, expertly manipulating his body, easing her way into his mind. "The world has a lot to offer. Don't force things. Take it slow and enjoy the ride." She traced his spine with her fingernails.

"If you say so." Matt responded more to her soothing touch than her words. "Hmm, that's nice. Just right." The warm Baja sun intensified her massage, and he relaxed, using a moment to rationalize his situation.

His current indecision had been more than one of those intellectual hiccups that came along when a class project did not go well or when he confronted a professor who should be selling used cars instead of teaching.

Matt realized that he had arrived at an academic cross-road and it was time for a serious change.

Protecting his eyes from the sun beneath Cindi's shadow, Matt watched her through vision blurred by too many Coronas. He scooted closer to her, hiding his uncertainties behind a large grin. "You're right. I've been a slug sizzling in the Mexican heat."

Matt placed his hand on the back of Cindi's neck and kissed her slowly on the lips. Then, with a wily smile, he released her and lifted the Corona he had been protecting. Three gulps later, the beer was gone. "And after all, this is the Mexican Riviera. I'm sure we can find something enjoyable to do—"

A blaring car horn and Matt bolted upright on his bed. The room was black and for a second he was lost, uncertain if he were home or still in Mexico. What a dream, but not only a dream. It was his trip to Cabo revisited; his indecision relived. The details were so vivid, the sensations so real: it gave him the creeps. Did he miss Cindi that much, or had the finality of his decision gotten to him? He rubbed his temples and rolled backwards, landing on the pillow, nearly grazing the side of his head on the nightstand.

Dangling over the edge of the bed, he grabbed the alarm clock. "Ten 'till four. Class in four hours—this sucks. I need . . . some . . . sleep." A long yawn, and he let the clock drop from his hand, barely hearing the thud when it hit the floor.

6:49 a.m.—Amazon Lowlands, Brazil

Hank Chism did not dare wipe away the sweat pouring down his face for fear of smearing his camouflage paint. The jungle was a giant green Turkish bathhouse, and mistakes came easily when on a mission in such a blistering place. Was that what had taken the other team down? A mistake? They were good, but whoever had gotten to them were better. Mistakes, the value of your life was measured by your mistakes. Stripes didn't make mistakes.

Chism switched the fire control on his Heckler and Koch MP10 submachine gun to semiautomatic, then moved his finger to the ready position. Squeezing the weapon's grip, he smiled. The Germans made efficient weapons.

His gun sight panned left to right as he listened to the report from his point man through his earpiece, "On perimeter, clear." Chism responded by triple tapping his throat microphone with his finger. He had given orders for his team to keep the talk down, standard tactics.

One foot at a time, Chism moved closer. His steps landed without a sound. Vegetation compressed beneath his boots, and he breathed in the smells of the jungle, extending his senses: overgrown plants, heavy damp air, animals prowling beyond the shadows. Another fifteen yards and his men would be in sight of where Team One had gone down. What would they find? Nothing organic lasted long in this green shit house.

He monitored the trail ahead. Would his men be better than the last? Now was not the time to question. They were on a hunt-and-destroy mission, a cleanup assignment. Chism assessed the trees, then the bushes, probing for any indication that they were not alone. The only sign of life was a small green-snake entwined on a branch within an arm's reach of his head. He ignored the reptile and moved on. "Three, spread left, four yards. Two, spread right, four yards." His orders flowed with authority. Did his men sense his own uncertainty?

Fear drew him to danger like a narcotic. He experienced the same sensation on every mission: the jungles of Cambodia, the diseased swamps of El Salvador. Knowing he might die brought that familiar heightened consciousness; his awareness had an unrestrained clarity. He slowed his advance, surveyed the perimeter, and assessed the positioning of his men. This time felt different. The Amazon was foreign and unnerving. An unnatural sense of foreboding invaded his thoughts, played with his judgment.

"Have location," his point man announced.

Chism clicked his mike, signaling he understood. He held up his Swiss Army watch. They were on schedule. "Three, hang back. Two, hold position."

Kneeling below the cover of a broadleaf frond, Chism read the signs: a broken branch, crushed leaves next to the trail. He inspected imprints left in the muddy clay soil. Military-type boots made one set, another, a half step to the right, was from bare feet. Team One had passed through here. He sensed the hint of a one-sided battle.

The attackers were still here, hidden amid the thick cover. They'd hit his team soon. How would they do it? Adrenalin surged inside his veins. His body temperature rose. Like a black panther prowling the jungle, his two hundred and fifty-pound hardened physique was primed.

Crouching on the fringe of the clearing, Chism stayed low; ready to return fire. On his immediate right were the remains of Team One. The high-pitched drone of a thousand insects swarming above the three corpses buzzed in his ears. The pungent smell of a bloody death lay heavily in his nostrils. He took a wary stride forward, then stopped.

Chism studied the location before moving closer to the bodies. Surrealistic; his Team One comrades lay side-by-side, their torsos partially covered by small shrubs. Evaluating the scene in more detail: broken branches, fresh imprints in the moist ground—his fighter's intuition began delivering danger signals faster than he could interpret them.

"Two, move right, five yards. Three, left flank. Lock and load; zone's hot." Chism checked his H&K, more from training than necessity. "I'm goin' in." He took a deep breath and exhaled slowly.

He passed among the wet plants; droplets of accumulated dew fell to the ground. His eyes panned left then right and back again in a well-trained pattern, never stalling on a single point. Chism scanned for a shape or a shadow line that did not match the natural surroundings.

Don't fixate, skim. They're out there, watching. The attack would be swift and quiet, but from where? Too much indecision, use your instincts—feel the attack. Crossfire, they would work his team into a crossfire. Stay low; don't give them a full target. Mentally considering all the possible angles, he used hand signals to advance his men in a staggered v-formation.

Within two yards of the bodies, he squatted on one knee. Team One all right, but why leave them here? Their attackers were making a statement. Blood everywhere, too much blood. Rising slightly, he clenched his teeth when the atrocity came into full view. "Sweet Mary."

5:14 a.m.—Arabela, New Mexico

"Meg, what's the situation with Team Two? It's taken them too long to switch to the new location. We aren't going to wait 24-hours. We don't have that kind of time." Rick leaned over her shoulder and read the mission status clock above her computer console.

Although Meg knew the answers, she referred to her notes. "Jaries relocated Ground Watch to the backup staging area, but it's not fully functional yet. He also said Team Two called in a half hour ago. They had Team One's last known location in sight. So we'll have something soon."

Meg looked up from her notes. Stress cast a grim shadow across everyone's expressions. Like her, the technicians weren't used to failure. Watching their comrades die had been devastating, a heartfelt blow that destroyed their own delusions of infallibility.

"Has anyone figured out why our cameras went down?" Rick paced behind her. "We're screwed without the minicams."

"We're on it," Dave Mires, one of the communication jocks, answered. "We lost the video links to all of the cams during the attack, which . . . "

"Are you saying the damn Indians found our equipment?" Rick picked up his pace. "We had over a hundred cameras. Hell, that's all I need."

Mires cast his eyes down. "I didn't say that, Rick. But we haven't found any problems on our end. The video equipment diagnostics came up negative. We should have feed."

"Meg, contact Ground Watch. I want to know if they've heard anything. This mission's gone to hell, and I don't want to lose anyone else."

She knew better than to cower in front of Rick. Being a field man, he didn't mesh well with cerebral types. His frustration often manifested itself by breaking things. In their best interest, everyone gave him room.

"No problem, Rick." Meg concentrated, blocking out the initial shock of seeing the brutal murders. Her panic held in check: concentrating on business, doing her job. They could beat this. The teams needed her. She pushed the transmitter switch on her satellite link. "Ground Watch, this is Northern Eyes. Ground Watch, this is Northern Eyes."

Crackle . . . "Go ahead, Northern Eyes. This is Ground Watch."

"Jaries, has Team Two called in?" She adjusted the transmission's gain and filtered the static.

"No," Jaries responded. "Contact broke off with them twelve minutes ago. We're assuming they switched to radio silence."

"Keep us posted."

"Will do. Ground Watch, clear."

"Northern Eyes, clear." Meg rotated her seat and faced Rick. "That's it, I guess. We know what he knows, which isn't much."

Two communications techs tiptoed by Meg, doing their best to keep busy—just like her. Rick's pacing circle had grown to encompass the entire room. He had been there, dodging ambushes, fighting for survival, and he knew more trouble was on the way. Unconsciously, Rick rubbed the scar above his right temple where a bullet had creased him on one such occasion. The teams were unprotected, isolated, and alone. Meg sensed his torment.

"Rick, Chism knows his job."

"He'd better."

His expression frightened her and she kept her voice low, to herself. "Chism has to safely recover Team One. They will return."

7:16 a.m.—Amazon Lowlands, Brazil

The sight of the three disfigured men made Hank Chism's stomach churn. His comrades' hearts had been gouged from their chests, leaving a mutilated cavity stuffed with broken bones and severed arteries. Their jaws smashed, and teeth gone. Worms probed their empty eye sockets. Roaches and ants invaded their blood-encrusted wounds. Chism nearly puked when he realized that they could have been alive when their organs were ripped from their bodies.

Slumping forward, hardly able to hold up his head, Chism could not face the repulsive display any longer. His breaths came short and fast. They had butchered his friends!

"Wait a damn minute." Chism shook his head. What the hell was going on? He wasn't an amateur who lost his cool at the sight of a little blood. Somehow this place had gotten to him. No time for remorse. Chism stood. The smell of death mixed with the jungle scents. Revenge cured—

All hell broke loose as arrows flew overhead. The attack came from every direction. He heard the stiletto crack of an H&K submachine gun fired in short bursts behind the bushes to his right. A thud in the center of his chest took his breath away.

He stared at the arrow's carved shaft impaled in his camouflaged vest, an inch below his heart. Events slowed while he analyzed the absurdity of being attacked by a band of Amazonian Indians. Arrows against automatic weapons, this was crazy, but deadly. If not for his Kevlar vest, he'd be a corpse. Ripping the arrow free, Chism dodged left, then shoulder rolled right.

"Status!" He trained his gun on the bushes in a tightly sweeping arc.

"Two, spotted movement. Six yards away, ten o'clock. They're everywhere."

"Three, target down, one o'clock."

Chism crouched next to a thick leafy bush. Ten o'clock was to his back. He fixed his position and put both locations in his sights. "Keep your heads. Two, sweep left. Three, sweep right. Circle at six." His instincts took over and he spun left. A rapid H&K burst and a half-naked native launched himself out of the trees, hitting the ground ten feet away—dead.

Three clicks told Chism his number three man was in position. He didn't need his earpiece to hear the guttural cry of pure terror that came from his left. His number two man was down and probably dead. Chism tapped his mike twice, but heard no reply. He repeated the signal and received a return of three clicks, not two. "Hold position. I'm working around." His every instinct said to run; experience kept him low to the ground and under control.

A branch rustled above his head, and he spun around, swinging his gun up to his line of sight. An arrow struck him in the side. He stumbled backward, falling next to the trunk of a giant cypress. Once more, his Kevlar flak vest had saved him. A short H&K burst was followed by a hollow thump. Three clicks in his mike told him his partner had smacked the son-of-a-bitch.

His team was losing a battle of attrition. It was only a matter of when until Chism and his men lay slaughtered next to Team One. They had to evade death long enough to turn the situation to their advantage. Throw them off balance.

He retreated into the thick growth of the rain forest. Number Three hid four yards to his back. Chism used a hand signal, a small circular movement, then pointed to the northwest. Waiting for Three to take the lead, he watched their rear. Two stealthy silhouettes, moving slowly, they covered each other and scouted the path ahead.

8:32 a.m.—Central Coast, California

Matt Wells had read the University's self-promoting propaganda, drawing his own conclusions. California's Central Coast had a unique mixture of tiny towns contending for their own individuality. Surfside communities, Avila Beach, Shell Beach, Pismo Beach, and Morro Bay, formed the western border. To the east, reminiscent of old Spanish California, the Coast Range Mountains surrounded villages, farms, and wineries tucked away in hidden grassy valleys. Central Coast townships radiated outward, like a pioneer's wagon wheel, with San Luis Obispo forming its cultural hub. In the center of that hub was Matt's new college, California Polytechnic State University; reputed to be a "hands-on" school, where students came before research.

"We'll see."

It had been only four days since his return to California from Cabo San Lucas, and as he stood outside his new academic advisor's office, doubts regarding his decision surfaced once again. Had he relied too much on emotion and not enough on analysis? Perhaps he should have discussed it with someone. His father? Yeah, maybe in his next life.

When Matt told Cindi of his decision to leave San Diego, she reacted with less of a response than he had expected. Somehow, she had known he was going to make a change. She had prepared for his departure, as if it had been a foregone conclusion. Women and their intuitive sense of things; how irritating. It disturbed him when everyone else was one emotional move ahead of him. Yet, she left him with a few amazing memories.

Recalling her intoxicating touch still made him light-headed. He laughed to himself. Those remaining hours with Cindi were truly remarkable.

After a sunset dinner on that last evening, they hadn't even made it into their Cabo bungalow before Cindi flung her arms around his neck. Responding to her heated moves, Matt kicked the door aside and they tumbled across the threshold locked in each other's arms. During the night the thunder of the waves breaking along Cabo's shoreline paled in comparison to their lovemaking. As the sun rose they parted for the first time, satiated and exhausted. Cindi had held nothing back. Matt rubbed his chin. Whoever said change was good for the soul must have been a masochist.

He read the nameplate on his advisor's door: Dr. Christian Ruhpor, Engineering Geology Department. The time had come. Regardless of how Matt felt, San Diego State and Cindi were gone forever.

Storing the memories, and to a degree, the uncertainties, Matt knocked on the doorjamb. He heard a mumbled, "Come in." The door was ajar, and he pushed it open.

The room was a chaotic mess overflowing with piles of loose papers and unevenly stacked books. Sunlight broke through a window half obscured by a pleated curtain, casting streaks across the random academic accumulation cluttering the floor. The streaming light and rich mahogany wall paneling gave the office a rustic Ivy League flavor.

Publications of all kinds filled the floor-to-ceiling oak bookshelves. Mathematics, engineering, geology, and microbiology were the most prevalent subjects. The floor was hardwood, and a brownish shag rug covered the center. A computer had been shoved into the corner and a worn walnut desk occupied the remaining space.

"I've seen neater dorm rooms," Matt muttered, and then wondered, had he entered the wrong office? While he surveyed the surroundings, a barely perceptible movement between two stacks of papers on the desk drew his attention.

"What was that, son?" A voice resonated behind the conglomeration. "Have a seat."

Had Dr. Ruhpor overheard his careless comment? Embarrassed, Matt did as instructed. He made space on the only available chair and took a seat among the stock of academic literature. While squirming to get comfortable his interest moved around the room, scrutinizing the decor. He repeated the rumors to himself, quieting his nerves, hoping they were true. "He's willing to buck the system, a real teacher; here for the students." Matt spied his new professor squinting at him over a pair of black horn-rimmed glasses.

"Good to see you again, son. How was the drive up?"

"Fine, Dr. Ruhpor. Only a few traffic slowdowns through Santa Barbara. They've ripped up the ramps to State Street." Crossing his legs, Matt attempted to find a more relaxed position. His efforts were wasted. He wondered how long this meeting would last. At best, it would be a quick introduction and he'd be cut loose. Then, the professor smiled. He sensed something there, in the Doc's body language—sincerity?

"I'm glad you arrived safely. Welcome to Cal Poly's

Engineering Geology program, son. By the way, I assume Cabo San Lucas went well?"

"You could say that." Matt touched the bruise on his shoulder. The one he received after falling through the bungalow's doorway wrapped in Cindi's arms. He smiled and pictured Cindi's firm naked body stretched across the floor. Her hair's golden strands shimmered in the soft light of Cabo's red evening sun. "It did give me an opportunity to deal with a few things. Your guest lecture and our talks before I left town also helped." Matt paused. No matter how well he hid his feelings, he was going to miss San Diego. "I must admit, I'm worried. Losing my scholarship will make things rough."

"Been taken care of. You have a job here in the Natural Sciences Department, helping me as a grader and lab tech. We've also passed your loan and grant documents on to financial aid." Dr. Ruhpor stood and stretched. Dressed in a white shirt, khaki pants, and a narrow tie painted to look like a trout, he strolled to the front of his desk and took a seat on the corner facing Matt. "Financial aid said you shouldn't have any difficulty qualifying for a work-study program. Eating is important."

"That's great." The professor's helpfulness unbalanced Matt. He didn't know quite how to respond. His experience with other Profs had convinced him they expected their students to starve their way through school—food came second to research. He listened intently and relaxed a little more once he accepted that his financial situation had been eased. Dr. Ruhpor might just be for real.

The office door swung open, banging into the wall. Shelves shook and dust puffed into the air. In dashed a young man carting a slew of books under one arm and waving a sheet of paper with his other. "Dr. Ruhpor, he's gone and done it again."

"Excuse me, Matt." The professor met the student before he stumbled into an uncharted pile. "Larry, what's got you all pumped up this time?"

"It's Dr. Theim. He nixed our Las Vegas article. You know the one, where we linked high uterine cancer rates to nuclear testing south of Las Vegas during the 50s. He said it was too controversial for the newspaper. What's his problem this time? Natural geologic isotope analyses confirm the results and the—"

"Calm yourself, son." Dr. Ruhpor set his hand on the young man's shoulder. "We'll get to the bottom of this during our three o'clock geology club meeting. Remember, Dr. Theim is slightly conservative when it comes to publishing."

"Slightly?"

"Don't get so stressed. I'll deal with it."

"Way cool, Dr. Ruhpor. I knew we could count on you. See you at three." Larry spun in the direction he had come from, fumbled with his books, and bolted through the doorway.

The professor returned to Matt, who was staring at the door. "Don't mind Larry. He's the excited editor of Soft Rocks, our geology club newspaper. Now where were we?" Matt shrugged. Dr. Ruhpor leaned on the ledge of his desk. "Oh, yes. I can also get you some added income tutoring, which when compared to flipping burgers, pays pretty well."

"I appreciate all your help. So what happens next, Doc?"

"Since you missed registration, we picked the rest of your courses for the fall quarter." The professor handed Matt his schedule. "Things are a little different here, but don't worry, you'll catch on quickly."

Matt stood and skimmed the course list—a total of five classes plus two labs. "Looks simple enough."

"I know you'll handle it just fine." Dr. Ruhpor set his hand in the middle of Matt's back and showed him to the door. "When you get a chance, stop by the front office and talk with our secretary. She'll get you headed in the right direction. Marcie's a whiz at anything you could need. She's also an ace at making the bureaucrats around here jump. So, son, you ready to do some serious work?"

"You bet."

"Then let's get moving. Science waits for no one."

"Thanks for your help, Doc." Matt waved on his way out the door. "See you in class tomorrow."

10:28 a.m.—Palo Alto, California

Dr. George Leland, the Head of the Archaeology Department, shuffled aside and gestured for a colleague, a smaller man wearing a beige, corduroy sport coat with suede elbow patches, to take the podium. Journalists representing more than ten San Francisco Bay area news media organizations and thirty or more students wedged themselves into Stanford University's modest pressroom. Heavy electrical cords trailed in all directions as television crews scrambled to get their equipment ready. Photographers wrestled among themselves to garner the best angle while the air conditioner labored to keep up with the sweaty madhouse. Positive publicity on this project had been a major emphasis, but no one had predicted such a massive turnout.

"Must be a slow news day, Henry."

Dr. Henry Isling smirked. "I'll do my best to entertain them, George." The professor pulled at his lapels, straightened his coat, adjusted his glasses and sauntered around Leland to the podium where he set his notes. A Professor Emeritus with Stanford's Archaeology Department, Dr. Isling was uneasy being in the public spotlight. . . . This was his moment.

"Professor!" an Oakland News reporter called. "Professor!" He was a faceless voice buried amidst the shoulder-to-shoulder crowd.

Lowering the microphone to better fit his height, Isling took the opportunity to observe the faces of the correspondents and students. To his relief many were familiar to him. Stanford's public relations staff had done well in their scheduling. This press conference would make the evening news.

Isling ran his hand across his butch-cut graying hair and straightened his thick, wire-rimmed glasses. "Yes, Sam." He gestured to the Oakland News reporter.

"Thank you, Professor." The reporter pointed a pocket tape-recorder at the podium. "Could you please give us an overview?"

Allowing his shoulders to roll forward, Isling's mannerism metamorphosed into a self-assured speaker—no longer the timid professor. He began to view the press conference as an academic lecture of sorts. "Well, Sam, this is a unique opportunity to study an ancient culture untarnished by industrial evolution. Keep in mind, we believe the Burbános have been exiled to the Amazon for over four hundred years. Their last contact with outsiders was brief, a marginal introduction during the mid-sixteenth century when the Spanish Conquistadors traversed the Amazon River and, later in the same century, when the Portuguese explored Brazil."

Robert Collinger yelled above the clamor, "What does this discovery mean to the archaeological world?"

Collinger represented Stanford's paper, The VIRTUAL Reporter, and Professor Isling had known him since he was a freshman reporter scrounging for copy. Isling beamed, pleased at seeing him. He was a good kid. The previous morning, his senior editor had collaborated with the Archaeology Department on the focus of Collinger's question. Besides wanting solid quotes for their story, they agreed the press conference was good experience for the burgeoning reporter and a convenient plug for their paper.

"Robert, we suspect the Burbános are the ancient ancestors of the Yucatán Maya. Documented Maya civilization dates older than 1000 BC, flourishing during Mesoamerica's Classic period beginning in the fourth century and ending during the tenth. For the last decade, archaeologists have theorized the early Maya were a migratory people, and it's very possible they expanded their territory to include portions of northern Mexico and parts of Brazil. This expedition could substantiate the Brazilian portion of that theory. It could also explain the sudden downfall of the Maya Empire. Which of course, has baffled archaeologists for decades."

"Thank you, Dr. Isling."

"Professor!" An Oakland Tribune reporter pushed her way in front of the crowd. "How can you be that confident this lost tribe really exists?"

Isling repositioned himself to the side of the podium, unintentionally giving the television cameras a better angle. He accepted the fact that he was not a commanding figure, more round than tall, standing a quarter of an inch less than five and a half feet, yet he addressed the crowd in his own special way. Maybe it was his academic presence or his informal demeanor, whatever the reason, he realized that he had astutely gained control of this group.

"Janet, finding the lost tribe was a stroke of good fortune. The Spaniards decimated the Burbános in the name of expansion and greed. They took many young men, women, and children to Spain as slaves. Records describing the barbaric action, and the possible existence of the Burbános, were found by a Dr. Salazar while visiting the Mission of São Gabriel da Anjo. Salazar's a sociopaleoanthropologist with USC currently on sabbatical in Brazil's Amazon Lowlands. He's mapping migration patterns of native Indian tribes." Isling slowed, building on the tension. "On his way back from an expedition to one of the villages he's studying, Dr. Salazar came across a distinctive Indian headdress. We studied the artifact and determined its style and inscriptions to be Maya. In our opinion, this is irrefutable evidence that the Burbános exist today." A wave of enthusiastic note taking circulated among the reporters.

"Dr. Isling," a San Francisco Chronicle correspondent interjected. "What do you suppose will happen when you meet your mysterious tribe of lost Indians?"

The professor became absorbed in his passion for the subject and waved his hands theatrically above the podium. "An excellent question. Like all adventures into the unknown, we're not certain. Although the documents provided by Dr. Salazar contained vivid historical accounts of murder and death, they remained incomplete with regard to the current disposition of the Burbános." By their expressions, the news crews loved the drama. Camera strobes lit the congested pressroom.

"Isn't this expedition dangerous? I assume the Burbános are already wary of Westerners."

"Yes, I'm sure the Spanish left them with a lasting impression. Please keep in mind, religious overtones aside, the primary mission of the sixteenth century Spanish Conquistador was to secure gold and slaves for their king. When they happened upon primitive Indian tribes, the Spanish viewed them simply as a commodity."

A journalist to the left of the podium waved. "Dr. Isling, how is it that in comparative numbers, an army of a few hundred Conquistadors was able to conquer the entire Maya empire, yet this tribe was able to flee?"

"Ladies and gentleman, we presume, based on both fact and theory, the Yucatán Maya and the Amazonian Burbános were easy prey for the Spaniards because of their religious beliefs. When Europeans arrived in the early 1500s, the Maya dynasty was disintegrating. Many of their cities in the southern Yucatán had been abandoned and they had foreseen the second coming of their god Kukulkán, also referred to by the Toltec-Aztec equivalent, Quetzalcóatl, as an omen for better times.

"For these reasons, they committed a grave, possibly desperate error, and unveiled their remaining cities to the Spaniards, mistaking them for gods. Normally the Maya's warlike culture didn't welcome uninvited visitations. We assume, after they discovered their mistake, their social decline delayed their ability to mount a unified defense.

"From within the Maya infrastructure, the Spanish conquered and eventually enslaved the entire region. But, the Maya did not go easily and the Yucatán became an enduring battleground, as Hernandez de Cordoba discovered when he landed during 1517 seeking slaves for Cuba. For political reasons Francisco de Montejo and the Conquistadores declared the continent subdued in 1542. In reality, the Maya waged war for control of their homeland for another 140 years. Therefore you can see, their conquest was rebellious and bloody, unlike the sudden downfalls of the Aztecs and Incas. And in some ways many Maya are still waging a war of independence today. It's just on a different scale."

Isling allowed the crowd time to assimilate the information while he evaluated how his lecture was being received. The reporters appeared to be genuinely enthralled with the discussion, taking meticulous notes and recording every passage. Pleased, he continued, "We have surmised, based on the available data, that of the more than 4,700 original Burbános fewer than 360 eluded the onslaught. Many of the tribes people who weren't either killed or taken captive died from diseases carried by the Spanish sailors. The ones who escaped death migrated deeper into the Amazon Lowlands, far from potential probes of the Spanish and any other inquisitive explorers. With a little help from modern technology, we will find the descendants of those remaining tribal members."

"Professor," Mary Bartenow of the Examiner shouted. "How does your work affect Eviel Wood's genetics theory?"

"You're well informed." Isling sorted and folded his notes in half, tucking them into an outside pocket of his sport coat. "As you might be aware, Dr. Wood mapped genetic similarities among many native Central American peoples. Currently, more than two million Maya Indians are suspected to be living in the northern Yucatán and Guatemalan highlands. If we compare social and physical developmental irregularities between the Burbános and the Yucatán Maya, we could prove Dr. Wood's genetic mixing theories."

Waving an outstretched arm, Stevie Walton of the San Francisco Times caught Isling's attention. She was quite attractive. Suddenly aware of himself, he shuffled his feet and readjusted his tie. "Yes, Miss Walton."

"It's Ms. Walton." She ignored the snickers among her colleagues. "When will you begin your expedition and what cultural differences do you think will be evident between the original Maya and the Burbános?"

"Um. Well, Ms. Walton, we've been preparing for more than six months. And unless something changes, we're sending our team into the Amazon Lowlands within the next two days." He adjusted his coat while the room quieted. "As for your second question, it's difficult to predict the evolutionary track of any culture; that's what makes this project so exciting. We suspect the Burbános might not have flourished like the Mesoamerica Yucatán Maya. They probably abandoned many of their ancient customs and adapted to the very different Amazonian environment. We've theorized, the cultural phenomenon enabling the Maya to achieve technological marvels might have bypassed the Burbános because of their South American seclusion. Essentially, we expect to find a primitive people, who have created a new world for themselves." He discerned a stirring in the crowd. "The modern Burbános most likely live the way they have for centuries, simply and instinctively. Our hope is that they are an unaltered window into the past; one that can provide answers to the ancient Maya's hidden secrets." Isling backed away from the podium.

Leland walked over and readjusted the microphone. He raised his hands, quieting the crowd. "Now, I know how exciting this upcoming expedition is; however, that concludes our press conference for today."

"Dr. Leland!" More than a dozen reporters clamored. "What about—"

"I'm sorry, but there will be no further discussion. The School of Archaeology has prepared a written statement, which can be picked up on the way out of the pressroom. Thank you all for coming."

"There's a moral issue here, Dr. Leland. Don't these people have the right to be left alone? Haven't they paid with enough lives in the name of exploration and conquest?"

The professor's eyes widened and he searched the faces in front of the podium. He placed his hand over the microphone. "Henry, who the hell said that?"

Before Isling could answer, a young woman made her way to the center of the hushed crowd. She wore faded jeans and a light-blue T-shirt. Her jet-black hair was styled short like a young boy's and her amber skin shone in the artificial light. The air conditioner's steady rumble echoed inside the pressroom. No one spoke, anticipating the woman's next verbal attack.

"Are you going to answer my questions, Dr. Leland, or not?"

"I'm not sure if I understand, miss." He knotted his fingers together to stop them from fidgeting behind the podium.

"I think you do. In the short history of western civilization, every time some scientist or moralistic explorer claimed a discovery was going to benefit the world, it turned into a self-glorifying endeavor. In the end, the newly found people were left devastated and filled with despair."

Blinding strobes flashed as reporters and their crews competed to get a microphone close to the woman.

"This is great stuff," Collinger whispered into his cameraman's ear. "Get a shot of the passion in her eyes."

Leland took a deep breath. "Miss, if you want to discuss this complex issue, I'd be happy to meet with you at your convenience. This press conference has ended."

She moved to the middle of the room. "I warn you, Professor. The world is tired of its children being raped in the name of scientific achievement."

"I have no further comment." Dr. Leland straightened his tie and with shaky hands pulled down the front of his pinstriped navy blue jacket, then lumbered backward.

Isling supported him by the elbow and the two professors walked away. The young woman's words had raised subconscious uncertainties within Professor Leland; uncertainties his friend had refused to face. Exiting the room by a side door, they left the journalists and their shouted questions behind.

10:42 a.m.—Sausalito, California

As Ben Singular gazed out his partner's office window, mentally gauging his company's brief history, a heavily loaded cargo ship traversed beneath the Oakland Bay Bridge. Out a ways, a blue schooner with a reefed white and orange main sail and sleek lines completed a sharp starboard tack to avoid the big ship's heavy wake. Sausalito's natural beauty had entranced Ben so much that he borrowed heavily and built his company in the northwest part of town to entice and stimulate the greatest minds in biogenetics.

It had been more than eight years since Ben first saw this same view. At that time, he knew this would be BenaTex's future. Secluded along the northern shore of San Francisco Bay, Sausalito had been a focal point for California artisans since the 1800s. The hillside community, with its turn-of-the-century architecture, offered visitors an unparalleled view of the Bay, the often-fog-enshrouded Oakland Bay Bridge, and the manmade Treasure Island.

Grumbling in the background, Nathan Donner, Ben's top genetics engineer, partner, and friend, sat on the other side of his oak desk. While Nathan continued to complain about Jolon Steele's new round of requirements, Ben recalled all that had gone into establishing BenaTex as a leading biogenetic engineering firm, the years of hardship, many bank loans, hunt for the right mix of talented scientists, and groundbreaking research in medical genetics. Until a day ago, he would not have traded the good or bad times for anything.

Ben turned from the window, searching the room for a comfortable chair. His partner had the second largest office floor space, and the least amount of furniture. Nathan's excuse had always been that he lived in the labs, so why did he require traditional occupational conveniences.

The scant three chairs Ben saw looked to be from a local yard sale. Some day he would bring Nathan into the corporate world, screaming and kicking most likely. Nathan's office did have a modest oak desk and matching credenza, and a four-foot round conference table—his rare concession to improving his image. The barren powder blue walls were decorated with two computer-generated renderings of double-helix DNA strands—Nathan's odd idea of modern art. The decor was an expression of a forlorn clinical bachelor.

"What! Did I hear you say he wants better than 90 percent by the end of the fiscal year? That's less than two weeks." Jumping up, Nathan slammed his knee into the desk. "Ouch, damn. We've been fortunate to get this far considering all of the secrecy requirements." He rubbed his knee. "By reverse-engineering a retrovirus, we're essentially creating a new viral species. One of the most difficult feats in science I must add. You don't just pull something like that past your sphincter muscle."

Ben shrugged him off. Nathan was experiencing another one of his famous moments. Everyone at BenaTex, Ben included, had grown accustomed to his rapid mood swings. He was a tall, lanky, Southern Californian, who dangled his emotions from his shirtsleeve, and if nothing else, Ben enjoyed the spice Nathan brought to an otherwise cold analytical world. He considered it a modest toll for employing a genius.

"You don't have to tell me," Ben retorted, throwing his hands up in the air. He crossed the room and closed the door. Their staff didn't need to overhear the conversation. He knew this meeting would be rough. All along Nathan had been opposed to taking on Steele's project.

"Ben, I can remember when BenaTex was a drunken concept we knocked around in our dorm room while downing three sixers of Bud. We wanted to build an idyllic research environment."

"Which we have," Ben said. "And your point?"

"My point is, our people are more like family than staff. If we put any more pressure on them, someone's going to start asking questions. We can't control everyone." Nathan's gaze locked with Ben's. "It's been hard enough to compartmentalize everything. We're swamped by this project and ready to burst." He shook his head in disbelief. "If we push for more overtime, it'll be impossible to keep the staff separated. What does Steele want, blood? Because if we keep this up that's what he's gonna get."

"Nathan, you of all people know empathy's not one of his greater virtues. We must meet the deadline, there's no other option. From here on out it's a seven-day work-week for all of us." Ambling to the other side of his part-ner's desk, Ben sat down on a blue secretarial chair and folded his arms. "We've got no choice, buddy."

"You surprise me, Ben. Have we dipped so low that our scientific decisions are based solely on Steele's whims and our bottom-line?" Continuing to stand, Na-than placed his overly large palms on the desktop and leaned toward Ben. "If that's true, we should revise our mission statement to more accurately reflect our eroded cor-porate philosophy." He slumped into his chair behind the desk.

Ben closed his eyes and slipped into deep thought. His partner's ranting reminded him of his graduate days with Yale's Biochemistry Department. Nearly a decade ago, one of Ben's professors had lectured on the values that drove the "real world." Dr. Berkhoff said those values frequently conflicted with scientific achievement, and he warned his young genetics students to choose their financial alliances carefully. To illustrate his point the professor quoted a respected peer, Dr. JD Copeland, "Science is the corruptible pursuit of discovery."

Over the past decade alone, the profitability and com-petitiveness of the genetics industry had increased three-fold. Genetic engineering had advanced at a pace simi-lar to the growth rate of computer technology twenty years earlier. Soon, like the evolutionary jump silicon chips created for computers, Ben predicted a similar break-through would occur in genetic engineering. His aspira-tion since graduate school was to make the discovery that propelled his industry into its own hyperspace.

Ben had deduced that a successful biogenetics com-pany mostly required money and out-of-the-box creativ-ity. In the last five years genetics had made monumental strides in biogenetically developed vegetables, insect-re-sistant plants, and organ cloning. The human genome had been mapped, which opened an unlimited potential for medical breakthroughs. Future triumphs were only limited by available funding. So when Steele offered him an extremely generous budget, bundled with the opportunity of creating a new life form by reverse-engineering a retrovirus, it had been impossible to refuse. At least that was what Ben had thought.

"Nathan, this project has been a geneticist's wish-come-true, a virtual wet dream, but we have to keep a-head of the financials if we're going to stay competitive."

"Finances, always finances." Nathan leaned back in his chair, temporarily pacified after venting his frustrations. "You know, Ben, it was blind luck that enabled us to isolate the right virus with literally hundreds to choose from."

"Luck was in finding an academic with soilborne virus expertise," Ben said. "It was a one-in-a-million that even Dr. Ruhpor was able to find us a suitable strain."

"We can't always depend on luck. It takes good research to stay on top, not just money."

"Yes, Nathan. I know."

"You do realize, Steele's the one squeezing our financial balls?" Ben did not respond. Nathan tilted his head back and stared out the window. "Okay, okay, if he wants 90, we'll give him 90. Who knows, maybe even more."

Ben reached across the desk and patted Nathan on the shoulder. "Thanks, buddy. I knew I could count on you."

10:43 a.m.—Central Coast, California

Tom Harden swung the office door open. "Dr. Ruhpor, sample N-T 2g3-2's scan is complete," the graduate student said as he poked his head through the doorway.

"Yes, yes . . . thank you, Tom." Dr. Ruhpor glanced over the stacks of papers littering his desk. "I'll be right there. Is Sheila behaving today?"

Tom grinned. Now in his second year, working on a doctorate in molecular biology, it still struck him funny when Dr. Ruhpor used the name Sheila for a machine as expensive as their scanning tunneling electron microscope. He suspected the name originated from a long lost love; obviously one with an attitude, because her electronic counterpart surely had one. Sheila always acted up, which was not too unusual for a machine sensitive enough to view molecular structures smaller than one angstrom—roughly one billionth of a centimeter.

"Yes, Dr. Ruhpor. An anomalous current fluctuation shorted the modulator unit. A technician came down last night and took care of it."

Closing his notepad, Dr. Ruhpor swapped it with another off one of the many stacks littering his desk and floor. The piles, he claimed, were a very complex filing system, one which boggled the minds of the most educated visitor. A rumor loose in the department hinted that the professor organized his office every couple of terms. The next cleaning date was an often-debated mystery. Although the clutter did not bother Tom nor Dr. Ruhpor, it disturbed the department head and a handful of the other faculty members. But that was their problem.

Dr. Ruhpor swept back his grayish-black Einsteinian hair, then rubbed the puffy circles under his eyes. Picking up his reading glasses, he moved easily among the paper mounds and met Tom in the hallway.

They entered the laboratory and Dr. Ruhpor sported an ear-to-ear grin as he closed the double-doors. Tom knew how proud the professor was of the Scanning Tunneling Electron Microscope Laboratory; it was one of his pet projects.

The school's administrators had argued in opposition to building the lab. They claimed not enough academic interest existed to support such a large investment. The administrators had been wrong. By the end of the second fiscal year, the revenues had repaid the loan, and the demand for the microscope continued to run near 93 percent, hardly allowing time for maintenance.

Upon inspection, the lab was rather plain, with its smooth off-white walls and polished concrete floor. In the center of the nearly empty room sat a large anchor-bolted black-steel-and-ceramic box. Next to the box were a gray steel desk and a putty-colored computer. The microscope's control interface was mounted on a stand to the right. At the far end of the room, a matched set of large, storage cabinets were lag-bolted to the wall. A steel door to the left of the cabinets led to the sample preparation laboratory. Not a lot to see, especially when he considered that the setup had cost the Natural Sciences Department more than three-quarters of a million dollars.

Much of the lab's technology was hidden behind the windowless walls. A HEPA air-filtration system recycled three equivalent room volumes every fifteen minutes, while removing suspended particles larger than one micron (half the size of a single-celled bacterium) from the climatically controlled atmosphere. The temperature never fluctuated more than a quarter of a degree from 72 degrees Fahrenheit. Relative humidity stayed within a comfortable range of 40 to 45 percent. When the thick, double front doors were closed, the lab was sound, dust, and vibration free—completely isolated from the outside. Thanks to Dr. Ruhpor, it was a place where Tom could go, be alone, and pursue his education and his interests.

In the center of the room the black-steel-and-ceramic box, or "black cube," as Tom called it, contained the scanning tunneling electron microscope—STEM. The microscope and box housing were an intricate concert of carbon fiber-steel, sound insulating foam, and ceramics. The box provided a resonance free, temperature-compensated environment that controlled the STEM's sensitivity to thermal drift. Dr. Ruhpor's design produced the highest degree of quantitative magnification available within the academic world.

Best of all, the STEM lab required no special sample handling equipment or protective technician clothing. Half of the time, Tom worked in a T-shirt, baggy shorts, and sandals. What a job.

Once the sample was prepped in the adjacent laboratory and transferred to the STEM, it never contacted the outside world until it was appropriately discarded. The system's sample isolation capability enabled guests to tour the lab during the school day without interfering with sensitive research or the scanning accuracy.

Dr. Ruhpor gave Tom an approving nod. "So, show me the latest."

Tom moved in front of the control interface, keyed in the commands and increased the magnification to 200,000 times the sample's original size. When the computations were finished, he pointed to a seventeen-inch, flat-screen monitor mounted above the keyboard. The enlarged image of the virus shown on the screen resembled a white cotton ball one centimeter in diameter resting on a loosely woven, fabric-like background.

"It's another quality sample, Dr. Ruhpor. The RNA sequencing is consistent, and the population count is stable. You were right. This strain's genetic character is well-adapted to the geothermal conditions near the San Andreas Fault system."

The professor took his glasses out of his shirt's front pocket and slid them in place. Bending toward the screen, he examined the STEM's enhanced viral image. "Excellent detail. What did you do differently?"

"Oh, the change, that was Nancy's suggestion. We dumped the directional gradient filter and replaced it with a Laplacian filter. What you see is the resulting real space sample analysis."

Smiling, Dr. Ruhpor patted Tom on the back. "Good

job. Very good."

He returned the smile, knowing it had been a long road for both of them. Almost three years earlier, as a last resort, Tom applied for entry into the Microbiology graduate program. He thought his life was over following a blown knee during his last season of collegiate football eligibility. The humiliation of leaving the field on a stretcher still brought painful memories. His pro career had fallen apart with one shattering blow. Up and until that time academics had not been a priority, so he held no illusions about his limited potential for a scholastic future.

Even though Tom had shown a mediocre aptitude, Dr. Ruhpor had taken a chance on him and ignored the recommendations of the Graduate School Committee. The professor must have seen something, for he pushed the approvals through and allowed Tom into the Soil Microbiology Research Program four months later. Neither man had regretted the decision. Tom was a dedicated graduate student, maintained straight A's, and demonstrated a mechanical ability unsurpassed by anyone else in the department. Dr. Ruhpor said Tom made the STEM possible, and he had taken the praise to heart.

"Have you set up the testing program to verify the virus' conditional boundaries?" Dr. Ruhpor asked.

"Yes, professor." Tom handed him the most recent logbook. "Are you anticipating any changes?"

The professor eased away from the computer monitor and perused the log. "Maybe, but nothing extreme." He made a notation in the margin of one page. "This strain should be more adaptable when compared to the last batch. I suspect we'll find it's less sensitive to natural climatic changes. However, let's be cautious and run the temperature tolerance to relative humidity and mortality analysis in triplicate. Its ultimate commercial viability will depend on those parameters."

Already aware of the requirements for the virus, Tom grinned. He envied Dr. Ruhpor's natural talent for mentoring. "Do you want to run the standard documentation tests before we hand the sample over to the BenaTex rep?"

"That'll be fine. Make certain you catalog this one as a new strain of retrovirus. While you're at it, make a split sample and store the copy in the prep lab."

Strange, Tom thought as he arched an eyebrow. "Whatever you say, Dr. Ruhpor."

11:52 a.m.—Arabela, New Mexico

"Meg, contact Ground Watch. We haven't heard from any-one in over three hours. I want thirty-minute updates until we get a handle on things." Rick gulped down his fourth extra large cup of coffee in the last hour, and his unsteady hands were beginning to show the effects.

"Right away." Meg punched the satellite uplink switch. "Ground Watch, this is Northern Eyes. How do you read? Ground Watch, do you copy?" They were too slow to respond. What was going on? Meg crossed her fin-gers—not them too. Rick stood behind her; his stare burned a hole in the back of her neck. The waiting was tearing him apart. What did he want her to do? She was no more in control of events than—

"Go ahead, Northern Eyes. This is Ground Watch."

Relieved, Meg quickly responded. "Ground Watch, how's Team Two's progress?" She felt her emotional con-trol skidding. Activity helped her escape the memories: the contorted expression on Stripes' face when he ripped off his protective mask, the astonished agony revealed by his eyes. The fear of losing field personnel was a job hazard she had kept suppressed in the recesses of her mind. Stripes was the best. Her teams were the best. They weren't supposed to die.

"Northern Eyes. . . . Sorry it took so long to re-spond. We've had a setback since our last communi-cation. . . . The locals ripped into the new base camp, and we haven't heard from Team Two."

Meg felt Rick move in closer. He bent down and listened over her shoulder. His warm breath distracted her. She stole a glance up at him. Fatigue had sunken his cheeks, and his tan features had gone ashen. "Ground Watch, what's your status? Do you have to abandon the location?"

The audio link speaker crackled. "Not yet. The last two attacks tested our defenses. If they strike us again, we might not have a choice."

"Ground Watch, hold on." Meg appealed to her boss. "What do I tell them?"

Rick was speechless. Only once before had they lost personnel, but that wasn't like this. They were rookies; Stripes and Chism were pros.

"Tell them they have four hours to complete the as-signment, and that's it. Then erase the operation and get out."

"And if they can't complete the assignment?"

"Then they are to save themselves any way they can."

11:28 a.m.—Sausalito, California

Ben Singular stood by his office window, gazing out-side while a light rain came down. He visualized the beginning of winter at Yale, sitting in the breezeway of Hadley Hall watching the snowflakes fall, the gothic ca-thedral towers capped with a thin layer of snow, the thick ivy growing on red brick walls gone dormant, and students pulling up the collars of their heavy coats as they sprinted to class. Those were good years, full of challenge and ex-citement. He achieved all his goals except one.

Even after graduating from Yale and starting his own

multibillion-dollar corporation, Ben never gave up hope on finding Lorie and his child, spending much of his money and time searching for them. He was determined to correct his mistake and make things right. School friends, professional detectives: no means was overlooked. Yet, as the years went by, his drive to be united with his lost family had waned.

The expense and false hopes were hard on him; his business ventures were unraveling. Circumstances forced Ben to forget the past and tend to his own needs. What other choice did he have? His life, his company, they required his full attention if he were to ever live his destiny.

He thought that once he married and had other children of his own, he could leave the stress and worries behind him, but then came the fullterm miscarriage. His wife Hannah was no longer able to bear children.

Ben closed his eyelids, shutting out the present, haunted by the past. He could still see her on the hospital bed; pain etched the dark creases encircling her eyes. She appeared so vulnerable, lost in a confused world, carrying the guilt of responsibility. It wasn't her fault, but she wouldn't listen. Never before had he felt this helpless. The realization of his own mortality renewed his need to seek out his firstborn son.

When Ben found Lorie, she lived in San Diego, had married, and their son, Matt, attended a local high school. He had grown to be a man. And to Ben's surprise, Lorie had not enlightened him about his real father, opting instead for their lives to evolve along a different path.

He leaned on his office windowsill and heard himself sigh. Lorie and Matt had discovered family symmetry, and Ben was not one to be selfish. No, he had made the ultimate sacrifice and had chosen to stay out of their lives. Lorie and her husband agreed with Ben's wishes and Matt never knew otherwise. Although best for his son, the decision had not come lightly. That fleeting moment had sanctioned him to a legacy with no legitimate heir, a lifetime without a father-son bond.

Had he made the right choice?

11:29 a.m.—San Francisco, California

"Send him up." Jolon Steele released the intercom button and sat poised behind his huge mahogany desk.

The door to his private elevator opened and a confident, yet common-looking man entered. He might have been over six feet tall and medium build, but never remained in one position long enough for an observer to be certain. His hair was a musty brown color. If not for the cold gleam of his light greenish eyes, this man could vanish unnoticed in any crowd.

"Mr. Osborne." He called the man by his current pseudonym. "Have a seat. How was your flight?" Steele feared no man; still, he closely watched this one. Osborne's reputation for clandestine espionage was unequaled. He was an enigma among his peers, a rogue with no apparent loyalties or exploitable vulnerabilities.

"Uneventful, Mr. Steele. Your message said you had a project of the utmost urgency." Osborne took a seat. "If we could proceed?"

"I appreciate your professionalism." Steele matched Osborne's dispassionate tone. " And I assure you, no one else knows of this meeting." He reached for a cigar, diverting his gaze from Osborne.

"I'll take your word for it, Mr. Steele. Now what can I do for you?"

Steele adjusted the angle of an embossed wooden plaque sitting on his desk. "I require your expertise on a project. I am concerned with our security—"

"Security's not my forte. You have the wrong man."

Osborne stood.

"Wait." Not the reaction Steele expected. "Hear what I have to say. If you do not want the job, you can walk." Osborne listened. "You are an expert at beating corporate surveillance systems, which makes your talents ideal for this assignment. In addition, discretion is required."

"In other words, you want someone outside of your own company." Osborne returned to his seat.

"You could say that, but most of all." Steele squirmed. "I want a professional who can covertly verify the security of a project of mine—ours."

Steele waited for a response as Osborne sat casually with his elbows perched on the chair's armrests, his fingers locked together in front of him. Did he catch the verbal lapse? No noticeable change surfaced in his expression. Osborne was too cool, a difficult one to judge. Trust came from control; there had to be a weakness, somewhere.

"What do I have to do?"

"You are to use whatever methods available to evaluate the reliability of everyone involved with this project. If you identify any problematic concerns, they are to be removed." Steele held out a thick file folder.

Osborne took the brown folder without viewing the contents. He locked onto Steele's gaze. "You know my fee. I'll be in touch within the week."

1:31 p.m.—Arabela, New Mexico

"Northern Eyes, come in, please!" The desperation of the plea hung in the air, amplified by the building's metal walls. Meg Hines was stunned, frozen where she stood, unable to respond. "Come in, please!"

Meg swung back into the present and tore across the room, lunging at the control console. "Go ahead, Ground Watch, we read." She punched another button by a blinking green light and activated the satellite video connection for the new base camp. The view showed a terrified Liam Jaries. His crazed glare made Meg's skin crawl. "Rick, come quick, it's Ground Watch. I have their commander on-line, and they're in trouble!"

Rick and two technicians raced from the next room to her side. "Get a lock on that signal! I don't want to lose him!"

With a nimble stroke of the computer's keys, Meg piggybacked the signal with another satellite. "It's ready. We got him."

"Northern Eyes, we're under attack. Chism was the only one to make it back alive!"

One of the technicians pointed to the video monitor. "His face, he's hysterical!" Blood caked the side of Jaries' scalp.

Rick donned a headset over one ear and switched a black knob on the communications board, muting the speakers. "Tell us your situation and we'll send help."

"You don't get it." Jaries shook his head, his image momentarily distorted. "The Indians waited until we called in the helicopters, then attacked. They used their earlier assaults to map our defenses. No one's getting in here and staying alive. We're all dead men."

"He's saying a lost group of Indians has beaten modern technology and fifteen of our best men." Listening on another headset, Meg gasped. "Impossible."

"Impossible or not," Rick said. "It's happened. Liam, can you hold on?"

"No . . . stay away. Chism, Taylor, and I are all that's left. Both helicopters were destroyed. Don't send anyone else in. They'll die, just—"

The screen flickered.

"Liam!"

The picture cleared.

"Rick."

"Yes, Liam."

"You're gonna have to write this one off."

"But—"

The screen flickered again and went blank. Horrified, Meg and Rick stood quietly. Their headphones hissed static. Frustrated rage reddened Rick's face. Meg collapsed backward into her chair as the shock sank deeper. Her heart ached like never before.

"We're out of business." Rick took one last glimpse at the blank screen. "Shut down the operation. I'll call Noble and our employer."

She stared up at him; tears flooded her eyes. Rick walked away.

October 5

12:21 p.m.—Sausalito, California

Sally Brinkman sat quietly eating her leftover stew in the far corner of the smallest of BenaTex's three lunchrooms. She heard the door open and glanced over to see Wade Fields enter. He headed her way. Her first instinct was to bolt for a safe hiding place, but he was too quick.

"Howdy, Sally, do you mind if I join you? Lunch is always better eat'n with a friend."

"Sure, Wade." Sally cringed and scouted the lunchroom for inquisitive stares. Although Wade was a handsome guy, standing an inch or two over six feet, with hazel eyes and a well-proportioned body, Sally disliked his nosiness. Wade was a gossip, always shoving his face into everyone else's business, a real flake. How he ever earned his doctorate in biochemistry was beyond her.

"Thanks." Wade pulled a chair up to the table and sat. "How's your day goin'?"

"Oh, the usual." Sally skirted a real conversation, then her eyes met his, and for a brief second, she caught a sensitive, caring expression on his rugged features. No, it had to be her imagination. She wiggled uncomfortably and fumbled for a reason to politely excuse herself. The lunchroom seemed to shrink, becoming claustrophobic, hardly able to hold its six medium-sized round tables, two vending machines, microwave, refrigerator, and sterile white Formica countertop.

"Your group's got a lot goin' on."

"Not really." Sally shrugged, avoiding further eye contact. His incessant probing irritated her. She groped for a way to put distance between them.

"That's not what I've heard." He scooted his chair over next to her. "Cooper's supposedly got y'all jumpin'."

Sally pulled away, trying to hide her uneasiness, knowing her body language had given her away. Her nose wrinkled along the bridge, the way it did when she was restless. As she gave the lunchroom another scan, her petite figure tensed defensively. He had trapped her into this conversation. Wade had ways of manipulating information out of people, and Sally refused to fall prey to him. She whisked her shoulder-length hair behind an ear and acted indifferent.

"Those are just rumors, and you know how they get started."

He brushed off her response with a sigh. "I even heard they've got y'all separated into teams to keep everythin' hush-hush. Blue team, red team, that kinda stuff. It sounds like overkill to me. Why all the darn secrecy?"

"Wade, I can't discuss an active project. You know that." Her shoulders pulled tight as she hoped no one had heard him. "It's against corporate policy."

"Wow, you guys on Blue Team are touchy." Wade rocked his chair onto two legs, feigning annoyance with her policy reference.

"I have to get to work." She pushed back her chair.

"Y'all haven't finished eatin'."

"I'll see you later, Wade." Standing abruptly, Sally grabbed her lunch bag and headed for the exit. Wade's knowledge of in-house secrets amazed her. She wondered how he found out about Blue Team. He had to be connected to someone at the top. Sally held the door and cast a glance at him sitting alone. Somehow, today was different. He had a strange air to him, one she hadn't noticed before. As the door closed, Wade looked up and held her gaze.

6:40 p.m.—San Francisco, California

Ben Singular finished his dinner, left the Tempura Palace Restaurant, and strolled onto the sidewalk. A pleasant evening breeze blew inland over the bay. He stopped at the curb, slipped out of his wool sport coat and slung it across his arm. Travelers heading home after a long day packed the street. Ben did his best to relax among them; loosening his tie and unbuttoning his collar. Removing his cellular phone from his coat pocket, he pressed the encryption button on the side and dialed a private number, and then he exhaled.

"This is Steele."

"Singular, Mr. Steele. We have to talk."

"Be at my office in one hour."

Five minutes later, Ben sat behind the steering wheel of his custom BMW 750i—fresh out of the repair shop. He exited the restaurant's parking lot onto Powell Street, eventually following a circuitous route that included Golden Gate Park. During the forty-minute drive, he collected his thoughts, but in the end was unable to come up with a way to mitigate Steele's predictable reaction to his news. The man never appreciated complications.

Ben left Market Street and drove into the underground parking garage beneath Janstone Pharmaceuticals' highrise where he slipped his car into a reserved space. He switched the ignition off and contemplated his next move.

Inside the BMW, the extreme quietness reminded him of an embalmer's office. A desolate feeling lodged in the pit of his stomach. The rapid thump of his heart throbbed in his ears. He smelled the rich leather seats and caressed the genuine wood trim, anything to clear his mind of his worries. Then for no reason, he laughed.

What could Steele do—fire him? Hardly. Taking a deep breath, Ben grabbed his briefcase and walked toward the garage elevators. Spent oil and exhaust fumes lingered and the tap of his leather soles on the floor echoed among the concrete walls.

A security guard passed him through to Steele's private elevator and Ben pressed the button for eighteen. The door shut and the carpeted floor lurched upward. Gripping his briefcase, Ben looked away from his reflection in the elevator's polished brass panels. Steele would recognize the fact that no one could have foreseen these events—right.

The elevator stopped and the doors parted at Steele's office. Ben saw him standing next to his mahogany conference table.

Steele pointed to a chair. "We have a slight complication," he said, rolling a Cuban cigar between his index finger and thumb. "Apparently a Stanford University professor is planning a trip to the Amazon. This Dr. Isling is on a pilgrimage to find our lost Indian tribe."

Ben didn't speak. Whose meeting was this anyway? Typical Steele; he always had to be in control. Ben took the seat and shook his head. Not another problem, he worried, but kept silent, trying to hide his reaction. What could go wrong next?

"This information does not impress you, Dr. Singular?"

"Uh . . . there've been other developments." Steele's eyes took on a strange yellowish glow. Was it the lighting or had their color changed? Ben downplayed the chilling apparition to his imagination.

"And?"

"It's the Amazon Project. A ground team was attacked."

"By whom?"

"We're not certain, but I should know soon. Most

likely the subject tribe." Steele had not moved, not even a twitch. Ben felt his hands tremble under the icy stare of Steele's yellow eyes. He tasted stomach acids fuming into his throat. His ulcer was taking a beating. Again, Steele showed no response to Ben's troubling information.

"Is this the news we had to discuss?"

Suppressing his surprise, Ben balled his right hand into a fist and kept his expression neutral. Somehow, Steele knew of the attack. The man had spies everywhere.

"I assume your covert Amazon team will remain on location?"

"Yes. They'll stay until the hospital testing and site decontamination are completed." That was basically the truth.

"I suggest, Dr. Singular, that you discover who has interfered with your Amazon project. Meanwhile, I will manage Dr. Isling's inconvenient expedition."

Ben sat transfixed by Steele's diabolical glower. He understood all too well what Steele meant by "manage."

Noticing Singular's hesitation, the executive scowled. "What do you think we have been doing these last eighteen months with your Amazonian test program?"

"That was in the name of science." Ben could not believe his own words. He had just vindicated the agonizing deaths of more than twenty innocent Indians in the name of scientific advancement. What kind of animal had he become? Dr. Ben Singular was no better than Dr. Mengele of Auschwitz! Steele simply smiled.

The private line sitting on Steele's desk rang and he picked it up. The interruption seemed to distract him some. "Yes. One moment." He pressed the hold button, then handed Ben a thin stack of papers. Their meeting had concluded.

"Before you leave, Dr. Singular."

"Yes."

Steele stroked his cigar. "Did you deliver the birthday present to your son?"

"Uh . . . no, not yet." Actually, he neglected to mention that he had tossed it off the Golden Gate Bridge.

"That is a shame." Steele rotated his chair toward the telephone, turning his back to Ben. "I expect to hear from you soon, Dr. Singular."

"You will." Ben shoved the papers inside his briefcase and left.

* * *

Jolon Steele watched the elevator doors close and groomed the end of his cigar in an ashtray. Dr. Singular would have to be cut loose sooner then planned. Steele mused; he would handle Singular with creative flair. He released the hold button.

"I am impressed, Mr. Osborne. I did not expect to hear from you this soon. What do you have for me?"

"As you requested, Mr. Steele, I've finished a preliminary assessment and found your presumption to be correct. There are significant security oversights, any one of which could bring down your project."

"Then, Mr. Osborne, the appropriate action is to surgically remove those oversights. You are therefore directed to execute the job promptly and professionally. I expect no delays. Do I make myself clear?"

"Consider it done." Osborne hung up.

7:53 p.m.—San Jose, California

Forty miles south of San Francisco, a gentle wind blew through a graffiti-tarnished phone booth. A woman ushered a small terrier across the street, briefly catching Osborne's attention as he passed a prepaid calling card through the slot and dialed another number. He listened to the phone ring while watching the woman pull the collar of her ankle length coat tight about her neck and lead the dog toward a distant park.

A gravelly voice answered. "Yeah."

"Your unique manpower services are required."

"How many?"

"Four to six."

"Should be doable."

"Meet me at the usual place to discuss the details."

"I'll be there nine tomorrow morning," the man confirmed, then hung up.

Pausing outside the phone booth, Osborne mentally set up his next move, recalling his trip to Steele's office, visualizing his observations for pertinent details. He assessed the furnishings for revealing clues, determining the decor was designed to intimidate. Photographs of powerful people shaking hands with Jolon Steele hung on a far wall opposite his desk. Most of the faces were men and women of right-wing political persuasions. Framed degrees, certificates, and awards covered another wall, establishing an air of technical competency, if not superiority. No plants. No signs of life.

He remembered noticing the jade sculpture of a Central American jaguar head. The antiquity sat alone in one corner, meticulously placed on a narrow wooden stand. The piece's violent expression and harshly carved features bothered Osborne. Its ethereal eyes and isolation from the main body of the office made him think of Steele. This was the game room of a corporate hunter.

Osborne sensed the meeting had been videotaped. He'd take care of that annoyance later. It was always prudent to be careful, and Osborne never took unnecessary risks. His training did not allow room for such simple mistakes in judgment.

An expert at his trade, Osborne had always watched for the smallest details, a remnant of his formal British education, where he had also undergone corporate espionage training with MI6 and then further indoctrination two years later with the Mossad. A natural skeptic anyway, he was wary of anything Steele might have said. Men in Osborne's position often acted on instinct and his warned him not to take Steele too lightly, which wasn't much of a surprise. Over the years, if nothing else, Osborne had learned that those who typically sought his services had their own secrets to hide.

On occasion, even Osborne had freelanced his talents to lone-wolf managers like Steele; the vermin of humanity, men who assumed they were above everyone else, compelled by insatiable greed, not greed for money, but for the kind of power measured in ruined lives. He recalled Steele's verbal lapse regarding the reference to his versus the company's project and was surprised that the executive had made the error. He didn't seem the type. By the end of their meeting, Steele had left no doubt that Janstone Pharmaceuticals had not sanctioned this project. But was this a setup? Was Steele providing misdirection on purpose? He made another mental note to protect himself and watch for a double cross.

Osborne scanned the area within sight of the telephone booth. The night had a pre-rain moistness, not a pleasant time to be outdoors. He zipped his navy blue flight jacket up half way; then canvassed his surroundings one more time. Leaves riding on a sudden gust swirled into the air. Cupping his hands in front of his face, he lit a cigarette and studied the street. A light sprinkle began to fall. Corner streetlights cast a yellow hue across parked cars and billowing trees. A scraping noise came from an alley on his right. He chucked his cigarette into the gutter and stepped next to the entrance, allowing a second for his eyes to adjust to the darkness.

He extracted a Smith & Wesson 9mm pistol from a holster hidden under his jacket. The gun had a natural fit to his hand. Another shuffling noise held him in place, and he slowed his breathing to one shallow lung full every three seconds. He concentrated, bringing his heart rate down to an average of forty-five beats per minute.

These calming abilities heightened his reactions and opened his senses. Rain splattered a metal awning to his left and wind whipped by his legs. Osborne extended his thoughts, visualizing, focusing down the alley. He detected a sound—denim pant legs rubbing together—he crept closer.

Quickly rounding the corner, he pointed his pistol ahead, covering the alley, finger in the ready position. His eyes swept side-to-side, never stopping for more than a fraction of a second: a banged-up trash dumpster, a dozen rain-soaked cardboard boxes piled next to the far building, a wooden pallet leaned against the boxes. The alley reeked of urine and other human excrement, but there were no signs of anyone. Then Osborne heard running footfalls splashing through puddles, and as he listened, the sound melted into the rhythmic beat of the rain. Logging the incident to a homeless vagrant, he waited, relaxed, holstered his weapon, and returned to the street.

Stopping at the curb, Osborne lit another cigarette. The problem with his line of work was someone always had an interest in him. He could never let his guard down. Yet, that very uncertainty was what gave him such a psychological rush. Always pushing, his survival hung in the balance of every decision.

October 6

7:01 a.m.—Central Coast, California

Matt Wells rubbed the remaining sleep from his eyes with the back of his hand and entered his first class. The analytical side of his brain did not function well until after ten o'clock in the morning, and a 300-level physics course at seven was cruel punishment. He assessed the classroom's available space, eventually taking a seat at the rear, near a side exit.

Professor Elbert arrived four minutes after the hour carrying notes and a coffee cup, which apparently had not seen a dishwasher for quite some time. The professor set his papers and cup on the front podium. He withdrew an electric razor from an inside pocket of his wrinkled sport coat. As Dr. Elbert shaved his graying stubble, he introduced himself, then distributed a course syllabus.

"This guy can't be for real." Matt sank into his seat and ran his index finger down the syllabus. "What have I gotten myself into? This is the last time that I let the Doc pick my classes." He read the clock on the wall above the professor's head and estimated the time left until class ended. Fifty minutes later, even before Elbert sputtered his last incomprehensible word, Matt was the first one through the doorway.

With an hour to kill before his next class, Matt

used the hiatus to investigate his new campus. The perfect weather, the perfect day: a clear blue sky, a mild southeasterly breeze, and a temperature in the low 70s. He grabbed a bagel at the cafeteria and wandered west along a horseshoe-shaped road spanning the school's interior.

A quick appraisal left him with the impression that Cal Poly lacked an identity. Every building projected a unique theme. The architecture ranged from early concrete bomb shelter to new-millennium glass works. It gave him visions of a student project gone mad. He laughed; if nothing else, the place had character.

Half way across the campus, Matt happened upon a large gathering area. He left the road and strolled onto a grassy expanse below a Spanish-style clock tower; the same one that he could see from the Doc's class the other day. He scanned the area, feeling at home.

Students roamed the lawn, tossed Frisbees, and threw footballs, anything to burn excess energy between classes. Others studied, visited with friends, or ate assorted snacks. The casual sight reminded him of good times at San Diego State.

Matt spotted a yellow flyer stapled to a shaded pillar bulletin board. For some reason it aroused his curiosity and he made his way over. The announcement described a classical music concert scheduled for the Performing Arts Center on Friday night. He arched an eyebrow.

A Matt Wells heaven included a warm evening with a seductive female and classical music lofting in the background. He sighed as more memories of the hot Cabo nights pervaded his thoughts; the vivid sensation of Cindi's sensual body lying entwined with his . . . Damn, he needed a date before he slipped into an emotional coma and began hallucinating about naked women dancing on his chest. Then again . . .

Casually perusing his immediate surroundings told him that his new school came furnished with many unattached female beauties. It shouldn't be too difficult to secure one for the night. A steamy blonde and a sultry brunette sitting on the lawn stopped their conversation and turned his direction. They gave him a slow inspection and he acknowledged their attention with a tip of his head. He smiled. Naw, it wouldn't be difficult at all.

10:58 a.m.—Manaus, Brazil

The Boeing 767 landed on the International Airport Eduardo Gomes' main runway with a sharp jolt, waking Dr. Isling. Pleased to have slept so well, he readjusted his glasses on his nose and returned an outdated Time Magazine to the seat rack. On his left, his young assistant James Monal was folded over snoring.

James had been Isling's assistant for the last three years. He was the brightest and youngest graduate student Isling had ever worked with. And in many ways, James reminded him of his son. They were both twenty-three and ready to conquer the world. Like his son, James was tall and thin, had brown hair, brown eyes, and loved the outdoors. Their only difference, was his son had gone into acting. Of all the careers he could have chosen, the positive contributions to society he could have made, why had his son shunned it all to become an actor? Isling would never understand that decision.

"My, boy." The professor nudged his assistant's shoulder. "We have arrived." Isling's baritone voice sounded like a Spanish explorer landing in the New World, and he chuckled at the implication.

"What? Oh yeah, seems so." James stretched his long legs into the aisle.

"Numb?"

"A little." He yawned and watched passengers in the adjacent rows begin readying themselves to disembark.

A small child a couple of seats away cried, and James groaned. "I feel the same way."

"Pardon?"

"Nothing, Dr. Isling. Just undoing the kinks."

"Get loosened up quickly, my boy. We've got a lot to do. When we pass customs," Dr. Isling pulled his brief-case onto his lap, "get the team together and remind everyone of our timetable. I don't want any delays."

James shed his residual sleep with another large yawn and a mild cough. The cabin air was stale and smoky. Many international flights, including their five-hour flight from Mexico City, had not adopted a nonsmoking policy. "Yes, sir. By the way, when I called the local embassy, they assured me the Brazilian Customs officials would work with us."

Dr. Isling gave his assistant a disbelieving smirk. "I'm not that confident, James. We've run into government bureaucrats before, and their unnecessary paperwork can bog things down."

"I'll take care of everything."

"I trust you will, my boy."

Staring out the window, Isling marveled at the horizon, painted with sculpted mountains and tree-blanketed slopes. Pico da Neblina, the highest peak in view, towered 9,800 feet above the jungle floor. The plane turned west off the main runway onto the third ramp, Sierra Three, and lurched to a stop. Tearing his gaze away from the entrancing scenery, he bent down and sifted through one of his carry-on bags.

Neither James nor Dr. Isling noticed the man two rows back eavesdropping on their conversation.

11:04 a.m.—Amazon Lowlands, Brazil

The high priest, Cocataél, looked down upon his subjects while they recited their devotions. He felt the power of the ages flow from him, spreading throughout the sacred ground, touching each soul, preparing them for their divine calling. Cizin, the death god, would be pleased with their preparations, and even more pleased with their actions. By the hundreds, Burbános worshipers had left four different villages, braving the dangerous nightlong trek through the jungle to be part of the ceremony. At sunrise they had gathered, eager to hear their god speak.

Two hundred and sixty bamboo torches burned along the boundary where their sacred site met the jungle. Fifty-two human skulls stacked in four pyramid groups of thirteen segregated an area for the high priest. Exuding the metaphysical aura of guardian spirits, the skulls marked the celestial corners: north, south, east, and west. Centered between the pyramids, a limestone altar, carved with effigies of bloody rituals, rested on a wooden platform waist high above the ground. Gifts of adornment, including gold, jewelry, food, and pottery had been placed at the base of the altar.

Cocataél lifted another warm human heart above his head; blood streamed between his fingers, splattering on the altar stone. Entranced by the ceremony's mystical ambiance, the chanting worshipers rocked back and forth, as their religious fervor intensified with the culmination of each successive human sacrifice. Cocataél seized the moment by walking to one of the platform's four corners, brandishing the severed heart and the majesty of his brightly colored feather-laden crocodile headdress before his subjects. The crowd hushed, then continued their chants of adoration as he moved on. Through him spoke the Feather Serpent man-god, Quetzalcóatl.

Faith in their heritage and future glory had helped Cocataél's people survive the merciless jungle for more than 480 calendar cycles, and for the last two moonrises, the gods had blessed them in battle. They had avenged their ancestors by conquering the White Devil. Now his warriors feasted on the hearts of their victims.

The tempo of the chanting increased when Cocataél stopped before the altar stone and squeezed the heart, draining the last of the dying organ's blood into a ceremonial bowl. He cut the muscle into small segments while two naked priestesses knelt on his right, lashing themselves with ragged strips of dry leather. In the crowd, a young warrior used a boned knife to carve a serpent icon into his bare chest. Cocataél smiled. Ah Chuy Kak the fire god of war would bless their offerings with more victories. The high priest laid the chunks of heart on a clay platter adjacent to the ceremonial bowl. He then whispered the words of eternal homage while watching another sacrificial victim being carried to the platform.

Four Burbános warriors held the White Devil by his arms and legs above the kneeling crowd. A path through the faithful parted and they approached the high priest. With their heads humbly bowed, the warriors went down on one knee before the platform. Cocataél motioned with his hand for them to place the body on the altar. The crowd hushed.

The white man lay stretched out flat on the cold stone, his eyes glazed with fear. He had an idea of what was happening and fought to move, but his muscles remained paralyzed. Same as the others before him, his alert mind screamed with terror at his helplessness.

The chanting returned, louder and louder. Perimeter drums began; their hypnotic beat drove the crowd on, faster and faster. They were peaking, reaching rapture. His people would be reborn, stronger, unstoppable.

Raising the scepter high above the white man's head, Cocataél called to the gods to accept this mortal sacrifice and guide his people into their new beginning. Once again, his people fell silent. The jungle fell silent.

With deadly precision, the high priest brought the

scepter crashing down into the man's mouth, crushing his jaw and knocking loose his teeth. Blood spewed from the cratered face.

Hank Chism's eyes bulged as if they were going to explode. They were silent windows to his torment. His screams went unheard, and he raged, powerless to escape his fate. Pain from his smashed jaw was unbearable. Blood clogged his throat. A serrated knife plunged downward; its uneven surface hacked into his chest. The world turned mercifully black as he sank into permanent peace.

A quiet hum permeated the worshipers and they swayed back-and-forth. The white warrior's spirit had been released, liberated. His incised chest lay wide open; blood seeped across the bare pale skin, dripping onto the altar stone. Cocataél pried apart the rib cage and exposed the heart. He gripped the pulsing muscle with both hands, drenching his fingers in the blood of his victim's immortal spirit. A satisfied smile crossed his face. He raised the heart with outstretched arms. Blood gushed onto the altar from the mutilated corpse. The gathering called out, their cries echoing: "Ah Chuy Kak!" . . . "Ah Chuy Kak!" . . . "Quetzalcóatl!" They undulated in a continuous human tide.

Blood poured from the amputated heart into the sacred bowl, slowly blending with the red fluid of the warrior's dead companions. Cocataél waited for the last drop to fall, then he used the ceremonial knife and sliced the muscle into thirty sections. The still warm pieces were arranged next to the other heart fillets already evenly distributed on the clay platter.

Cocataél removed his own penis from behind its protective leather covering, draping his genitals above the sacred bowl. A quick slash with the ceremonial knife opened a small laceration behind the head. The crowd screamed with ecstasy. Blood coursed down his organ. His own life force flowed into the bowl, becoming one with that of the white warriors'. Cocataél wiped his penis and bound the laceration with a ribbon of blue cloth. He then ripped another length of white fabric into short strips, soaking each in the bloody mixture. The cloths were held high for the crowd to view. The drums beat softly in the background.

Once dried, Cocataél would give a length of cloth and segment of heart to every Burbános warrior, exemplifying the great valor they had shown in defeating the White Devil. His warriors would consume the heart and burn the cloth, communicating directly with the Sky World. In this way, they captured the spirit and strength of their enemies and bonded with the gods.

The ceremony had been a success. All had gone as planned. Quetzalcóatl showed Cocataél's people his will. The White Devil would never again haunt the Burbános.

12:06 p.m.—Manaus, Brazil

James Monal sat with his eyes closed and his head resting on the seat. Being stuck in a smoky smelly airplane was not his idea of an Amazon adventure. If nothing else, he wanted to check out the local sights. From what he had read, seldom did mainstream tourists frequent Manaus, the gateway to the Amazon Lowlands. Its isolated location attracted the more courageous souls—people seeking challenges capable of taking them to the limit. James assumed, regardless of the tourist hype, the Amazon existed as untamed today as it had for centuries. Fierce and exotic creatures, searing weather, and bloodsucking insects lingered, waiting for the ignorant visitor.

"Are you sure this is an 'International' airport?" Dr. Isling asked. "We've been parked on the tarmac for more than an hour, and this silly place has weeds growing through cracks in the runway."

"That's what they call it." James shrugged. "But I'm

not surprised. The school's travel agency warned that even though the outlying population has over a million people, modern conveniences were still scarce. During the 1920s Manaus was a boomtown for rubber barons, and I assume some of that wild exuberance still exists. Although, it's supposed to have mellowed over the years and become more touristy." James peered down the aisle for any sign of movement. "It might not be all bad. When I spoke with Dr. Leland, he mentioned the Teatro Amazonas. He thought the opera house's neoclassic design might catch your architectural eye."

"What does an old-fart department antique like him understand of neoclassic design? Humph." Dr. Isling scowled while reconnoitering the tropical surroundings through the plane's port window. He turned his back on James and shook his head. "I'd hate to disappoint him. Maybe we can visit the theater on the return trip."

James snickered, knowing Dr. Isling's curiosity always got the better of him.

"I'm glad we came prepared, my boy. Looks like the clouds are thickening. I suspect we're in for rough weather. What do you think?"

"Pretty nasty stuff. I'll unpack our personal jungle gear right after the baggage is unloaded."

Dr. Isling ran his hand across his nubby gray hair. "James, when can we catch our flight to São Gabriel da Anjo?"

"If things go as we prescheduled, it shouldn't be too long. On Tuesday before we left, I spoke with the local immigration officials. They said we'd clear customs and be on our way within 24-hours after touchdown." James unzipped his planner and reviewed his notes. "Although it sounded great at the time, I assumed nothing was too definitive. I hope we're not in for a delay."

Gesturing impatiently, Dr. Isling tapped the seat's armrests with his fingertips. "I do believe we're closing in on a stupendous find, and I don't want any setbacks."

Dr. Isling's driving enthusiasm bordered on obsessive. At the start of every expedition, Isling experienced a euphoric phase. In James' view, it was akin to a kid pressing his face on the front window of a closed toy store, counting away the minutes until it opened.

"I guess I shouldn't get too anxious. Remember our Mexico dig south of Chichén Itzá two summers ago?"

"How could I forget?" The expedition to Chichén Itzá was the first major excursion James had been on with Dr. Isling; a grueling adventure into the core of the Yucatán peninsula. James retained vivid memories of trudging in mud up to his kneecaps, using tree branches to inspect his boots for snakes, avoiding a sun that broiled everything in sight, and hacking through a jungle that seemed to have a will of its own. In the end, when they had unearthed the ruins and James climbed through the tomb's arched entry, he realized that he would endure any hardship to experience such a discovery again.

"I was afraid we weren't ever going to get our travel papers approved," James said as he leaned into the aisle and pulled his carry-on bag down from the overhead bin. "One minute the Mexican government loved us, the next, they treated us like we had the plague. The Yucatán's regional unrest didn't help matters either."

"Nothing good comes easy, my boy. It took effort, but we eventually won them over." Dr. Isling stood and stretched, then moved into the aisle next to James and winked. "When we uncovered the tomb of the second known female Maya ruler, the Mexican Archaeological Society went crazy over our find. And remember, we used science, not the Palenque psychic hotline." He rolled his eyes in disgust.

James smiled.

A psychic had helped find the first female Maya ruler at Palenque, Chiapas. The breakthrough had shaken the archaeological world, and James still remembered the article in Archaeology Magazine.

"The royal tomb and skeleton of the first documented female Maya ruler were uncovered beneath Temple 13. This spectacular discovery was the result of 'energy' sensations felt by a French psychic visiting Palenque. The psychic informed the ruin's archaeologist of her 'feeling' and warned they must ask 'permission' of the dead souls before entering. An archaeological team followed the psychic's instructions and found the royal tomb intact. . . ."

"Even though you don't believe a psychic helped locate the tomb, facts are facts, Dr. Isling. The archaeological team found everything where she had predicted."

"Humph, superstitious garbage. I'm just glad our more astute scientific colleagues chided the idea of an archaeological psychic network." Preparing to leave the plane, Dr. Isling put on an old, moth-eaten khaki green bucket hat, adjusting its angle to shade his eyes. The hat was his good luck bald-spot protector, and he wore it on every expedition.

"Dr. Isling, you have to admit there are many unexplained revelations regarding the Maya beyond their extraordinary mathematical ability." James recalled the vibrations emanating from the female ruler's tomb. Though he was touched by the sensation, he had not mentioned it to anyone.

"What now, are we going to have that alien debate? Or maybe the more esoteric one, suggesting the Maya Feather Serpent man-god Quetzalcóatl is an Atlantian?" Uncomfortable with the conversation's direction, Dr. Isling shuffled his feet.

"Are you saying, in the more than thirty-three years that you've been studying the Maya, you've never considered a non-terrestrial source for their technology?"

His mentor's restricted views regarding the potential metaphysical origins of some cultures frustrated James.

"Never." Dr. Isling proudly smiled. "I will admit that the ancient Maya were remarkable, even gifted; however, in every case, we've been able to discover a scientific basis for our findings."

James rifled through his carry-on bag for his passport, wondering how Dr. Isling, an accomplished archaeologist and anthropologist, could be that narrowminded. But this was not a debate he wanted to suffer through while stuck in a plane on the Manaus airport tarmac. "Either way the expedition went well. And thanks to our findings the Mexican government preserved the ruins and their antiquities before modern grave robbers had stolen anything."

"Don't forget Stanford was graciously allowed to showcase the artifacts. Yes, James, despite your naïve scientific beliefs, we make an incredible team." Dr. Isling patted his graduate student on the shoulder. Passengers migrated in the direction of the forward exit. "So let's get our anthropologic rear ends on the road. More wonders await us."

10:15 a.m.—Sausalito, California

Ben Singular entered the A-Wing laboratory where he found his partner sitting alone at one of the computer stations. Nathan Donner was the brightest genetics engineer in the business, and a good friend. He was, however, a typical mega-nerd. Even in college, except for fantasizing about how to alter their DNA, Nathan had little to do with other organic forms of life. In those hormonal-driven early days, Ben's charismatic appeal and handsome features were all it had taken to seduce the women of his choice. He shook his head, saddened; that had been almost ten years ago, and things change.

One thing that had not changed was Ben and Nathan's opposite personalities, a key ingredient to their effective business relationship. Ben handled the public affairs, financial, and personnel aspects of the company, while Nathan focused on the technical issues. On occasion, they had their differences, but for the most part their alliance created a solid team.

"Why don't you turn on the lights?" Ben asked, surveying the lab to ensure their privacy. "That puny desk lamp can't do the job. Live a little. I'm pretty sure we paid last month's electric bill."

"Funny." Nathan showed Ben a half smile. "I perform better in the dark." He laughed. "It helps unclutter my mind of your lousy jokes. Besides, I hate the resonate noise the ceiling lights produce." Nathan motioned upward with his eyes.

He was so damn hypercritical. It drove their staff crazy, and Ben was always mitigating the tension. Everything Nathan came in contact with had to function perfectly, otherwise he whined like a toddler with dirty underwear. Ben imagined his youngest daughter running to the bathroom screaming while a soupy brown liquid streamed down her leg. He chuckled.

Regardless, putting up with his partner's peculiarities went with the job. Nathan was brilliant; no one could touch him when it came to analyzing the functionality of a retrovirus' capability to reverse its genetic transcription from RNA to DNA, versus adhering to the standard DNA to RNA pathway.

"How are the stats on the latest batch?" Ben asked.

"Good, good. The new viral strain has a unique thermal resilience."

Nathan puffed up his chest. Ben could see how proud he was of their progress. He knew that before long Nathan would make the necessary breakthrough and bring him a genetically altered retrovirus.

"Thanks to the professor, I think we have found the one

with the right baseline properties. Dr. Ruhpor knows his stuff." Nathan pointed to his computer monitor. "Take a look at these and tell me what you think."

Ben peeked over Nathan's shoulder. "Are you comfortable with the numbers?"

"Ran them twice, but a decisive conclusion is premature." Nathan scrolled up the screen, showing Ben the entire data set. "We'll have a more detailed picture tomorrow morning when I get the final computer analysis."

"I want you to push the data through the numerical model right away. The Amazon project is having difficulties." Ben did not dare tell him the whole truth, though he assumed Nathan suspected something. Although his partner was a gifted scientist, his prerogative to do the right thing would just get in the way. He'd never understand that self-sacrifice was often necessary. If Nathan ever discovered that many of the Indians had died as a result of their work. . . . My God, Ben stopped himself. All life was precious. Steele had brought this moral decline upon him. Ben's jaw muscles tightened as he forced himself to stay composed.

"Okay, Nathan. Keep the lid screwed on tight. We'll review the results after you've modeled the final data."

"Are we going to field test the last viral adjustment?"

Regret overcame his thoughts as he saw Nathan's innocent expression. What had he done? Ben took a breath, accepting there was no turning back. He'd take care of everything. "I'll do my best, Nathan, but it doesn't appear too hopeful."

2:46 p.m.—Manaus, Brazil

Even after America's 9/11 terrorist attack the industrialized nations had not devised a foolproof system to protect air transportation from a determined saboteur.

And by comparison, security in Third World countries was dismal, anyone with a few skills could roam the grounds of an interior Brazilian airport. The laxed controls at the International Airport Eduardo Gomes were no exception.

The Chameleon had gone unchallenged while posing as a flight service technician. His dirt-stained buff-colored fatigues matched those worn by the other maintenance workers scattered throughout the airport. Even his naturally darkened features had taken on a more native Indian appearance. A wave to a guard at the front gate and the impostor passed through without question.

The Chameleon's shoulders sagged forward and he relaxed into a casual stride. His ability to ease into a disguise and complete an assignment was unequaled. That after all was why the American, Osborne, had hired him.

Heat currents danced in waves above the hot asphalt surface. Making his way across the tarmac, the Chameleon approached the charter plane from the south. He stopped to wipe his forehead before circling the tail section of the multi-engine King Air 200. If anyone watched, he would be just another member of the ground crew conducting the airplane's preflight check. He canvassed the fuselage using his peripheral vision, verifying it was free of any unwanted intrusion by airport personnel.

The Chameleon moved behind the starboard engine, eyeing the three-bladed prop. His hand followed the tapered margin of the left aileron, then he walked to the front of the plane and ducked beneath the curved surface of the wing's leading edge. Squatting down, he examined the retractable landing gear.

His fingers traced the gear's center shaft into a large circular aperture under the wing, and from there, he inspected the available space, searching for obstructions. He visualized how the landing gear would hang after takeoff, concluding, the wheel-well opening provided a perfect hiding place for his package.

Carefully, the Chameleon produced a tiny white box from a side pocket of his coveralls. Finding a location where his gift would not be disturbed, he slid it into place. A magnet grabbed the reinforced metal surface of a wing strut with a clank.

He studied the configuration of critical in-flight control components in relation to the placement of the device. It would sit amongst the wing's hydraulic lines, a few inches below the right fuel tank. He pushed the box deep into the wheel-well and depressed a concealed button, arming the unit. When the airplane reached an altitude of nine thousand feet, a pressure-sensitive preprogrammed destruct sequence would be initiated. A bead of sweat trickled down his forehead and a crooked grin crossed his face. Even if someone detected the package prior to takeoff, it resembled any number of parts making up the plane's mechanical system. It would pass unnoticed.

The airplane's schedule indicated no charters until tomorrow morning. That was good, because the next flight this King Air made would be its last. His employer would be satisfied. The Chameleon finished the preflight inspection and disappeared across the tarmac.

October 7

10:23 a.m.—Manaus, Brazil

James Monal stretched and Dr. Isling dumped his duffel bag on a desk in the middle of the room while the rest of the archaeology team settled into their temporary accommodation.

"Nice of the airport manager to let us use this office to get organized. James, when you get an opportunity, see to it the school sends the local officials a thank-you card."

"I've made a note to do so, professor." Tilting his head to the side, James eyeballed the humble surroundings. Spiders, dust, and mildew seemed to be the inspired themes. Most likely, the room had stored greasy airplane parts until a few hours earlier.

"Thanks, James. Now, everyone." Dr. Isling clapped his hands together. "Attention everyone. We've had a good night's rest and it's time to get busy. Let's inspect our equipment and make certain everything arrived safely."

While the other archaeological team members unpacked boxes and crates, James realized how awed he was of this prestigious group; possibly the finest ever assembled. Besides himself there were five members, each an expert in their field: Dr. Henry Isling, a leading anthropologist with Stanford University and an authority on Mesoamerica cultures, Dr. Aidan MacKiernan, a medical doctor with the University of San Francisco and a revered researcher on tropical diseases, Dr. Ann Wright, a paleobotanist on sabbatical from the University of California, Los Angeles and a well-published tropical plant specialist, and the newest member to sign onto their team, Dr. David Sooner, an archaeologist with Purdue University and a scholar of Post Mesoamerica Maya architectural design and construction. Keeping up with this group was going to be a challenge.

The telephone on the desk rang. James answered. He cupped the receiver and motioned to catch Dr. Isling's attention. "Yes, thank you. I'll tell him." James hung up.

"Excuse me, Aidan." Dr. Isling crossed the room, leaving Dr. MacKiernan to inventory his medical equipment. "Yes, James."

"Sorry to interrupt. I thought you'd want to know. That was airport security."

"Is there a problem?" Dr. Isling straightened his glasses. He was anxious.

"No. Nothing, sir. I didn't mean to worry you. They wanted to tell us Customs was finished with our passports and the plane would be ready to board in forty-five minutes."

"Good. When we get our hands on the mission's files, I'll rest a lot better. There's nothing like being on the brink."

Even though the professor hid it well, James appreciated how uneasy Dr. Isling felt. This expedition was very important to him and to Stanford's Archaeology Department. Every year, financing for field research became more difficult to secure. Competition for scarce funding was fierce, and a failed expedition would be financially disastrous.

7:32 a.m.—Sausalito, California

With a glance, Wade Fields confirmed the office was empty. He hurried in and shut the door. Wade considered himself to be a mediocre biochemist and these diversions endeared him to powerful people outside the company. Besides, the excitement relieved his occasional boredom.

To avoid detection, Wade rarely used the same phone or office more than once. Recently vacated offices were his favorites, and this particular one belonged to a chemist who had taken a leave-of-absence to pursue her doctorate. All of her personal items had been removed, leaving a barren metal desk, chair, and black touch-tone telephone. The space was small by BenaTex's standards, but then, many of the offices for the entry-level staff were. Wade laughed. Had he been spoiled over the years?

"Never," he whispered and hurried to the chemist's desk where he picked up her private line. Dialing a secured number, he waited.

A woman's voice answered, "Yes."

"This is two-two-four-six. Tell her that she was right." Wade spoke softly into the receiver, cupping the mouthpiece with his hand. Talk had circulated among his friends that many of the high-tech companies used electronic surveillance equipment to protect corporate secrets. Although BenaTex was not like most other companies, there was always the possibility that they would someday start tapping office telephones. This would be his last call from work. Wade wasn't going to take any unnecessary chances.

"A clandestine project is being run. I haven't discovered who's involved. My guess is they're high up."

"I'll pass your message along."

Wade hung up and wiped the phone clean with a handkerchief, being careful not to disturb anything. Before leaving, he smoothed his hair and calmed himself by allowing time for his adrenalin surge to subside. This spy stuff was something else. Prowling vacant offices, collecting tidbits of information from wherever they could be found, pretty cool. He smiled and headed out, ready for another day at the office.

11:36 a.m.—Manaus, Brazil

The pilot completed the engine run-up and pushed both throttle levers to their full forward positions. The blue-on-white King Air 200 multi-engine aircraft pitched upward then sped down the runway. Thermal currents radiating above the asphalt bounced the plane twice as it rotated and lifted into the air. The landing gear retracted with a loud clunk.

James Monal watched the pilot through the cockpit doorway as he executed his flight ritual. Besides a love for collecting rocks and uncovering ancient ruins, James obsessed over airplanes, to the point where he had almost joined the Air Force rather than enter Stanford's archaeology program.

His eyes scanned the plane's instruments starting on the right and moving left. He followed the pilots' hands as they moved across the control panel. He verified the condition of the vertical speed indicator, heading indicator, altimeter, and attitude indicator. The plane continued to climb through the humid air at a standard rate of 500 feet per minute. An envious pout crossed James' face when he saw the Trimble 200 color radar mounted in the avionics panel, then the Collins ADF60 & S1Y-7A ADF. "Nice plane," he sighed. Envying the pilot's way of life, James reclined into his high-back leather swivel chair, enjoying the comfortable furnishings and the ride. The rest of the archaeological team had already done the same.

While boarding, the copilot explained that a southern Brazilian cattle rancher had owned the plane before it became a charter. The cattleman had intriguing tastes in amenities, stocking the main cabin with a plush, beige leather interior that comfortably sat eight. He also added small overhead and under-the-seat storage compartments, a center cabin built to conduct business, and the latest avionics. Even though the rancher might have been rather bizarre in some of his additions, James still admired the interior workmanship.

He imagined himself ripping down the runway in his own King Air, its twin-turbo Pratt & Whitneys screaming at full throttle. A steady pull on the wheel and the plane would rotate, eating altitude on its way to 30,000 feet. Then would come the true feel of the plane's performance capability as the airspeed pegged 300 knots. What a sensation. "Humm."

"Like to fly, James?" Dr. Isling asked.

"Huh, what?"

"I saw the keen attention you paid the cockpit crew during takeoff, and that euphoric glaze that came over your face afterward."

"That bad?"

"Pretty much. I didn't even know you flew."

"Yes, sir. I just don't talk about it much." He shrugged. "I've had my private pilot's license since my second year at Stanford."

"How often do you go?"

"When we're home, a couple of times a week. I joined a flying club last term to keep the cost down."

"I understand why it intrigues you; there's nothing like the view of the world from a small plane." Sitting across the carpeted aisle, Dr. Isling shifted his attention to the panorama outside his oval window. "See there. It's the Rio Negro." The professor pointed to the sleek river running more than 8,000 feet below them. "Nowhere else in the world can you find a natural body of water with such rich black color."

James swayed across the aisle and knelt on one knee next to Dr. Isling. "It's fantastic."

The swirling ebony river and the serpentine jungle vegetation created a magical contrast. The river's striated meanders were hypnotic, and James understood why the Burbános had chosen this place. "I've never seen water glisten like that before."

"Ah, 'Rio Negro,' the black river. It's a magnificent sight. The jungle's unique ecology creates the river's color."

A yearning in Dr. Isling's expression reminded James of their shared enthusiasm for new adventures. Dr. Isling had told James he often felt it was not that long ago when he had first ventured beyond the confines of a college classroom. His mentor, Dr. Abrams, had taken him on an Egyptian dig in the Valley of the Kings. The moment he entered the Valley, Isling was hooked on archaeology forever. Uncovering ancient worlds became more than a pursuit—it turned into a passion. A classic case of archaeological nirvana. James identified with those emotions, for he had the same drive and desire to experience the past firsthand.

They moved their heads away from the window. "You see, James, over the centuries the dense jungle vegetation has fallen to the ground and decayed. Heavy rains come along and leach minerals out of the thick organic muck causing rich flows to enter the river."

"Humm." James' eyebrows arched upward as he visualized the process. "It's analogous to water percolating through tea leaves."

"Very good." Dr. Isling slapped James on the top of his knee. "As always, your ability to deduce my meaning is outstanding."

James crawled onto his own seat as Dr. Isling continued.

"The Rio Negro doesn't get overloaded with the suspended silt and clay found in the Amazon River because of geologic differences. The Negro's headwaters stream over resistant crystalline rocks in the mountains of northern Brazil, Guyana, and Venezuela. Whereas the Amazon River—"

A violent tremor erupted. The cabin dipped steeply to the right. James saw the cockpit crew react to alarm buzzers and flashing red lights. The plane stalled, shuddered, then plunged nose first into a rapid spiral. The pilot and copilot scrambled to correct the catastrophe. They adjusted the trim, increased the airspeed, and pounded the rudder. Nothing helped.

Their copilot shouted into the plane's microphone, "Manaus Tower, King Air, niner-two-three-zero-five-hotel has an emergency. Repeat, we have an in-flight emergency." He punched the International Emergency Distress frequency, 7700, into the plane's transponder. To his left, the pilot's hands moved across dials and switches in a mad blur. He slammed the rudder pedal to the floor and shoved the wheel forward, driving the nose down even more. His efforts failed. Drag on the right wing was too great.

"King Air zero-five-hotel, this is Manaus Tower." The Portuguese accent resounded in the headset, and the Vermont-born copilot had never been so glad the required universal language for air traffic controllers was English.

"Manaus Tower, we're fifteen miles west, descending through eight-seven-zero. Have severe right wing damage and in an uncontrolled spin. Do you have us on radar?" The copilot stopped and stared through the main window, his eyes riveted on the twisted jungle canopy, racing toward them at over 4,800 feet per minute.

"Manaus Tower, copied. Emergency equipment on the way. We confirm your position on radar." The voice was metallic and far away.

"Impact in less than two minutes!" The copilot glanced over his shoulder at the carnage blasting the main cabin.

The centrifugal force generated by the spin smashed James into his seat. He fought for air as his lungs constricted. Across the aisle, Dr. Isling braced himself, stuffing his feet under the teak drink table and craning toward James.

"What's happening?"

"Right wing's damaged!" James wrenched his head and looked out the window. He released one hand from his grip on the armrest and pointed. "Fluid's squirting through a crack in the wing. We've stalled and are cork-screwing."

Another tremor ripped the plane, widening the tear in the wing's upper surface. Hydraulic fluid splattered the starboard side passengers' windows.

"We're gonna crash!" Aidan shouted as an overhead bin burst open and showered him with field gear. He snagged a dangling pillow, held it on his lap, and buried his face, praying for divine intervention.

"Watch out, James!" Ann Wright screamed a second before a brown suitcase smashed into James' head. Clothing, luggage, and seat cushions came loose everywhere. An airborne camera case barely missed Ann's ear.

A swirling updraft buffeted the plane to the right. The sudden change in momentum hurled the flailing passengers to the left. Ann whacked her forehead on the side of the cabin wall, and then launched headfirst into a forward seat, where she lay dangling by her seatbelt.

David Sooner saw her go down and cast aside his seatbelt, suddenly grasping his mistake when he was catapulted into the air and slammed into a rear bulkhead. Bouncing from the impact, he sprawled into the aisle. A sharp object on a broken seat frame sliced his hip. Sooner screamed and clenched the wound, but was ripped off the floor and flung into another bulkhead. He fell toward the aisle, landing draped across the top of a leather armrest. Semiconscious, he grabbed the nearest seat, clinging for survival.

The pilot altered the left engine torque setting to compensate for the unbalanced lift. He pushed his foot to the floorboard, giving the plane all the left rudder he could squeeze out of her. The wings leveled and the spin broke. The pilot yanked the King Air's nose up, but it continued to sideslip, heading for the treetops. The plane's underbelly skirted a whisper above the wicked tentacles. Skidding in midair, branches scraped the nose section, scarcely missing the spinning props. A violent rumble vibrated the fuselage and the blue and white King Air shot over the jungle, stalling fifty yards above the churning Rio Negro. The plane hung in the air, suspended.

"Everyone!" Dr. Isling yelled while straining across the aisle to hold a towel against the gash on James' head. "Grab anything. Cushion your impact. We're gonna hit!"

Yawing right, the King Air lurched and fell. The right wingtip's white running light vanished under the water's black surface and the plane tumbled into a violent cartwheel. The five passengers slammed into walls and bulkheads. Mounts sheared loose and leather seats became flying weapons. A second end-over-end loop and the damaged wing ripped apart.

With the cutting bite of a biserrate anchor, the remaining stub dug below the water. A mountainous splash, then the plane came to a sudden halt. The twin-engine King Air floated, momentarily buoyed by the surge. The plane settled partially submerged along the river's muddy bank. Concentric ripples radiated outward across the Rio Negro.

*   *   *

Stars spun and the laceration above James' right temple pounded. Blood trickled down his cheek as he unlatched his seatbelt and slumped into the warm water rising within the plane's interior. Sunlight blazed through four port side windows, the others lost under the river. Bare wires and torn leather upholstery dangled from the ceiling. Stumbling over a smashed seat, he forced back his dizziness, shoved aside the broken teak table and lifted Dr. Isling's head above the water's surface.

"Professor!" He hung limp in his arms. James groped for a pulse and located a weak one throbbing along the carotid artery, then verified he was breathing. After checking for broken bones with the blind touch of his hands, and finding none, he lifted and floated the professor through the debris-laden water to an emergency ceiling exit, another welcome addition made by the previous owner.

Holding Dr. Isling with one arm around his waist, James disengaged the locking mechanism and pushed the exit hatch open. He hoisted the professor through and climbed out next to him. James cleared the escape portal and lowered the professor onto a dry section of the left wing, then he returned and dropped into the main cabin.

James worked his way to the front of the plane, combing for survivors. Suitcases, blankets, and pillows floated everywhere. He angled into the cockpit. The entire nose section had been crushed. The pilot and copilot were dead. A river streamed through the broken windows. Water rose above his waist. His head swirled from the smell of hydraulic fluid and high-octane fuel.

He swam to the center of the main cabin and crawled over a dislodged seat where he found Dr. Sooner's dead body bobbing facedown behind a starboard bulkhead. A massive blow to the base of his skull oozed with thick dark red blood. James took a deep breath and forced himself to stay calm. Humanlike groans came from the tailsection. "Dr. MacKiernan! Hold on. I'm on my way."

Lunging past another broken seat, James stubbed his foot, tripped, and sank beneath the warm water. He struggled to the surface, plowing into more floating suitcases and seat cushions. "Aidan, I'm coming." James coughed and ducked past a smashed overhead bin, two yards from the rear of the plane. He threw a suitcase to the side. A body bumped into him and his eyes met Ann

Wright's pasty bruised face and purple lips. Screaming, he recoiled as vomit rose in his throat.

He raised Ann's head above the water and felt her delicate throat, hoping for a pulse. Nothing. Ann had been so full of passion. What a waste. Gently, he moved her aside and fought his way to Aidan, reaching him seconds later.

"Pry me free! My leg's stuck! The seat!"

"I'll see what I can find. Hold on a little longer."

"Like I have a choice?"

James grimaced, turned, and scoured overhead bins, tearing apart their remaining contents searching for tools, anything he could use. Frustrated, he slammed his fist into the plastic bin. His fruitless effort had left him short on options. Water slapped his chest, scarcely an inch from Aidan's chin. The man would drown if James didn't hurry.

Two deep breaths and James dove into the muddy water. He grabbed the seat's headrest and crammed his feet into an arched slot in the plane's rear bulkhead. Something slimy slithered across his face. James shot above the water, cracking his shoulder on the sharp edge of a portside window frame.

"Yuck! What the hell was that?"

Aidan didn't respond, his green eyes remained glazed and his skin had a bluish-white hue. Oily black water sloshed beneath his trembling lower lip.

"Shit, shit." James took a deep breath and ducked under the surface once again. The murky water forced him to go slow, to feel his way. He snagged another finger on a sharp object. His lungs burned with the searing pain of oxygen deprivation. This would be his last try, Aidan's only hope. James tensed his body, giving the seat a muscle-ripping pull. Screaming with fear and rage, he pulled again as the remaining ounces of reserve oxygen drained away and his mind became woozy. A bolt snapped and the seat blasted free, sending him flying backwards with Aidan in tow. Their heads burst above the water's surface. James gasped and spit black muck.

Aidan gagged up his portion of river water while bobbing next to him. "Thanks, James. You saved my life."

"I wish," James took a deep breath, "I could have helped Dr. Wright and Dr. Sooner." Blood dribbled from the cut on his shoulder, coalescing with the rising surge.

Wincing, Aidan placed his arm on James' good shoulder. "We're lucky to be alive. I saw you save Henry. If not for you, he and I would be dead."

"Dr. Isling!" James looked to the open hatch.

"Go ahead, I'll be all right." He gave James a gentle shove and watched as he plunged through the cabin.

James pulled himself through the breach and sprawled exhausted onto the fuselage. The sun's intensity hit him full force, and he used his hand to block the glimmering reflection bouncing off the mangled wing. Steam rose above his battered body as hot air heated his soggy wet chest. He took a moment and allowed the tropical warmth to soothe his aches. When James regained his awareness, he saw Dr. Isling perched on one elbow staring down the river.

"How're you doing?" James asked, sliding next to him on the wing.

"I . . . I don't know. My . . . my ankle might be broken. My god, James, what happened?" Dr. Isling massaged a spongy purplish patch, and his eyes reddened.

"I have no idea, professor."

Aidan crawled out of the escape hatch and over the fuselage, favoring his gouged leg. A big Irish smile creased his ruddy face when he saw his friends, but then, he turned solemn. "Gentlemen." He slumped onto his back. "It's good to see the two of you."

"You too, Aidan," Dr. Isling said as he observed the battered condition of his two comrades. "Are we all that made . . . ?"

"Yes," James answered. "I'm afraid so."

The three men mulled the tragic loss of their friends.

James watched water drip from his pant legs onto the wing's metal surface. Aidan gazed at cumulus clouds floating in the deep blue South American sky. Henry's eyes trailed the river's current as it eddied beside the wrecked plane. With a common thought, they stared at the escape hatch. Was this the way it would end?

The rotary thump-thump-thump of a helicopter reverberated up the river.

10:10 a.m.—Central Coast, California

After his second class, Matt Wells found Dr. Ruhpor energetically waving in the hallway outside his office. Matt stepped into the mass of bodies and carved a path to meet him.

"Yeah, Doc? Marcie said you wanted to see me."

The professor led him away from the crowd.

"I'd like you to meet someone." He gestured toward an exotic young woman standing next to a row of metal lockers. A curvaceous athlete . . . interesting combination. She's simply beautiful. Her tan, olive skin—Matt's gaze was instantly held by her almond-shaped honey brown eyes. "Whoa, Doc."

She glared.

"Matt, this is Allyx Katero." She shot him one of those, "I'm not interested looks." Dr. Ruhpor caught the exchange and smirked. Matt shrank back a little. "She's a biology student, with a minor in genetics."

He put on a serious face. "Hi, Allyx."

"Mr. Wells." He shook her offered hand politely. Her response was anything except warm. She nodded and coolly smiled, exuding the negative energy of a dedicated man-hater. Maybe the Doc had blown this one.

She was the one who had spoken during class the other day—the special one who connected with the Doc.

What was Ruhpor scheming? This guy was full of surprises. Another thing he had heard was that the Doc always manipulated his immediate surroundings; Matt assumed for the better.

"Matt . . . Matt? Pay attention."

"Sorry, Doc, thought I was."

Ruhpor shook his head and laughed. "Okay, Matt, Allyx, I'd like the two of you to team on the midterm project. Your individual talents will make for a great combination."

"But, Doc—"

"That's not such a good idea," Allyx interrupted. "I've developed an approach that—"

"If you'd please let me finish. I agree with her. I have my own ideas, and she wouldn't fit."

Allyx focused her attention on Matt. "Are you implying that I can't handle you—it?" She encroached on his space, pressing him.

Matt edged backwards. Her intensity deflated his defenses. How did she do that? "No, that's not—"

"Then you have a problem with women scientists?" Allyx's scowl darkened.

"Hey, I don't have a problem with women, scientists or otherwise." Her aggressiveness made him even more apprehensive. The opposite sex was typically easy prey to his seductive charms. Matt wasn't used to being challenged by a woman. He considered himself an enlightened male, a man of the new millennia, one who intellectually respected the female gender. Whom did she think she was attacking? Was this some sort of test? "Look babe—"

Allyx growled at him, "Don't call me—"

"Now, you two." Dr. Ruhpor polished his glasses with his forest green Cal Poly tie. "Let's take a moment and calm a little."

The Doc was using his "Jedi voice." He had smoozed them with a soothing parental tone, and Matt visualized Obi-wan Kanobi in the first Star Wars manipulating a pair of brainless storm troopers. Matt suppressed a laugh when he caught a subtle grin form on the professor's face.

"You both need to learn how to be team players. Everyone's got issues, let's get beyond them. Allyx, your strength in microbiology complements Matt's engineering background."

"But, Dr. Ruhpor—"

"No buts from either of you." The professor gave them a stern look. "My decision is not up for negotiation." He watched for any further argument. "Both of you are to research soilborne viruses that specifically target the human immune system. I want to know if there is sufficient scientific evidence to demonstrate that these invaders occur naturally. Rethink a methodology and get a draft outline to me by next Tuesday."

"Yes, Dr. Ruhpor," Allyx said.

"Do you have any questions, Matt?"

"No, Dr. Ruhpor."

"Then I'll see you two in class next week. Matt, there's a pile of homework papers on my desk. Please grade them when you can."

"Sure thing, Doc."

Matt's chin drooped. He scowled and watched Dr. Ruhpor walk down the hallway toward his office. It would take a miracle for Matt to survive this class. Headstrong women made him uncomfortable, and this one was a terror. Maybe it wouldn't be so bad—a change for once. He looked at Allyx. Not a chance. Matt dipped and shook his head, staring at the tile floor. He was in for nothing but trouble. "That was fun," he grumbled.

"Get over it," Allyx retorted as she pulled a silver PDA from her backpack. "When do you want to get started?"

"Huh? What? Whenever you want."

"That's decisive. I can tell this is going to be fulfilling." She skimmed her schedule. "What if we meet in front of the Student Union at six tonight? We'll have to cut it short though, I have a seven o'clock appointment."

"Six is okay with me. Uh, I have plans afterwards too."

"I'm sure you do. Don't be late." Allyx blocked time on her calendar, then spun on one foot and headed for the exit before Matt could utter another word.

Stunned by the ease at which Allyx took charge, Matt stood cemented in place, watching her, his adrenalin pumping. She had touched a nerve, or two. Never before had he been that argumentative with anyone other than his dad. The last sounds Matt heard were Allyx's white cross-trainers squeaking on the polished vinyl floor as she left the building. What had Dr. Ruhpor done to him?

11:15 a.m.—Los Angeles, California

Kelly Karrie adjusted her hips to the left and pulled her business suit jacket under her bottom. The movement helped square her shoulders, straighten her spine, and gave her a more regal posture.

"Forty-five seconds; you look great," the program manager said.

She smiled curtly.

An Independent News Network evening anchor did not do late morning reports; they were beneath her. Come to think of it, management had not given her a choice in the matter. The decision supposedly came down from the top. These last-minute program changes were especially irritating. Her comfort zone did not include adlibbing the news before lunch. A schedule swap was a ratings game designed to bump up the sagging morning numbers.

Kelly unconsciously brushed her fingertips against her hair and a frazzled hairdresser came running.

"Don't touch," the woman said. "Don't touch."

"Twenty seconds."

If INN had stuck to their original hard-news format, Kelly would not have the prime time evening slot. Beauty and style were her expertise, not her news savvy.

A former Miss New York, and a perfect five-foot eight, size four; Kelly Karrie blew through television news with the finesse of a storm slamming into a quiet Tahitian shore. With no effort at all, she could convince the world Osama Bin Laden had been on a humanitarian mission. When she tossed back her long auburn hair, the American male lost track of time. The perceived sensitivity in her blue eyes and the tenderness exuded by her full red lips enchanted television viewers into believing she spoke directly to them. INN's management was convinced miraculous things happened when Kelly spun a news story, and far be it for her to question their wisdom.

She listened for her cue as the business report droned on.

". . . another unpredictable day on Wall Street for the high-techs. By midmorning, the Dow had risen 43 points, fueled by above expected earnings from the pharmaceuticals. Researching cancer and exotic diseases has created a—We interrupt this news segment for a special bulletin with Kelly Karrie. . . ."

"Three, two, one. . . ."

There's nothing like a little drama to start your morning. The Teleprompter rolled, and Kelly moved smoothly into her monologue. "Before nine o'clock, Pacific Time this morning, an expedition sent by Stanford University into the Amazon Jungle came to a tragic end when the plane carrying Dr. Henry Isling and his archaeological team crashed. Rescue workers and equipment have been flown into the region. But according to the chief spokesperson for the Brazilian government, Ramone Peres, the probability of finding anyone alive is not very high."

Kelly paused. A red light on camera two blinked and she rotated her upper torso in the appropriate direction. "At six o'clock tomorrow evening INN will broadcast a special segment devoted to this courageous group. We will also monitor the rescue activities as they take place. Stay tuned for any late breaking news. We now resume our business report with Simon Zeigler."

Finishing her story Kelly removed her earpiece and dropped it on the countertop. She held her head with both hands and twisted it to the left until her neck cracked. Since college, she had used this technique to relax. A habit her producer, Mikhail Haines, considered disgusting. Kelly rotated the opposite direction until she heard another pop.

2:18 p.m.—Manaus General Hospital, Brazil

The Brazilian Army helicopter lifted off, and James Monal covered his eyes, protecting them from the rotor wash. When the dust settled, he helped Dr. Isling into a wheelchair. Aidan limped away to make arrangements with the Manaus General Hospital.

"Damn, James, it feels good to be on familiar ground, even if it is back where we started. Thank God the Army was doing maneuvers nearby."

James nodded. "By the way Dr. Isling, before I forget, I have something of yours." He reached into his hip pocket and removed a waded green bundle. "Found it floating on the river." James held out his hand.

"My hat!" Dr. Isling ran his hand over his hair and slid the beat-up chapeau into place. "If I didn't thank you already, James, then I want to say it now. Thanks."

"Any time, Dr. Isling."

This was their first resemblance of a real conversation since the helicopter arrived. Images of the plane crash, and sloshing about within the drowned interior, were all too vivid in James' memory. Aidan's voice still called to him. Ann's vacant eyes . . .

Sunlight shone through the plane's oval windows,

flickering when dangling cables and torn leather upholstery swung across its path. The stench of burnt wiring and wet upholstery choked the main cabin. James' courage weakened the more he pondered the horrible disaster that had befallen his friends. He tried to block the memories and focus on the wheelchair as it bounced along the pathway.

A med-tech met the pair at the hospital's entrance. He took the handles on Dr. Isling's wheelchair and guided them to a private room where Aidan waited. Their initial action, once settled in, was to contact relatives and friends. The hospital provided a telephone line for their exclusive use, but before long, their optimism switched to frustration when they realized it would take hours to make all the calls. The Manaus phone system was more than forty years old and barely operational by modern standards. During their extended idle periods the attending physician, Dr. Cortese, put the three explorers through exhaustive examinations.

"Gentlemen," Dr. Cortese said, his voice highlighted with a New England accent and his handsome amber features accentuated by a standard issue white hospital coat. "Besides bruises and abrasions, you're fit for duty."

"That's the best news we've had lately," Dr. Isling replied. "How's my ankle?"

Dr. Cortese held the professor's calf; his right hand supported the Achilles tendon.

"Based on the mobility and swelling pattern, it's a sprain. Now, because it's not broken, doesn't mean it's not going to hurt. If your ankle's not noticeably better in two days, come see me and we'll take an X-ray. Scheduling the machine is difficult I'm afraid. Unfortunately, we have just one."

"Doctor," Aidan said, admiring the bandage on his own leg. "Your accent, are you a native?"

"Yes, I was born twenty miles east of here. However,

I spent many years in the States. I received my medical degree from Dartmouth and served my residency at Johns Hopkins. I haven't quite lost my Yankee inflection, but I'm working on it."

Aidan laughed. "We appreciate your forthright manner. If you ever visit California, you'll have to be our guest."

"Thanks for the offer. You gentlemen take it easy. The next time I see the three of you, I want it to be under better circumstances." Dr. Cortese stopped on his way out. "You can leave when you're ready. I'll authorize your release at the front desk."

No sooner had the door closed when James looked to Dr. Isling. "This might not be a good time." Hesitating, he felt awkward broaching the subject. "Are we continuing the expedition?"

"I honestly don't know. Aidan, where do you stand?"

He thoughtfully rubbed his chin. "Almost getting killed, and losing good friends, does require introspection. We've reached one of those junctures when you have to weigh individual frailty against academic curiosity." Aidan glanced up at the tan ceiling, then at Dr. Isling. "With that bit of philosophy said, I want to finish what we started. We owe it to Ann and David."

Dr. Isling acknowledged James. "And your vote, my boy?"

"Although I agree with Dr. MacKiernan and want to continue the expedition, I go where you go, Dr. Isling."

"Thank you, James. I concur with Aidan, we owe our friends." Dr. Isling forced a smile. "However, before a final decision is made, there's a lot to consider. Let's sleep on it and finish this discussion in the morning." The professor adjusted his hat, folding its wrinkled brim down over his eyes. He gave James and Aidan another manufactured smile. Supported by wooden crutches, he hobbled through the doorway, leaving his two friends behind with their thoughts.

"He's right, James. I'm beat and our hotel rooms should be ready by now." James sighed just as Aidan turned around. "It'll be okay, lad. I'll see you in the morning."

The door closed and James crashed on the hospital bed, exhausted. He wondered if the expedition should continue. Had he read doubt in Dr. Isling's weary eyes? The weight of responsibility had taken a heavy toll on the professor's conscience. Four people were already dead. How many more might die?

4:18 p.m.—Central Coast, California

"Why'd you stick me with that testosterone-loaded jerk?" Allyx Katero closed Dr. Ruhpor's office door. "He's going to bog me down and I already have enough of a load to carry this quarter."

Dr. Ruhpor sat on the edge of his desk and proceeded to clean his glasses. His lack of immediate response frustrated Allyx even more. Was this another one of his tests? She never could figure him out.

"Aren't you going to say anything?"

"Seems you're talking enough for both of us." He glanced up.

Allyx balled her hands into fists and suppressed a scream. "You're such a pain." She pouted, held her comments in check, and crossed the room and sat. "Okay, I'm calm. Now can we discuss why you saddled me with that male macho creep?"

"Much better."

"Are we taking in another stray?"

"Something like that." Dr. Ruhpor straightened his tie. That was a subconscious hint that he might have been unsure about his decision. Allyx smiled at his rare showing of uncertainty. He was such a poop. It wasn't too often that Allyx got the upper hand. She had intended on helping him all along, but first, she had to put him on notice not to assume.

"I don't pick up stray puppies; not my nature. That's your calling, professor."

"Oh, it's in you, Allyx. You just hide it well." He gave her a devilish grin. "And I should know."

This time, Allyx experienced a blush. "That was the old me, but I'm listening."

"I know what you think of him, Allyx, but Matt's a good kid." Dr. Ruhpor looked at her over the rim of his glasses.

She cringed; Ruhpor was about to go all paternal. "Of course he is, for a lost lug nut."

He smiled and shrugged off her comment. "Who knows? Matt might even teach you a thing or two." Allyx frowned, as he continued. "Watch what you say. The kid's bright—a Mensan. Caltech and three other top schools offered him a full-ride scholarship. He turned them down, preferring to stay close to home. I'd cut him some slack."

"We'll see."

"With the right guidance, he has no limits."

"And I'm supposed to help guide him?" Allyx sank back into her chair. Maybe this time the great Dr. Ruhpor had made a mistake. "I'm a little short on my people skills. Why not get someone who's sensitive to the male ego? I've been burned enough."

"You have what it takes."

"Yeah, right."

"Have I ever led you astray?"

"Not lately."

He pulled a chair up next to her. "I'll let you in on something. He's got some baggage."

"Don't they all?"

"This one's different."

"So you say."

Ruhpor frowned.

She smiled.

"I talked with his mom."

"And?" Allyx softened her approach. She could see the compassion in Dr. Ruhpor's expression. Apparently, this one was different.

"Besides the normal emotional bumps associated with a parental divorce and all, he lost someone close to him. The friend was a girl he had known for years."

Allyx refrained from making a girlfriend joke. She sensed the intensity shift in Dr. Ruhpor's emotions and the suddenness unsettled her.

"A Great White Shark attacked the poor girl. You might remember reading about the accident in the news."

"No, but keep going."

"Matt was surfing with her along the San Diego Jetty. It was 1995, around the same time as an incident up in Monterey, another one of those not so uncommon occurrences off our coastline. For your information, from 1928 to 1996, California experienced 69 reported shark attacks."

"You and your damn statistics." Allyx blurted her thoughts before she could stop herself.

He grimaced.

"Sorry. Tell me what happened."

"She would have died if not for Matt. He saved her by distracting the shark, which almost cost him his life. His quick action allowed time for a wave to carry her in to shore. Lifeguards pulled her out of the water, provided emergency services, and medivaced her to the hospital."

"So he's a hero."

"In a sense. The girl lost part of her leg. Amputated below the knee"

"Oh, jeez. That's awful."

"She was seventeen and beautiful. He was sixteen."

"At least she was alive."

"Sometimes that's not enough. The injury wrecked her mentally. She told Matt she preferred death over being crippled."

"But—"

Dr. Ruhpor held up his hand, gently quieting Allyx. "She committed suicide a month later."

"My, God . . ." Allyx covered her mouth.

"No one blamed him, but still, Matt took it hard. It changed him."

"It wasn't his fault. He saved the girl."

"I know that, and now so do you. Matt's the one who doesn't."

"Doesn't he need counseling or something?"

"No, just a chance here-and-there. Mostly, he needs a real friend."

"You mean me?"

He smiled."

"I'll try."

"He has difficulty with commitment."

"Like I said, don't they all?"

Dr. Ruhpor gave her a displeased frown.

She sighed. "Okay, okay. I'll try harder."

"Be yourself and you'll do fine." They stood and Dr. Ruhpor put his arm around Allyx's waist. "Again, be yourself. That's all I ask. The rest will find a way."

"If you say so. I guess I owe you at least one."

Dr. Ruhpor chuckled. "Yeah, at least one." He accompanied her to the door. "I have a class in twenty minutes."

Allyx shook her head. "I can't believe I'm doing this. I'll do my best to be patient."

"I know you will. Now get moving or I'll be late."

"You knew I'd help all along, didn't you?"

"Maybe. Now get out of here or else." He gave her a gentle nudge as she passed by him.

She giggled on her way out. "You're too much. I'll see you in lab class tomorrow morning."

4:30 p.m.—Palo Alto, California

The press conference had just started and Dr. Leland was already in a sweat. Dampness grew under his armpits and spread down his spine. It had been one crisis after another ever since the news had reached his office six hours earlier. He was dazed after the hundreds of phone calls. It seemed everyone in the world had seen the INN news story. Making the Amazon expedition a media event had been a mistake. Leland wiped his forehead with a handkerchief.

He was spent and no longer cared how he looked for the cameras. His normally impeccable presence was marred by a wrinkled, dark-gray wool suit and unkempt hair. As his pained gaze descended upon the crowd, the clatter of shouting reporters blended together. With any luck, he hoped this public showing would put an end to the questions.

"Is it true the plane went down under mysterious circumstances?" a Herald reporter yelled.

Leland scowled at the man. "At this time, we have no information supporting that rumor. Difficulties with the international phone system have made it impossible for my staff to confirm the condition of our team with the Brazilian authorities. We only learned of the accident shortly before INN announced it late this morning." Dr. Leland shifted his weight, one leg, then the other. This public discussion of such a personal tragedy was very difficult for him; these were his colleagues, his friends. He wiped away the perspiration on his forehead with a monogrammed white handkerchief, a birthday gift from his best friend—Henry Isling.

"The early reports said all the passengers were killed in the crash," a Tribune journalist interjected. "Do you have any comments?"

"We have the same information you do." Dr. Leland grappled with his emotions. "I was, am, very close to Dr. Isling and his team. When we have something credible, we'll contact their families."

A reporter shouted, "What are their chances if they didn't die in the plane crash?"

Another yelled, "How many people were on the plane when it went down?"

The Media's lust for disaster sensationalism was a vile side that Dr. Leland didn't care for. He overheard murmuring among the journalists. If he wasn't cautious, tomorrow's headlines would be awash with gruesome suppositions. A failed expedition would destroy any future funding. Jobs were also on the line—so much to consider.

Strobes flashing from a dozen cameras captured Leland's pained expression, his sunken tired eyes with their dark circles, and the pale hue in his cheeks.

"I have no further comment regarding the status of our team. We'll provide a press release only after we receive additional information and notify relatives accordingly." Leland scowled at the journalists' intrusive questioning. They were vultures. As if the possibility his longtime friend and colleague, Dr. Henry Isling, could be gone was not punishment enough, standing before this cretinous crowd had become unbearable. "Is there anything else?"

A hand went up, preventing Leland from lashing out with his damaged feelings. "Yes, Shannon." He gestured to a woman representing Stanford's newspaper.

She pointed a microcassette recorder in his direction. "Is the Archaeology Department going to send another group into the Amazon?"

The question he had dreaded. When does the risk outweigh scientific gain? What would Henry have wanted? "Until we verify the safety of our people, all future expedition activities are halted. Next question please." Countless hands shot into the air.

Hearing the answer he sought, a man standing unnoticed at the rear of the pressroom eased out a side door. He entered an empty hallway and made his call.

"Yes, Mr. Osborne. . . . They're not scheduling any more trips into the jungle for a while." He slid the phone into his breast coat pocket and left the building.

5:52 p.m.—Central Coast, California

While Matt Wells stood in the narrow foyer near Dr. Ruhpor's office, he rummaged through his pocket for a key and fumed over being coerced into working with Allyx. She was trouble. There had to be a way out. On top of everything else, grading papers would crater his weekend. Matt checked his watch; less than ten minutes until he was supposed to meet with her.

He inserted his key into the lock and the door swung open. Puzzled, his lips crinkled into a deep frown and he scratched his head. The Doc had never left his office unlocked before. Attributing the oversight to the professor's absentmindedness, Matt ducked into the room and reached for the light switch. A scuffling noise stopped him.

The room remained pitch black. A blur exploded through the darkness, slamming Matt headfirst into the wall. The attacker grabbed his shoulders and drove him against the doorjamb, where he slugged him in the stomach and sent him crumpling to the floor.

A burst of bright light was followed by a hazy darkness as Matt coughed and rolled over onto his back. Passing into unconsciousness; rapid footsteps faded away.

6:00 p.m.—Sausalito, California

"Ben, this is Nathan. I'm in my office. Why don't you come by? I have the final statistics and the initial modeling results. I'm printing them both right now."

"Great, you're ahead of schedule. I'll be right over."

"See you." Nathan switched off his speakerphone, then visually skimmed the computer screen. The retrovirus' development modeling had run perfectly. Their goal was within reach, and he should have been ecstatic. Still, something did not feel right. Ben's uneasiness during their last meeting bothered him. Nathan kicked his left foot up onto his oak desk and plopped the computer keyboard into his lap. He moved the roller ball with his thumb and selected the print icon, sending the graphs to a color LaserJet concealed in a credenza on the opposite side of the room. His partner was hiding something. The office door opened.

"Hey, Ben. Here's the latest." Nathan crossed the room, grabbed the graphs and laid them on his conference table, handing Ben the spreadsheets he had run earlier.

"These numbers are impressive, Nathan." Ben lifted a yellow highlighter from his shirt pocket and underscored key points. "Can we use this recent viral strain to outmaneuver the mortality rate problem and achieve the 90 percent ECR?" He tapped his highlighter on top of the paper.

Nathan scrunched his lips together. "Keep in mind that at this stage there are no certainties, but, yeah, I am confident the RNA resequencing will show that this retrovirus can meet Steele's project parameters. And, yes, our final product will have an Effective Contraction Rate well over 90 percent. After the initial exposure, there will be a guaranteed nine-in-ten chance the subject will get the disease; that alone should make Steele happy. Depending of course on his plans for this thing."

Ben stayed silent, unresponsive.

"Whatever." Nathan pointed a pencil at one of the line graphs. "You can see here that the regression of survivability to temperature has a relatively flat slope and a narrow cluster. Similar analyses of our original test ret-rovirus showed a much steeper slope and the data points were more scattered. That random fit demonstrated sta-tistically why we originally had a high mortality rate as we increased the temperature and other stress factors. Fortunately, the unique thermal resilience of this new strain has helped us overcome those previous limita-tions." He dropped the pencil on the graph and watched Ben's response. None. "Okay, then. To make a long story short, essentially yes to all your questions with only a few reservations. Thanks to Dr. Ruhpor, this one fits the bill."

"That's all that matters," Ben insisted. "We have to meet Steele's requirements with sufficient latitude to ac-count for any unforeseen problems."

"I'm on it." Nathan exhaled, loudly. "Damn, Ben. We've made a major breakthrough in recombinant genetics. What in the name of science does Steele want? Mir-acles?"

Ben placed his hand on Nathan's shoulder. "Steele bought miracles when he hired us."

Nathan groaned. His eyebrows dipped down, darken-ing his facial features. He did not care for the increasing influence Mr. Steele exerted on BenaTex's technical deci-sions.

"We won't be able to field-test this batch," Ben said as he took a seat at the conference table. "Is that going to be a problem?" He gave Nathan an opportunity to con-sider the change. "What kind of probability can we at-tach to the result without the testing?"

Nathan scratched the side of his head. "Based on the other RNA alignment data and the test subject re-actions, the model can be recalibrated to give us a prob-ability above the 93rd percentile."

"I like it. We'll have to pass the new statistics by Steele. Since you're so close, I'll send an e-mail to the staff that tightens security another notch. I want to make

certain there's no sharing of information. Has anyone else been involved at this level?"

"No." Was Ben being overly cautious? Nathan
wondered. "I've done all the modeling. We've compartmentalized the RNA resequencing to the point that
no one knows what anyone else is doing. And I'm the
one who pulls it all together."

"Who's handling shipping and receiving of the original virus?"

"Our intermediary. Why? What's troubling you?"

"Nothing. It sounds fine. Make certain you double-
check everything."

With so many different people involved at so many
different levels, it amazed Nathan how Ben managed to
keep things running smoothly. Nathan watched him twirl
the highlighter. He did not envy his partner's job. "Hey,
buddy, come on. We've known each other a long time.
We endured graduate school together. We started this
company then watched it go public. Hell, Ben, I even
guarded the john when you blew chunks at your bachelor party."

"So what's your point?" Ben retreated closer to the
door.

"My point is, there's a problem here and you're holding out on me." The threatening scowl on Ben's face
reminded Nathan of a trapped animal. Whom was he trying to fool? He had never seen his friend this uneasy.
Ben had always taken things in stride. Somehow, Steele
had changed him.

"Back off, Nathan. Just some loose ends. I'm on top
of them. You do your job. I'll keep everything else glued
together." He reached for the doorknob. "Don't worry.
It's under control."

Nathan suspected otherwise. "Look, Ben, don't cut
out on me. We've got a lot of data to review." Ben stopped. "I promise to lighten up. Why don't we take a break

and meet back here in ten minutes?"

"Sounds fine. I could use a few minutes."

6:41 p.m.—Central Coast, California

The echo of footsteps disappeared and Matt Wells slipped into unconsciousness. . . .

La Macarena's beat pulsated in the background while California's finest college coeds expressed their modern dance dexterity on the warm sand fronting Cabos San Lucas' Las Margaritas Bar. The stress of higher education required an occasional rescue and the old section of Cabo's resort community was a picturesque escape. Aiding in their journey to uninhibited relaxation, the beach-front bars gladly supplied alcohol to the willing students, similar to paramedics pumping whole blood into incoherent accident victims.

Oblivious to the bodily motions swaying nearby, Matt peeled free of Cindi's embrace and blazed a winding path down to the inviting ocean. With three rapid skips, he dove below an approaching wave. The water was in the mid-seventies and clear as crystal. Two strong strokes and his muscled six-foot-two-inch frame cut through the water, surfacing ten feet beyond the passing wave. Matt crested at the same instant a parasail passed overhead.

He watched the lone person dangle from the tethered lines, admiring the brilliant contrast between the airfoil's neon greens and yellows and the powder blue Mexican sky. Floating serenely on his back, Matt had a sudden desire to dump the college life and become a permanent Cabo fixture. But as always, his pragmatic side kicked in, preventing such leisurely considerations from taking their final form. He hoped his brief interlude into Baja's carefree lifestyle was enough of a diversion to last him until the end of the term. The end of the term . . . such a long way away.

At the moment, his most immediate challenge languished on the beach. Cindi deserved to know the truth. Matt gathered his courage. Do not fear introspection, experience it, and move on. Lately, however, that same introspection clouded his mind with indirection. Could the truth be, he was afraid to let Cindi go? Communicating with women on an intimate level had not been one of his strengths. Matt remembered that his previous girlfriend had accused him of being emotionally retarded. He scoffed at the notion, preferring instead to blame their relationship problems on her crappy attitude. But that had always been . . .

Lights flickered, and a constant ringing had his head throbbing to the beat of his heart. He slouched to one side and groped for a comfortable angle to hold himself. Had he been dreaming? Matt bumped his shoulder on something hard and moaned.

"Don't move, son."

The voice sounded familiar. A gentle hand held him still. Matt squinted, filtering the bright fluorescent lights. Slowly an oval face with horn-rimmed glasses and wild grayish-black hair came into focus.

"Are you all right, son?"

"Hi . . . Doc. It depends . . . I assume I'm not in Cabo?" Matt rubbed the lump on his forehead.

"No, not quite . . . more like the floor of my office doorway."

"That's what I was afraid of."

"Are you sure you're okay?"

"I guess so."

"Take it easy and don't move, son. The school's EMTs are here. They suspect you have a concussion."

"That would explain the pain." The concern in Dr. Ruhpor's tone unsettled Matt. "I think somebody tried to remove my head." He wobbled to the left and multicolored specs sparkled before him.

Dr. Ruhpor squatted next to him. "What happened, son? I came to get the notes for my six-thirty class and that's when I found you sprawled on the ground."

"I don't know. . . . I entered your office." Matt remembered his anger over being coerced into working with Allyx. "No wait. The door was ajar, which struck me as kind of weird."

"It should have been locked." Ruhpor surveyed his office. "I never leave it unlocked." He scratched his head, trying to jog his memory. "I'm getting feeble-minded. Maybe I forgot."

Matt sensed the Doc's guilt. "When I reached for the light somebody hammered me." He pressed on his throbbing forehead with his palms. "I guess I didn't put up much of a defense."

"Don't worry about it, son."

Another dizzy spell and the nausea struck. Matt concentrated, refusing to barf. How embarrassing would that be?

A campus police officer squatted on his haunches by Dr. Ruhpor. "Did you notice anything unusual, Mr. Wells?" The cop was young, no more than nineteen. His partner, who was investigating the crime scene on the other side of the room, had to be in his forties. Matt would have been more comfortable talking with the older guy. He might have been more understanding; there was nothing Matt could have done.

"No. I didn't have time to take notes." Matt managed his temper and the nausea, while massaging his head to purge the lingering fog. "Sorry, it happened too fast."

"Yeah, but you must have noticed something."

"The door swung open, a noise, then wham, I was blindsided. Not a lot to notice."

"Looks like a typical break-in, Professor," the older officer said, standing in the doorway. "Probably a student looking for test scores or answers. Was anything stolen?"

"Sit still, son. I'll be right back." Ruhpor stood and followed the officer into his office.

A paramedic faced Matt. "We'd like to examine you more thoroughly." He flicked a penlight into Matt's pupils. Twitching the light back and forth, the paramedic watched the dilation. He timed his pulse. "Tell me how you're feeling."

"Like a baseball after extra innings. My head's throbbing and my stomach's doing flips."

The paramedic ran his hands along Matt's scalp. "No obvious fractures, but you might have a mild concussion. To be safe you should go to the hospital for a complete evaluation."

Dr. Ruhpor bent down on one knee next to Matt. "Nothing was taken."

"How can you tell?" the younger officer mumbled as he stood. His partner gave him a displeased frown, and he shrugged.

"What time is it?" Matt asked.

"About fifteen minutes 'til seven," the older officer responded.

Matt pushed his shoulder against the wall and picked himself up. Unbalanced, but standing, he moved slowly.

"Take it easy, son." Ruhpor held onto Matt's arm and steadied him. "That's a sizable knot on your forehead. You should follow the paramedic's advice and take a trip to the hospital. I'll be glad to give you a ride."

"It's no big deal; I'm okay." Matt rested, using the wall for a brace. The paramedic handed him a clipboard.

"Please sign this and we'll cut you loose."

He read the general liability release. They wanted a signature in case he turned up dead. Matt sighed, signed the form, and handed it back. His fingers began to tingle and his face felt warm. The paramedic's features blurred. The room began to spin and Matt's knees sagged. Ruhpor grabbed him with both hands.

"Maybe you're right, Doc. The hospital's beginning to sound better already." As Matt's vision improved, he saw the frown on Dr. Ruhpor's face. "If you don't mind, I'll take that ride."

"Let me help you to my car. The police can finish up here."

8:21 p.m.—Sausalito, California

Ben Singular handed Nathan another cup of coffee. They had been reviewing the viral statistics for more than two hours. The chance of getting home at a reasonable time had vanished long ago. Ben sighed. Late nights at the office were adding up. He couldn't even remember the last good night kiss he had given his kids.

"The medical data on the most recent test subject is rather critical," Nathan said. "To verify the success of our previous and current RNA adjustments, we need that data."

"I realize that," Ben answered, shaking his head. "Quarantine requirements continue to slow everything. You just don't slap a postage stamp on a sick Indian and ship him via Brazilian mail." Nathan slouched in his chair, jolted by Ben's defensive outburst. "Sorry, Nathan. I shouldn't have snapped. We'll have the final lab results by tomorrow."

It continued to disturb Ben that he misled his partner. From day one the logistics had been a nightmare, and Ben was glad this was the last test subject. Every phase of the program had been painstakingly orchestrated and well financed. The dead Indians were collected and prepared before some jungle animal scavenged lunch. Each corpse was smuggled to a specially equipped hospital in Manaus for an autopsy. A fictitious corporation reserved a private wing to isolate the infected bodies. Since doctors loved to talk, the discretion of the attending physician had been secured. Enough American dollars silenced almost anyone, especially in that part of the world.

When the physician finished each autopsy, the results, including a blood sample, were passed to a private laboratory south of San Francisco. The bodies were incinerated. During the last eighteen months, twenty-three test subjects had been processed. And through it all, Nathan was unaware of the true nature of the Amazon Project. Ben would just have to learn how to live with the responsibility and the burden of guilt.

"It's okay, Ben. I understand. Do we have the doctor's initial findings?"

"No. There have been, uh, delays." Ben's eyes wandered around the room. "The last subject died from a brain aneurysm."

"Oh my . . . How did it happen?"

"Preliminary results indicate it started as a sinus infection, then migrated north breaking down the brain's defensive systems. The infection weakened the blood vessel walls in his right frontal lobe, and well, you can guess the rest."

"What happened to the medical precautions?"

"Occurred too fast." Ben glanced away. "A terrible tragedy." Nathan said nothing. He had insisted on testing their virus under realistic conditions, a scientific approach. Yet, when Steele suggested the Amazon site, Nathan was dubious, questioning whether they could establish adequate medical restrictions. Ben admitted that human testing was always risky, but what other choice did they have? The FDA would never approve of the testing within the US. Eventually Nathan caved to Ben's pressure. If Nathan only knew the whole story, and how he had been manipulated, there'd be hell to pay.

Ben never told his partner that Steele had demanded the human control group. He even suggested the Burbános. Nathan assumed that he had been the driving force behind the testing. Truth was, Steele had argued that he would not buy the results unless they were verified with real people, not lab mice.

"At least we only lost one."

"Yeah, one," Ben said, knowing otherwise.

Nathan gave him a curious look.

"What I meant to say was, this is a dangerous business and anything can happen."

"Sure you did."

He gave Nathan a harsh look, but refrained. The stress was getting to him and Ben started to pace; physical movement helped him cope with difficult issues. He stopped at the window overlooking the Bay and watched the boat traffic. Red and green bow lights glowed brightly as the vessels navigated the deep swells of the black sea. What a beautiful night to be on the water. He could almost feel the damp breeze on his face.

"Ben, are you okay with what happened?"

"As best as I can be." Ben stared at the lights of the city as they reflected off the water's surface. "It's one of the few downsides to our business."

"Yeah, I guess."

Astonishingly enough, less than sixty years ago, before the proliferation of modern antibiotics, a sinus infection could become deadly. Those same infections were now curable with modern medications. Damn, the world had changed a lot. It had taken sacrifice. Ben often questioned if early antibiotic researchers had experienced testing constraints similar to those plaguing modern geneticists. Probably not.

"What a way to run a business," Ben grumbled. How in the hell were they supposed to function in a society afraid of its own shadow? Discovery took guts, not bureaucratic stupidity. Over the last decade Congress had created numerous laws restricting the genetics industry's ability to test their theories using the most realistic scenarios possible. With such stringent constraints, how did they expect him to compete with foreign corporations? Ben hated the ignorance of the general public, knowing the great things he could achieve if he had a freer hand. The country's anxieties over genetic experimentation had pushed much of the research outside the United States, where the rules were not as strict. In Ben's view, the government should stay out of things they did not understand.

"Nathan, when the final data arrives, I want a record of the reactions for each vict—, uh subject."

"Whatever you want." Nathan stared at Ben. "Are you expecting anything in particular?"

"No. I want a handle on how this altered virus would react in an unprepared host. Sinus infections are treatable, as are many of the other immune deficiency related symptoms observed within the test group. I'm looking for a discernible pattern." Ben privately chastised himself. Thanks to BenaTex, the common cold could decimate the entire Burbános' race. Was his company worth the lives of twenty-three dead Indians? This was not the BenaTex future Ben had envisioned.

"On to another subject. Nathan, have you ever wondered how Steele knew of the Burbános? Until recently, no one else had even heard of them."

"I assumed . . . I don't know." Nathan shook his head. "Is that important right now?"

"Probably not." Ben returned to his pacing. Could their virus be eradicated if it were accidentally unleashed into the general population? He had assumed all along that Janstone Pharmaceuticals wanted the retrovirus for vaccine research or development. Had he misjudged their motives? Steele would never . . .

October 8

7:48 a.m.—Manaus, Brazil

James Monal entered the tiny café near the Manaus docks and removed his soft-brim outback hat, knocking the dust away with a quick whack against his pant leg. The remote location drew from a more intimate clientele, and was well suited for their meeting. Inspecting the interior, he surmised by the heavily spiced smell of chili peppers and freshly cut jalapeños that the food was the only thing more rustic then the building's exposed wood-on-adobe brick walls. He dropped his hat on a small, carved wooden table, his rucksack on the dusty floor. James then pulled up a chair and sat between Dr. MacKiernan and Dr. Isling, taking note of their apprehensive expressions.

"Good morning, gentlemen," Dr. Isling said. "Now that we're all here, what look's good for breakfast?" Neither James nor Aidan answered immediately.

"The eggs are lively," Aidan said before taking another bite of his breakfast.

James forced a smile. He dreaded discussing details of the expedition. It was difficult for him to concentrate on the future when he had not yet let go of the past. At least the quietness of the café fit his dreary mood.

A waiter wearing an open-chested, sweat-stained shirt ambled up to the table. "Sim, senhor?" He greeted the archaeologists in Portuguese.

"Si," Dr. Isling answered in Spanish. "Muchos gracias. Yo quiero sus mejores huevos rancheros y un vaso grande de jugo de naranja, por favor."

"Si, señor," the waiter responded in Spanish after taking down the order.

"Although the locals primarily speak both Spanish and Portuguese, I'm more comfortable with Spanish. Must be all my time in the Yucatán." Dr. Isling set his menu on the table. "I hope the two of you had a restful night."

James shrugged, then ordered in Portuguese.

Uncomfortable with the awkward silence, Aidan responded, "I have more pains than body parts, but I'll endure."

Dr. Isling gave him an empathetic grimace. "I finally got hold of Dr. Leland this morning. At first, the sound of my voice sent him into shock, but he recovered. And while not completely awake, he confirmed that he'll support our decision, which leaves it up to us. So gentlemen, if you're still game, we'll finish the expedition. What do you say?"

The answer to come was obvious. To not finish, would be like abandoning those friends who had given their lives. James felt it and saw it on the faces of the other two men. They would never quit.

"I'm ready to complete what we started," Aidan answered, glancing at James.

"Me too, Dr. Isling," James said with an underlying uncertainty now that he had voiced his decision. The memory of Ann Wright had haunted his sleep.

In his nightmare, trapped in the wrecked King Air, he slogged his way through smelly water chest deep. In the center of the plane, Ann's bruised face floated to the surface. Her sunken brown eyes called to him and he did his best to reach her behind a wall of floating luggage, frayed wires, and broken seats. Slimy things rubbed his legs and he tripped over invisible obstacles. He grabbed her hand, it dissolved in his grasp as she slowly sank below the water's surface. If he had been quicker, stronger, Ann would be alive. The horrid dream repeated itself all night. His hands rubbed together beneath the table, he could still feel the clammy touch of her cold, lifeless skin.

"Are you okay, James?"

"It's nothing," he assured. "I had a rough night's sleep." Diverting his eyes, he used his fingers to examine a long split in the surface of the wooden table. Dr. Isling would ship him home if he ever suspected the nightmares.

"James, contact Leland and tell him we're continuing."

"Yes, sir." James picked up his leather planner and peeled apart the pages. The pitiful thing got wasted during the crash and all the pages had stuck together.

"We'll have to get new supplies sent in," Aidan added helpfully.

"Was anything salvaged?" Dr. Isling asked.

"Let's see." James leafed through his notepad to an inventory list. Thankfully, he had followed another of Dr. Isling's field requirements and wrote everything down with waterproof ink. He scrolled across the page, mentally adjusting the tally. "The heavy objects were shipped ahead and are at the mission. Smaller stuff we carried with us, including the communications equipment and medical supplies. Nothing of any use was recovered. We also lost portions of the sampling gear and a few personal items."

"All right then," Dr. Isling said. "Hook up with Aidan and work the details, then when you talk with Leland, give him a breakdown of our needs."

"Do you want everything sent here?" James asked.

"A good question. Probably not. Aidan?"

Aidan removed his Boston Red Sox baseball cap and

wiped his sweaty forehead with his shirtsleeve. The café was not air-conditioned, and the temperature, although cooler than outside, was rising under the intense morning sun. "It might be best if the supplies met us in São Gabriel da Anjo. It'd be one less thing to worry about."

"Excellent suggestion. Don't you agree, James?"

"I'll make the arrangements with Dr. Leland." He cocked an eyebrow at Dr. Isling's indecision. His mentor was typically more forthright; bordering on tyrannical. "Keep my breakfast warm, and I'll be right back. I want to catch Dr. Leland at home. The local phones aren't too dependable and I don't want to miss him." James stood, wondering what other changes Dr. Isling had in store for them.

"Oh, and, James, tell Leland we'll be going by river to São Gabriel da Anjo. Since we need a little recuperation time, why don't you secure us a leisurely boat ride. I'm done with planes for a while."

Now he knew. "Sounds good to me." James nodded and left the café.

6:20 a.m.—Sausalito, California

Wade Fields spent a sleepless night mentally reciting his planned excursion into one of BenaTex's more secretive research sections. Biogenetic discoveries were coveted more than diamonds, and as a result, BenaTex's laboratory security had grown into a religious fanaticism. Management's most recent paranoid psychosis had gone beyond belief. Everywhere Wade went there were hallway cameras, door lock checks by armed personnel, extra lighting, new access cards, and the latest in retinal eye-scanners and thumbprint readers. It was creepy.

"Security?" he murmured. "Jesus." This was unbelievable. BenaTex was on the verge of becoming tighter than a military stockade. "What in the hell am I doing?"

Considering the increased precautions, Wade was taking a high-risk gamble poking his nose into a Level 4 authorized area. As a rule, he was more comfortable gaining information during idle conversations with other BenaTex staff, not pillaging vacant laboratories at odd hours of the morning. But the scent of a conspiracy drove his curiosity, and he had no time to gather information through normal channels. He downplayed the dangers of the Level 4 safeguards, believing it was possible to snoop early in the day, when few people were at work. The morning crew tended to operate a little looser.

Wade rounded a corner and entered a nondescript gray hallway twenty feet from his intended target. Using his peripheral vision, he spied two ceiling cameras monitoring his movements. Mounted at opposite ends of the corridor, their muffled electric motors whirred. He closed his eyes and focused his thoughts. Presenting a blasé demeanor was a valuable and necessary guise; someone always watched, and there would be more hidden cameras inside the laboratory. He adjusted his face into an assured, yet carefree pose, which was not too difficult. Wade Fields was not a thief. On the contrary, he provided an essential scientific service.

Tension gripped his body and Wade chuckled, reluctantly admitting, he was getting too old for this secret agent business. He approached the laboratory's polished steel door and pulled a forged access card out of his pants pocket, then slid it through the slot of the magnetic strip reader set next to the door lock. The card didn't work and he began to sweat. He visualized his daughter's smiling face, her new orthodontia, and relaxed, then passed the card through again. A red light in the upper right corner of the electronic pad switched to green, followed by a welcomed clunk. The door lock had disengaged. He was in.

First thing he noticed upon entering was the odor of disinfectants common to the applied laboratories. Only on one previous occasion, while delivering a new procedure to a technician, had Wade frequented this particular lab. Wade's specialty was theoretical recombinant processes and this lab was dedicated to applied genetics, which meant, there was no legitimate work-related reason for him to be there.

The lab was one of four at BenaTex designed for data analyses using various biostatistical methods. Six dry chemistry work areas, each complete with a mini-tower computer, refractory microscope, and sterilized sample handling tools, took up most of the space. Scattered among them were three wet chemistry workstations, where technicians performed nonhazardous biological testing and analysis.

Stopping at the first available computer, Wade wheeled a chair over and planted himself at the keyboard. He called up a file list and skimmed the information. His attempts to view the most recently run reports and programs were met with "Access Denied." Not a surprise, rarely could Wade break into private archives, which didn't matter, he was very adept at guessing their content. His familiarity with BenaTex's proprietary file naming system gave clues to many sensitive details. Wade copied the names of the newest documents onto a notepad, calming his trembling hand by squeezing the pencil between his fingers.

He slid a compact disk into the computer and retrieved the latest deleted files. While these files were blocked from view, they had not yet been erased. Every month, as a general security precaution and to remove outdated information, BenaTex's computer technicians reformatted all the company's hard drives. The next scheduled sweep was in four days. Wade initiated a special program and burned the ten most recent deletions to his CD while concealing his movements behind his lab coat. His heart pounded and he felt the cold lenses of the monitoring cameras spying down on him. Taking a slow breath, his composure returned.

An active work area by a portable biological isolation unit attracted his attention. Wade removed the CD and borrowed a clipboard and notepad hanging on a hook above the desk. He then sauntered over to the area, carrying himself with the confident manner of a scientist conducting an important experiment. He took a seat at the polished stainless steel table and evaluated the setup, quickly sketching the layout for later reference. On a similar incursion into another lab, he had tried using a miniature camera, but his poor quality photographs were an embarrassment. Wade smirked. James Bond he was not.

The biotechnical materials were neatly sorted and various components of sampling equipment were organized to one side. Specific manuals and journals, applicable to earlier experiments, were pushed to the front. Each image hinted at the type of research being conducted. The setting showed a familiar pattern, suggesting enzyme-chemical assays were being evaluated. He flipped his sketch over and jotted notes on the next page.

How long had he been in the lab? Wade glanced at his wristwatch, then at his arms and hands, realizing that his skin had turned clammy. Eleven minutes had elapsed. He had stayed too long. With a forced casual stride, he returned to the first workstation and replaced the clipboard in its holder, shoving the notes into his lab coat pocket.

A noisy metallic clunk echoed through the room. Wade's heart sank when a mid-level manager entered and approached him.

"What are you doing here, Fields?" Ed Cooper asked, scowling. "Are you authorized for this lab?"

"Sure am." Wade handed Cooper his access card.

10:05 a.m.—Central Coast, California

Matt Wells' first class of the day ended and students poured into the hallway. He followed them out and pulled his San Diego State sweatshirt off, wincing when he brushed his forehead. He sighed, threw his backpack over his shoulder and merged with the crowd. It was going to be one of those days.

The mass of bodies closed around him and his temples began to throb. Hot irons jabbed the backs of his eyeballs. The emergency room doctor had said to be patient, take the painkillers and the headaches would go away in a couple of days. The only problem was, Matt had an inborn intolerance for patience and a natural distaste for medication of any kind—alcohol possibly, but not pills. He'd rather endure the pain; it made him stronger, a man thing.

As for adhering to his doctor's advice, Matt stopped at a trashcan, where he quickly deposited the prescription. "That should about do it."

"Matt Wells!"

"Oh, crap. Speaking of headaches." If Allyx's stilted stiff-legged strut was anything to go by, here came another one. Matt met her halfway. "Hi, Allyx."

Squaring her shoulders, Allyx stopped in front of him. "Hi, Allyx?" She gave him an indignant grunt. "That's the best you can do?"

His eyes panned the hallway for emotional support. Allyx seemed to have a talent for making him uncomfortable. "What's wrong now? We haven't even started working together yet."

She glowered. "You could say that. Where were you at six last night? I'm not going to carry you on this project."

"Oh, no."

Allyx's face reddened. "And because of you, I was late to my seven o'clock appointment."

"I'm so sorry. I forgot." Matt dipped his head and gawked at his beat up running shoes. "A mishap got in the way."

"What mishap?" Puzzled, she frowned. "Your head. What happened to your head?"

"It's nothing." He touched the lump. The dull pounding increased and the hallway swirled with pretty streaming colors. "I, uh . . ."

"Matt!" Allyx caught hold of him.

"Whoa," he said, waiting for his equilibrium to re-establish itself.

"Are you okay?"

"Yeah, a dizzy spell. No big deal. Thanks." The worried grimace on Allyx's face made him feel awkward. He tried to shrug it off, but her soft hand gripped his arm, distracting him. Allyx traced the subject of his curiosity and quickly let go.

"Didn't want you to fall, that's all." She averted her attention, looking down the hallway, away from Matt. "I'm still mad at you."

"I would expect no less." Allyx's embarrassment gave her smooth olive skin a warm glow, softening the intensity of her features. Maybe she had a heart after all.

Allyx did her best to avoid eye contact. Her uncomfortable reaction was cute, and very uncharacteristic.

"You should probably sit down. Why don't we go to the Student Union and have coffee or something?"

He smirked. "If that would make you more comfortable."

"You're impossible." She stomped away, toward the Union.

*   *   *

The Union was a massive three-story concrete structure. An arcade, bowling alley, and pool hall were on the ground level. The upper two floors held food service facilities and meeting rooms. To support the erratic schedules of many students, the Union operated day and night. After purchasing two large black coffees, Matt and Allyx searched for a quiet location. They found a vacant corner on the second floor furnished with a padded blue couch and a circular wooden table.

Matt set his cup on the table, his backpack on the floor, and sat a foot or so from Allyx. He was still ill at ease being near her and reconsidered getting too close. "If we're stuck together . . . uh, going to work together, shouldn't I get to know you better?" Great move, Wells. Nothing but style today. I'm sure she's impressed.

Why couldn't he hold a simple conversation with this woman? What was it about her that rendered him incapable of casual speech? It's not like he was telling her his deepest secrets. He sniffed the rich coffee and tried to relax.

Allyx smiled at his clumsy move. How nice. She had noticed his awkwardness. He could feel his temperature rise. The embarrassment registering on his face had to be obvious. If they were going to spend time together, he had to get himself under control. Otherwise, she'd turn him into a babbling idiot.

She held her cup with both hands and sipped. "Not too fast, Matt Wells."

"What?"

"Tell me about this mishap of yours."

"Oh that." He suppressed a sigh of relief. "It's no big thing, really. Someone jumped me when I entered the Doc's, Dr. Ruhpor's office last night. The police said it looked like I stumbled upon a student break-in." Allyx didn't push him for more. Contrary to what he expected, she reacted to his explanation as though they were discussing an everyday occurrence.

Gently moving a lock of hair away from his lump, she studied the injury. "Black and blue are definitely your colors. The knot adds character."

Matt squirmed. What was it with this woman? Why did she affect him so? Allyx was full of awkward surprises, constantly keeping him off balance. "I'm glad you approve. . . . So uh, now that we've gotten beyond the appeal of my new forehead, tell me about yourself."

"Whatever." She sipped her coffee. "Not much to tell. I'm a neglected fourth generation Greek offspring of a doctor and a lawyer. My father's a military physician assigned to the CDC in Atlanta, and my mother's an associate with a small environmental legal defense firm."

"The CDC?"

"Sorry. I always assume everyone's heard of them. It's the Centers for Disease Control." She set her coffee on the table and turned toward him.

He wondered, observing her mannerisms, had she finally lowered her guard? "Go on."

"Basically, I've been here for two years, and I'm working on my bachelors in biology. My goal is to get my doctorate in biogenetics. . . ."

Allyx and Matt shared life stories for more than two hours. When they said good-bye outside the Student Union, they parted as friends. She headed to her next class and he returned to the Natural Sciences Department. They apparently had a few things in common, and for once, she hadn't grilled him. He had even found the nerve to ask her to Friday night's classical music concert, and she had accepted—another surprise.

His mind still pondered Friday night when he stopped at the department secretary's office. Embedded in the wall by the door was a mailbox rack made of varnished oak. Grading papers and lab teching for the Doc had earned him one of the twenty-four bins reserved for faculty and staff. He dug through his slot and emptied the contents on a table below the rack; mostly junk mail, except for a curious handwritten note.

"Matt: I'm going to be on sabbatical for a couple of weeks dealing with research issues. While I'm gone, keep an eye on Allyx and help Tom Harden. It's a world filled with nasty, ubiquitous little creatures. Good health and good hunting to you. Dr. Ruhpor."

He rechecked his empty slot. "That's it? Kind of strange." Professors don't pack up and suddenly leave town without making appropriate arrangements, at least not for simple academic reasons. Class schedules and other commitments had to be handled. Besides, Harden was a graduate student whose projects were well beyond Matt's comprehension, and Allyx could definitely take care of herself. This was unlike the Dr. Ruhpor that Matt thought he had gotten to know. Or did he really know him at all?

10:10 a.m.—San Francisco, California

Ben Singular hated these update meetings and grumbled accordingly while leaving the elevator's solitude to enter Steele's office. He flicked lint off his jacket lapel and smoothed his hair. The consummate micromanager, Steele had to have a hand in every aspect of the retrovirus project. It drove Ben crazy to have his work censored by another. As his client was not yet in, he took a seat at a large cherrywood conference table.

Jolon Steele arrived a minute later. "Dr. Singular, what news do you have for me today?"

"Actually, we've made a significant leap forward." Ben laid his calfskin briefcase on the conference table. Popping the locks and lifting the lid, he took out Nathan's graphs.

"Oh?" Steele straightened some sort of Indian war shield hanging on his wall, then removed one of his Cuban cigars from a carved ivory case and strolled to the table, taking a seat at its head. He clipped the end of the cigar and lit a wooden match by striking it against a corrugated brass plate mounted on the corner of the table. Steele let the match burn down until there was no lingering sulfur aroma, then fired the end of his cigar, gently puffing.

Steele's cavalier attitude made Ben uneasy. "As I was saying, we've had a breakthrough. The latest viral strain provided by the professor has the necessary thermal resiliency." He arranged the graphs into their appropriate sequence.

The executive remained quiet.

Ben wriggled in his seat. "The modeling results show the ECR will exceed 90 percent."

"The human testing?" Steele asked.

"It won't be necessary. When we analyze the latest test subject's autopsy results, we'll have enough data to make the final RNA adjustments using the computer model."

The executive leaned forward. "Acceptable, but I have received troubling news."

Ben cleared his throat. "What might that be? We're nearing the end and everything's going well—"

"Hardly. The Amazonian site has fallen apart, and Dr. Ruhpor is getting too inquisitive. But that is not what concerns me."

"Then you already know we've shut down the Amazon project?"

Steele tapped the ashes into an antique ceramic tray. "So I understand. However, my current interest is more domestic. You and BenaTex have a mole. This person is an insider working for one of your board members."

"Giles!" Ben blurted. Where did Steele get his information? "It has to be her."

"I see you are familiar with the board member I am referring to." Steele puffed on his cigar, noting Ben's reactions.

"Not that well. She was voted in last year by the Board of Directors, and most of our interaction has been limited to financial battles on other projects. Her name is Naomi Giles."

"Was she the one who authored that ridiculous JAMA paper last fall?" Steele's features darkened and his eyes seemed to take on that same yellowish color Ben had noticed before. The image unsettled him.

"Dr. Singular?"

"Uh, yes. That's the woman. Her article was entitled 'Ethics Versus Biotech: Is There a Conflict?' "

Steele studied Ben for a moment. "Find Giles' mole and take care of him. Here is the name of the man we suspect. Check him out, but do not take too long. We think your employee might run. You can call this number at four-thirty today for assistance." Steele handed Ben a torn strip of paper. "You have two days to eliminate the problem. I will deal with the Stanford expedition and the Cal Poly professor."

Oh shit, now what had he gotten himself into? Dr. Ben Singular, a renowned biochemist, Yale Honors Graduate, and president of his own biogenetics company, was adding cold-blooded-murderer to his résumé.

Steele stood; the meeting had ended. Ben was stunned, speechless. If he followed orders as directed, he'd be trapped and under Steele's thumb for the rest of his professional career. He thought for a moment, searching his options. First the Indians, now this new development, who or what would be next? Not his son? Ben couldn't think straight, there was too much at stake. Sweat beaded on his upper lip.

"That will be all, Dr. Singular."

10:28 a.m.—Sausalito, California

Wade Field's accidental encounter with Cooper had been

too close. Luckily, Cooper had bought his excuse for being in the applied laboratory. Locked away in his own office, the laptop's screen prompt flashed and Wade typed in a command that listed the records on the CD. Those were the deleted files he had copied off the laboratory computer. Nine complete files in all; the tenth had been damaged and was unrecoverable.

Wade used a commercially available software package to reconstruct the data. The first character of each original file name had been replaced with a question mark when they were deleted, making them unreadable by the computer's bios system. His software gave him the capability to restore the missing character. The nine files were designated: ?iraltest.rpt, ?ccount.rpt, ?ubject.dat, ?ewvirus.doc, ?estrun29.dat, ?ilestone.dat, ?naseq.tbl, ?esequenc.dat, and ?quipment.sum.

Following a superficial scan, Wade concluded it shouldn't take him too long to sort through the data. One at a time, he accessed each record and reviewed its contents. He then compared his lab notes to information collected during casual conversations with coworkers and to other technical tidbits gleaned from various offices. The accounting Wade had amassed painted a tale of scientific intrigue; one that said BenaTex's upper management had embarked on a new business line. He shut down the laptop and closed the case.

Picking up a genuine 1968 Willy Mays autographed baseball from its brass holder on his desk, Wade stood and tossed the ball into the air, catching it with one hand then the other. Reengineered viral genetics had been lucrative, and looked to be the financial wave of BenaTex's future. The extreme secrecy still bothered him.

Retroviruses were complex and dangerous, requiring very special handling. Unless there were strong financial incentives, most genetics firms opted to avoid them. A shiver hit him. Could it be a military application?

10:46 a.m.—San Francisco, California

Osborne strolled into Steel's private office.

"Have a seat." Steele pointed to chair.

As Osborne approached the conference table, the stench of Steele's cigar assaulted his sinuses. He suppressed a sneeze, and surmised the obnoxious habit was another extension of the man's compulsion to intimidate. What an arrogant ass, so full of himself.

"Mr. Osborne, I am not pleased with your handling of the Stanford group. You are supposed to be the best."

A brief pause occurred while Osborne carefully observed Steele. He appeared calm and calculated. Osborne understood the man could not afford mistakes, therefore, neither could he. Like most perfectionists, Osborne preferred to work directly, limiting his contracted intermediaries to muscle jobs, where he could keep his own hands clean. Except for the Chameleon, the scummy non-questioning types he had been relying on lately tended to run short on brain mass. As always, there were never any guarantees, and the trouble with middlemen was in maintaining their quality. No matter how well planned or thought through, miscalculations happened—even for the Chameleon.

"The pilot was better than we had anticipated." He kept his expression neutral. Steele sought to dominate, but Osborne was familiar with that game, and he refused to give ground. "Our man sabotaged the plane in a professional manner, leaving no sign of his workmanship. If the rescue team adheres to standard Brazilian crash investigation procedures, they'll never find our device. Even if they do, it doesn't matter. The damage resembles an in-flight electrical circuit meltdown and metal fatigue in the wing. No one will be the wiser."

Even though Osborne was practiced in observing body language, Steele was a difficult man to read.

There was something strange about him.

"So far, Mr. Steele, the radio transmissions we've intercepted from the rescue aircraft have counted three survivors."

"I am unimpressed." Steele puffed on his cigar, allowing smoke swirls to rise into the air. "I require a higher level of performance if we are going to continue our relationship. You came well recommended, and this is not the quality I expected."

"We're on top of things, I assure you."

"You are paid to account for every possibility. How are you handling Ruhpor?"

A perceptible eye twitch and slight apprehension in his tone, had given Steele away. So, that Cal Poly professor, Dr. Ruhpor, had gotten to him. But how? Osborne watched Steele involuntarily blink to his left, suggesting he had heard something that made him anxious. His subconscious reflex showed someone was keeping him current. Why had he suddenly let his guard down? He knew the professor had slipped through Osborne's net, but he had decided to keep that bit of information private. The game had escalated. Steele was measuring him, playing him.

"Ruhpor will be handled."

"Discreetly," Steele instructed. "I will not tolerate any more entanglements. Too many outsiders possess sensitive pieces of the puzzle, and I want them all removed."

That was Steele's agenda. Sparring over the plane crash, although important, was simply a challenge to verify Osborne's resolve to complete the rest of his assignment. He had been warned. Yet, there was something else, a subtle and dangerous change in Steele's demeanor. Along with shutting down the Stanford expedition, he was to take Dr. Ruhpor and his graduate student, Tom Harden, out. Based on the intensity in Steele's eyes, Osborne's own life might hang in the balance of another failure.

"I'll take care of it."

"You had better." The tone in Steele's voice sharpened. "What happened to the professor?"

"He dropped from sight yesterday evening after one of his classes. My people are hunting for him and his assistant."

Steele frowned. "I do not like it. Allowing Ruhpor and his graduate student to run loose could become problematic."

For the first time, Osborne experienced a twinge of anxiety. The Amazon plane crash was an unpredictable roll of the dice. The failed hit on Dr. Ruhpor was an embarrassment. "We hope to have him in our hands within the next 24-hours."

"I do not barter in hope. I deal in results. Steele pointed the red tip of his cigar at Osborne's face and he flinched. "Find them."

"It . . . it will be handled." There was murderous rage in Steele's yellow eyes. Osborne had never seen such an evil look.

"In addition, take your men off BenaTex's mole."

"Immediately?"

"Correct. You will get a call at four-thirty. The man will ask for directions on how to find Fields. Hand over the information and keep your people in reserve."

"I'll make the adjustment," Osborne responded coldly, wanting nothing more than to put some distance between Steele and himself. "Is there anything else?"

"Not at this time."

11:35 a.m.—Sausalito, California

Wade Fields smiled warmly, landing in the chair next to Sally Brinkman before she could object. "Fancy seein' y'all here."

"Oh, hi, Wade." Preoccupied, Sally picked at her potato salad with a fork. She pushed the pale mush to the center of her plate. "It's not like I go anywhere else for my lunch break."

"You sound mighty low." Sally's droopy expression showed she carried a heavy load, and Wade Fields was just the guy to dump it on. "What's bothering you? Y'all are usually a ball-o'-fire. Is there anythin' I can do?" Sally was an intelligent and attractive woman, and taking advantage of her when she was vulnerable made him feel like a sleaze. If the situation had been different, he would have asked her to dinner or something more human, anything other than simply pumping her for information.

"It's . . ." She visually swept the nearest table. A technician sat alone, engrossed in the San Francisco Chronicle, oblivious to their conversation. "Ever since Ben, I mean, Dr. Singular, sent his last e-mail, the place has been turned upside down. Security in our section has more than doubled. We're at the point where we can hardly get our jobs done." She redirected the potato salad to the left side of her plate.

"Heck, it won't last long. Nothin' 'round here ever does." Mentally, he retraced his trip to the Level 4, A-Wing lab. The company couldn't be on to him. Maybe Cooper had said something. Naw, paranoia clouded his perspective, that's all. No one suspected. "Do you know what's got 'em all riled?"

She shook her head. "We're on a big project that's bringing in a lot of money and they're freaked over corporate espionage. They've isolated everyone. There's no communication among the teams and no central core group. Singular and Donner are handling everything themselves."

"Interesting," Wade commented.

11:50 a.m.—Central Coast, California

Matt Wells squatted on a metal stool outside of the

STEM lab and waited for Tom Harden, hopeful that he might shed light on the Doc's sudden departure. If anyone knew where the Doc was it would be Tom. The two men were close, so much so, that Matt was shocked when he heard Tom had been a football star. He had considered Harden to be more akin to Dr. Ruhpor, a typical egghead, but an okay guy. Matt glanced at his watch. According to the schedule posted on a corkboard by the door, Tom should have been there twenty minutes ago. Apparently, he also had the Doc's gift of running late. Which didn't make a whole lot of sense, especially when he considered the demanding deadlines of the various STEM projects.

Matt inserted the master key Marcie had given him and turned the knob until the laboratory's double doors clicked open. He switched on the lights and scouted the room. The heavily filtered atmosphere gave the air a tainted metallic taste. The floor had been swept clean. Except for residual dirt staining a hand auger, shovel, and other miscellaneous soil sampling equipment hanging on a rack by the storage cabinets, the lab had a sanitized look. It just didn't feel right and Matt couldn't put his finger on why.

Loose papers cluttered the desk next to the electron microscope's computer interface. The piles reminded Matt of the Doc's filing system, which the professor had named "stacks and stacks of technical facts." Matt called it chaos.

Two-dimensional colored line graphs covered the pages, and the margins on many had notes scribbled in cursive. The handwriting resembled the Doc's scrawl. Matt picked up the microscope's most recent usage log and thumbed through the first dozen pages. No one had been in the lab for more than eighteen hours. Before then, the STEM had not seen a break. A dirty coffee cup held his attention. This was not the sparkling—

A hand touched his shoulder. Matt jerked in the opposite direction, fists raised. He wasn't going down twice in one week.

At the last second, he pulled his punch and scrambled backward, stumbling into the desk. A slew of reference books toppled over on an attached shelf. "Oh, Dr. Theim, I'm very sorry." Matt sensed his face had turned bright red. "You startled me. I didn't . . . I mean, again, I'm so sorry."

Stopped by the aggressive reaction, Dr. Theim hid his surprise well. "It's okay. I heard about the bump on your head. It must have made you anxious. If not jumpy."

"To say the least." To regain his balance and work on his composure, Matt stepped away from the desk. "Did . . . did the police catch Dr. Ruhpor's burglar?"

"No. Probably just a prank."

"Kind of a nasty one." Matt ran a fingertip across his forehead and shied away, straightening the shelf and re-aligning the logbooks; that's when he noticed one had been placed in the wrong order. The other twenty or more logbooks were chronologically sorted. Except for the papers, graphs, and two logbooks—one on the desk and one on the shelf—everything else in the lab was filed or stored away.

Uncomfortable with the Dean's prying gaze, Matt diverted attention elsewhere, away from the bookshelf. "Is there something I can help you with, Dr. Theim?"

Theim stiffened. "No, that's all right. I was nearby and saw the lights were on, so I stopped in to see who was here."

The short hair on Matt's neck tingled. The Dean had lied. The lab lights were not visible from the hallway. Just the other morning the Doc had explained how he had customized the lighting system specifically for the STEM lab. Each recessed ceiling lamp contained a low-amp tungsten filament that drew power through an ultra-low frequency capacitor. Dr. Ruhpor's approach lacked the annoying resonant frequency cycling associated with most commercial systems, which in turn, would have interfered with the microscope's sensitive electronics.

Every square-foot of the lab had an equal degree of brightness, thereby eliminating shadows. When standing in the hallway the lights always appeared to be off because of their unique illumination pattern and the absence of defined shadows. Catching the Dean in a lie was unsettling.

"Dr. Theim, have you seen Tom Harden?"

"Tom, no . . . can't say that I have." Dr. Theim shoved one hand into his pocket and fidgeted with his change. His distracted eyes darted around the room. He acted as if this were his first visit to the lab, or was it that he had expected to find someone other than Matt?

"According to the schedule, he should be here by now." Matt watched the Dean's eyes as they continued to flit about. "I wanted to talk to him and Dr. Ruhpor about a project." The Dean's melancholy expression turned stern. The passing reference to Dr. Ruhpor had apparently piqued his attention in a negative way.

"They're very busy. Grad students and professors have little interest in keeping schedules."

"Funny," Matt said, narrowing the distance between him and the Dean, trying another tact. "Tom impressed me as the punctual type. I guess not."

The Dean rattled coins in his pocket. "Maybe Dr. Ruhpor sent him to do field work. He does that a lot." His attention swung toward the door, and he took note of his watch.

"If you say so." Matt judged it doubtful that Tom enjoyed the field. Tromping across the boonies on a bad knee couldn't be much fun. He figured him to be more at home behind a computer or tinkering with the STEM. "With Dr. Ruhpor's sudden departure, I doubt he had a chance to give Tom a field project." Matt was becoming more confused and more emboldened the longer their conversation continued. The Dean appeared perplexed.

"Ah, yes . . . well . . . you're probably right."

"Dean Theim, did Dr. Ruhpor mention how long he'd be gone?" Matt assumed the school's administration required the Dean to preapprove sabbaticals.

"Yes, he did." He checked his watch again. "A couple of days was all."

The note had said two weeks, not a couple of days; another lie. Even though Matt stood directly in front of him, the Dean avoided him. Why was he lying? "Then who's teaching his classes while he's gone? I have him for Soil Microbiology. And then there's my grading responsibilities."

"At the moment, Matt, I don't recall. I'm sure it will all work itself out soon. You can speak with Marcie tomorrow. Well, I have to go. I'll let you get back to work." He quickly left the lab.

"This is screwy." Matt rubbed the side of his jaw with his fingers, mumbling to himself. "I get jacked then play mind games with the department head. What's next?" He pursed his lips, snatching up the two logbooks, one on the shelf, then the other on the desk. Their front covers were stenciled with *Scanning Tunneling Electron Microscope Usage Log*. He skimmed a few pages of the most recent addition while absentmindedly thinking about the Doc and the Dean.

"Get focused, Matt. You're not getting anywhere." He concentrated on the books. The log entries were in scientific shorthand, and the gist of the notations had to do with viruses, which made sense when he considered the Doc's expertise. He took his lucky Mexican peso, a keepsake remembrance of his last night in Cabo, and flipped it into the air.

"Heads I borrow the lab stuff, tails I don't." Matt caught the coin one-handed. "Tails. Oh well, I guess I'll do it anyway. It might be a stretch, but what other choice do I have?" He put the books into his backpack and scooped up the papers.

As Matt left the lab and entered the main hallway,

he caught a glimpse of someone ducking down an adjacent corridor. The silhouette's portly shape resembled Dr. Theim.

1:08 p.m.—Sausalito, California

Ben Singular rocked his chair back, holding the telephone receiver in one hand and a photograph of his family with the other. Baby Jenny nestled in his wife's arms, and Sarah, his six-year-old, stood by her side. Ben readjusted his chair and gently set the picture on the corner of his desk. The time spent away from his family was getting lonelier and longer with the passing of each day.

"Donner, here."

"Hi, Nathan, I've got the final parameters for the model. The retrovirus analogy still flies, only a minor adjustment or two. Steele's provided specific requirements for its premutagen characteristics."

"I'll be over in a second," Nathan replied.

Ben set the phone receiver in its holder, organized his notes, and waited. The meeting with Steele had been another grueling emotional drain, and he wasn't sure how many more he'd be able to take. Steele's manipulations gained greater control over Ben and BenaTex the closer they came to finishing the retrovirus project. What a mistake it was to get involved with that monster.

How Ben wished for unhampered thoughts away from Steele. He longed for the ability to choose his own way, not to be subjected to the demands of another. Patience, he told himself. The day he could say good-bye to Steele was near. Then maybe, his life would regain some balance.

He glanced at the family photograph, then thought of Matt. His fatherly affairs had been put on hold for too long. Lorie had been divorced for the last few years and Matt had grown into his own man. The time had come to tell him the truth. Matt deserved to know his real father. Ben deserved a son.

* * *

Nathan Donner bounded through the door, letting it slam shut behind him.

"That was fast," Ben said. "You must've flown down."

"My calls were forwarded to my cell phone. When yours came in, I was around the corner in Conference Room 103." He stood next to the desk and faced Ben. "I'm as pumped as a college kid prepping for an on-line computer date. Developing a reengineered retrovirus is an awesome feat, and the end is so close. Damn, I love this stuff."

"I'm the same way. Now why don't you take a seat before you burst a brain cell?" Ben handed Nathan his meeting summary. "It's too bad we'll never be able to share our accomplishment with anyone else."

"You sure know how to kill a moment." Nathan scrunched his lips together. "Our accomplishments should be shared with the world."

"That wasn't the agreement we brokered."

"I might have agreed to that, but I never liked it. He took advantage of us" Steele hamstrung them with all the secrecy requirements. He hadn't even deemed it necessary to discuss his intentions once they delivered the virus. The closer they came to completing their project, the more perplexed Nathan became over its limited pharmaceutical value. Often, the only thing that kept him going was the far-reaching applications of their research.

The data they had collected affected a string of retroviruses and might even lead to cures or vaccines for many. Steele couldn't restrict the use of their new knowledge. He wasn't God.

"Rigid requirements." Nathan analyzed his partner's meticulous notes. He lifted a pen off the desk and made a few comments in the margin. "We can handle them. I'm also working on an idea for the viral dormancy."

"Prepare a summary analysis of what we have; we're short on time." Ben skimmed the pages of his Dilbert desk calendar, a subliminal gift from his wife. "How long until the new modeling parameters are programmed? We're still running in the shadow of the ECR requirement."

Removing a PDA from his sport coat pocket, Nathan punched in some reference numbers. "We've refined the boundary conditions for the reverse transcriptase enzyme based on the previous model runs. The difficulty lies in limiting the precursor virus' influence on the immune system. Steele wants a maximum dormancy of six months with restricted pathway mobility." He compared his computations with the notes. "I suspect we'll be ready for a recalibration run within the next twelve hours and a final run within twenty four."

"Good." Ben reached for a pencil and began to tap it against the top of his desk. "Considering the virus' ability to mutate, can we guarantee the results? BenaTex could be delivering an uncontrollable predator. Does Steele understand he's going to have a deadly organism in his possession?"

"Doubt it." Somewhat surprised by the question, Nathan shook his head while continuing with his calculations. "Business types generally focus on the financial angle and tend to disregard other realities." He swept his hand through his unkempt hair and looked at Ben. "Options are within reach to protect us. I can do a DNA modification that will affect the virus' sensitivity to oxygen. The tweak limits its life expectancy outside the host. We can also modify the messenger RNA to regulate the relationship between the virus and host's cell function."

"I like your suggestions, but won't there be a cell

mortality problem if we allow the virus to replicate inside the host without preprogrammed limitations?"

Nathan bowed his head respectfully. Businessman and geneticist, Ben Singular was still the best in both worlds. "That was the limitation with the earlier strains. This new virus will enable us to create a symbiosis within the host's cell membrane, which will curtail cell death and promote viral replication." Nathan showed Ben a satisfied grin. His enthusiasm made it difficult to sit still. Creating a self-sufficient life form starting at the cellular level was incredible. This must have been how God felt.

"We can then limit the proliferation of the virus by introducing an abnormality into its messenger RNA; one that promotes random incomplete genetic coding. This adjustment statistically reduces the number of viable viral particles in the blood stream at any given moment."

"Your configuration impedes viral growth as a predictable geometric progression," Ben added.

"Exactly. When we're finished, we'll have knocked the six-month dormancy and restricted the available transmission pathways." Nathan loved being in the center of free-flowing ideas. When they formed BenaTex, he and Ben met weekly to brainstorm new approaches and ventures. As their clientele base expanded, the sessions were pushed back to monthly. Soon business demands seemed to always get in the way and they stopped scheduling meetings all together. Nowadays, conferencing was no more than an afterthought; their Board of Directors oversaw everything, scrutinizing each approach on all new projects—or so the Board thought. Even they were kept in the dark on some things. If they had been made aware of all the details, this retrovirus affair would not have been approved. Nathan missed those energized days before BenaTex had gone public.

Rising, Ben pressed his hands flat on the desk and leaned forward, giving his back a stretch. "If we pull the preliminary data together by tomorrow, I can control Steele. I'll need the final model run within two days."

"Should be no problem. I'll push the recalibration up and the rest can be easily handled." Nathan jumped up and headed for the doorway. Abruptly stopping, he turned and faced his friend. "I still don't like all the security requirements. Our people won't put up with the constraints much longer."

Ben sauntered to the front of his desk. "You concentrate on the virus, staff's my problem."

"If you say so, Ben. I'll take care of my end." Nathan closed the door and stood in the hallway next to Ben's office. The housekeeping crew must have just come through; their trademark floral fragrance lingered in the air. Nathan closed his eyes and reflected. The reality of their situation was difficult to accept. Ben no longer had a sensitive finger on the BenaTex pulse. He had changed; many things had changed.

1:23 p.m.—San Francisco, California

Jolon Steele shut the door to his office and slowed as he walked past his "ego wall." He picked up a color eight-by-ten photograph of him shaking hands with ex-President Reagan. Most men toil for a lifetime and do not achieve a fraction of what Steele had in half of one. Heads of nine countries knew him personally, and he had been an advisor to five presidents, three while still in office. Returning the photograph to its appropriate spot on the display shelf, he aligned its viewing angle. The second major part of Steele's master plan was in place. Within twenty-four hours he'd trigger a multibillion-dollar financial coup d'état and no one would ever be the wiser—that was real power and a test of what was to come.

Steele crossed the room to his desk and sat in his brass-studded executive chair. He caressed his custom-carved ivory cigar case with his fingertips, outlining the intricate pictorial of a cheetah taking down a water buffalo on an African plain. Lifting the lid he removed a cigar, but left it unlit. He pushed the remaining cigars aside and took out an object wrapped in a worn brown cloth. A smile formed on his face as he set the cigar and object together on the desk. He held down the intercom button.

"I'm ready."

A moment later the door to his office opened. His secretary entered, locked the door, picked up the cigar and object, then walked to the conference table. A Brazilian beauty queen; she said nothing.

He pressed an encryption button on the side of his telephone followed by the autodial.

A raspy voice answered, "Yes."

"Ambassador, this is Steele."

"How much longer, Mr. Steele?"

"My last meeting with Singular verified that we will have a viable retrovirus before the deadline."

"Are you on top of the deliverables we discussed?"

"Osborne is handling them. Singular shut down the Amazon project and the group we contracted is removing any evidence of their activities." Steele omitted details relating to the attack on the mercenaries and the inconvenient Stanford expedition. "No one will know of our involvement."

"That's acceptable." The raspy voice deepened as the man hacked a thick phlegmy cough. "Any potential link to Janstone would be inappropriate. And the BenaTex mole?"

"Being handled. The transfer to Singular will be this evening." Unaccustomed to being on the defensive Steele's left eye twitched.

"Send the virus data to the Houston group for risk

modeling the moment it is available."

"Understood." Steele jotted a coded reminder in his scheduling book to call Houston. "They will have the necessary information before the deadline." He hung up and weighed the exchange. Singular had better produce.

His secretary remained still during the conversation, trained to wait. He approached her and she removed the protective cloth wrap, exposing a small dagger with a jade hilt. She laid the cigar and cloth on the conference table, then took hold of the hand Steele offered and pressed it against her chest.

He felt the beat of her heart through the thin blouse, the deep curve of her firm breasts. She trembled—anticipation. Her dark eyes stared straight ahead, expressionless. Steele watched as she raised the knife and his hand together, running the tip of the blade across his scarred palm. The pain gave him an expected thrill. Blood streamed across the dagger. She licked the blade clean, and then eased her tongue between his bloody fingers, caressing each of them with her lips. Her head dipped into a submissive bow as she handed him the weapon.

Steele held the dagger to her throat and shoved her back onto the conference table, hiking her leather skirt up and exposing a black lace thong. She moaned ever so slightly as he pushed apart her legs. He pinned her hands above her head, then slid the razor sharp blade between her breasts. She flinched when he nicked her skin.

With methodic slowness, he cut away the buttons on her blouse, the straps on her sheer black bra, and then outlined her breasts with the tip of the blade. A few small marks were visible on her smooth, tan skin; scars from their previous encounters. Blood dripped from his hand, splattering her nipples. He sliced through the remaining strands of clothing, unveiling her completely.

Her hips began to undulate as he held the knife against her stomach and squeezed her wrists down hard against the table. The more he pressed with the blade the more intense were her thrusts. He set the knife on the cloth and picked up the cigar.

4:10 p.m.—Sausalito, California

Wade Fields grabbed his briefcase and laptop and slammed the office door shut. The implications of his findings were alarming. He worried about sharing the information using an unsecured BenaTex telephone line. Circumnavigating the last corner into the foyer, Wade passed by the security station. As he approached the exit, his briefcase felt heavier than usual. Smuggling dynamite through airport customs had to be easier.

"Mr. Fields," the BenaTex security guard called.

Wade's heart pounded. He stopped one long stride from the exit. If he bolted for freedom, would the guard chase him? Could he get away? His mouth went dry.

"Yes." Wade didn't dare face him.

"You forgot to sign out." The guard dropped a pencil and clipboard on the counter. The noise of the impact seemed awfully loud.

"Oh . . . sorry." Wade returned to the counter. His knees swayed and he hoped the guard didn't notice the sweat accumulating on his forehead. "Work's been crazy lately. I've even considered bringing a sleeping bag and staying all night."

The guard shoved the sign-out sheet across the countertop. "If you'd please, Mr. Fields."

"Thanks for reminding me." His hands trembled. Had the guard ever seen his signature before? Wade quickly finished and scurried through the main door without looking back.

Traffic congested the street, making Wade more uneasy. His car was parked in the company's private garage around the corner, but a sixth sense told him to take an alternate route. He swiftly measured his choices, crossed the street, then jogged two blocks and entered a Chicago Deli.

Wade bought a soda and sat in a corner seat with a strategic view of the deli's front door. A small group of college students had assembled at the order counter. His pulse raced and his awareness became ultra-alert—colors brightened and sounds were crisp. Wade listened to the crackle of a tungsten ceiling light. He smelled the sweet deli meats. With swift movements, his eyes assessed the patrons.

Two men dressed in jogging suits, one in charcoal gray and the other in royal blue, entered the deli. They ordered drinks, and then sat on the opposite side of the room. Their awkward movements were out-of-place among the college crowd. Wade's body temperature began to climb. Paranoia, he had to stay calm.

When his eyes skimmed the joggers for the second time, the two men ducked away. Had they come for him? Wade maneuvered a cellular phone from his coat's inside pocket. Hiding the small device behind the table, he punched memory one, then whispered into the mouthpiece. A plastic floral arrangement covered his actions.

The flap quietly closed and he placed the cell phone back in his pocket. His timing had to be perfect. He sweated out eight long minutes then strolled to the order counter and stood an arm's length from the deli's double-door entrance.

"I'd like a chocolate chip cookie please." Stupid as it sounded, a cookie was the first thing that came to mind. As the two men he had been watching shielded their faces, a yellow and black taxicab pulled up outside the deli. A young woman keyed in his purchase. He placed a dollar on the counter. The cash register drawer banged open, and at the same moment, Wade flew through the doorway.

"Hey!" the cashier yelled. "What about your cookie?"

Taken by surprise the two joggers jumped to their feet, smashed into chairs and customers, and raced after him hurling themselves onto the street just as the taxi pulled away. One of the men kicked a rock into the road; the other spoke into a cellular phone.

4:13 p.m.—Sausalito, California

The clock on the wall ticked away another minute; Ben Singular picked up his pace. His six hundred square-foot rectangular office appeared to shrink with each stride. The responsibility of running a corporation, especially the people it employed, had taken a heavy toll on his health. Every day he made decisions affecting their lives, and college had never prepared him for the stress of those decisions. No school taught the lessons of failure. No school imparted the rules of where fiscal responsibility ended and human responsibility began. What was the cost of success? How far did his commitment to his employees and shareholders go? He walked alone, conflicted and confused.

Ben pushed the intercom button. "Julie, have Mr. Latch come see me right away."

"Yes, Dr. Singular."

Pushing the retrovirus project to completion was his only option. Its revenue guaranteed BenaTex's financial future for the next five years; his company would be safe, his employees secure, and the stockholders happy. One man could not be allowed to stand in the way, even if he was one of his own.

"Come in," Ben responded to a knock at his door.

"You wanted to see me, sir?"

"Mr. Latch." He stopped pacing. "Shut the door."

Latch closed the door and took a seat next to the conference table. A stuffy, all business, ex-military type, he had the stocky frame and puffy face of a seasoned boxer, and the cold glower of a man with few friends. Before financial gain had lured him into the private sector, Latch served with the Army's special forces, then the San Francisco Police Department. He had been head of BenaTex's security going on four years. Many of the employees considered him too rigid, and most left him alone. He was the quintessential security chief: dark and scary.

"What can I do for you, sir?"

"I have a delicate matter to discuss with you." Ben went back to pacing. "It has come to my attention that we've had a security breach."

Shifting in his chair, Latch asked, "Can you give me the details, sir?"

"This morning, one of our employees used a fake access card to enter a high-security laboratory. While there, he copied documents pertaining to a confidential project."

"I take full responsibility for any lapse, sir."

Ben watched his head of security as he considered his next move. Mr. Latch was a dedicated BenaTex man; would he do what was necessary? "For the sake of the company, this has to be rectified, Mr. Latch. Find Wade Fields and recover our property."

"Fields . . . I know him. Yes, sir. I'll take care of it."

"Call this number at four-thirty and you'll get a lead on Fields. You have about five minutes." Ben handed Latch a sealed envelope. "Here are additional instructions and something for your expenses." He showed his security chief to the door. "Thank you, Mr. Latch. I know I can count on you."

5:42 p.m.—San Rafael, California

The taxi left Wade Fields on the east side of San

Rafael, at the front door of a rundown bar. A reddish neon sign crackled Bob's Place in the cool evening air. One taxi after another, he had been on the run since leaving the deli. He did not dare go home, fearing the company would be waiting for him. His first task was to shed any ties with his normal routine, then find a temporary sanctuary. Wade chucked his cellular phone into a trash dumpster down an alley adjacent to the bar. They would scan for his calls.

He entered the bar and scrutinized the surroundings: a dive, with one broken-down pool table and a decrepit jukebox. Stale smoke and sweat filled the room. Faded and cracked, maroon wallpaper trimmed with walnut crown molding covered the walls: a throwback to the disco '70s. Two old winos sat at the counter. A nearly naked woman fondled a man wearing a cream-colored polyester suit in a booth at the far end of the room. The bartender had the empty stare of a '60s burnout—too many drugs. Wade crossed the faintly lit space and propped his foot up on a barstool.

"Can I get whatever you've got on draft?"

The bartender poured a clean glass and slid the cold Miller down the cigarette burned counter. Skidding to a halt in front of Wade, the beer's foamy head slopped over the lip onto the wooden countertop.

"That'll be a buck fifty."

Wade laid two dollars on the worn surface. "Keep the change." Supported on one elbow, the beer in his left hand, he assessed the room. "You got a phone?"

"In the rear, by the head."

"Thanks." Wade took his beer and rustled for change in his pants pocket. He fed the telephone and called another taxi company. The dispatcher said the cab would arrive within fifteen minutes. He hung up then staggered wearily into the men's restroom.

Following a quick peek that the single stall was

vacant, Wade set his beer on the rim of a cracked sink. He held onto the sink and inspected his face in the polished piece of stainless steel substituting for a mirror. His eyes were haggard gray around the fringe; he had looked better. Cold water streamed across his hands and he splashed his cheeks. The chill jolted him.

Wade returned to the bar, ducking into a secluded booth. A long gulp of his beer and he mentally reran the day's events. Someone on the inside was on to him, which meant seeing his daughter was not an option. He had to protect his family. His only chance was to contact his other employer and get help, but he first had to analyze the data and verify his suspicions. Closing his eyes, Wade rested his head on the booth's torn padding and sighed, accepting his momentary reprieve while silently waiting for the cab.

10:12 p.m.—Central Coast, California

A cold wind swept through the telephone booth. Central California's other season, winter, was making its presence known. Matt Wells fished two quarters from his shirt pocket and dropped them into the slot. He pulled his Levi jacket closed and listened for the dial tone, then punched in the number.

"Hello," a woman's tired voice answered.

"Hi, Allyx." Matt swallowed hard. What if she wouldn't help him, or worse, said he was crazy? He had wasted hours reading the lab information, and in the end, the logbooks and graphs had meant nothing to him. Allyx was his only connection to the Doc.

"Yes . . . , who is this?"

"Matt. Matt Wells." A pitiful yawn followed the silence. "Sorry I woke you."

"How . . . how did you get my number?"

"I called Marcie, our department secretary."

"You bothered her tonight, for my number?"

"Guess you could put it that way." Marcie had not been too happy to get a phone call just before ten on a weeknight when she was trying to get her kids to sleep—being a single mother had to be tough. He had profusely apologized during their brief conversation. The exchange reminded him of the tough times his own mom had gone through raising two boys.

"This had better be important, Matt."

"I have a situation and need your help." Through the receiver, he heard the familiar sound of rustling bedsheets.

"What do you want?"

"Can you meet me at my townhouse?" Matt crossed his fingers. "Right now I'm outside the Science building, freezing to death."

"Are you serious? I'm not exactly dressed."

Allyx, naked in a warm bed? Matt took a breath and slowly let it go. The worst she could say was no. "Allyx, I think Dr. Ruhpor's in trouble. He's disappeared. Even Marcie doesn't know how to get hold of him. I'm not sure what—"

"Give me your address."

10:15 p.m.—San Mateo, California

Wade Fields pulled the tattered shade down. Turning on the nightstand light, he assessed his new surroundings. The motel room was abysmal, chipped paint on the walls and worn paths in the carpet, but it served his purpose. He had selected this location for its discreet renting policy, not its decor. This kind of room could be paid for by the hour and he did not intend on staying long. Wade plopped on the bed, spent.

His briefcase lay next to him and he let loose his iron grip on it for the first time since leaving the bar.

He treated the case with delicate care, as though it held a precious metal, knowing its real content might be even more valuable. Regardless of what he carried, his suspected knowledge worried someone at BenaTex.

The computer data he had copied was heavy on viral genetics, although the specific details were sketchy. Monetary gain in genetics generally came when deciphering an existing problem virus, not in creating a new one. If there was no obvious purpose or application for BenaTex's retrovirus research and development, then Wade had to find a fringe financial angle. Humanity's health requirements hardly ever motivated business decisions. Profit potential always moved projects one direction or another. Therefore, the question was, who could make a profit with a reverse engineered retrovirus? Bioterrorism? The military?

He emptied his briefcase and spread the contents on the bed. BenaTex had broken down the project into more than a dozen isolated elements. No one ever saw anything other than what they were working on, and interaction among the staff was not allowed. An unusual approach, especially when he considered that the synergistic sharing of information had brought about many discoveries, which was also a standard in the industry. This project had the characteristics of a Black Hole operation run by the Department of Defense. It reminded him of his old DOD days.

While serving as an Army captain in the early 1990s for the CDC evaluating biological warfare agents, Wade had gained insights into the military mentality. DOD often sequestered workers on sensitive programs to maintain security, but that precaution also pushed up the cost. Unless the BenaTex research was government sponsored, their project was too compartmentalized to be economically effective. He wondered what they were hiding, and who provided the funding. Answers, he needed answers.

Wade tumbled backward onto the bed. His head sank into the soft pillow, and his eyes closed, shutting out the world. He vowed to find the answer. Did he have time? For the past five years, he had been able to stay one move ahead of the company. Had his luck run out? The telephone by the bed rang.

"Mr. Layman?"

"Yes." Layman was the pseudonym he had used to register.

"This is the front desk."

He recognized the night clerk's squeaky voice and tensed.

"Three men are on their way to your room, and they ain't the police." The line went dead.

Wade stuffed the papers, laptop, the CD into his briefcase and slammed it shut. His mind raced. How had they found him? Credit card? No. He had paid cash. Somehow, he had left a trail. They had trapped him, then maybe not. He ran for the bathroom and praised his luck when he found a small window. Judging the size, and propelled by enough fear, he could squeeze through.

A metallic crunch echoed from the parking lot. Startled, Wade flinched, tripped on the stained toilet bowl, and landed flat on his back inside the mildewy shower stall. The stall smelled awful, and Wade was certain he had seen cleaner restrooms at rundown gas stations. Outside, voices argued, followed by the blast of a car horn. Damn, he'd overreacted, jumped at shadows. Get a grip Fields.

Wade climbed off the sticky floor and onto the toilet seat where he inspected the window mechanism. He grabbed the frame, shoved the glass pane aside until it stopped, yanked it free from its track and chucked it into the shower. His left foot on the dilapidated sink, his right on the toilet, he lifted his head above the windowsill; six feet below, compacted dirt and scattered weeds covered the ground. A hurried assessment told him no one was watching the rear.

He bent down, retrieved his briefcase and heaved it outside. An audible click came from the other room. Someone was at the door. Wade pushed against the sink and dove headfirst through the rectangular space, smacking the hard ground with a groan. "I'm too old for this crap," he grumbled, ignoring a sharp shooting pain trouncing his right hip.

Fields crouched low and surveyed the surroundings—no sign of his uninvited visitors. A wind gust ripped through an alley on his left, carrying the fetid odor of rotten garbage. He hoisted his briefcase out of the weeds, then dashed past the alley to a deserted side street and disappeared.

10:48 p.m.—Central Coast, California

When Matt Wells arrived at his townhouse, he found Allyx Katero leaning on the wall by his front door with her arms crossed. Sleepy, wearing baggy jeans and a green Notre Dame sweatshirt, her natural beauty still shone through.

"Have you been here long?"

She yawned. "A few minutes."

Matt should have felt guilty for dragging Allyx out at this late hour, but seeing her spurred selfish thoughts. "I'm glad you came." A biting breeze blew across the porch. "It's chilly out here."

He unlocked the front door, reached around the corner and switched on a light. "Be my guest." Matt gave Allyx a slight bow and rolled his hand toward the inside. She brushed up against him on her way by and his pulse jumped. He closed the door.

"Nice place, Matt." Allyx evaluated his modest quarters while standing on the edge of the living room.

"Did your cleaning lady quit?"

"What—?" Matt spun around and stubbed his toe on a dictionary. His jaw drooped as he assessed the disaster. His things lay shattered on the floor. Even his houseplants had been tipped over and crushed. He moved through the debris, trying to make sense of the carnage. The room smelled of spilt potting soil. Hard to believe that this used to be his home. Shock bleached his face a pasty white, but anger quickly restored the color.

"You live this way?"

Matt grimaced.

"I was only joking."

"Someone trashed my place."

He picked up his calculus book and placed it on a shelf.

"Much better," Allyx said.

"It must have just happened," he muttered. "I went to the Union, ate dinner, and reviewed some stuff; I was gone only an hour or two."

"I don't get it, Matt. What's going on?"

"I have no idea." He glanced around the room. "My guess is it has to do with Dr. Ruhpor." Violated by the invasion of his private world, his head pounded. "I should call the police."

"It's obvious you can't stay here." Allyx gave him a concerned look. "Make the call, then come to my place."

"Huh, yeah, sure." Muddled, he stared at her, sure that the concussion had affected his mind. Had Allyx just invited him to spend the night? Was he hallucinating? The emergency room doctor had warned him that cognitive loss was a common occurrence and that he might find himself confused or disoriented.

"Here." Allyx handed him the phone. "Report the break in."

11:24 p.m.—Santa Cruz, California

Wade Fields headed south after diving through the motel window. Following three random taxicab changes, he settled on Santa Cruz's boardwalk, where he had hidden among the beach-going drifters for the last half hour. His disheveled appearance blended in with the wandering souls enjoying the crisp fall night. Visitors gathered there from across the southern Bay, strolling in groups or by themselves along the concrete walkway.

Boisterous teenagers, hanging on surfboards as they stood next to a public restroom wall, argued among themselves, mocking each other's ability, the day's rides, and the cut of the waves. Their raised voices challenged the crash of the surf. A long-legged brunette, gliding on inline skates sped past Wade to his left, leaving the scintillating scent of her flowery perfume. An elderly homeless woman, shoving an overstuffed shopping cart, spun him around while imparting her own special odor. Wade had to laugh. This crazy human microcosm had no concept of material responsibility or bad guys with guns. These people moved within a world separate from the mainstream populace, a world that spawned existential life during the black of night.

A hundred-and-fifty yards to the west of where Wade stood, the ocean slammed the shoreline with all its might. To the southwest, the rugged coastal cliffs brought the North American continent to an abrupt and jagged halt. To the southeast, ancient stands of Monterey pines saturated the night with their nocturnal energy. The downtown lights of Santa Cruz cast a golden glow onto the star-streaked northeast sky. Wade watched the smiles of those who passed, wishing that he were there for any other reason. Santa Cruz's serenity provided a conduit for its inhabitants to escape the evils of the daylight hours.

He squeezed his briefcase to his chest and surveyed the boardwalk for curious eyes. Although no one suspicious had caught his attention since escaping from the motel, he was uncertain. Could they already be in the crowd, watching, waiting? They had found him before, and they could find him again.

Another quick glance and Wade ducked into an isolated telephone booth beneath the Santa Cruz wharf. After fumbling for change, he entered an emergency number. His hands shook uncontrollably. Ironically, his very survival wavered in the balance of another phone call. A stranger had saved him at the motel; hopefully, someone could help him now. Wade shuffled his feet and shivered when a cool ocean gust penetrated his thin wool sport coat.

A woman's voice answered. "This is two-four-eight-three. Please give your ID and password."

He hesitated, "Two-two-four-six and my password is, Adrienne." Using his daughter's name was not the smartest decision he had ever made. But then, he never thought this call would come either.

Interesting how one's life evolved. Since his wife's death in a car accident six years earlier, his daughter had become everything to him. Losing his wife had been emotionally devastating, but thanks to Adrienne's love, he had been able to resolve his personal pain. And, because of his other more specialized kind of work, he had built up a tidy nest egg. Adrienne would be taken care of for the rest of her life. He thought of his daughter's bright brown eyes. By a stroke of good fortune, she was visiting his sister, hidden away in Los Angeles. It seemed that all his affairs were in order.

The woman on the phone responded moments later. "Your password cleared. This number is for emergencies."

"This is a damn emergency! I'm on the run in Santa Cruz and have information the company wants bad enough to send hired killers after me. I need a safe haven and I want it now!"

"Hold please." The phone became unnervingly quiet.

"You've got to be kidding?" Wade felt stranded.

"Go to the Old Mission Plaza. Your contact will meet you at forty minutes past midnight. Don't be late, and make sure you're not followed. When he signals, provide the appropriate countersign." She hung up.

Wade replaced the receiver and left the booth. Now all he had to do was hide among the shadows for another hour—no problem.

11:28 p.m.—Central Coast, California

Officer Ryan McCuvey, representing the San Luis Obispo Police Department's Burglary Division, stood in the doorway and shook Matt's hand. With a polite nod at Allyx, he said good night.

The police had descended on the townhouse with the speed and sensitivity of a swarm of locusts. They sifted through his belongings, hunting for clues, and in the end, were more frustrated than Matt was. The police found no apparent reason for the break in; nothing had been stolen. They logged the incident as an act of unsolved vandalism—just like Dr. Ruhpor's office, another dead end.

"Matt." Allyx touched his forearm.

"What? Oh, hi."

"Are you ready to go?" She appraised their surroundings one last time. "We can take care of this mess tomorrow."

"I guess. Feel like I'm abandoning the place."

Allyx looped her hand under his arm. "Let's leave before you have us both in tears." She led him outside and locked the door.

A light wind blew inland off the ocean twenty miles

west of them. Matt inhaled, expanding his chest to its limit. Salt carried in on the night's drifting currents. The back of his throat tickled and the moist air felt crisp on his face. He was glad to be away from the carnage that used to be his home.

"Thanks, Allyx."

"For what?"

"For being here. For being a friend." She smiled and gently pulled on his arm, guiding him to her car, an older model red Karmann Ghia.

They drove three blocks before Matt spoke. "The Doc left on a sabbatical. The Dean didn't know anything about it. And Tom Harden, a grad student who works with the Doc, he's missing too."

"I've met Tom."

"Well, I found a cryptic note in my box when I got back from the Union. The Doc must have left the note and disappeared shortly after the attack outside his office."

"Matt, I'm sure there's a simple explanation for all this."

He shook his head. "The Doc wouldn't just leave like that. Not without saying something at least to Marcie."

"You never know. I've seen professors do stranger things." Allyx spoke in an even tone, close to condescending. "I don't want to scare you, but all things considered, you sound like one of those conspiracy nuts." He sighed and sank into the car seat. "Matt, a lot has happened to you in the last forty-eight hours, and I think you're seeing things that don't really exist. It's natural after what you've been through. Relax and give it a day or two. I'm sure everything will be fine."

"Maybe." Allyx had one good point. On the surface, the Doc's abrupt absence didn't seem sinister, and a thousand things could have delayed Tom. Who's to say the guy who thumped him was involved? The ransacking of his townhouse could have been a coincidence, except Matt Wells did not believe in coincidences. If only the throbbing in his head would go away.

"Pull over!"

"Say what? Why?" Allyx swerved to the side of the road, stopping next to the curb.

"Do you want ice cream?"

"Do I want what? Jeez." Allyx took a deep breath. "Have you lost your grasp on reality?" She calmed herself. "Look, Matt, I know you've been through hell, but you almost caused an accident for some ice cream. Have you lost it?"

"Most likely. Hungry?" He hopped out.

Her eyes rolled toward the ceiling of the car. "Another man driven by his stomach." Turning the ignition off, she dropped the car keys into her pocket.

They entered Stephsons Ice Cream Parlor, ordered, and found a corner booth. Matt laid his backpack on the table before taking a seat facing Allyx. Undoing its flap, he removed the notes and graphs, then pushed the papers and logbooks across the table.

"Now what?" Allyx scooped a spoonful of her hot fudge sundae and skimmed the material.

"This place closes in about fifteen minutes, which doesn't give us much time. Before we go, there's some stuff I'd like you to look at. Maybe I am crazy, you tell me." He pointed. "This is what I called you about. I picked this stuff up at the STEM lab, and after hours of pounding my brain, I couldn't make anything of it."

"I'm not surprised."

Matt grimaced.

"So what are these?" Allyx picked up the papers and skimmed the top one.

"I was hoping you could tell me. That's why I borrowed 'em. They might be tied to the Doc's sudden departure. A clue or something." He watched two men wearing black clothing enter the ice cream parlor and take seats three booths away. A server made her way to their table.

Allyx scrutinized one of the graphs, trading her skeptical sarcasm for a quizzical expression. Her brow crinkled into a frown. "These two," she pointed, then leafed through the rest of the papers, "are time-series plots of viral replication under variable conditions. It's a test to see how well the virus reproduces when the temperature changes. Or as Dr. Ruhpor would say, affect the humidity, modify the nutrient base, and then monitor what the ubiquitous little critters do next."

"Is this an unusual approach or something?" His eyes swept the parlor. The bright lights made him uneasy; he and Allyx were too exposed.

She shook her head. "No. Dr. Ruhpor is big on geology and soils. So it's a natural conclusion that he'd be involved with soil borne viruses as part of his research. And these tests are pretty standard."

"Then there's nothing out of the ordinary?"

"Not really. Well, maybe. But it's a stretch." She frowned.

"Little help here, please. I don't quite get it."

"It does appear he was very interested in the influence of temperature on a specific viral strain. Almost to the extreme." Allyx rotated the graphs for Matt to see. "This virus, marked 2g3-2, was worked to death. Humidity, alkalinity, and hosts of other tests were also run."

"Just a second, Allyx."

A young server stopped at their booth. "Can I get you anything else?" she asked. A smudge of chocolate fudge on her left breast marred her pink uniform. She smelled of candy and ice cream. Her demeanor was that of a junior in high school. Matt used her body as a shield and spied on the two men in black suits. When one of them turned his way, he jerked his head back.

Matt read the girl's nametag. "I'm sorry, Andrea, I wasn't paying attention. What did you say?" His rudeness had annoyed her, but that faded as soon as she heard him mention her name and saw his smile.

"That's all right. All I said, was can I get you anything else?" She licked a polished red fingernail and swept a tuft of tight brown curls behind an ear.

"Give me a break," Allyx muttered.

"No thanks," Matt interrupted. "We're fine."

"But, I—"

He frowned at Allyx. "We're okay for right now. Maybe later."

"Call me if you want anything." The server showed Matt a flirtatious smirk and twirled away. He was used to such reactions and hardly noticed. Her short pink skirt fluttered side-to-side as she swayed to the order counter.

Allyx's eyebrows dipped low and menacing.

"Sorry, Allyx, but we're not staying long."

"You're a heck of a date, Matt Wells."

"What can I say?" He fumbled with the graphs. "Too bad you didn't find anything unusual with these? It might have helped."

"I'm not sure what you expect to find, but that's not exactly what I said." She grabbed a pencil out of Matt's backpack and traced the graph's x-axis. "Okay, pay attention. This data plot focused on a very restricted temperature range. The low end's 93 degrees and the high's 107." Allyx circled the tick marks on the y-axis of the graph. "If I analyzed a virus' limitations, I'd test the extremes to verify dependent mortality. In other words, what ranges of natural conditions are optimal for the virus' proliferation. When viewed from an academic perspective, and considering how many tests were run, the data collected are awfully narrow in their scope."

One of the two men stood and swaggered to the order counter. Matt motioned with his hand for Allyx to be quiet.

"Are you listening?"

"Don't look around. Two men came in right after us.

They took a booth and have looked our way more than a half dozen times in the last two minutes."

Allyx scowled. "Are we now getting paranoid?" She placed her hand on top of his. "These graphs are interesting, but as for having hidden secrets that explain the whereabouts of Dr. Ruhpor and Tom Harden, I don't think so. You've run into a string of crappy luck, that's all. It happens. A coincidence of sorts."

Matt took notice of Allyx's hand. Her skin felt soft, and her touch warm. "Remind me to show you a book I have. It expounds on the underlying truth behind coincidences. Come on, we're leaving." He shoved everything into his backpack, dropped a two-dollar tip on the table, and hooked Allyx by the arm.

"This way. We're using the rear exit." Before the back door clanged shut, Matt heard heavy footsteps running their direction.

They sprinted across the Stephsons' parking lot to the street. Allyx jumped into the driver's seat of the Karmann Ghia and Matt slammed the passenger's door shut. "Start this thing and go!"

Allyx cranked the engine over. The sports car lurched forward. She spun the wheel hard left and they picked up speed, zipping past street signs and closed businesses in a blur. The whine of the four-cylinder, rear-mounted engine increased as the amber dashboard lights cast a muted glow across Allyx's intense features.

He kept one eye on the road and the other on her. "Slow down before you get us killed." His voice sounded unnaturally calm.

"What . . . ?" She gave him a disbelieving scowl. "Not again. We left Stephsons like it was on fire." Allyx shook her head. "You'd better do some fast talking, mister. Otherwise, I'm gonna explode, and then kick your flaky butt out of my car."

"I'll try." Matt composed himself. "I don't know what's going on. All I really have is a nagging hunch.

Make a left there." He pointed ahead, while monitoring the road behind them. A sickening premonition gnawed at him. Someone shadowed them, back there, just beyond his line of sight. Matt could feel them, or was it his imagination. Was he going over the edge?

"I can't explain why. I'm convinced the Doc and Tom Harden are in trouble and those men I saw back there are involved. And I'm just as certain that the Doc's disappearance is tied to my getting whacked and my place being demolished."

"Okay, I'll give you the benefit of the doubt, but where to now?"

"All I want is to put distance between us and the ice cream parlor, after that, I'll entertain suggestions."

A dark blue sedan moved to within two blocks of the Karmann Ghia.

"My apartment. We can review your 'stuff' in more detail and sort through things."

He shook his head. "If I am being followed, they could know we're together and your place might not be safe."

"I said I'd give you the benefit of the doubt, but to be honest, Matt, I'm not convinced there is a 'they.' I didn't see anyone suspicious at the ice cream parlor. And now that we've settled down, let's remain calm before you invent a real crisis without any hard evidence."

"I . . . maybe you're right. My head's killing me." His brain swirled like burnt mush. "Maybe the crack I took," he massaged his temples, "is making me delusional." Matt closed his eyes. "I need rest." He slumped in the seat, ran his hands over the smooth leather upholstery and listened to the rhythmic sputter of the Karmann Ghia's engine. "Your apartment sounds fine."

*   *   *

"We've got the sports car in sight. . . . Hell no, of course he's not alone. It's some babe. . . . Yeah, another student. . . . Yeah, we're gonna take care of her too." He slammed the car phone into its console holder. "That guy gets on my nerves. If Osborne's that damn smart, why don't he do them himself? I wish he'd chill long enough tuh let us get the job done."

"What did he say?" the driver asked.

"Keep loose 'til they stop, and then pick the dude up. He wants to pump this guy, Wells, before we smack him."

"What about the girl?"

"He said, he didn't care about the babe. I guess that makes her ours." The man cackled, visualizing the things he could do with her young supple body. "It'll be like that creamy-fine high schooler we snatched last month."

"I can't wait," the driver chuckled.

October 9

12:15 a.m.—Central Coast, California

Matt Wells checked the road behind and in front of them as the Karmann Ghia turned south at the intersection, about a hundred feet from the nearest apartment building. Matt spied more than two-dozen multistory, red brick apartments positioned along the elm-lined street. Their overgrown ivy-covered walls blended into a continuous mélange of red and green. Differentiating between buildings would be difficult during the day; at night it was impossible. Adding to the visual confusion, the next three blocks were crammed with hundreds of parked cars—another overpopulated student-housing project. When street space had been exhausted, the locals garnered the first available patch of grass.

"Don't park too close to your place."

"Why? Did you see somebody?" Allyx's head swung back-and-forth, skimming the neighborhood for strangers.

"No, and I know you think I'm crazy, but I'd rather not take any unnecessary chances." Matt pointed to a vacant plot of lawn. "How's that?"

"It'll do." Allyx dodged two trashcans, a tree, a frightened cat, and swerved into the grassy slot.

"Nice neighborhood." Matt exited the car.

"I guess; if you like being pickled together like dead fish. My apartment's in the next building." She led the way under a white trestle and followed a walkway illuminated by planter lights and lined with dormant rose bushes.

Swinging a large, black iron gate to the side, they passed between a pair of three-story apartments. The layout and architectural style were the same for each building, and the narrow passages running between them formed an intricate maze. After a few turns, Matt was hopelessly lost. Allyx stopped at the fringe of the glow cast down by a yellow porch light.

"Are we home?"

She smiled and unlocked the oak door, then removed a message attached to the knob.

"Is it important?"

"No. The telephone company's doing an emergency repair on a trunk line and my phone will be off until noon tomorrow." She shut the door behind Matt and locked the deadbolt. "Make yourself comfortable."

Allyx set her keys on the counter separating the kitchen and the dining area, while Matt tossed his Levi jacket over the back of her tweed couch. He stretched and looked around. A modest apartment with one small bedroom, tiny kitchenette, cramped bathroom, and a large living room that doubled as an extra bedroom and dining area.

"Do you want some hot tea?" she asked.

"Sure, thanks."

"I'll only be a minute." Allyx ducked behind the counter and Matt heard pots and pans bang together. "I hope herbal's okay." She placed a copper teapot on the stove's burner.

"Sound's fine." Matt sat at the small dining table and emptied his backpack. "How long have you lived here?"

"About a month. I lost my roommate at my old apartment and had to find a place I could afford on my own."

"It's cozy," Matt said.

Allyx handed him a cup of tea and placed a bowl of cut apples in the middle of the table. She dropped a biochemistry book and a stack of class notes on the floor, then took a seat beside him. With one foot propped up on the chair, she hugged her bent knee. "It's not very big, but I don't require a lot. I spend most of my time at school or in the library."

"I understand." Smiling, he sipped his tea. "This is good. Thanks."

"Why don't we recap your grand conspiracy theory? You believe Dr. Ruhpor and Tom have disappeared. It's tied to the bump on your head and to your townhouse being torn apart. And the answers can be found in all this biotech information you brought me. Do I have it right?"

Matt's uncertain fingers flipped through the pages of one logbook. "Does it sound that crazy?"

She snickered. "I've heard worse pickup lines than this. But I have to admit, yours is the most creative."

"You don't think. . . ." He blushed.

"You should see your face." Allyx laughed. Yet, she was obviously touched by his embarrassment. "I'm sorry, that was insensitive of me. No, I really don't believe it's a cheap line."

Quietly, he nursed a bruised ego while butterflies fluttered inside his intestinal tract. Yeah, she was only teasing, but that didn't help. Rejection was the worst of all pains, more deadly than the swiftest bullet, and exposing himself was not worth the risk. Contrary to what his friends had said, he often became tongue-tied when with beautiful women, emotionally illiterate in his ability to articulate his feelings. His confident attitude was a guise, protecting many buried uncertainties. Matt took comfort in keeping his emotions at a distance, remaining safe and unchallenged. Perception had been his shield.

While Allyx might not have that modelesque beauty that usually caught his interest, she did have a smoldering sensuality, giving her striking athletic features an exotic quality. What set her apart from most of the women he had known, besides the little-girl freckles across the bridge of her perfect nose and the shine of her tanned olive skin, was an unprotected gleam that twinkled in the corner of her honey brown eyes; a hint to deeply buried emotions, a hint to vulnerability.

Every thought, every action, carried more depth with Allyx. One moment she was sensitive and caring, and the next, she sliced and diced his ego with ease. She had the uncanny ability to heighten his awareness of himself, while exposing his weaknesses. If he could only understand why. Matt sipped his tea and studied her movements as she pushed her long wavy golden brown hair behind one ear. Allyx was nothing like any other woman he had known.

"Hmm . . . well, I'm . . . I'm glad you don't think I'd stoop that low." He blushed again. Damn, he was losing his grip. "Can we get back to Dr. Ruhpor?" Allyx's proximity added to his growing awkwardness. Relax, do what comes naturally, which, around her included tripping over his tongue.

"Matt," she touched his forearm; he tensed, "it's after midnight and I'm exhausted. Why don't I throw a blanket and pillow on the couch for you? We can discuss this in the morning when we're rested."

The reprieve helped him relax. "That'd be great. Perfect. Good idea." Matt realized that he was babbling. He hoped Allyx didn't know how she affected him. Had it become obvious? She's just another female. Allyx smiled and his stress seemed to evaporate. How did she do that?

"I'll only be a minute."

"Huh, okay. I'll pick up a little."

She glanced inquisitively, then shrugged and smirked. "Whatever."

God, she must think I'm a freakin' goofball. He arranged the papers on the table and organized the logbooks, then flopped onto her couch. One good thing, his headache had eased for the first time since leaving the townhouse.

"Here's a . . ." Allyx set the bedding down when she

saw Matt had fallen asleep. She raised his head and slid a pillow underneath, then placed a blanket over him. Stepping back, she gave her guest the once-over.

"Given a chance, Matt Wells, you might be okay after all."

*   *   *

The dark blue sedan skidded to a stop in the middle of the intersection.

"If you don't shut the fuck up," the driver griped, "I'm gonna stuff this steering wheel down your throat! You whine more than my old lady. How could you lose them?"

"All I said was these damn streets all look the same. How do I know what way they went? You're supposed to be watchin' them too. Besides, the address we got off the run on her license plate was crap."

"Give me that." The driver ripped the sheet out of his partner's hands. "Her name is Allyx Katero. She's twenty-two, five-foot seven, one hundred twenty-one pounds. It gives a Georgia address. Hell, it's not even from California. She's another damn student with a new address every couple of months. What good are these stupid DMV computer hack jobs if the info's shit?"

The passenger snatched the Department of Motor Vehicle information sheet back. "Nice lookin' babe. I'm gonna take my time and enjoy her. What're we gonna do now?"

"Cruise the streets and hope we score."

12:33 a.m.—Mission de la Santa Cruz, California

Wade Fields hid under the cover of a juniper bush next to the main walkway leading into the Old Mission Plaza

Park. Crouched on a slight knoll, he used his vantage to monitor the major access points. A grassy lawn, sparsely covered with magnolia, cedar, pepper trees, and a spindly date palm or two, sloped to his left. The bell tower of the Mission de la Santa Cruz stood straight ahead. Wade shivered, nervous in the cold early morning air.

Plaza Park formed a neighborhood gathering area, half the size of a football field, where a dozen footpaths ended. One of the many secondary brick pathways passing near Wade's hiding place encompassed a large circular fountain and terminated at the mission. The fountain, made of brick and rock and lined with varying shades of blue ceramic tiles, marked the approximate center of the park. About sixty feet to his right, the restored annex of the original mission, known as "the Old Adobe," occupied the full length of the park's northern boundary.

He strained his eyes and picked out more details. The only usable light came from a few lamps scattered here and there around the park and along neighboring streets. Tree branches snarled above his hiding place shredded the light from a single street lamp located on School Street. The distant lights threw a desolate mood over the park. A coastal fog encroached from the west; its wispy gray tendrils crept down the annex's red tile roof, adding an air of intrigue to the Spanish Californian architecture. The building's whitewashed walls radiated a yellowish-gray glow in the misty air.

His imagination surged wild with visions. Spirits of missionary Indians danced in the foggy night. Killers sent by BenaTex hid in the moonlit shadows. Pounding in his chest outpaced the tempo of his racing mind. Before he went crazy, Wade slowed down. He had to relax, take it easy, think positive thoughts. No more killers, only the good guys were out there.

Wade had watched the park while huddled behind

the thick juniper bush for the better part of a half hour. He probably knew every shadow by heart. Behind him, hidden by the juniper's thick branches, stood a brass plaque mounted on a brown adobe-brick edifice. Covering his hand with his coat sleeve, he shoved aside a bristled limb and read "Hard Luck Mission" embossed across the top. It figures. Just what he needed; a meeting in a place remembered for its rotten luck. Was the whole world against him?

Another quick glance across the park told him his contact had not yet arrived. Passing the time, and keeping his mind occupied, he took a pen light out of his briefcase. He shined the narrow beam over the plaque, hiding the reflection from view of the trail with his hand. Beneath the inscription, the Mission de la Santa Cruz's turbulent history had been summarized for the tourists.

Since its founding in 1791 by Father Fermin Lasuen the mission had experienced devastating floods, robberies, earthquakes, and financial woes, falling into disrepair in the early 1900s. According to the writing on the plaque—

Movement about one hundred and fifty feet away attracted his attention. A man wearing a black trench coat emerged from the fog. He stopped under the light of a street lamp and lit a cigarette, then pitched it onto the grass and adjusted his narrow-brim hat to one side. The melodramatic scene was cloned from a cheap, detective film noir, but it was the signal Wade had expected. He clicked off the penlight and shoved it into his pocket. Questioning the wisdom of this late-night rendezvous, Wade waited an extra second before leaving his bushy sanctuary.

Before long, he stood and weaved a passage through the bushes onto the brick walkway, clutching his briefcase under his arm. Fear compressed his chest and his breathing labored in the cold air. Plagued by doubts, Wade analyzed his reasoning for putting himself in jeopardy. What had gone wrong? It used to be simple: get the information and pass it on. Now his life was on the line. Would his daughter be proud of her daddy? Wade drew closer to the man standing under the light.

A voice nagged at him, warning him, he shouldn't be there. What did he think he was doing? He was a Ph.D., a man of science, not some espionage operative. Wade stopped. Had the fog made him hesitant?

Wade hung back as another man, wearing jeans and a flight jacket, stepped from behind the far wall of the Annex. Did they send a team? The woman on the phone said one contact, not two. He battled an urge to go for the trees. The man in the trench coat angled his direction. Wade moved slowly, keeping both men in sight, noticing the one in the trench coat had not acknowledged the new man.

Two rapid thwap-like sounds distracted Wade. The noise resembled the muted thud of a flat tire rolling on wet asphalt. He watched the first man stumble when one of his legs teetered in front of the other, then he caught himself and continued walking. An expanding gray wall of fog absorbed the light of the street lamp.

The man in the trench coat, now a yard or two away, faltered again. He wrenched to one side. Wade glimpsed an agonized expression stitched across his face—a boy, twenty at most! Stunned, Wade leaped backwards, but the young man lunged and grabbed him by the coat sleeve. His grip was like iron. Warm liquid spread across Wade's hand—blood! His contact released him as he buckled to his knees. Blood seeped through the boy's shirt, splashing on the red brick walkway. He raised his head. Wade's throat constricted.

"Please . . . !" The boy coughed. Blood and saliva dribbled from the corner of his mouth. His pleading eyes were unbearable. "Ru . . . run! Get help!" The boy doubled over, landing facedown.

Confused, terrified, Wade's head jerked left to right, canvassing the plaza for the other man, but he was gone. Wade leaned toward the boy. His weakened knees wobbled. He could do this. He had to do this.

The other man emerged from the shadows. Tainted gray light angled across the killer's legs. Although the thickening fog concealed his face, his mannerisms seemed vaguely familiar. Not knowing what else to do, Wade inched closer to the trees, away from the man and the boy.

"You have something that belongs to us," the killer said in a deep and husky tone.

"That voice," Wade blurted as light glinted off a metallic object in the man's hand. His eyes widened. "Oh shit, he's going to shoot me too. Stupid. Stupid."

"I said you have something we want."

Wade strained to see beyond the unsettling shadows. The Mission was too far away, while on his left, the scattered trees provided minimal cover. Wade saw a bright yellowish flash, then heard a dull thump. He staggered sideways; a searing pain burned his right shoulder, and he held his left hand on the spot. Warm blood pooled beneath his shirt. Shit, it hurt. Of course the killer had a silenced gun. Think, Wells, think. No more stupid mistakes. The pain cleared his mind, helped him to think.

"If you don't give me what I want, the next one'll kill you." The assailant stepped closer.

Wade feinted toward the Old Adobe, then something in him snapped and he went for the trees. An oak branch exploded inches above his head. Rounding a sprawling trunk, he dug his fingers into the rough bark, catapulted himself to the left and darted for another tree. He slowed, sucked in a breath, and ran on, vanishing into the fog.

* * *

For what seemed like hours, probably only minutes, Wade dodged down side streets and between closed businesses. He passed a mini-mall and a clock tower on his right. His shoulder throbbed and his hand had gone numb, but he kept running. A sloshing noise sounded in the distance; an instant later a wrought iron railing slammed into his thighs. Flying over the top, Wade sprawled rump first into a swirling mass of frigid water.

Sinking under the saturated weight of his sport coat, holding his briefcase with his injured arm, Wade kicked and flailed to the surface. His head bobbed above the water, that's when he realized he had landed in the San Lorenzo river; a glorified stream about four feet deep during this time of the year. He coughed up a mouthful of rancid liquid, then rolled onto his back while the current floated him downstream.

Pain wracked his shoulder, and he grimaced. Blood seeped through his shirt. Concentrating, Wade visualized his daughter's innocent face, drawing on her strength. He had to fight the drowsiness. The adrenalin rush faded, his efforts to stay awake failed and his will weakened. Sleep sounded so good. Swept up by the intervening hand of God, Wade's body rode the current as his mind drifted toward darkness.

12:36 a.m.—Sausalito, California

Midnight came and went, and except for Sally Brinkman, most of BenaTex had been empty for hours. The geneticists on her side of the building started early and left late to avoid the rush-hour traffic. At the moment, she was glad that only on a rare occasion did any of them pull an all-nighter.

Sally entered Fields' office and appraised the sparse furnishings—not unusual for a Ph.D. She thought of Nathan Donner and his peculiar habits. They all had their own quirky eccentricities. Although their offices tended to be large, creature comforts, especially furniture, were not a priority among many of the male doctorate level staff.

She strolled across the room, having no idea of what to look for. Wade's sudden strangeness had not set right with her. When they bumped into each other just before three-thirty in the hallway, he hardly spoke. His hazel eyes were glassy and nervous. The guy was always in a good mood. What had changed? He was not the same man who had sat with her in the lunchroom earlier. While their last meeting was brief, Sally had experienced an awkward tenderness toward him, as if she sensed he was in trouble. The feeling haunted her for the rest of the day, prompting this midnight visit.

His desk was even more barren than the rest of the bland gray office: scratch pad, touch-tone telephone, desk calendar, Rolodex stuffed with business cards, and a framed eight-by-ten photograph. Wade held a young girl in his arms. Sally guessed no more than six. The image said everything. His captured expression had a protective paternal bearing, giving him a vulnerable attractiveness Sally hadn't noticed before. She was unaware that this side of Wade even existed. A message was written in the lower left corner with a black marker:

> Daddy,
> I will love you forever.
> Your cuddle bear,
> Adrienne

Was Wade divorced, or a widower? Did Sally really know him at all? She searched for any details on his desk that might shed light on his sudden personality shift, a hint to the man behind the mystique. His laptop computer and briefcase were gone. She rummaged through his desk, but found no clues. Still pondering the picture of Wade and his daughter, she picked it up for a closer inspection.

When Sally flipped the frame on its side, the photograph dropped out the bottom. As she replaced the picture in its track, a small yellow post-it hidden inside the frame landed on the desktop. She read the handwritten note: 38-26-35. Could be a girlfriend's measurements? She frowned. Or a combination to a safe? Whatever it meant, it was important enough to hide. Now what, break into his home hunting for a safe, and maybe find the girlfriend? Sally shook her head. She was getting in too deep.

Wade's problems were not her responsibility. Sally checked her watch; it was late and she had to be sharp for work at eight-thirty. Her house was a long drive. One day, she vowed to move closer to BenaTex.

Sally restored his desk to the way she had found it. "There's always tomorrow." She switched off the light on her way out the door.

5:58 a.m.—Manaus, Brazil

A fiery morning sun burned above the Amazonian horizon as James Monal, Dr. Henry Isling, and Dr. Aidan MacKiernan strolled along the waterfront leading to the Manaus wharf. On the Rio Negro, an oil tanker made its way to a refinery outside of town. Fishing boats crowded the docks, preparing for a day's run. James saw the vessel they sought moored to the north side of a floating platform. He cocked an eye at the outlandish vision. This was their new form of transportation?

The craft was a bit of a sensory shock. An antique sixty-foot, double-deck barge would have been a better description of the medieval apparition. The American Consulate had said that the old river trawler had been converted into a floating laboratory that housed an eight-person academic team and a five-person crew. The view of the craft from the shore did little to verify its human carrying capability much less its seaworthiness. James wondered if their planned water excursion was such a good idea.

Supposedly, an American-funded biological team had chartered the boat to sample the Rio Negro and catalog fish species. They swept the river scooping up specimens using a deep channel net attached to a boom with 250 yards of steel dragline cable. In preparation for their next trip upriver, the scow was heaped with boxes, electronic equipment, food supplies, and fish storage chests. It had been described to James as very high-tech. He couldn't tell.

The dock buzzed with activity. Local laborers jostled crates onto the trawler faster than the lone man waving his arms could direct them. The barrel-chested foreman stood on the crowded wooden dock and bellowed orders in a variety of languages. Every time he barked a command, the mass of sparsely clothed amber bodies responded faster than the change in a politician's agenda. James observed that each movement was a well-orchestrated scramble.

"That monster in shorts waving his arms in the middle of the mess is one of the men we're supposed to meet," James said and pointed. "He's an Australian guide hired by the University of Arizona's Biological Diversity team. They're conducting aquatic studies on the Rio Negro."

"I suppose we were fortunate they had space for us," Dr. Isling said. "By the looks of things, air travel might not have been a bad idea."

James shot him a worried scowl. Until his nightmares ended, he planned to give up flying. His idea of a restful night's sleep did not include waking up shivering in a cold sweat.

"Calm yourself, son," Dr. Isling reassured him. "Only kidding."

Activities on the dock attracted James' curiosity and he walked away without responding. A blond man, a good foot taller than the native workers, deftly made his way through the crowd. He waved and called above the clamor. "Are you the Isling group?"

"Yes, we are," James answered, sounding like a tourist boarding a cruise ship.

"I'm Brian Beacher." He stuck his massive right paw in front of James.

"Nice to meet you, Brian." James grabbed his hand, and Brian squeezed with such enthusiasm James worried his fingers might dislodge. "I'm James Monal and this is Dr. Henry Isling. Dr. Aidan MacKiernan is over there somewhere cataloging our equipment."

The man was a muscled giant. James guessed he was near six-feet, six-inches tall, and at least two hundred and forty pounds. His eyes were blue crystals and he had a disarming smile on a clean-shaven tanned face. James' first impression was he could trust Brian Beacher with his kid sister, if he had one.

"I'm proud to meet you, gentlemen. I've read your theories, Dr. Isling, and enjoyed your revolutionary accomplishments in reconstructing the latter history of the Yucatán Maya." He vigorously shook the professor's hand.

Another man approached the group. "Did you introduce yourself appropriately, Brian?"

"Sure did, Dr. Thorne."

"Doubtful. Brian wants everyone to think he's a crew roadie." He gave Brian an affectionate slap on the back. "Actually, Dr. Beacher is a key member on our team. He's our surfer dude, UCLA marine biologist, on loan." Thorne stepped next to Dr. Isling. "Ha, the renown skeleton hunter, Dr. Henry Isling. Your presence brings great honor to this lonely biologist. So good—"

"Dr. Peter Thorne, you old sea weasel." Isling grasped the burly man by the shoulders. "Are you part of this floating circus?"

"Hey," Thorne retorted. "At least we're doing real-world research, not that bone-picking guesswork you call science."

"Thorne you haven't changed a bit." Dr. Isling gave him an ear-to-ear grin. He leaned toward James. "Peter and I have been friends—"

"Just friends, Henry? Drinking buddies is—"

"Shut up, Peter. Humph, as I was saying, friends since our graduate days at Stanford. Thorne has dipped his sun-dried body into every major river in the world, so I guess it's not a complete surprise to bump into him on the Rio Negro. When it comes to river aquatics the man's a living encyclopedia, a freshwater version of the late Jacques-Yves Cousteau." Dr. Isling grinned. "Peter's also a robust beer connoisseur who loves to speak his mind. And too bad not everyone shares Peter's views, as you can see by the scars on his crooked nose."

Thorne grumbled. "If I remember correctly, there were a few occasions where I wasn't the one—"

"Humph, yes, well," Dr. Isling gestured toward James. "Peter, this is my gifted graduate student and assistant, James Monal. You already know Aidan. He's on the dock poking through our gear. We were able to scrounge a few supplies here and the rest of our stuff is being flown to São Gabriel da Anjo."

Swatting a hungry mosquito on his leathery cheek, Thorne visually canvassed the dock for MacKiernan. "I won't ever get used to these darn insects." He gave the archaeological team a playful grin and rubbed the stubble on his chin. "Henry, when I heard your group needed a ride upriver, I couldn't wait to find you."

"You're the one who offered to help us?" James asked.

"Actually, it was Dr. Beacher. He's our troubleshooter extraordinaire. Brian contacted the local American Consulate and put the word out we could give you a ride up the Rio Negro."

"We're very grateful, Peter." Dr. Isling craned his neck around, inspecting the flat-decked boat. "I think."

"Don't worry, Henry, she floats. I'll send Leland a bill for your passage later." Thorne laughed and slapped his friend on the back. "Tell that old grump, Aidan, to get with Salvo over your supply needs. That's him, the big, half-naked gorilla in the middle of the rabble." He pointed to the foreman. "The local folk are helpful, but they tend to be a bit rough with the equipment. Salvo gives them firm direction."

Placing his hand on Isling's shoulder, Thorne motioned his friend to one side. "Henry, we were downriver when the news of your tragic accident, and the loss of your associates and friends, found us. If there is anything I can do, please ask."

"You're doing it now. Thanks, Peter."

"Alright then, you old relic," Thorne said. "Get your crustaceous butt onboard. We shove off in an hour."

5:23 a.m.—Santa Cruz, California

Icy cold water sloshed over Wade Fields' injured shoulder, slowing the blood loss. His head dipped below the river as he drifted in-and-out of consciousness. Floating to the surface once more, he swung his legs around and bounced against another rock. He had no idea how long he had been in the water, nor how far he had gone. The foggy sky had cleared, and he tried to get his bearings, but was too tired after fighting the current.

Straining his way to shore, Wade grabbed the root of a willow tree and flung his briefcase onto a narrow mud beach. He pulled his weathered body from the water and collapsed below the overhang of a small footbridge. His lungs heaved with exhaustion while his legs dangled knee-deep in the frigid water. The muddy beach had a sewage stench to it, and he crawled onto his side, coughing up more of the San Lorenzo River. A trickle of blood landed on the mud. Shock would take him, if he let it. He had to stay alert, but his eyelids drooped closed.

A strong shudder shook his body and his head shot

up. Trees within his field of vision wobbled on long
sinewy stocks. How long had he dozed? Sleep meant
bleeding to death; he had to stay awake. Rolling onto
his back, Wade's thoughts strayed to his daughter and
the aspirations they shared. When his wife died, it
had been hard on him and Adrienne. Laura had been
a wonderful woman, his soul mate. Her compassion-
ate smile, full of kindness, always made him feel
warm and safe inside. With his wife gone, he had relied on his daughter's love more than ever. All he
wanted was to see his little girl, hold her tight, and
tell her everything was all right.

The ground around him was glazed with morning dew.
Wade struggled onto his knees, then rose to his feet, using
his one good arm for support. His legs cramped and he
staggered, forcing himself to stand. He spied the river for
prying eyes. Although no one was in sight, he was not
going to take any chances and chose to move slowly
along the shoreline, shielding his torn body among the
bushes and trees.

Gray light of dawn cast reflective glitters along the rip-
pling water. When the sun crested the horizon, he would
be a target. He had to find somewhere to hide.

Footing along the grassy riverbank was treacherous. It
took every once of his will to keep moving and not stumble.
Wade glanced in the direction he had come from, watching
for the shooter. As he spun back around, his vision blurred.
He swayed and tripped on the creeping root of a huge
cottonwood. Landing on his wounded shoulder, the jolt
took his breath away and he folded against the tree's
uneven trunk, trembling.

Balanced on his knees, Wade bent at the waist, bracing
his shoulder with his hand. God, it hurt. He scrunched
his eyelids together, concentrating, knowing he would
die without help. Don't give in. If he could only get to
the street. It couldn't be far, just on the other side of the
river's high-water embankment. He could make one last

climb.

Wade slid, regained his footing, and crawled up the muddy slope. Two steps then rest, two steps then rest were all he could manage. When he reached the top, along the northern boundary of an expansive park, his spent muscles caved and he crumpled to the ground. Huddled on the wet grass, he listened to his lungs wheeze. Never before had his physical and mental strengths been so tested. But Wade refused to quit, and he lifted himself up again.

A few cars sped along the nearby street; it was early. He scraped the gunk off his pants and coat, then searched for a ride, realizing he resembled a mugging victim who had been left to rot in the gutter. Covering his injured shoulder with his coat, he approached the nearest corner. The second taxicab he waved down stopped, but even that driver would have sped away if Wade had not jumped into the backseat.

With strong coaxing and the promise of an extra thirty dollars, the cabdriver begrudgingly agreed to take his grubby fare where he wanted. Wade gave him the general location for a residence in a fishing village nestled by Half Moon Bay, thirty miles south of San Francisco. The cab pulled onto the street and Wade slipped into dreamless sleep.

An hour and fifteen minutes later, the cabdriver shook him awake. "We're here," he said.

Wade raised his groggy head. "Thanks." He handed the man cash, including the extra thirty, with the accompanying instructions to forget he had ever seen him. The cabdriver let him out two blocks from the address, and Wade used the walk to scout the location, contemplating an excuse for arriving unannounced before seven-thirty in the morning.

Dogs barked behind fenced yards and a woman wrapped in a turquoise flannel robe lugged a large green trash container to the curb three houses away. Smoke billowed above stone chimneys, flowers in fertilized beds reached for the sun, dew clung to the grassy tips of groomed lawns, and the salty ocean air carried on a gentle breeze: a quiet middle-America neighborhood preparing for a new day. Homes lining the streets in Half Moon Bay's eastern section were modest, wood-frame colonials. The serene familiarity soothed his conflicted mind and aching body.

He straightened his posture and adjusted his sport coat, doing his best to project the demeanor of a man who belonged there, less like a bum fishing through trashcans for a meal. Within fifty feet of his destination, insecurity gnawed at his stomach, and the throb in his shoulder sent stinging pulses up his neck. The pain peaked and his vision clouded. What was he thinking? She might panic and call the police, if the sight of him didn't first cause her to faint. He had no other choice. To give up now . . . he would surely die.

When Wade reached a well-kept home, he slowed and watched the windows for signs of life. An occasional paint chip in the house's sky-blue siding was the only indication of age. Someone who had a touch for such things had manicured the yard; Wade was not one of those people.

What would her reaction be when she saw him? Would she be able to handle his sudden grotesque appearance on her doorstep? He crossed the covered porch. His head swam and his confidence sank lower by the second. He tugged at his sport coat and adjusted his shoulders, pointed a finger, hesitated, then rang the bell. The door opened.

"Wade . . . ?"

"Hi, Sally. You have a beautiful home—" He plummeted through the doorway, landing sprawled and unconscious on a woven wool rug.

7:28 a.m.—Sausalito, California

"You did what!" Ben Singular's pace quickened as he shouted into the receiver. "I don't give a shit about the fog! You'd better find him. He witnessed the whole damn thing, you idiot! . . . No, don't call me on this line again. Use the other number." He slammed the receiver into its cradle. His intercom light flickered and he pressed the talk button.

"What is it?"

"Dr. Singular, your seven-thirty appointment is here."

"I'll be ready in a minute." Ben used the time to calm his nerves. Latch had blown the pickup and let Fields get away. Now, they had a murder to contend with. The senseless murder of a kid no less. . . . The same age as his son.

He kicked the desk corner with the side of his wingtip shoe, disgusted with what he had become. Ben raised his family photograph above the desk and contemplated his future through their unknowing eyes, asking himself, how had things gone this wrong? Steele had done this to him.

7:29 a.m.—Half Moon Bay, California

Sally Brinkman wrapped the corners of her prized Malaysian wool rug around her fists and hauled Wade's limp body into the living room. His suit was stained with black muck, and her nose crinkled from the stench. Blood dripped onto the rug, spreading quickly within the fine weave. She gasped, then sank to her knees next to him.

"Wade," Sally whispered, glad she lived alone. "What have you gotten yourself into?" She lifted his lapel and peeked. The sight was a gruesome mix of blood and mud. His grimy clothing made it impossible to tell how badly or how long he had been bleeding. With effort, she pulled off his sport coat and stripped him down to the waist. After covering him with fresh blankets retrieved from an upstairs linen closet, she placed a small pillow under his head. She then probed with her hands for broken or shattered bones, surmising, although battered in various places, his shoulder injury was the most serious problem.

Wiping away mud and clotted blood with a damp cloth soaked in rubbing alcohol, Sally gently massaged the wound with her hands. It was neither torn nor jagged, and was roughly the size of a dime. She guessed he had been shot, based on the hole's rounded shape. The bullet had passed through his shoulder without creating any obvious major internal damage, and partial coagulation had slowed the bleeding.

She poured half of a bottle of three-percent hydrogen peroxide into the hole, and manipulated his shoulder to disinfect the wound as deeply as possible. Wade moaned and winced when the cold liquid sizzled its way past his punctured flesh. Rolling him onto his side, she examined the exit wound. The hole was larger, the size of a quarter, and the skin had more damage. The horrible tearing reminded her of a circular plug, which had been hacked away using a serrated cookie cutter. She flushed the exit wound.

Folding a white bath towel, she placed it under his upper back, elevating the damaged shoulder blade above his heart. She cut four strips of one-inch wide first aid tape and snipped them into butterfly bandages. One at a time, she pinched the wounds closed, using the bandages to keep the damaged edges together and maintain tension on the skin. He winced. Sally inhaled and wiped the sweat off her forehead with the back of her hand. She then taped two thick gauze pads on both sides of his shoulder. Glad the difficult part was finally over, Sally rubbed the tense muscles along her shoulders. No time to rest, he was still a mess.

She dipped a washcloth into a pan of warm water and swabbed his face and upper body. After a quick cleaning, aside from his features being disturbingly pale, he at least looked nearly human. "That's all I can do for now. I only hope it's enough."

Sally placed two fingers on his wrist and rechecked his pulse—still strong and regular. His breathing had stabilized and his pulse remained constant at 63 beats per minute. She tucked a blanket around him, then squatted on the floor, releasing a depleted sigh. Her hands shook and she squeezed them tightly together, folding them into her lap. An uncontrolled shiver ran up her spine. What had he gotten himself into? She stared at the ceiling, thinking of BenaTex. If she called in sick, would they get suspicious? It might not be as noticeable if she went to work and left early.

She read the mantel clock above the fireplace, and then looked over at Wade. The blanket rose and fell with his breathing. He seemed peaceful enough, but would he be all right if she left him alone? "Wade, you've thrown me into one hell of a situation here. I hope you know, worrying about you is going to make this day the longest of my life."

9:12 a.m.—Central Coast, California

Matt Wells woke to the noise of a metallic clang. He stiffly rolled to the left, falling and landing on the floor. As he rose, he bumped his head on the white pine coffee table. A dull thud preceded the ringing in his ears. Totally disoriented, he opted not to move again and curled up next to the couch on the soft carpet with his blanket and pillow.

Popping her head above the kitchen counter, Allyx laughed. "Do you always wake up that way? It must be dangerous."

"Only when I'm with you." He moaned and rubbed a new knot forming on the back of his head, then buried his face beneath the pillow. "I think I'll lie here for a while."

"If you can peel yourself from the comfort of my floor, I've made us something to eat. I hope you like it." She placed a bowl of sliced cantaloupe, two plates with fried eggs and whole-wheat toast on the dining table. "It's not often that I get to cook for someone."

Rising tentatively, Matt smiled and flexed his achy body. "Thanks. It's nice not to have to do it myself. Ooh, that's not what I wanted to say."

"Don't worry about it."

"I'll just keep my mouth shut and eat." The food was ambrosia, and before long, it was gone. "I must've been hungry."

"I'm glad you finally have a full stomach." Allyx gave him a teasing smile. "I want you to know, I didn't sleep very well last night."

"Sorry to hear that. You should have joined me. I slept like a rock. "

"Yeah, and you landed on my floor like one too."

"At least I slept."

"It was because of you that I didn't. I wrestled with some lame conspiracy theory all night." She moved the plates over and spread the biotech data across the table. "You said Dr. Ruhpor left you a note?"

"Then you believe me?"

"Let's just say I'm intrigued."

"If you say so." He smirked.

"Do you remember what it said?"

"What?"

"The note." She glared at him.

"Just kidding. Better than that, I have it with me." He emptied a side pocket in his backpack and handed her the message.

"Matt: I'm going to be on sabbatical for a couple of weeks dealing with research issues. While I'm gone, keep an eye on Allyx and help Tom Harden. It's a world filled with nasty, ubiquitous little creatures. Good health and good hunting to you. Dr. Ruhpor."

Allyx read to herself. "Why would he want you to keep an eye on me?"

"I assumed it to be a fatherly thing."

"I don't want you as a father, thank you." She shook her head. "I disagree—"

"You would."

"Don't interrupt." Allyx reread the note. "He must have had a reason for getting Tom and the two of us together. We have abilities or knowledge he considered important. Otherwise, we don't have anything academically in common."

"Did the Doc ever explain why he teamed us on the soil microbiology project?"

"Not really. I did learn that we're the only students he asked to pair up."

"Oh?" Matt's left eyebrow arched upward. "I don't get it."

"Teaming with you has confused me from day one." It was Matt's turn to glare. She ignored him. "Dr. Ruhpor must have had a good reason for his decision."

"One comes to mind." Matt gave her a devilish grin.

"Don't fool around or I'll have to hurt you." She jabbed him in the ribs with an elbow. "What do the three of us have in common?"

"Or not have," Matt interjected.

"Another possible twist." Allyx tugged a chain and switched on the lamp above the table. "The graphs you found represent the results of viral experiments."

"When it comes to viruses, I'm pretty ignorant."

"We'll add that to the list." Allyx smiled. "Which could be one reason why he put us together." She grabbed a STEM Operations Logbook. "These don't appear to contain anything unusual. A clue has to be hidden within the message. Otherwise, why leave it?"

"The reference to a sabbatical doesn't say much," Matt said. "But I think we guessed correctly at the reason he wanted to get the three of us together."

"Maybe, maybe not. What if mentioning Tom was simply intended to get you to the lab? Then that brings us back to the graphs and logbooks."

"Possibly. What do you think of 'nasty, ubiquitous little creatures?' He uses that phrase a lot."

"Ubiquitous refers to many or present everywhere."

"Isn't that redundant with world filled?" Matt asked.

"Yes, so, I don't get the point. He could have been in a hurry."

"The Doc was a stickler for accuracy. I can't see him making a simple grammatical error. If it's there, he intended for us to see it." Matt picked up the note. "Based on his lectures, I assume nasty and little creatures refer to viruses, and at the same time, he's trying to enforce the point that they're everywhere."

"You might be onto something."

"If I am, then that leaves 'good health.' The Doc's disturbed about the coming flu season?"

"Cute." Allyx shook her head. "That's not exactly what I meant."

"Hey, I'm trying."

"Sure you are. Still, it is another reference to a virus."

"Hold it a second." Matt slid the most recent logbook over from in front of Allyx and fanned the pages until he reached a specific date. "I read a passage in the margin of the page for October fourth. I remember, because it struck me as odd. I blew it off since it didn't make sense. Here it is. 'Concerns arising. Splitting the last sample as a control. Not going to tell the rep. Mortality requirements unusually narrow.' "

"Is that all?"

"Yeah. Didn't you also mention the limited mortality, or temperature, or something?"

"Yes, I—"

"Wait, Allyx, before we do anything else, I just got an idea. If we find the group who's funding this latest research, that could give us a lead. The grant money had to come from somewhere."

"We?"

Matt was speechless. Had she been stringing him along, messing with his head?

"Don't look so pitiful, Matt."

"I have no clue what you mean."

"Yes, you do."

"No, I—"

"And while I'm sure that innocent, puppy-dog pout of yours has won many hearts, just don't try it on me. What I meant by 'we' is that if we're going to work together, we don't play any games. This is strictly business."

"Of course it's only business. I wouldn't have it any other way." Matt gave her his hand and they shook. What was it with this woman? It was as if she read his thoughts, tapped into his uncertainties, umasked his defenses.

"Good, now back to work." She smiled and skimmed the second book. "Here it is. This was six months ago. Originally, the grant summary pages were included before each analysis. The earliest listing mentions Bena-Tex. Later summaries neglect to reference the financial source. According to this entry, Dr. Ruhpor's doing a sort of viral isolation project for them."

"BenaTex?" Matt shrugged. "Never heard of 'em."

"They're a premier genetics company located in the Bay Area. Sausalito, I think." Allyx left the table and went into the kitchen. She returned with a map of Northern California.

"Road maps in the kitchen? I assume your laundry's hanging in the bathroom?"

"Where else?" Allyx unfolded the accordion-style map and laid it on the table.

"Don't tell me, we're going to Sausalito?"

"It's your conspiracy theory. BenaTex could have answers. Besides, Dr. Ruhpor did say 'good hunting.' "

"Now I know why the Doc wanted me to watch you. Someone has to keep you out of trouble." She growled at him. He ducked away and slid the STEM lab materials into his backpack. "If you hurry, we can leave for Sausalito before noon."

Allyx paused and surveyed the room. "I'll have a friend get my class notes. Otherwise, I'm ready now."

"Since you don't have a telephone, we can go by my place and grab my cell." Matt stood and contemplated their next move. "While we're there, I'll pack some necessary travel supplies."

"Then let's do it." He didn't move. "What's wrong?" she asked.

"Before we begin chasing who-knows-what." Matt held her attention, assessing her mind-set. "You got your assurances, now I want mine."

She shrugged. "Okay."

"That day in the hallway, when you tried to rip my head off."

"Yes."

"What was all that about? And why all of a sudden are you interested in helping me?"

Allyx dropped her backpack on the floor. He stayed his ground, watching her body tense. Their initial meeting was a sensitive chord; one they had to get behind them. Matt had to know he could trust her.

"If you insist, I'll tell you." She seemed to be searching for the right words. He read uncertainty on her face, something he had never seen before. "I've known Dr. Ruhpor for over two years. I met him during a sabbatical to

Mono Lake. We were investigating a new species of angiosperm. He had a theory the lake pollution had created a geologic microenvironment which spawned the mutation of this new plant. I was there to evaluate soil and water biology." Matt saw the tentativeness in her expression hadn't changed.

"You don't have to do this."

Her gaze trailed past him as though she was reliving a painful memory, and Matt was not an important consideration. "We became friends. He was someone I could talk to, and I really needed him. Dr. Ruhpor helped me find myself. Through his strength I discovered what I truly wanted." She looked at Matt and he hoped she saw his sincerity. "That's why I'm helping you."

"But why did you snarl at me when we first met?"

"Oh, that. I figured you for a brainless muscle head, and I wasn't in the mood to carry you."

"Well, uh, that answers everything." Layers of complexity built on more layers of complexity; Matt shook his head. He was even more mystified about Allyx and her relationship with the Doc. "I feel much better now."

"I'm glad for you. Let's get moving." Allyx grabbed her backpack and headed for the door.

1:48 p.m.—Rio Negro, Brazil

James Monal sat next to the port side railing of the trawler's upper deck and watched the jungle pass by as they chugged up the Rio Negro. The boat's bow sliced through the black water, sending v-shaped wavelets cascading along the muddy tree-choked shoreline. This was the first opportunity since leaving Stanford when James had nothing to do but relax. Propped up against a wooden crate, he closed his eyes and listened to the slap of water on the hull and the steady rumble of the trawler's diesel engine.

Toucans squawked along the river's fringe. Monkeys squealed in their treetop hideaways. Waves splashed in the trawler's wake as the boat moved past another shoal. Exotic plant aromas and animal sounds saturated his senses.

The early afternoon temperature had climbed its way into the high eighties, and a layer of sweat coated James' chest while his body labored to cool itself. He pulled off his shirt, relishing the breeze against his skin. The rhythmic rocking of the boat and the alien sounds of the jungle were hypnotic, reminding him how at ease he became when on an archaeological expedition; with all that had happened, he had almost forgotten.

James hung over the railing and sucked in the rich air. Sweeping palms and impenetrable hardwoods lined the shore, making it impossible to judge where the jungle started and the river ended. How did Francisco de Orellana, a simple Sixteenth Century Spanish explorer, ever traverse the Amazon Lowlands? Even modern man, with all his vast technology, could hardly compete with the rigors of the jungle's extreme conditions. Twenty feet in front of the trawler's bow, a huge peacock bass jumped into the air, snatched an insect, and disappeared beneath the black water. James watched intently.

"How you doing, compañero?" Brain asked, stepping up behind him.

"Not bad."

"Here's one of our simple pleasures." Brian set a cold beer on a crate behind James and placed two additional bottles next to his feet. "Because we store our aquatic specimens onboard, we run our own icemaker on the lower deck. We also make it a point to have cold beer on hand for emergencies." Smiling broadly, Brian rested his elbows on the railing, his back to the river.

"Perfect," James said. "It doesn't get much better than this."

"Enjoy it while you can. Things can still turn wild this time of year. It's the tail end of the rainy season and floods are routine."

"I thought the rainy season started in December?"

"That's on the coast and southeast of us. As you move inland from here, the Andes exert their influence and create a summer low pressure zone which draws warm moisture in from the Atlantic, essentially north and south of Brazil." Brian symbolically pointed to the west. "The rains get pretty heavy during the summer, usually mellowing some from September through the beginning of December. They pick up again after March. Nowadays, though, we're never quite sure what's gonna happen. The recent El Niño in the Pacific has rearranged everything."

"Interesting." James twisted off the cap on his beer and took a large gulp, then noticed the logo. "Different."

"Botafogo," Brian said. "It's a local Brazilian brew named after one of their soccer teams. It takes getting used to, but it's not bad."

James cradled the beer in his lap. "So what are you guys doing here? The consulate gave me a general run-down."

"Fishing."

"Fishing?" James dipped his head between the boat's double railings and watched the bow glide through the mineral-rich water, wondering what dark secrets the river held below its depths.

"We've contracted with the Brazilians to catalog as many aquatic species as we can find during a three-year period. This is our last trip upriver this season and we're hoping to get a grant extension for next year."

"What a job." James rolled his eyes and pulled his head back from under the railing. "I spend sweaty days on my hands and knees digging in the dirt for small bits of dead civilizations, while you play in the water and drink cold beer."

"Yeah, right. Swimming with piranhas, being chased by hungry crocs, and ducking river wolves—I guess you could call it playing."

"I can see crocs and piranhas, but come on, a river wolf?" James explored the jungle for wild beasts. "Are we talkin' werewolf here?"

"Come on, I'm serious. The locals call them river wolves." Brian had the gaze of a man visualizing a mythical being. "I've yet to meet one, but basically, they're giant otters. From what I gather, they're cranky little devils. The native tribes don't mess with them. On occasion, though, a few of the crazier poachers collect their pelts."

"Sorry to hear that; I hate poachers. But an otter, you're kidding, right?"

"No, really. I've seen photographs. They can grow to be six feet long. And teeth . . ." He laughed. "Get used to it, James. This place has all types of unusual and unique animals." Brian's hand swept the horizon. "Even the two-legged kind. To the north, there's a tribe of small people called Yansomani. They're like pygmies, but friendlier. They provided valuable help on one of our trips upriver last month."

"This is too weird for me. I'll stick with the dead. They don't bite, and I don't have to worry about their eating habits."

Brian gave him a mischievous smile. "You're not the only one who's not used to this river stuff. Heck, I'm a California coastal boy. The last seven months of my Ph.D. dissertation, I spent at Scripps Institute in San Diego doing blue-water exploration two miles past the continental shelf. I catalogued squid populations and tube worm colonies all day long."

James arched an eyebrow. "My brother's in La Jolla right now. Great place." He went back to watching the river. "How in the heck did you get involved with this project if you're a Diego saltwater dog?"

"Here, have another beer and I'll tell you my long, sad story." The trawler rolled to port. James grabbed the railing, and Brian laughed, "You landlubbers'll get your river legs soon." He scowled at the jungle with mock exasperation. "Peter Thorne shanghaied me with the unwitting help of a friend at UCLA. He wanted me for my exotic fish background, and for my stingray studies. My Master's thesis was on coastal stingray evolution."

"Are you inferring stingrays in freshwater?" James shook his head and chugged his beer. "Get real."

"Now you understand how they suckered me. Dutifully hooked on the possibility of a freshwater stingray, I was ocean chum waiting to be harvested and didn't read the fine print. Ah, besides, I had to find one for myself."

"Did you?"

"Yeah, you bet. We've documented four different species. They're oceangoing rays which have adapted over the millennia to freshwater. They've got handy bodily functions, like salt-secreting rectal glands and a killer sting."

James studied the jungle's formidable green foliage. "How many other fish species have you found?"

"More than 2,500. It's incredible. We've found everything from the tiniest serpa tetra to the largest and ugliest electric eel I've ever—"

The trawler's motor stopped. Everything, including the jungle, became silent, as if all had ceased to exist. Static electricity charged the air. "What the—"

"Hold still." Brian waved his hand to quiet James. "Bejas asesinas are swarming. Don't make any noise. They're drawn to certain sounds."

A dark brown shape emerged above the jungle canopy. The mass began to overtake the sky. Then came a pulsating buzz that grew louder with the passing of each second.

10:50 a.m.—Central Coast, California

"This is a nice car," Matt Wells said. "You don't see too many Karmann Ghias on the road anymore, especially not in mint condition."

"Thanks. I do all the work on her myself."

The woman amazed him. "When you get close to my place, park a couple of blocks down the street. No reason to announce ourselves."

"Still paranoid?"

"Cautious." He loosened his seatbelt. "I'll run in, grab my cell, and take care of business." She scowled at the rearview mirror. "Allyx, are you listening?"

"Sort of. When we left my apartment, did you catch sight of a dark blue sedan parked on the street?"

"With all those cars, are you kidding?" He heard her serious tone and saw the deep furrow form on her brow as she checked the rearview mirror. "Why?"

"There's one behind us now. It's been tailing us for quite some time." She grabbed the wooden shift knob and slid the car into third gear.

"Now who's paranoid?"

"Stuff it. This is for real."

"In that case take a right here." Matt pointed.

Allyx downshifted into second and sped around the corner while watching the rearview mirror. "They're still there. Any ideas?"

"I wish you'd quit asking me that." He gave her a teasing smirk. "Can you find Lee Hun Low's Chinese restaurant?"

"Yes, it's wedged between two banks three streets away. Why?" She increased her speed.

"Get us there, and stay below the speed limit. I don't want this guy to get even a hint we know he's behind us."

Late morning traffic was light, making it easy for Allyx to maintain her distance ahead of the sedan.

"Our shadow's keeping pace."

"That's good. In an hour this part of town will be swamped with people."

They passed through the second intersection and saw the restaurant. "Hungry again? Sorry, I'm afraid they're closed for brunch."

"Concentrate on your driving and speed up." Matt showed her a mocking frown, crinkling his nose and curling the left side of his upper lip like Elvis. "Okay, Mama, when I tell you to take a left, go like hell until I say stop. And whatever you do, don't hesitate." Matt watched the sedan make the corner behind them. His timing had to be perfect. "Turn now!"

Allyx spun the wheel hard left and panicked. She went for the brake.

"Do it!" Matt grabbed the dashboard. "Take the alley!"

"That's not an alley. It's a hallway!" Her eyes widened as the Karmann Ghia rocketed into the narrow passage. Strangling the steering wheel, veins bulged on the backs of her hands; she dared a glimpse and gasped. There couldn't have been more than an inch between her precious car and the red brick wall of United Federal Bank.

"Watch the road," Matt ordered, "and gun it."

The sedan careened into the narrow alley behind them. A deafening screech preceded the sound of grinding metal echoing between the brick walls of the restaurant and bank. Within seconds, their pursuers had come to a sudden halt less than twenty feet from the alley entrance.

"We're okay. You can slow down now. They're not going anywhere soon."

Allyx leered at him, then checked the rearview mirror for herself. She released a nervous laugh at seeing the comic sight of the two men trapped in their car. Her hold on the steering wheel relaxed. "They don't look happy. I guess they didn't fit."

"Too bad. Stay in the alley for another block. Then take a left, followed by your first right."

The Karmann Ghia burst onto Monterey Street, and Allyx lifted her foot off the gas pedal, letting the car slow on its own. She inhaled deeply as the alley disappeared behind them.

He watched Allyx appreciatively. "Good reflexes."

"Thanks."

10:54 a.m.—Sausalito, California

Ed Cooper entered the B-Wing laboratory and was struck by the tension gripping the room. Some of the most gifted people he had ever associated with were here, and upper management had pushed them too hard. He could read the signs on the somber faces and sagging bodies of the biotechnicians working at the computer stations.

Cooper approached Sally Brinkman from behind. He was glad she was not alone. It bothered him when he thought of her and all the long hours. She deserved better. "How's it going?"

Sally rose slightly. "Hi, Ed. You surprised me."

"My fault. I shouldn't have snuck up on you like that. We're all a little fried and tensions are running high."

"That's okay. When are the guys at the top going to relax the extra security?"

"I'm afraid not soon enough. Section Three's incident rate numbers have almost doubled. We had a near accident in BioLab 2 earlier this morning. Big Brother's probing eyes have the entire staff jumping at their own shadows." Cooper peeked over her shoulder, inspecting her progress. He was her supervisor after all. "So, how are you doing?"

Sally swept her hair away from her face and rubbed her temples. "Tired, but getting things done." She swung around in her chair.

"You look beat, lady. Take a rest for a moment."

"If it's all right with you, I'll probably head home a little early for lunch. Have some personal things to do."

"Sure. I think we can spare you for a couple of hours." Cooper didn't mind bending the rules for Sally. "How's the fingerprinting?"

"Same as always, nothing special to report and no complaints. Except, I'd rather use the electron microscope to identify indicator viral characteristics, but I guess, for all the extra effort, the enzyme-chemical assays are doing fine." Cooper was about to speak when Sally cut him off with a shake of her head. "And you don't have to remind me. I know Nathan prefers the assays as a verification of the microscope's results. Besides, after a thousand or so your brain melts into green mush and dribbles out your ears."

"I've been there." He gave her a sympathetic pat on the shoulder. "Don't worry, we have this one about wrapped up."

She watched him closely. "Ed, I have a favor to ask."

"Sure, anything."

"Nothing big, just there's a rumor Wade Fields is in trouble. Have you heard anything?" For all she knew Wade had done something terrible. What if—

Cooper gave her a concerned look, turned serious, and then quickly scanned the room. "Sally, listen to me carefully. Don't ask those kinds of questions." Placing a hand on the back of her chair, he moved closer and whispered. "Take some good advice from a friend who cares. Keep your nose buried in your work and stay away from things that don't involve you."

Too late, she was already involved.

1:56 p.m.—Rio Negro, Brazil

Dr. Isling inspected the small cabin as he wiped his forehead with a torn hand towel. Although the captain's quarters onboard the trawler were air-conditioned, the temperature verged on intolerable. Most of the cool air escaped through cracks in the flimsy plywood door and the multi-pane windows. Isling mopped up more sweat while reaching for an iced tea. "Nice digs, Peter."

"Thanks. So, Henry, what brings you to the heart of the Amazon? And don't tell me it's the weather." Thorne faced Isling, standing on the opposite side of the cabin's teak chart table.

"It's simple; we're here to find, document, and study a rediscovered tribe."

"I thought you dealt with the dead, not the living."

Isling frowned. "It's all relative, Peter."

"Since you're a Maya guru, I assume this lost race is a distant ancestor of theirs?"

"You're as sharp as ever." Isling sipped his tea.

Thorne pulled a chair up to the table. "Anyone who's been on the Amazon for more than a day has come across stories of ancient tribes hidden deep within the jungle. Since Spanish explorers roamed this land there've been wild stories of beautiful tribal women, deadly pygmies, and even interplanetary alien visitors. I remember one story—"

"Peter, you're not going to lecture me about chasing mythical beings who exist in the fertile imaginations of local Indians and undernourished college students are you?"

Thorne laughed. "There's rough country where you're going. We'll be on station for a couple of weeks in the upper reaches of the Rio Negro. If you need help, call us."

"Thanks for—"

The air-conditioner stopped and in burst a native crewman shouting, "Bejas asesinas! Bejas asesinas!"

Isling jumped up from his chair. "What the . . . Peter? What's the matter? Did he say bees?"

The crewman bolted out of the cabin, accidentally slamming the door behind him. Flakes of white paint sprinkled down from the ceiling, mingling with the dust on the floor.

"Henry, remain absolutely quiet. Killer bees are swarming and headed our way. The captain's shutting down the engines and anchoring us in place. These Africanized bees go nuts over the hum of a motor."

"Killer bees," Isling whispered. Scientific curiosity, combined with morbid fascination, made it difficult for him not to raise his voice or look out the window. "I had no idea they were in these parts."

Thorne scanned the door for large cracks and closed the slatted window shutters. "It's not advertised, but some rather large colonies are scattered along the river. Three Southern California academic groups are studying them, which in turn, gets us a marginal forewarning when they swarm."

"Absolutely incredible." A loud buzz was followed by a shadow that overtook the trawler. The room darkened. "What do we do?" To Isling, the tiny cabin became even smaller, hardly able to hold the two men.

"Stay very quiet. They usually just fly on by."

11:03 a.m.—Sausalito, California

"Here you go, Ben." Nathan Donner entered his partner's office and handed him the latest model runs. "RNA resequencing for the new viral strain was successful. Even better than I'd hoped. "He grinned, framing two rows of perfect teeth.

"Did we achieve the required parameters?" Ben thumbed through the computer sheets. "He's pushing hard for the Houston submittal."

"We're getting there." Nathan was tired of all the pressure and his smile waned. Quality genetics required patience and tenacity, and under their current constraints, a few breaks mixed in with some good luck wouldn't hurt. "Doesn't Steele realize it's only been three years since the industry learned how to decode retroviruses with any degree of success? This effort is on the absolute high end of our technology."

"He doesn't care. His money speaks for him."

The subject had evolved into a festering burr between Ben and Nathan, and Nathan gave up the argument. Not much he could do; his partner had placed the fate of Bena-Tex in Steele's hands. "Maybe he'll relax when you tell him we've finished the prototype testing. That should get him the hell off our backs."

"Possibly. Steele wants a billing statement. I'm dropping it by after office hours this evening. Will we have anything by then?"

"I wouldn't count on it."

"When will there be enough data for Houston?" Ben seemed to ignore Nathan's frustration, choosing instead to watch an antigravity toy float across his desktop. The brushed-metal top spun on its own, centimeters above the flat surface.

Sometimes Ben's ability to tune him out drove Nathan crazy, but deep inside a part of him understood. In order to cope with the stress, his friend had to disengage every so often. In many ways, Nathan had it easier than his partner. Nathan was the technical machine within the company. He handled the physical sciences, where there were reliable processes and predictable rules, while his friend bartered with the financial world, where the rules were clouded and often flowed in the direction of fast cash. If a buck could be made, alliances shifted rapidly, as did the impetus of the genetics industry. Pressure to guide BenaTex in the right direction was tremendous, and Nathan had observed Ben's trips into non-reality had become more frequent. The stress was getting to him.

"Houston? I don't know, Ben. From the beginning, this project has been one major squirrel show. Steele tosses us a few nuts whenever he wants and we jump. We're better than this."

Ben said nothing, and Nathan gave up hope for a response. He couldn't force his friend to face the truth.

"Since you're not going to express an opinion and since Steele thought it best not to enlighten us regarding Houston's requirements, I guess the statistical data are almost ready, but we need verification."

Nathan crossed his legs and placed his hands on the chair's rubberized armrests. This whole process irritated him. He had always thought Steele demanded too much secrecy, and testing the virus on human subjects without adequate controls had been a huge gamble, resulting in a terrible tragedy. The medical precautions were supposed to protect the Indians and prevent accidents. Why had they failed? Nathan always found it difficult to empathize with the mistakes of others. If he had been handling the Amazon project, this would not have happened. They had given Steele too much control.

Admittedly, in the beginning, Ben and he had been blinded by the dollar signs offered by Steele. Desperate to keep BenaTex afloat, they had closed their eyes and mortgaged their future. Had they gone too far by climbing into bed with Steele? It didn't matter; Nathan refused to give up on BenaTex or Ben. They always had options. He'd find a way to redeem their good name and beat Steele at his own game—

"Nathan?

"Huh, what?"

"Are you paying attention?"

"Sure. What were we talking about?"

"I asked about the timing of the submittal. And I thought I was the spacey one. Are you okay?"

"Hey, no problem. Just got derailed for a moment." Nathan scratched his cheek and considered an idea that he had been pondering. "At the latest, the electronic data will be ready by midmorning tomorrow. The hard-copy documentation will take a day or two. Are we delivering to an intermediary?"

"Yes, as we discussed before, Steele will assign someone to handle the transfer." The top stopped and Ben looked up, making Nathan self-conscious. "Besides, Nathan, just like you, Steele doesn't tell me everything." Ben gave him an exasperated shrug. "Personally, I bet he's avoiding a paper trail. The logical next move is for Houston to run a risk model. Whom do we know?"

"The cream is Greg Gunder."

"Gunder's too obvious," Ben said.

"You could be right. He might want someone with a lower profile." Nathan's distrust for Steele had increased threefold over the past month, which was one reason he had kept a few of the virus' RNA traits to himself. Two could dabble at this secrecy game.

"You think it's Gunder, don't you?" Nathan didn't answer and Ben squirmed in his seat. "He's a good man, Nathan, and a sharp modeler, but Steele would guess we'd think of him. When you come right down to it, there aren't a whole lot of choices with Gunder's capabilities."

"Ben, Steele doesn't give a shit what we think. Either way, I'd be more comfortable if he was freer with his intentions." Nathan noticed his partner's obvious discomfort with their conversation. His fidgeting suggested Ben knew more than he was willing to tell. Hell, he had probably guessed Steele's intentions long ago, and if that were the case, his friend was living on very dangerous ground.

2:04 p.m.—Rio Negro, Brazil

James Monal could not believe his eyes. A speckled brown

cloud moved with an amorphous discontinuity, spreading above the tree line, blotting out the sun. Hair on his arms prickled as the whir of tiny wings charged the air. The mass moved overhead and its pitch increased, until the sound was unbearably loud. The boat rocked within the river's current, tugging on its anchor. Something whizzed by his head. He ducked and saw a wild drone plow into one of the single-pane windows protecting the bridge, then a dozen more brown bodies hit the glass. James started to rise, but Brian laid a firm hand on his shoulder.

Countless blurred shapes swarmed overhead. The noise was tremendous, a million miniature buzz saws. They were everywhere. James' uncertainties became too strong, the sight too overwhelming, and he glanced at Brian for reassurance. Brain nodded encouragingly, leaving a firm hand on James' shoulder.

The cloud hung in midair, wavering ten yards above the trawler's upper deck. James was convinced the bees were going to attack. Just as he was about to dive for the wheelhouse, the bees changed direction and without warning headed downriver. The ear-pounding buzz receded and everyone on the trawler exhaled an audible sigh of relief.

James drained the rest of his Brazilian beer, then turned to Brian. "Does this happen often?"

"Not too." Brian laughed while he popped the top on another brew.

"How do you take it? I wanted to race for cover."

"We all felt that way at one time or another. You get used to it I guess."

"If you say so." James shrugged and gazed beyond the bow at the expansive Rio Negro.

"Welcome to the Amazon, James. From here on, all you have to do is relax and enjoy the ride. We'll reach São Gabriel da Anjo by late tomorrow afternoon."

"I hope things settle down then," James said as he sagged

next to his adopted crate, closing his eyes, and contemplating all that had happened since they arrived in the Amazon. No more surprises, please.

11:06 a.m.—Central Coast, California

Matt Wells unfastened his seatbelt and tried to mask the anxiousness in his voice. "If they're hunting for me, my place might be watched. I should go in on my own. I'll get everything together and be back before you know I'm even gone."

"I don't like it, Matt." Allyx scowled. "I'm not the type that sits and waits."

"Glad you care. Now stay put." He swung the Karmann Ghia door shut.

Allyx frowned, obviously unhappy. Matt sensed her probing stare as he strolled along a side street behind his townhouse. He checked the perimeter for strangers. The car door opened and he saw Allyx's feet swing onto the curb. Patience was obviously not one of her notable strengths. He had better hurry.

The morning sun warmed the neighborhood, heating lawns and sending steam swirling above the ground. A gentle gust rustled leaves through the breezeway running between the townhouse buildings. The air was fresh with chrysanthemums and other morning scents of fall-blooming flowers. Matt's comfort level had gone up a notch when he entered familiar surroundings, yet not knowing what to expect, he cautiously approached his home.

He tiptoed between two buildings, approaching his place from a blind side. A hurried inspection told him no one was around, which figured. Most of his student neighbors would be at school or asleep; a noon wake-up was early for many of them. Pulling down a fire escape ladder, he cringed when the rusted hinges creaked. The squeak of metal-on-metal echoed between the buildings. Matt waited, exhaled, and climbed to a second story window, where he swept away the dusty cobwebs growing on the sill. He slid his Swiss army knife under the wooden frame, tripped the latch and lifted the window. Following another uncertain read of his neighborhood, he climbed inside.

This was not what he had expected. His home felt alien and hostile; the only sound was the gentle bubbling of his fish tank's aerator. Matt shrugged and attributed his worries to the vandalism. He greeted his tropical friends in their abode atop his dresser, sprinkling food into their floating feeder and blowing pretend bubbles with puckered lips. A new Plecostomus algae-eater was doing a good job keeping the muck down. The diversion calmed his nerves, but a disquieting feeling persisted as visions of a restless Allyx returned.

Hastily jogging across the room to his bed, Matt emptied a wad of cash stashed in an old gym sock hidden under his mattress; he then nabbed a debit card from his dresser underwear drawer. He shoved apart the double doors of his closet, hunting for his cellular phone, only to confront a mound of dirty laundry. The moldy stink tickled his nose as he launched clothes over his head onto the floor behind him. The last dirty shirt floated by and Matt remembered his cell phone was on the kitchen counter downstairs. He grabbed a gym bag and two changes of clothes and left his bedroom.

So far, there had been no signs that suggested anyone had entered the townhouse since the previous night, which eased his apprehension. He crossed the hallway and pulled back the curtain of a window that overlooked the shaded front yard. Had his home been placed under surveillance?

Fresh footprints marked the dew-covered lawn. He backed away from the window. The curtain floated closed.

Numerous possibilities invaded his thoughts, few of them good.

Matt dreaded going downstairs and listened for any hint of an intruder. The ticktock of an antique wall clock his mother had given him made its way up the stairwell. He waited, taking his time, extending his senses and picking his way through the familiar sounds. Nothing abnormal registered, but a renewed uncertainty grew inside him. He crept downstairs, one-step then another, gliding along the banister, avoiding the floorboards' squeaky spots.

Before descending the last step, Matt hesitated and considered the living room. He had forgotten just how bad the mess was. An elephant stampede could have passed through last night and he'd never have known the difference. What a disaster. His visual sweep reached the kitchen, where he saw the cell sitting on the counter. If he were fast, he could grab it and get back to Allyx before her patience reached its limit. He rushed for the phone.

"Hey, Matt, glad you stopped by. You really should clean this place yuh know."

Shocked, and to a degree pissed for being caught, Matt froze in mid-stride. His right hand rested on the phone and he gradually turned. If there was, a next time, he'd trust his instincts.

"No fast moves. I don't wanna hurt yuh; not yet anyway. Step back. Leave the phone on the counter and raise your hands. Remember, no fast moves."

A stocky man, wearing a black windbreaker and baggy blue jeans stepped from the downstairs bathroom. His bulky clothing made his pockmarked features appear even more menacing. The man's mouth was a grotesque distortion, caused by a large scar, which originated under his chin, outlined his jaw, and terminated at his left ear, where a chunk was missing. He pointed a handgun at Matt's chest and circled to the left, blocking the kitchen doorway, trapping him inside. The gunman's evil grin made it obvious that he wouldn't even break a sweat after blowing a massive hole right through Matt.

Matt did as he was told. He carefully watched the gunman, searching for a weakness he could exploit. The man was a pro and Matt didn't expect him to make a simple mistake. His mind raced through escape scenarios, dumping them one by one.

"Yuh've been a pain in the ass." The man pulled a small flip-phone from an inside jacket pocket. His gun never wavered from Matt's chest. "I can see it in your eyes; don't even consider making a move. Yuh'd be dead before yuh got a foot. Where's your girlfriend?"

"She ditched me," Matt moaned.

He heard the familiar squeak of loose floorboards rubbing on nails. The startled gunman reeled toward the sound. A dull thud followed. The man spun around and slammed headfirst into the wall, landing on the floor by Matt's feet. He shook his head and stepped over the body, not sure what to do next.

"Are you going to stand there gawking at him or can we leave?" Allyx asked.

Matt's head turned quickly and he sighed. "You were supposed to stay in the car."

"Good for you, I got bored. You should fix those steps." Allyx looked down at the man. "Wow, a grand slam." She frowned at her handiwork. "Is he dead?"

"Could be." Matt squatted next to the gunman and picked his pockets. "If it's any help, and not that I care, the guy's still breathing. But he's not carrying any ID."

"Here," Allyx said, handing Matt his Louisville Slugger baseball bat. Her hands shook. "I hope you don't mind; I found it upstairs."

"Whatever gets the job done." Matt wiped down the bat with a dishtowel, and then threw the towel into the kitchen and the bat into the living room with the rest of the clutter. When he looked back, he saw Allyx standing over the man. Her hands continued to tremble.

"Now's not the time to deal with it. He had a phone and others might be watching the front. Time to leave, you can count your runs later." Grabbing his cell phone with one hand and Allyx's waist with the other, Matt flew up the stairs, two steps at a time. They reached the Karmann Ghia minutes later and sped away.

"Where to?" Allyx asked, keeping her eyes on the road.

"You doing—?"

"I'm fine."

"If you say so. Then it's Sausalito." Matt unfolded the road map. "First, we'll dump this rolling red stop sign."

"What's wrong with my car?"

"Color's a little bright, that's all. Besides, our new friends probably have a description."

Allyx guided the Karmann Ghia into the left lane and watched for the 101 Freeway on ramp. "There's a rental place north of town. Their cars aren't fancy, but they run."

"Works for me." He removed his wallet. "Stop at an ATM and I'll use my debit card to get us some money. That way we can pay cash for everything."

"Matt." Her tone softened. "Do you have any idea what we're getting ourselves into?"

What could he say? It was his fault she was involved. "Allyx, I really don't know." An uncomfortable silence followed, then he said, "But we might be the Doc's only hope."

"Thanks for at least being honest with me."

11:14 a.m.—Sausalito, California

The phone rang, startling her. "Yes, this is Sally. . . . Hi, Ed. . . . I'm on my way over right now." Sally Brinkman put down the telephone receiver and wondered why Cooper wanted a meeting. She had talked to him in the lab not twenty minutes ago. His tone on the telephone had been very businesslike, sharp and to the point. Placing a notepad under her arm, she headed to her boss's office.

* * *

Cooper stood by his window skimming a genetics trade journal when Sally entered. Fresh coffee brewed in the far corner. "Have a seat." He motioned her to a chair by his standard-issue gray steel desk. Cooper busied himself with a stack of papers while she took a seat.

"Sally, it's come to my attention that you entered Wade Fields' office." Cooper watched for a reaction. Her expression held constant. "Can you explain?" He had warned her. Doesn't she understand the danger? She was an attractive single woman, approaching middle age; it didn't seem fair for her to be alone.

"Mr. Fields acted restless yesterday. I thought someone should try to reach him and make sure he's okay."

The answer sounded reasonable; he hoped they'd buy it. "Did you find anything when you were there?"

"No, I didn't," she said firmly.

Cooper lowered his eyes. She had lied; he was almost certain of it. "Sally, please, for me." He stepped closer and placed his hand on her arm. "Stay away from Fields and don't ask any more questions. He's gone and got himself into big trouble."

"Is that all?"

"For now."

"Can I go?"

Cooper could not tear his eyes from her. Everything, her touch, her smell, was intoxicating. He wanted to help, but she was making it difficult. Damn woman. Couldn't she tell how he felt, how much he cared? "Yes, Sally. That'll be all for now." He escorted her to the door.

"If I can do anything for you, please ask. Call on me."

Without responding, she left. Cooper held the door open and watched her walk away. So much love trapped in his heart. . . . He would protect her.

The door swung closed.

*   *   *

Safe in her own office, Sally flopped onto the nearest chair. Her mind analyzed the situation, while her fingers tugged on a clump of hair dangling beside her face. They couldn't know Wade was at her house, unless he had been followed. Had she made a mistake by leaving him? Stupid girl, you should have called the police. She read the clock. In a little less than half of an hour, she'd sneak home and check on him.

Could she trust Ed? Could she trust anyone?

1:02 p.m.—Half Moon Bay, California

The front door creaked open and Sally Brinkman held her breath. The foyer was empty. Wade's shoes were visible as they protruded beyond the arched entrance leading to her living room. Sally stepped around the corner and saw he was sound asleep. The crackers and water were gone, which was a good sign. She knelt, then gently shook him, careful not to disturb his damaged shoulder. "Wade, wake up."

Sluggishly, Wade blinked. A weak smile formed on his pale face. "My angel cometh," he said in a gravelly tone. "Sorry for dropping in unannounced."

Sally covered his bare chest with the blanket. His skin color was slightly better, not too pasty anymore. "You might live after all, but don't get too excited. That shoulder's a mess. We'll have to immobilize it."

"Your bedside manner's a bit rough." He shifted, seeking a comfortable spot.

"Conserve your strength. We're going to move you upstairs."

Wade twisted his head side-to-side, then caved onto the pillow. "Where's my briefcase?"

"I put it in a safe place." She weighed her thoughts. "Wade, I don't understand what's happened to you, but I've decided to help. Don't ask me why."

She explored his vulnerable hazel eyes. He was too weak to argue with her. Why was she doing this? Her actions didn't make sense. Wade of all people; he hadn't meant anything to her before, except that her heart had been touched when she saw the photograph of him with his daughter. She could not deny her feelings had changed, or maybe, they had been there all along.

His persistent attention used to bother her, but looking back, it was kind of flattering. It had been nice to have a handsome man notice her. Geez, she chastised, questioning what was going on with her head. Wade's been hurt and all she could think about were her feminine needs. Sally sighed.

"Oh, Wade, you are a pain."

He smiled, his sad eyes looking up at her while she examined the bandages. One had a small dried bloodstain. "The bleeding has stopped. How does your shoulder feel?"

The tension drained from his face and the crow's feet at the corners of his eyes softened. "Stiff and sore." The rug wasn't padded, and he moaned when her hardwood floor rubbed against his hip. "You saved my life."

"We'll see." Sally removed the old bandage and applied a new one. "Seems you're on everyone's mind today. Cooper asked about you. He suspects something's up with us. I'll move you to a safer location after the sun goes down." She straightened the bandage. "You should see a doctor."

"No doctor!" He grabbed her hand and squeezed. "They'll be watching for me." His eyes rolled back and his face contorted.

She held his hand. "Don't worry. No one's going to find you." I won't let them, she thought, but was she truly willing to protect him at any cost? How far had she fallen? His eyes refocused and another weak smile reformed. Far, very far, was her answer.

"You did a great job on my shoulder."

"A minor in premed helped." Sally's expression became more businesslike. "You're not completely out of trouble. An infection remains a real possibility. I have an unused antibiotic prescription the doctor gave me for a deep cut on my knee. I'll give it to you. Is there anything else I can get you?"

"No, you've already done too much." Wade became still and quiet, and very serious. "Sally, these are very dangerous men. You could get hurt. I should go." He sat up, then sagged, dropping onto the pillow.

Seated and leaning on one arm next to him, Sally carefully chose her words. "Wade, you're not going anywhere in that condition. As I said before, I'm involved, and for me, there's no other choice or turning back." She maneuvered her hand under his arm. "Right now, no more arguments. I want you upstairs where you'll be more comfortable."

"You're the boss."

Struggling with Wade's awkward bulkiness, Sally got him to his feet. They climbed the stairs to her bedroom, his arm over her shoulder and hers holding his waist. She laid him on her bed, fluffed the pillows and pulled the blankets up under his chin.

"I'll be right back."

Sally returned with a bowl of chicken soup and a pitcher of water. She handed Wade two antibiotic capsules and inspected his wound for the last time.

"You stay put and take these." She poured a glass of water and handed it to him. "I'll be home within four hours. Leave the glass on the nightstand and don't wait up."

He lifted his head. "Sally."

"Yes, Wade."

"Be cautious. You're not safe at BenaTex; none of us are anymore."

2:08 p.m.—Highway 1, South of Santa Cruz, California

Many of the most scenic vistas in North America could be found along California's Coast Highway 1. Its winding curves paralleled a rough coastal margin, described as both treacherous and enchanting. Thick groves of hillside oaks, lush grassy valleys, sweeping flowery meadows, and rugged rocky cliffs extended for miles. A beautiful woman, a coastal setting, and classical music piping through the radio: Matt should have been in heaven.

"Do you have a plan?" Allyx asked, jetting the rental car through another sharp curve.

"I had a plan at my townhouse and almost got killed." He gave her a sly wink. "We'll develop the next one together."

Allyx turned away and murmured, "We'll see."

The sun sank lower on the horizon, while a fog bank lingered offshore. Matt rolled down his window, listening to the waves slam the ragged coastline. A sliver of an adjacent hillside had succumbed to the pull of gravity, forcing Allyx to avoid a small landslide crowding the road. Along Highway 1, nature remained unfettered, in a constant state of dynamic change.

Gazing at the fading skyline, Matt said, "I'm beginning to understand the real reason why the Doc wanted us to team."

"Which is?"

"We work well together."

"Was that a compliment?"

She seemed surprised.

"Could have been." He smiled.

No comment from Allyx and Matt recognized her need for some space while searching for answers. He assumed she would speak when ready, then maybe not. Their situation had grown more complex, nothing was simple, and patience was required. How he hated to be patient.

The remainder of the winding route passed with occasional small talk. Matt offered to take the wheel, but Allyx declined, saying it relaxed her to drive. Outwardly, they watched the many sights along the way: Cayucas' seal preserve, playful otters lounging on isolated beaches, dramatic bridge spans, and Hearst Castle's expensive charm. Inwardly, they attempted to make sense of what had happened and what they might be walking into.

Ten miles south of Santa Cruz, Matt touched Allyx's hand. "How are you doing?"

"Not too bad."

"It's a long drive."

"I wish we could have taken our time and enjoyed it more."

"Tell you what, when this is finished, we're coming back and doing Big Sur the right way."

She gave him a warm, yet probing smile. "I look forward to it."

3:03 p.m.—A Motel, Southeast San Francisco, California

"You're a bunch of ignorant fuck-ups." Osborne held the phone receiver away from his ear. "No more excuses." He had reached his limit with hired thugs and their incompetence. Lowering himself to their subhuman level gave him a migraine. "I don't care if she almost killed the dumb son-of-a-bitch with that bat. Listen to me. If you screw up again, you're going to have more to worry about than some college chick with a stick. I'll make sure you have serious trouble swallowing your next meal. Do I need to make myself any clearer?"

Osborne was not used to losing his temper; it affected his judgment. Calm and decisive actions were his trademarks. He lamented over having to rely on outsiders, but sadly, brain-dead muscle was often necessary in his business—a regrettable necessity. "I don't care how they got away. These are two lousy college students. What seems to be the problem?"

The sniveling excuses on the other end of the phone continued.

"I don't give a crap if she sent the dumbass to the hospital. You'd better find those two. I'll contact our Northern California people and have them pick up their trail. If these kids are as smart as you say, they're probably onto the BenaTex connection by now. But just in case, get a team to Cal Poly. They might show up there. . . . That's right. Call me at this number if you find them." Osborne hung up and scowled at the telephone, contemplating his next move.

He pondered his growing dilemma. Steele pushed harder every meeting to take people down. Espionage was Osborne's game, not body removal. He had to finish this job before Steele snared him too—no loose ends.

4:05 p.m.—Outside BenaTex, Sausalito, California

Matt Wells pointed and Allyx pulled over to the curb, around the corner and two blocks down the street from BenaTex. The car's engine was still running when Matt jumped out and scaled a small hill. He ducked beneath the cover of an oak tree and surveyed the territory.

The BenaTex building had to be more than forty thousand square feet. In spite of its size, the architecture blended effortlessly with Sausalito's expensively artistic and tranquil ambiance. Imaginative landscaping combined trees and shrubs with local perennial flowers to create a secluded setting. Matt approved of the building's gray and white art-nouveau façade, which used curvilinear lines to merge aesthetically with three other light industrial structures angling to the north.

Two tinted Palladian windows bordered the main entrance. In the center was a smoked-glass French door capped by a stilted arch. The building angled to give the front windows an unimpeded panoramic view of the eastern San Francisco Bay.

He panned toward the city. There was no traffic. Most of Sausalito remained fairly calm. Those who were not at work were downtown enjoying a late season fine arts festival and music by Carlos Santana and his brother Jorge. Matt heard Santana's vibrant rock sound in the distance as he scouted another location with a more encompassing view. He jumped down from his perch and jogged a hundred feet to his left.

After three more location adjustments, Matt surmised that he would not glean any useful information by spying on their front door. So far, all he had collected were foxtail stickers embedded in his running shoes. The real answers they sought were on the inside. He sensed a clandestine mission was in the making; although, Allyx might not necessarily see things his way.

Matt descended the hill and met her at the car, plopping down on the passenger's seat. He pulled a burr from his shoelaces. "We have to get a peek inside. I have a plan."

"I bet you do." Allyx shuffled in her seat and faced him. "Like you said, we'll discuss the details together, and just remember, here on out, we're inseparable."

"That could be fun."

She rolled her eyes. "Stick to business."

He shrugged. "If you insist."

"I do. Now what's this plan?"

"I'll tell you on the way. Let's go."

Allyx moved the rental car to the front of BenaTex and parked. Together they approached the building, passing beyond the double-front doors into the foyer. The reception counter formed a half circle, bounded on the ends by two dwarf palmetto palms. Matt noted the expansive entry was finished in the same gray-and-white color scheme as the exterior. A young, pretty, and preoccupied blonde sat behind the counter. On her left, a uniformed security guard stood vigilantly. The guard watched a bank of video monitors and scrutinized incoming visitors.

"Excuse me," Matt said.

The receptionist puckered her thick red lips. "Yes."

"I'm Steve Tyler and this is Vana Black." Matt motioned to Allyx. She was not pleased. He had neglected to mention their new aliases when they discussed his plan. "We're with the Berkeley Daily Californian."

"Do you have an appointment?"

"Yes, my editor scheduled one for four-fifteen with your public relations department." Matt showed her a frustrated expression as his eyes fell to his watch. The receptionist scrunched her lips together and skimmed her appointment book.

"Your names aren't on my list." She rubbed her temple with the eraser end of her pencil. "A four-fifteen appointment is a little unusual. You see, our normal business day ends at four-thirty. However, let me make a call. One minute, please."

"I hope we're not causing an inconvenience. We'll just take a seat in the waiting area."

Allyx grabbed Matt's arm; her cheeks pulsed red. "This is your plan?" she hissed. "It's not exactly the way you explained it to me. False identities? Do you have any idea how much trouble we'll be in if . . . ?"

"Get a grip; it's going fine. Here, read a magazine." He handed her a Sports Illustrated with a large breasted, bikini-clad model on the cover; bad decision based on Allyx's eviscerating expression.

"Mr. Tyler," the receptionist called. "Mr. Largent, our Public Relations Manager, will see you now." She pointed down the hall. "Room 115."

Exchanging Allyx's magazine for a notebook, Matt smiled. "Are we having fun yet?" He preferred to have her mad at him rather than worrying about being nabbed by BenaTex security. "Can't keep Mr. Largent waiting." Allyx held back and let Matt lead the way.

As they walked the hallway to Largent's office, Matt motioned her attention to the many photographs and plaques lining the walls. Among them were images of BenaTex's executive officers, plaques representing the local Chamber of Commerce and the Rotary Club, and awards from the National Science Foundation and the American Medical Association—an impressive showing. They stopped at the last photograph, a picture of two men shaking hands in front of the BenaTex building. A brass plate below the walnut frame identified them as the founders, Nathan Donner and Ben Singular. In the still scene, the two celebrated the grand opening of their new facility.

Largent's office was to the left of the photograph. Allyx reached by Matt and knocked.

"Come in."

Allyx pushed the door open and sidestepped, encouraging Matt to go first. She whispered, "This is your game, stud."

"My pleasure." On the way past, he curled the corner of his lip and squinted at her.

Matt entered and was overwhelmed by Largent's large and expensively furnished office. The decorations included a tasteful combination of forest greens trimmed with dark mahogany and maple wood. Besides the baroque wood trappings, Matt counted five collector paintings by three master impressionists. He assumed they were high quality, oil reproductions, since at least one of the originals was at the Louvre in Paris. Claude Monet's *Waterloo Bridge* and *Charing Cross Bridge* hung opposite Pierre-Auguste Renior's *Diana the Huntress* and *Umbrellas*. On the wall between Monet and Renoir was an exquisite example of Camille Pissarro's inspired painting *Landscape at Louveciennes*. Matt suppressed an appreciative sigh. He had a fondness for impressionistic art.

Recessed ceiling lights provided the precise degree of illumination necessary to draw a visitor's eye. The atmosphere was sublime and the artwork smooth in its presentation. Matt had entered a room totally isolated from Bena-Tex's day-to-day operations. As they moved into the middle of the office, he glimpsed the awed expression on Allyx's face.

Largent stood and strolled around his antique mahogany desk. "Sorry for the mix-up. Please, have a seat." He motioned toward two plushly cushioned chairs next to a handcrafted mahogany table. The table had a waxy fresh lemon smell.

Not giving in to the distractions of the elaborate furnishings, Matt scribbled nonsense in his notepad. He had to keep on track, realizing the elaborate décor lulled visitors into a more receptive mood. Matt was just as certain additional rooms existed elsewhere in the building with similarly strong themes, each prepared to provide a variety of impressions depending on how BenaTex wanted to influence their guest—corporate mind manipulation at its finest.

"Now, Mr. Tyler—"

"Please, call me Steve, and this is Vana."

"And I'm Neal. Now, what is it I can do for you?"

"Okay, Neal. We're running a story on the biotech industry and want to showcase local standouts like Bena-Tex. We're interested in your approach, special projects, and general background information." Matt flipped to the next page on his notepad. "We understand you can't provide specifics because of trade secrets, but we'd appreciate any information you could share with our student readers."

Largent reached under the table and removed an assortment of colorful brochures. "Why don't you take these? We can discuss the rest while I show you around Bena-Tex."

This was going better than Matt had hoped. "That'll be great." He hid his relief behind a frozen smile.

The group left and followed a long hallway outside Largent's office, and the farther they progressed, the more animated Largent became, pointing out various areas of possible interest. "I won't bore you with all the specifics. Let's just say we have more than two hundred million dollars invested in our state-of-the-art equipment. For example, we have the top gas chromatography machines, electron microscopes, elemental analyzers, and gene splicers in the industry. Our technological capability is unsurpassed."

Matt and Allyx took notes while he talked.

"Am I going too fast for you?"

"No," Matt said. "Please, continue."

"Our building's floor plan is a horseshoe loop." Largent went on. "Along the inside perimeter, you'll find mostly laboratories. The outside ring contains our staff offices. As we continue, you'll notice each laboratory section supports the next one in the series. The system forms a sort of genetics assembly line. We're separated into four primary divisions based on our business focus: Discovery Research, Clinical Development, Process Science, and Quality Manufacturing." Largent described each activity, identifying characteristics unique to BenaTex.

Some of the laboratories had glass fronts, which enabled Matt to observe employees performing various experiments. Many of the technicians wore plain white laboratory coats over street clothes, while others worked behind thick transparent walls wearing light green, self-contained protective biological suits hooked to multicolored tubes and lines. Near the end of the tour, Matt watched technicians guiding robotic arms within specialized enclosures as they handled containers marked "Biohazardous Materials."

"Hasn't BenaTex pioneered significant discoveries with bacteria and viruses?" Matt asked.

"That's correct. When the founders started the company, they first tackled a bacterium's genome. Bacteria have a matched pair of chromosomes with approximately four million base pairs, which is relatively simple when compared to a human or a mouse with more than three billion base pairs. So mapping a bacterium's genetic character was an easier challenge for us. During our groundbreaking work, we were the first to map the genetic structure of Prokaryotic bacteria. Before long, everyone began copying our approach, and now new breakthroughs are occurring nearly every day."

"Amazing," Matt said, feigning interest. He was here for other reasons, ones that had not yet yielded any promising information.

"Viruses, on the other hand, have an even simpler genetic makeup, although they tend to be more complex when it comes to decoding their messenger RNA. At least half of our business centers on medical research, making it quite natural for us to work with many different viral and bacterial forms. Tell you what; I'll introduce you to our lead biotechnician. She's an expert with gene splicing and statistical verification."

Largent retraced his path along the horseshoe loop and stopped at a plain gray steel door. Room 127 was stenciled on the front. He knocked. A woman's voice instructed them to enter.

"Steve and Vana, this is Sally Brinkman. Sally, these two are with the Daily Cal. Being a fellow Berkeley alum, I wondered if you had a minute to talk to them regarding your work. They mentioned an interest in bacteria and viruses."

Sally's eyebrows arched upward. She twisted in her seat and blinked toward the clock on her desk; the hands were closing in on four-forty. "This isn't—"

"Consider it a favor to me, Sally."

She sighed. "Okay, Neal, no problem."

4:53 p.m.—San Francisco, California

The elevator doors closed behind Ben Singular as he entered Steele's office. His eyes adjusted to the dimmed lights while he scanned the empty room. Ben checked his watch, noting that he was a few minutes early. He stopped at the conference table and set down his briefcase. A deep clunk sounded and Ben turned around. The main double doors to Steele's office opened.

"Dr. Singular." A well-dressed woman approached him.

"Yes."

"I'm Ms. Peña, Mr. Steele's Personal Assistant. Your meeting has been canceled. Mr. Steele had a prior commitment."

"That's too bad." Although grateful not to have to deal with Steele, Ben could not quite decipher the uncomfortable sensation he felt while in the presence of Ms. Peña. Was it her association with Steele that troubled him? Outwardly, she was an attractive woman, very businesslike and professional. Her tailored dark suede suit fit perfectly, accenting a trim feminine figure. Her long black hair hung in a tapered wave just above her breasts, but there was more. He noticed her actions were very stiff and guarded as her untrusting black eyes intently monitored his movements. Ben tapped his fingertips on the conference table next to his briefcase. There was something about her: an underlying cruelness.

"Mr. Steele wants to see you in two days. He expects the retrovirus results to be delivered at that time."

Ben's hand swept over a smudge on the conference table as he absentmindedly scraped the surface clean with his fingernail. "Two days would be fine." He handed her the billing statements Steele had requested.

"Then I'll show you to the elevator, Dr. Singular."

He picked up his briefcase and followed her, glancing at the dry material collected under his fingernail. Blood?

"Thank you for coming, Dr. Singular. Mr. Steele will be expecting you in two days." She pressed the down button, then walked away.

5:00 p.m.—Sausalito, California

Sally Brinkman closed the door at precisely five o'clock, thirty minutes later than she had intended. Bewildered by her meeting with those college kids, she leaned on the corridor wall outside her office and stared at the royal blue carpet under her feet. They had been persistent with their questions relating to viral genetics and it had struck a sensitive nerve with her. Exhausted, she tried to dismiss her worries, but was only able to go a couple of yards before she had to stop again. She felt unbalanced by everything that had happened.

What if Wade was one of the bad guys? God, that was all she needed. A cold chill shook her, as if someone was watching.

The hallway leading to BenaTex's foyer was vacant. Staff always stayed after hours to discuss the day's events. Those were the old days. The emptiness heightened her worries. Sally balled her hand around her briefcase handle and hurried along the horseshoe curve, headed for the exit.

A heavyset man stepped in front of her, blocking the

passageway. His bloodshot black eyes leered at her and Sally experienced another anxious shiver.

"Ms. Brinkman."

"Yes." A second man moved in behind her. The one she faced brandished a government employee identification card.

"My name is Billings and this is my partner, Special Agent Thomas. We're with the Federal Bureau of Investigation, and we'd like to ask you some questions."

Now what? They couldn't already know about Wade. Where was everyone? She felt defenseless.

"Do you have a minute?" the agent asked.

"I guess. Does Ben Singular know you're talking with me? Has this passed BenaTex security?"

"Yes it has, Ms. Brinkman," the man standing behind her said, too forcefully. "Please step into this office." Her attention bounced between them. They weren't going to take anything but yes for an answer.

"Whatever you say."

"This way, please." The FBI agents ushered her into a side office. She glanced up; 132 was printed on the door. The room was unfamiliar, simply furnished with a gray steel table and a single chair. Even the light gray walls were bare, which was strange. BenaTex's management encouraged personalized decorations. They believed it raised morale and increased productivity. The room's starkness unnerved Sally, reminding her of Wade's lifeless office. She sat next to the table and crossed her legs, trying to appear composed, but the nervous cramping in her calves made it difficult.

The two men stood to each side, ogling her, as though she had committed a crime. She glanced from one to the other. "What do you want?"

Thomas switched on a second overhead light. Sally jumped. "No reason to be alarmed, Ms. Brinkman," Billings said.

She wasn't convinced.

"What's your position here at BenaTex?" Thomas asked.

They should know that. Shouldn't they? "I'm a Senior Biotechnician."

"Two students came to visit you," Billings said, crowding her. "What did they want?"

His overpowering aftershave almost gagged her, a low-class cheap brand. Hardly the quality you would expect from a starched FBI man. "They were student reporters doing an article on biogenetics firms."

"Yes, we're aware of what they claimed to be. If you'd please repeat your conversation?"

"Well . . . they were interested in our processes, what projects we worked on, whether any of those projects had commercial applications, and what type of virus research we're involved with. Their questions were pretty general." She had been audited on other sensitive projects by various government and corporate managers, but it had been nothing like this. Her eyes moved toward the door. She was trapped and afraid to give them any specifics.

"We want examples of the kinds of questions they asked," Billings pushed.

Sally retreated into the chair, feeling very small under the harsh light. "Mostly nothing. A lot about commercial applications and whether there's any hot research going on right now. They also wanted to know if we ever contracted academic support on projects."

Thomas and Billings swaggered to one side of the room, whispering. After a long two minutes, they returned to Sally. "That'll be all, Ms. Brinkman. You can go, but remain close by; we might have more questions later."

Dismayed, Sally could not believe that was all they wanted. Thankful for her change in fortune, she grabbed her briefcase, and hustled out of the office. Their suspicious stares held her until the door swung closed.

Once in the corridor, she sprinted to the front counter.

"Harry, you've been on security all afternoon."

"Yes, ma'am."

Her pulse raced as she slammed her briefcase on the counter. "Who . . . ," she took a deep breath, "who let the FBI in?"

The guard gave her a skeptical frown. "Sure, Sally, see ya tomorrow."

"Harry, two guys flashed an ID and grilled me with questions not two minutes ago."

He scratched his forehead. "Sally, no one's been past this desk except you in the last half hour. Look for yourself. Here's the sign-in sheet."

Scanning the page, Sally shook her head, then dropped the pad on the counter and ran down the hallway. Shoving the door open, she found a vacant room—just the table and chair. She leaned back and eyed the office number, 132. Who were those people? Wade had warned her to be careful. Sally sprinted back to the front counter, signed her name and dashed through the exit.

The security guard scrunched his face all up. "They're all a little crazy 'round here." Not giving it another thought, he plopped in his chair and continued skimming his latest NRA newsletter.

6:11 p.m.—Interstate 80, South of Milpitas, Northern California

"Boss was right; these kids are smart." Rob Spanks rolled down the car window. "They're gettin' too close. We're gonna have to take 'em fast like."

"No problem, Rob, I mean Mr. Billings—FBI agent." Baker Barns laughed. "You should have been an actor."

"Don't knock it. By tomorrow mornin' the dumb bitch won't even remember what we looked like. Osborne must have a major connection to pass us by security like that."

Spanks lit a cigarette and folded his arms across his chest. The longer this Wells dude and his woman danced free, the more complications he had to handle. Whacking them would be a simple task. He had killed before without blinking an eye; after all, it was strictly business and a couple more bodies didn't matter. But that Sally woman had seen them and he didn't believe she'd forget their faces, another loose end. Osborne's threat to tie this one up weighed heavily on his mind. A smart man didn't cross Osborne. And Rob Spanks liked to think he was a smart man.

"Hit the gas, Barns. We're gonna do our college boy and his girlfriend." He took a long drag on his cigarette and bit down on the end. "We're gonna nail his ass."

"You know where they are?" Barns asked.

"No, but I've got an idea where they're headin'. So, if we get it on, we might catch 'em on the way."

6:12 p.m.—Highway 17, West of San Jose, California

Matt Wells drove the rented Neon; it was his turn to unwind and put events at BenaTex in perspective. He and Allyx had kept to themselves since returning to the car. Unanswered questions trailed through his thoughts, most of which implied they were going nowhere fast. They had no real clues, and only a handful of ambiguous hints. Frustration was beginning to pick away at him, weakening his resolve, fostering doubts. He wondered if they'd ever find the Doc and Tom Harden alive.

"Where are we headed?" Allyx asked.

"How about school? There's nothing more for us here." Beyond her obvious silent treatment, he sensed Allyx was upset. "Are you all right?"

"Yes, I'm all right, you insensitive butt! Your macho-garbage attitude at BenaTex could've gotten us into major trouble."

"But it didn't."

"By pure luck."

"And?"

"And, you said we were going to grab a few brochures and leave. I had no idea you planned on moving in." She frowned and then gave him a steely glare. "Don't ever pull a stunt like that again."

Matt smiled sheepishly. "I won't."

She scrunched her eyebrows down—a skeptical face.

"I promise."

"You're crazy; you know that?" Allyx shook her head.

"So says my mom." He remembered how his mom used to tease and chastise him for being too spontaneous for his own good. She had nightmares, worrying that he might take up skydiving, or worse, that he would head to some foreign country in the middle of a civil war because their beaches had good surfing. Matt assured her, the way a convicted criminal reassured a judge of his innocence, that each count was a figment of her imagination. Mom always knew otherwise. He laughed aloud at the memory, and Allyx squinted curiously.

"It's a genetic defect. A dip in a warm hot tub seems to help."

"In your dreams, Matt Wells."

He caught her watching him. The tiny lines around her eyes relaxed, showing a hint of trust, a small one. Had he gotten to her?

"What am I going to do with you, Matt?"

"I guess the hot tub's not an option?" He saw Allyx nod. "Oh well, I still have my fantasies." She slugged him in the ribs. "Ouch! Okay, okay, they're gone too." So much for sensitive and vulnerable.

Allyx smiled. "That's much better. I like you more when you're a gentleman."

"I'm here to please." He grinned, a devilish grin.

"Yeah, right." She sneered.

"Okay, partner, I'll behave. Besides I can see I'm not going to get you to lighten up anytime soon."

"Business, Matt. Stick to business."

"Simply business. And, I also get a sense you suspect something's not kosher with BenaTex."

"You could say that. Like your hunch about Dr. Ruhpor, I get the feeling that things at BenaTex weren't the way they appeared. They were too rigid, not the casual think-tank atmosphere you'd expect to find in a young and aggressive high-tech firm. These people are big money."

As Matt slowed the car on Highway 17, taking an off ramp leading to Coast Highway 1, Allyx continued. "The place had an obvious undercurrent of tension. While that alone doesn't suggest they're rotten, I'm sure they're hiding something. We just don't know what. And keep in mind, for there to be a crime, there needs to be a motive."

"Maybe their big money is running thin."

"Doesn't seem to be. They were awfully generous with Dr. Ruhpor's grant."

"We need a sinister connection between the Doc's research and BenaTex."

"What do you suggest?"

"Frankly, I don't have a clue."

"Then let's keep it simple. We might find that connection if we strip down BenaTex's bureaucratic layers." His eyebrows perked up. "Get out of the gutter, Matt."

"You're no fun."

"Humph. You'll never know."

Matt shrugged and smirked. "I can only hope."

Allyx looked out the window and shook her head. "Sometimes you're so trying, but you might be right about one thing. We can use the school's library resources to dig into BenaTex's financials."

He rubbed his chin. "Good idea. If they're not listed on

the Web, Nexis-Lexis® should have something. If you can get an electronic copy, I'll run the numbers by a business major friend in San Diego. She could give us a lead." Although talking with Cindi might be awkward. Nervously, he adjusted the position of his hands on the steering wheel. Maintaining relations with ex-girlfriends was another diplomacy technique he had not yet mastered.

Matt pressed on the accelerator and the car sped up to sixty-five. "Do you remember when Sally Brinkman mentioned viral genetics being the wave of the future and that genetic procedures would replace commercial drug treatments? She was so matter-of-fact, so persuasive. All I had to do was close my eyes and it could have been one of the Doc's lectures."

"I have it right here." Allyx grabbed her notebook. "She mentioned how competitive her business had gotten and that the first genetics company to patent a process to combat viruses was going to leave the rest of the industry in the dark ages. Do you remember how animated she became when we probed the potential for a breakthrough? BenaTex's onto something."

They drove past a road sign for the University of Santa Cruz. "Now there's an awesome location for a college. I'd never get any studying done this close to the beach."

Allyx scowled. "I realize it's difficult for you, Matt, but could you please stay on one subject. If you recall, Ms. Brinkman began the interview in a cooperative mood, but by the end, she seemed stiff and uncomfortable with the conversation. Her mood swing was pretty sudden."

"Our questioning got to her, Allyx. Something's there, hidden from view. The Doc's disappearance and BenaTex are tied together. I just know it."

Staring at the passing scenery, Allyx shook her head. "Sally Brinkman's moodiness doesn't prove anything.

There has to be something we missed."

"Yeah, but what?"

"I wish I knew."

"So do I." He said nothing more, chasing random worries. The Pacific Ocean had swallowed the sun and twilight engulfed the coastline. He drove along Highway 1, his left elbow resting on the windowsill. Cool air rushed through his open window followed by the thunder of the sea pounding the rocky cliffs. Nature's beauty surrounded him, calming his restlessness. His mind strayed to Allyx.

A remarkable woman, determined, smart, and in possession of a sharp wit. Her strength made him feel strange. How could he define it? Secure? Complete? Definitely confused. The feelings were unsettling. He watched her in the glow of the green speedometer light. What was going through her mind. Did she have a clue how he felt? How she affected him?

"I know Dr. Ruhpor," Allyx said, "and if he suspected BenaTex might not be on the level, he'd devise a means to expose them."

"And somehow, their exposure included us." Matt smiled to himself. He was glad Allyx was here. "The Doc must have left us more of a clue than the note. A trip to his office might help."

"Then, that's where we'll start." Allyx sagged against the car seat. "Wake me in a couple of hours."

"No problem. Get some rest."

6:40 p.m.—Half Moon Bay, California

Sally Brinkman shoved her key into the lock, glad to be home; no more prying eyes or probing questions. Thoughts of Wade had surfaced throughout the day, creating a myriad of mixed emotions. It had been difficult for Sally to hide her worries when those kids from

Berkeley touched on BenaTex's viral projects, especially after Cooper's interrogation. And then there was being cornered by those FBI agents. What was that all about, or were they really even FBI? Nothing made sense. Viruses and Wade seemed to be the only consistent theme. Sally had barely passed through the doorway when her phone rang. She picked it up.

"Hello."

"Sally, this is Ed."

"Ed, what's wrong?" Cooper never called her at home.

"I'm taking a big risk by contacting you. Your house has been wired and your phone's tapped. The company knows you've helped Wade, and they're coming for you. Get out now! I'm sorry." He hung up.

Dazed, Sally backed away from the phone and studied the room as though it belonged to someone else. She imagined listening devices hidden behind every fixture. Creaks, groans, and crackles echoed as the house cooled from the day's heat. Her bloodstained throw rug was still on the living room floor. The woodsy aromas of her home's hardwood trimmings smelled strangely foreign.

Letting go of her briefcase next to the hand-carved birch banister, Sally hurried upstairs and turned the corner heading toward her bedroom. The door was ajar, and the lights out. She eased closer to the doorway and hesitated. The strong odor of rubbing alcohol made its way to her. Wade could be asleep or maybe even dead. What if he had died? Was she more afraid to find his lifeless body or of her growing closeness to him?

Footsteps resonated up the stairwell to Sally's right. Someone was coming. She ducked into the room. The bed was unoccupied; the sheets and blankets bunched in a pile. Where was Wade? Another noise in the hallway; they're coming. Too late to run. A weapon? She had to defend herself. Sally was a hardened anti-gun activist, and at the moment, she reconsidered that conviction.

Sally grabbed a brass Victorian lamp from the dresser by the bed. The lamp had been her mother's favorite. Knowing she would have only one chance, Sally hugged the doorframe and held the weapon high above her head. A worried thought occurred to her; what if it was Wade?

The intruder poked his head into the room and Sally swung the lamp with all her strength. He looked up. She met his astonished gaze and pulled back on her swing. Not soon enough, as the lamp clubbed him above the left ear. He doubled over and landed in a fetal position at her feet.

"Wade!" As Sally knelt by him, the lamp dropped to the floor cracking the base. He groaned and she gently lifted his head, examining the damage. "Oh, Wade. What have I done?"

He rolled onto his side and peered at her from the corner of one eye. "Glad to see you too."

"My, God, I thought I'd killed you. Here, let me help you up." He was heavy and unsteady. "Are you sure you're all right? You sound . . . different."

"I'll be okay." Wade avoided eye contact. "You only grazed me."

She frowned at him. "A change in speech pattern often indicates a concussion."

He collapsed onto the soft bed. "I'm okay." Sally sat beside him and touched his hand. Anguish etched his face.

"Wade, we have to leave immediately. The phone call was a warning. They're on their way here." Sally went to the walk-in closet where she grabbed a large canvas suitcase. She threw it on the bed and worked the locks. "I'm not going to ask you to explain what's going on. At least not now. If I continue to help you, which I will, all I want is for you to be honest with me." Her probing gaze searched his expression for sincerity. "Do we have a deal?" The corners of Wade's mouth curled into a smile.

"Deal."

6:42 p.m.—Motel Off Highway 101, North of San Jose, California

Ed Cooper stared at the black telephone, and then at the moldy motel room. He was only doing his job, why was that wrong? It was wrong because he couldn't protect her. He had promised himself that he wouldn't let anything happen to her, he wouldn't let them get to her. What a joke. They were too powerful.

Another swig of the tea-colored liquid and he gritted his teeth as it burned its way down his throat. A forced laugh; the funny thing was, now she would never know how he felt, what they could have had together, or the fact he had just given up his career for her . . . soon his life. One last slug and he set the glass on the nightstand next to the empty bottle of Wild Turkey. They were not supposed to go after Sally. Fields was the target.

Trucks hauling their cross-country loads rumbled along the highway fifty yards east of the motel room's front door. He reached for the single-action Dan Wesson 357-magnum resting on the nightstand, cradling it delicately in his lap. All his desires had died with that phone call. Fields had ruined everything. If things had been different . . .

Cooper held the weapon's hammer back and spun the chamber. What a waste to have six bullets when he only needed one. Lifting the gun to his head, he rested the muzzle on his hairline, above his right ear and along a patch of new gray hair. He loved her.

The empty glass and bottle stared up at him. Would she miss him? He pulled the trigger.

8:35 p.m.—Highway 1, Big Sur, Northern California

Matt Wells slowed the car as the road narrowed. He didn't want to have an accident on one of the highway's sharp curves. Rubbing his eyes and yawning, he willed himself to stay awake. A glance at the dashboard clock told him they had been on the road for about three hours.

Allyx had curled up next to him and fallen asleep a few miles back. Matt thought he could hear her gentle breathing above the steady rumble of the Neon's engine. He took his jacket from the backseat and laid it across her shoulders. Their current closeness gave him a calming sense of himself, a definite change over the tension she usually spurred.

Headlights crossed the rearview mirror. How long had someone been back there? The sight gave Matt concern.

"Wake up, Allyx." He shook her. "A car is coming."

"What . . . a car?" She stretched and yawned. "Slow down and let it pass." Her head nestled against his shoulder and she went back to sleep.

Maybe the scenic twists and turns of Highway 1 weren't such a great idea after all. Matt scoured the narrow two-lane roadway. No one else in sight. A second sweep past the mirror told him the car had moved closer, maybe less than fifty yards away. He quickly weighed their options. Visions of sharp curves, narrow bridges, and steep cliffs troubled him. What if it was just another traveler? The other car was now forty yards back.

"Wake up, Allyx, and get your seatbelt on now." Matt pointed at the belt. "I've got a bad feeling about this."

He pressed the accelerator and the engine belched a puff of black exhaust. "Piece of junk." Eyes wide, he gripped the steering wheel and whispered a childhood prayer. The Neon rental car surged ahead, picking up speed, 45 miles per hour, then 50. A bend in the road came into view and a sign read sharp curve—35 mph. His momentum held into the turn, the tires lost traction and the car skidded to the left. Matt steered into the slide and punched the gas on the way out of the curve.

Allyx's head jerked back, her shoulders slammed into the car seat. "Matt, slow down!" He didn't respond.

Their headlights panned across huge boulders lining the left roadside, nothing but a black void existed beyond the artificial light. On the right side of the road was a rugged cliff, the ocean raged two hundred feet below. The other car's headlights lit the interior of the Neon, and as the road straightened, Matt saw Allyx squeeze the lip of the cheap vinyl seat. Her tan features had gone pale, but he saw determination in her expression, a coldness in her eyes. She shuddered and dug her nails deep into the vinyl. The distance between the two cars shrank to thirty yards . . . not just another traveler.

The black sedan was faster than the Neon, as it swerved next to them, no more than a few feet from Matt's window. He gave the two men an innocent smile. The passenger responded with a nasty grin and shoved the black barrel of a sawed-off shotgun through an open side window.

"Uh, oh. I think I pissed them off." Matt jerked the steering wheel left, smashing into the front quarter panel of the other car. The shotgun blast went wild, tearing into the rental, exploding the side mirror and peppering the dashboard. Matt swerved, grimacing at all the holes. These dudes were serious. He turned and hit the other car again, sending the rental veering right and the sedan careening left into an embankment.

He forced a laugh and yelled, "Take that asshole!" Allyx's head swung toward him; Matt shrugged.

The Neon's tires skidded, muddy gravel sprayed over the rim of the cliff, a heartbeat away. He saw Allyx sneak a peek outside. The moon's reflection glowed brightly above the ocean's white caps as thunderous waves crashed into black boulders lining the shore.

Allyx met Matt's gaze. "Do what you have to, but get us the hell out of here!"

"Consider it done." A loner for most of his life, Matt had always believed commitment equaled a slow death, right now, nothing else mattered except Allyx and seeing another sunrise. He'd kill if he had to. Matt shoved the gas pedal to the floor.

The car coughed and lurched forward. Spinning the steering wheel toward the road; the rear tires ripped into the soft ground. He pumped the gas and the car screeched onto the pavement. The other driver had also recovered and was bearing down on them. Matt's head flung backward when the sedan rammed them from behind. The steering went mushy, as if he had lost linkage to the tires. He heard the crunch of metal from behind. Matt shoved the brake pedal to the floor, then gunned the gas. They broke free. The front wheels grabbed the road and he sliced into the left lane. Each erratic maneuver put distance between him and the sedan. His triumphs were short-lived, buying a few precious seconds.

He straddled the centerline and flew into another tight curve. The sedan whipped to his right, wedging itself on the inside of the Neon. Matt anticipated the move and squeezed him back. This dude was good.

Then Matt saw a chance to get rid of his new friends. The Neon's headlights painted the concrete girders of a bridge a hundred yards ahead. It was risky. Quickly, he rammed into the passenger's door of the sedan, pushing the car farther to the left. Their uninvited guests fell behind.

Matt hugged the middle of the road, working his way left, blocking his pursuer's view of the oncoming bridge. He swerved, riding on the edge of control, keeping the other driver off balance, stalling. The sedan was trapped between the Neon and the cliff, and Matt hit the accelerator, racing for the bridge, now less than forty yards away.

The weather-stained concrete girders spanned a deep v-shaped canyon. A fog bank carpeted the top of the seaward abutment. Matt strained to memorize details before the entire structure was lost behind the thickening gray wall. The sedan smacked the back of the rental car, breaking his concentration and slinging him forward. The shoulder harness cut deep into his neck. He winced. A trickle of blood wet his collar. When he looked up, the bridge had vanished.

His sweaty palms slipped on the plastic steering wheel. He watched the rearview mirror, monitoring the sedan, knowing his move had to be perfect. How far ahead was the bridge? Twenty-five yards? He hoped not more. Matt eased his car a couple feet to the left and slowed.

"What the hell are you doing?" Allyx shouted.

"Offering bait! Come and get it, sucker."

The sedan was only a yard from the Neon's right rear bumper, preparing for another charge. The bridge burst into view, outlined in the fog by his low beams. Matt slammed the brake pedal to the floor, then cranked the steering wheel and ripped into the sedan. The other driver jerked his car to the right. His tires spun on the soft shoulder. Matt pushed closer, until the cars raced side-by-side.

"You can't!" Allyx screamed. "It's murder!"

There was a quick glimpse of the sedan's terrified driver, when at the last minute, he understood there was nowhere to go. The sedan clipped the abutment and rocketed over the cliff. Matt hit the brakes and the Neon slid sideways onto the bridge, skidding to a stop.

Neither Matt nor Allyx moved, hardly able to believe. They sat silently, dazed, stunned, listening to the rumble of the Neon's engine and the thunder of distant waves. A foggy void thickened around them. Matt eased the car into reverse and backed onto the side of the road. "Allyx, I've got to be sure." She didn't speak. Her fingers still clenched the seat. "I'll be right back."

Matt pushed open the banged-up door with his shoulder and sucked in the damp salty air. Pausing long enough for his knees to stop wobbling, he staggered onto the road. The Neon's headlights pierced the fog in front of him. Fresh tire tracks led along the shoulder of the road, tracing the sedan's final path. He reached the bridge abutment, squatted down, and touched a chipped section of concrete marred by ribbons of fresh black paint. The tire marks continued across the damp ground on his right.

"Oh, crap." Matt froze, unable to believe his eyes. He jumped up and ran to the Neon.

"What happened?" Allyx asked as Matt dove inside the car and slammed the door closed.

"They didn't go over the cliff." He steered into the right lane and accelerated. "Their tire tracks lead to a dirt service road that goes under the bridge to the beach below."

"What?" Allyx twisted around. "They're alive?"

Matt looked in the rearview mirror, where all he saw was a curtain of gray.

9:06 p.m.—Coast Highway 1, South of Big Sur, California

Whir, whir . . . rear tires spun in the dry sand. The car rocked, but did not budge. Rob Spanks shut the engine off and slammed the steering wheel with his fist.

"That's a good one." Baker Barns slapped his leg and laughed. "You were just out driven by a college punk. What a crack up."

Spanks snarled, showing his partner a mouth full of crooked teeth. "You say another word and I'll snap that pencil-dick neck of yours! Go dig or we'll be here all fucking night."

"Okay, okay, man. Lighten up." Barns slid backwards out of the car. "What an asshole."

Ripping the phone from its floorboard mount, Spanks dialed and bounced a signal through a satellite connection. "Lawyer, Spanks. We missed 'em. . . . Yeah, they're on their way back. . . . No way, Osborne's your problem."

October 10

5:55 a.m.—Central Coast, California

Matt Wells yawned and scanned the Cal Poly Library parking lot. Theirs was the only car. He read the dashboard clock: five minutes before six. They had slept for barely four hours. Morning classes did not start until seven, which left them time to get organized. He stretched, taking care not to wake Allyx. She had fallen asleep shortly after they had arrived. His stomach growled and he licked his dry lips.

Allyx lifted her head, rubbed her eyes, and rose up. "Was that you making all the noise? What time is it?" She twisted right then left.

He massaged his hungry stomach. "A few minutes before six."

"I must look awful." Allyx pulled down the sun visor and inspected her hair in the mirror. She ran a hand over her scalp, giving her hair a quick fluff.

She looked beautiful. "You, uh, look fine to me."

"Gee, thanks. You sound so convincing. Have you seen any sign of our friends in the black car?"

"Not since the bridge." Matt put on his jacket and questioned whether he'd ever find the right words around Allyx. Half the time he sounded like an adolescent, which was not exactly the image he wanted. If he could relax and express his feelings, maybe she'd see the real Matt

Wells. That would be a good thing, he hoped.

Allyx assessed the parking lot for herself. "Okay Mr. Earnhart, what next?"

"Food—"

"Figures."

"At least I'm consistent." He grinned. "We'll hide this car and get another. And while it's quiet, I want to rummage through the STEM lab. We might get lucky."

"We should also follow-up on last night's brainstorm and visit Dr. Ruhpor's office. We can swing by the cafeteria on the way to both and take care of your stomach."

"Sounds good. Before we leave the campus, we should do the library." Matt reached for his backpack and climbed out of the car.

Shaking her head, Allyx met him on the driver's side. "The rental company's going to have serious heartburn when they see the damage we inflicted on their poor car."

"Yeah, I know." Matt smiled slyly. "I'm glad we rented it in your name." He slung the backpack over his shoulder, cinched it up and headed to the cafeteria, ignoring Allyx's irritated grimace.

6:30 a.m.—Highway 101, North of Los Angeles

Morning sunlight streamed through the car's closed window, warming Wade Field's face. He rolled onto his side in the backseat of Sally's Volvo and pulled a seatbelt clasp from the middle of his ribs. Wade blinked once, then twice, as he brought events into perspective.

"Where are we?" he asked Sally.

"My family owns a beach house in Malibu, which I never told anyone at BenaTex about. I haven't been there for years. It's safe." She turned from Highway 101 onto Topanga Canyon Boulevard. "How's the shoulder?"

"It's been better. The extra sleep helped. Have we been on the road long?"

"Almost eleven hours. I stopped and napped outside of Carpenteria. The beach house isn't far from here, another twenty or thirty minutes."

Wade nodded off without finishing their conversation, and Sally left him alone. She had her own ghosts to exorcize. Apprehensive at seeing the beach house, a surge of childhood memories came flooding back. Malibu used to be a happy place. Sally remembered her daddy and brother romping in the surf, her mom lounging on a beach towel reading a magazine, and Eclipse, their black Labrador retriever, chasing sticks Sally threw for him.

The sickness had come on suddenly. The doctors thought the shadow on Mom's lung was Valley Fever— *coccidiodomycosis*; a leftover from her visit with Daddy while he worked for Getty Oil on Shark's Tooth Mountain up in the San Joaquin Valley. The experts were convincing. They showed Daddy studies where people had contracted the airborne disease by simply riding on a train passing through Bakersfield. They said not to worry. She didn't smoke.

Mom had always been strong and healthy; the family pillar who was not allowed to get sick. Her symptoms had been more flu-like than anything else. No one questioned, and the trips to Malibu continued. Then a new batch of X-rays came back. She had another shadow on her lung.

Within two months of the initial medical evaluation, her health took a dramatic shift, and the entire family noticed how small things began to upset her. She grumbled at everyone, often staying alone in her bedroom crying for hours. Dad couldn't handle the change.

Her breathing was what had been so unsettling. Mom struggled, unable to catch her breath, wheezing and coughing. Sally still heard the wet thick sound.

All the experts performed their tests, while the sickness continued to spread unchecked. The doctors experimented with exotic drug and chemotherapy treatments. They thought they could get the disease under control. They had seemed so very confident.

The family held together, struggling with the knowledge that Mom was dying a slow horrible death. Publicly, they avoided the truth, putting on a face that said she'd pull through. She's our mom. Nothing ever stopped Mom.

Then the physical changes began and it became more difficult to hide the obvious. Her beautiful sandy-brown hair dropped in clumps, leaving her completely bald. Her trim figure dwindled from a lithe one hundred and ten pounds to an emaciated eighty. Her creamy smooth facial features turned hollow, a mere skull covered with a thin plastic coating. What Sally remembered most of all, was the sullen bluish hue of her skin.

Her lung spots were the unrecognized signs of a cancer that had taken over her entire body, an untreatable form of lymphoma. Just before she died, five months later, the only thing left was a vacant shell. Even now, as an adult, Sally relived the nightmares of helplessly watching her mother being eaten away by an invisible disease—the paralysis of inaction. She could never imagine a worse way to die.

After the funeral, her father withdrew into himself, abandoning Sally and her brother when they needed him most. Dad was determined to drown in his own misery, and that devastated the siblings. They blamed themselves for the family's widening emotional chasm, wrongly assuming that they were somehow responsible for their mom's death.

That was sixteen years ago, and it had taken nearly the entire time for Sally and her brother to deal with their father's anguish. Mom had built a legacy of caring and compassion, and that legacy eventually provided the strength to bridge the emptiness that had grown between them. But because of its strong ties to the past and to their mom, they never returned to the Malibu beach house. Yet despite all the painful memories, Dad could not bring himself to sell the place. Maybe even he remembered the good times.

As she turned north onto Malibu's Coast Highway 1, Sally's memories became stronger, more vivid. A kaleidoscope of feelings, both happy and sad, filled her mind. She focused on the better times, before her mom had fallen ill. Sally was good at blocking the painful thoughts, the same ones that had motivated her into obtaining Bachelor and Master's degrees in medical genetics from Berkeley by age twenty-three.

Her hope, although overly idealistic, was like that of many of her colleagues, she wanted to be on the team that found a way to beat cancer. That dream was what had drawn her to Dr. Ben Singular and his group; they were the leaders, innovative and creative. She believed a cure was close. Advanced research had already shown a unique strain of viruses caused many cancers. Her work could help someone else's mom, but now, that might never happen.

The years of dedication, an education from a top school; had it all been for nothing? Why was she suddenly willing to forget her dream? What was it about Wade that persuaded her to risk her future and completely change her life?

Leaning over the seat, Sally watched him sleep. He looked so helpless and in need of a friend. That was when a slow realization came over her. She was as committed to helping Wade, just as she had been committed to helping her mother.

6:35 a.m.—Central Coast, California

Matt Wells pushed on the door with his fingertips until

it bumped into a stack of books and stopped. He entered the room, noticing the musty odor of undisturbed dust. The office had been locked up tight for a couple of days and the air had gone stale. He shut the door and crossed to his right; Allyx moved left. They initiated a haphazard search, rummaging through the professor's personal things.

A green philodendron sitting on the windowsill had wilted, its heart-shaped leaves curled inward, drooping over the lip of the plastic pot. Random file folders were strewn across the desk. Numerous books with yellow highlighted passages remained open on a table beside the computer. Crumpled in the far corner lay a faded, computer dust cover. The room had a suddenly vacated feel to it, an unintended emptiness without Dr. Ruhpor. Matt skimmed the files and Allyx scanned the reference materials.

"Find anything?" he asked.

"Nope. What about the computer?" Allyx motioned toward the machine.

"Does he ever use the thing?"

"Reluctantly."

Matt shrugged and grabbed a chair. "It's worth a try." He pressed a lighted red button on the electric power strip. A department logo danced across the screen and a simple menu appeared. "Obviously, the Doc never heard of Windows™."

Allyx watched over his shoulder as Matt listed the files on the hard drive. He highlighted one that had been accessed the night he was clobbered outside the Doc's office. "Allyx, please get me a diskette. I want to copy these files. All of the department's programs are standardized. We can borrow a laptop from the STEM lab and review this stuff later."

She found a diskette in one of the desk drawers and handed it to him, then returned to perusing the reference materials. "These open books and files relate to soilborne diseases and genetics. Apparently, Dr. Ruhpor's interest went beyond simple virus collection." She held one of the texts. "This one explores the medical applications of genetic engineering."

"Bring it with you. I've got the diskette. Let's go." Matt shut down the computer and headed for the door.

"Somebody's there."

"I didn't hear anything."

Allyx's face squeezed into an impatient grimace, then she put a finger to her lips and eased Dr. Ruhpor's door back. "Come on, Matt, follow me."

"That's the Department Head, Dr. Theim. What are you doing, Allyx? We don't have time for this."

"Yeah, yeah. Whatever." Allyx moved by Matt and inched her way next to Theim's door, peering through a crack under the uppermost hinge. He was on the telephone and she waved Matt over. "He's an early bird."

"Are you nuts?"

"Hush. Listen. He sounds upset."

". . . I don't know. . . . Not my responsibility. You paid me to watch Ruhpor, not some students. . . . Sounds like you're the one with a problem. Nothing had better happen to him. . . . Don't threaten me. . . . I can make a phone call too and you won't be . . ."

Dr. Ruhpor's phone rang and Matt heard the Dean say, "One minute."

A chair skidded across the floor. The phone rang again as Theim's fingers flexed around the edge of the door. Allyx froze. The door swung closed.

Matt hooked Allyx by the arm and yanked her into the main hallway. He shook his head, giving her an incredulous laugh. "And you talk about me?"

"Hey, it was a spur-of-the-moment thing." Like an excited cat, her eyes skipped between Matt and the offices. "I must admit, I was worried he might catch us."

"Us?"

She snickered. "You were there too, buddy. I tell you

what, when I saw his fingers curl around the door, my heart skipped a beat.

"Mine skipped more than that." He frowned. She shrugged.

"Okay, okay, I get the hint. But what was that conversation all about, Matt? He gave me the creeps."

"I can only guess, and it didn't sound good. Let's go. We can analyze later. Right now, we've got to get moving." Matt led Allyx down the hallway to the lab, where he used his master key. He quickly shut the door behind them.

"Grab anything interesting," Matt said. "I'll get the laptop." He jogged to the storage cabinets while Allyx skimmed the logbooks and files.

"Matt," she whispered. "Matt."

"Not so loud."

"We have company."

He shifted his attention to the entrance. A shadow crossed the frosted glass window of the double doors. Matt cringed, then realized, whoever was out there couldn't see inside the lab; too bad that wouldn't last long. With a hurried wave, he signaled for Allyx to come to his end of the room. She rushed to him, and before she could react, he hauled her stunned body into a storage cabinet and latched the metal door closed.

"You planned this, didn't you?"

He squirmed within the confined space. "How did you ever guess? Since I first met you, it's been my fantasy to get you alone inside a dark, metal closet."

"Well?" Allyx wriggled to her left.

"Well, what?"

"Is it everything you thought it would be?"

"Almost." Matt groaned. "Shh."

"You, shh. And while you're at it," she shifted to the right, "please remove your elbow from my ear."

"What? Oh." He lifted his arm and grimaced, glad she couldn't see him. "Sorry." Mixed emotions began to build. Their relationship teetered on comfortable, natural, still her words often cut to the heart of his hidden insecurities. It didn't figure. Matt had spent intimate time with other beautiful and intelligent women; what was it with this one? She made him feel like an imbecile. Yet, there was something there, between them. Right now, it was his elbow.

A wisp of her hair brushed his face. Her sweet scent saturated the small cabinet space. Allyx had become strangely still. Matt's heart fluttered, then he heard the laboratory door open and close. Multiple footsteps echoed on the concrete floor.

"Voices," Allyx whispered. Straining to listen, she pushed on the steel door. "I can hear two."

"Take the journals and any notes."

"How're we gonna know we've gotten everythin'?"

"I don't know. Osborne'll have to decide when he sees what we bring him."

"Don't forget we have to clean out that professor's office."

"I got it handled."

"How 'bout the computer?"

"I'll reformat the hard drive and we won't have to worry."

"Damn." Matt reached for the door. Allyx stopped him. "Reformatting the hard drive will wipe the disk clean. There's information for hundreds of projects on that computer."

"They could be armed. Then what?"

"I can't just stand here."

"Have a better suggestion?"

"No comment."

A shuffling noise. The laboratory door banged closed. Matt waited for an excruciatingly long minute before chancing a look. He eased the cabinet door open. Its metal hinges squeaked and he hesitated, then peeked into the laboratory. Too late, the computer monitor flashed "*format in progress.*"

"They're gone."

"And we're still alive."

6:52 a.m.—Malibu, California

In a strange sense, pulling onto the beach house's drive-way felt comfortable, a long overdue, spontaneous act—a rebirth of sorts. Had enough time passed for Sally Brinkman to confront her tormenting ghost on its own terms? She remained behind the steering wheel, absorbing the familiar view. A shame she had stayed away all those years, their home was beautiful. . . .

The house was modest by Malibu standards: a 2,500 square foot, split-level, three-story built by Sally's grand-father in the late 1960s, before Proposition 20 created the Coastal Commission and construction standards weren't as stringent. During the expansion boon of the late '60s and early '70s, plundering Malibu homeowners grabbed all the valuable beach access for themselves. Homes were placed almost on top of each other, so close, many of the roofs overlapped. This unchecked construc-tion greediness created a beachfront of million-dollar row houses.

Behind the manufactured beauty, Sally knew the price to live in Malibu came high. During heavy rains, the cliffs to the east often disintegrated under their own weight, sending thick mudflows teeming with rocks through unsuspecting living rooms. On one such occa-sion, the State of California closed off access to their home for weeks while the Department of Transporta-tion pondered a way to remove a boulder larger than a house from the middle of the road.

As if the wrath of unstable cliffs was not enough, the Pacific Ocean held no sympathy for the trials of the lo-cal inhabitants. Many of the homes had been recon-structed more than once during the last decade. Strong winter waves had either eroded house foundations or slapped the sides of buildings until they surrendered. As a result, Malibu homeowners spent millions for engineered defenses designed to combat the menacing Pacific.

Concrete walls, stacked boulders, and steel sheet piles protected the belowground portions of exposed houses from the seasonally high wave erosion and the annually vanishing beach. Half of Sally's home sat on the road's shoulder, while the other upon deeply anchored concrete abutments and steel pilings. These supports secured the house to the ground and extended the main floor skyward above the beach. Yet, no matter how high the lower balcony stood or how well constructed, it remained a chilling experience during a high tide to hang over the railing and watch the sandy beach disappear beneath your feet. Chicken rail-hanging had been one of her favorite games.

She recalled the afternoon Daddy caught her playing hide-and-seek with her brother under their neighbor's house. He ranted, "These concrete pylons and giant rocks protect our homes. They're not toys for your amusement, nor are they safe. Things can happen. People have gotten hurt." When Daddy finished his tirade, he grounded them for an entire week. She snickered. The old softy caved three days later, and she was back on the beach body surfing with her brother.

Sally smiled. Those were good times. She reached into the backseat and gently shook Wade's thigh.

"Wake up. We're here."

8:43 a.m.—Los Angeles, California

A bank of soundless television monitors, all tuned to different news networks, played along the rear wall of INN's war room. The group sitting at the oval oak table had been going at each other for almost two hours, and the tone had eroded into open hostility. Kelly Karrie's producer, Mikhail Hains, stood, draped his brown sport coat over a chair, and paced around the table for the third time in the last fifteen minutes.

"What are you suggesting? I'm not a location reporter!" Kelly's face reddened. "This is not in my contract. You want to abandon me in the middle of some snake-infested jungle?" She snarled at Mikhail. "Two days ago we were worried that they were all killed in a plane crash. Now you want me to join them. I refuse to go!" She scowled at the four men sitting across from her.

"Think what this could do for your career." Their Program Manager, Don Prague, used his most mollifying tone—a salesman's voice. "We have the opportunity to scoop everyone on an historic event. It would add substance to your image."

"If it's such a great idea, then you go, Don. I'm staying in LA." Now she understood why no one sat by her. This meeting had been a setup from the moment she entered the war room. They knew she'd be mad as hell. If Kelly could grab one of the weasels, she'd strangle him.

"Ms. Karrie," INN's legal counsel interrupted.

She slowly licked her lips while uncrossing and recrossing her legs.

"If . . . if . . . uuhm." The attorney cleared his throat, and Don Prague snickered. "Like I was saying Ms. Karrie; if you read your contract in detail, you'll find a clause which states, at our discretion, we can assign you selective location projects to help promote your commercial viability." The legal worm leaned forward, glancing at her legs. "It is management's opinion that this assignment will promote your commercial viability."

"Kelly." Mikhail suppressed his amusement. "Dr. Isling's group is on the verge of the greatest archaeological find of the last seventy years. Imagine being at the discovery of the first Egyptian tomb. This is the same fantastic opportunity. Besides, Stanford has already agreed to give us exclusive coverage."

"Mikhail, I don't care about your stupid exclusive. I'm not going." Kelly twisted her hands together in her lap, then dug her spiked high heel into the beige shag carpet, imagining it was his forehead. She saw that he wasn't going to back down. The possibility of getting lost in the Amazon jungle suddenly became very real and very scary.

Kelly searched the faces of the men sitting around the table. All of them, except for the corporate ambulance chaser, looked away. Even her agent wouldn't make eye contact. He hadn't said a word. "Leon, can they do this to me?"

"Afraid so, babe. I suggest you pack your summer clothes. The INN jet leaves in two hours."

"Leon, you and the rest of these pigs are pond scum." Kelly slouched in the swivel chair, defeated and abandoned.

10:23 a.m.—San Francisco, California

"Osborne, this is Steele. Plans have changed. You are to forget the Stanford expedition. . . . That is correct. I have decided to let nature run its course. If additional services are required on that aspect, I will contact you. . . . Yes, stamp out the other fires as previously instructed."

Jolon Steele hung up and lit his cigar. Everything was going nicely. To sit atop the world, controlling governments, people, who would have thought it possible? Steele chuckled and puffed on his cigar. His people would soon be liberated. Some things came too easy.

4:00 p.m.—Rio Negro, Brazil

James Monal watched while the trawler rounded a bend in the black river and the mission's whitewashed walls came into view. Lying more than 260 nautical miles northwest of Manaus, São Gabriel da Anjo had the ambiance of a safari way station, not an inhabited town. Ramshackle wooden and adobe buildings were arranged in a random circular pattern encompassing the mission. Compacted dirt roads rutted by six months of torrential rains angled between the structures. A couple of passable streets were feebly paved with black asphalt. The jungle intruded on all but the river's side of the small settlement. Lacking in any of the more obvious modern amenities, São Gabriel da Anjo was still a welcome sight. His tired river legs ached for firm ground.

"How do you like our new temporary home?" Dr. Isling stepped up from below deck.

"Not a lot to it, but it does have character." James propped his elbows on the boat's railing.

Dr. Isling laughed. "To say the least. A sanctuary for river pirates is more like it. Our first venture into the Amazonian past. And where would you place the mission?"

"I'd guess it to be early 1700s."

"Not bad." Dr. Isling patted James on the shoulder. "Jesuits raised the original mission in 1718."

"Right now, Dr. Isling, my first priority is to get on solid ground with shade trees above my head." Dangling over the trawler's bow, James spied an amber-skinned man dressed in a white robe standing on the tiny wooden dock. Compared to the mud-stained buildings and tangled jungle, his pristine attire was strikingly out-of-place. The man waved as the trawler approached.

Dr. Isling returned the wave. There's our contact, Father Ismailia DeLeon. He's the local Jesuit Missionary. Dr. Leland notified him of our delayed arrival."

James looked away from the priest as the trawler approached the dock. Native crew members scurried among the crates stacked on the congested lower deck. They rearranged the supplies, making room to receive additional provisions. One of the crew dogs grabbed a length of coiled rope and threw an end to a man standing on the dock. When the native Indian holding the rope below deck turned his head, a recognition of sorts passed between him and James. Curious? A subtle shift in the boat's position and the sun's water reflection blinded James. He regained his sight and scrutinized the lower deck, but the Indian had vanished.

"Dr. Isling." James scrunched his eyebrows down, scanning the deck and the dock.

"Yes, James."

"Uh, never mind." What would he tell him? That he saw a native with piercing black eyes and it gave him the chills? Dr. Isling would have him on a plane to the States before he finished his sentence. "When will we get access to the mission's records?"

"This is a switch. I'm usually the one who asks those questions." The professor glanced toward the dock. "And I thought I was the anxious one. You and Aidan have me beat. He's already organizing our equipment." When Dr. Isling turned back around, James did his best to hide a grimace. He had to get his mind on the expedition and forget what happened to the others. The professor gave him a probing frown, which James ignored. "All right, my boy, I bet we can cut a corner here and there." Dr. Isling patted James on the back. "Tomorrow morning should be a reasonable request."

Nodding, James grabbed the railing. "I'm eager to get going. It's been frustrating being cooped up on this barge."

"I agree, just don't tell Dr. Thorne or his team. They might think we didn't enjoy the ride, and we don't want to hurt their feelings." The two men laughed.

"My feelings, Henry?" Dr. Thorne placed his arm across his friend's shoulders. "We save you from a swarm of killer bees, give you a leisurely river ride, and now I find you worrying about my feelings. I'm touched."

"Probably something you ate. Don't worry, Peter, it'll pass."

"Thanks, Henry."

"It was me, Dr. Thorne." James interrupted their bantering. "I long for dry, stable land under my feet." He stomped his foot on the boat's wooden deck.

"Ah, yes, I remember dry land." Thorne chuckled. "Isn't that where they serve up delicious tropical delicacies? Show me the way, lad. This boat brew goes flat after a while." All three men laughingly agreed. The bow of the trawler rebounded on the pier's padded pylons, which for some reason made them laugh even louder.

As the dockworkers secured the bow and stern lines, James noticed that Father DeLeon had climbed aboard. Reaching amidship, the missionary shaded his eyes with his hand and scouted the boat. The heat was relentless, even though the sun had dipped low on the horizon. The temperature held constant at roughly 88 degrees Fahrenheit throughout the day, and the relative humidity had peaked by early afternoon at 98 percent. Dressed in his wool robe, the priest did not seem to mind the blistering climate. He was here to do his god's work and physical penance came with the territory. Father DeLeon made his way to the upper deck, maneuvering between the boxes and crates.

"Good afternoon, Father." Dr. Isling extended his hand. "So nice of you to greet us."

When their turn came, James and the others shook the missionary's hand. He had a strong grip and a worried expression. James sensed the tension in his sweaty touch.

"I have disastrous news," Father DeLeon said.

Concern mirrored the faces of the three scientists as

they exchanged awkward glances. Disaster had become too commonplace. Dr. Isling watched the missionary, assessing his sincerity. "What's happened?"

Father DeLeon's gaze wandered toward the jungle. "Word has made its way to my church. The people you seek have been touched by their gods. They fought and defeated an ancient tormentor, gaining renewed spiritual power."

"Bah, jungle superstition." Dr. Isling removed his glasses and wiped them with his shirttail.

"Local Indians warn, if anyone interferes with this tribe, they will meet a deadly fate. No one has gone into the Amazon for days." The missionary's intense black eyes burned. "If you continue your quest, you will not see the sun rise again."

October 11

9:38 a.m.—São Gabriel da Anjo, Brazil

The mission stood alone in the center of town, erected as a monument to the courageous accomplishments of the Christian pioneers. Its grand double-bell tower shone like a sacred beacon fending back the jungle's relentless encroachment. Thick green vines assaulted its whitewashed walls and clay tile roof. God's work took constant vigilance. Before the sun had risen above the treetops each day, Indian laborers, under the watchful guidance of Father Ismailia DeLeon, tended the well-vegetated grounds.

Inside, behind the mission's thick adobe walls, it was comfortable, almost pleasant, and more than fifteen degrees cooler than the Amazon's steamy outdoors. When James queried Father DeLeon, he explained that the cooler indoor temperature was courtesy of a 280-year-old air conditioner designed and constructed by the founding Jesuits.

Vented eaves in the high-pitched, open-beam ceiling allowed heat to escape. As the hot air exited, it created a current that drew outside air into the mission through wide subterranean shafts burrowed into the soil under the plank floor. The shafts descended three feet, and then trailed horizontally for hundreds of feet. Within these tunnels, the hot and humid air cooled and dried as it

streamed into the mission. The ventilation system functioned on a high-to-low pressure flow principal. Local
Indians used this technique to circulate treated air
through their tribal meeting lodges, much in the same
way the Hopi Indians of the southwestern United States
cooled theirs.

Continuing to combat the difficult Amazon temperatures, the missionaries expanded a good portion of their
church underground. The largest substructure was a multi-
room basement, buried deep beneath the mission's religious services area. Massive solid-wood doors, reinforced
with monolithic black iron hinges, separated the subterranean rooms from an octagonal anteroom. White plaster
coated the bare walls and the floor was inlaid with chis-
eled basalt cobbles. Three bare-wired bulbs dangled from
the ceiling. The room had the musty odor and appearance
of an abandoned crypt. Standing alone in the basement's
sparsely lit antechamber and facing the eight closed doors
was unsettling.

Although his tour of the mission had been informa-
tive, James was relieved to be out of the antechamber
and away from the priest. The missionary had been very
vivid in his portrayal of the Burbános' wrath, conjuring
mental visions of feathered serpents and brutal sacrifices.
Even though Dr. Isling and Dr. MacKiernan downplayed
their worries, James perceived that they had been affected, as he had been. James and the others knew too
well the Maya's bloodcurdling rituals, and the missionary's conviction had rekindled their fears, creating an
undercurrent of uncertainty.

Only by immersing himself into his work was James
able to set aside the discouraging meeting with Father
DeLeon. Locked away behind one of the basement's thick
wooden doors researching the archives with Dr. Isling
and Dr. MacKiernan had given James cause to unwind
for the first time since landing in São Gabriel da Anjo.
When James had entered the mission's archive room two

hours earlier, he quickly lost his misgivings among the thousands of documents. Huddled among the room's Spanish and Portuguese drawings and exploration records, the three researchers were all business.

Written accounts dating back to the early sixteenth century neatly stocked the rough-cut wooden cabinets and floor-to-ceiling shelves. The Jesuits were very strict record keepers, meticulously filing everything in chronological order with cross-indexing by subject matter. Even though the missionaries kept detailed transcripts covering the events occurring in their region, the team was cautious to separate religious and political overtones from historical fact. Theirs was an arduous task, and they welcomed the mental challenge.

"It's like reading their private diaries," James said to Aidan. "We're viewing events with their eyes. I envy their trials and admire their dedication."

Aidan gave James an appreciative smile as he lifted another historical record from the mound he had compiled. "You're an archaeological romantic, secretly wishing to have been there in person."

"And you aren't?" James smirked. "I don't see the problem." The two men laughed.

Aidan pointed to the ornate cover of a leather-bound journal he had just handed James. "That's an interesting one."

James held the journal in his lap. He wore cotton gloves, and was mindful not to disturb or miss the slightest detail. The Spanish cover alluded to the events shaping Francisco de Orellana's 1541 AD descent from the mountains of Quito, Ecuador, through the Amazon Lowlands to the Atlantic Ocean. James rolled his shoulders back. Goose bumps covered his arms as he untied the leather straps. He leafed through the ancient pages, using only his fingertips.

His eyes narrowed while he read the Castillan text. The pages held vivid details of bloody battles, hidden

Indian tribes, unusual flora, torrential rains, and deadly animals. Realization of what he possessed—an archaeologist's treasure trove—began to take hold. James finished and closed the book, smiling at Aidan.

"Dr. Isling, Aidan and I have found something." The floppy expedition hat was the only thing James could see of the professor's head as he rummaged through a wooden crate on the other side of the room.

"Dr. Isling," James repeated. "We found—"

"Yes, yes, James. I heard you. Uh, here we go." Dr. Isling stood. "I had hold of this artifact and didn't want to lose it." He showed him a carved effigy. "Look familiar?"

"A little. More curious than anything." James inspected the artwork, while Aidan watched.

Isling flipped the artifact over. "Notice the center is a skull with a deformed cranial configuration, and the outer portion demonstrates an artistic use of pyrite rather than gold." He pointed his finger, outlining the perimeter of the circular piece of jewelry. "Does it remind you of anything?"

"Egyptian?" James replied. "Strange."

"An interesting possibility." Dr. Isling dropped the amulet into the front pocket of his field vest. "What do you have there?"

"It's our first real clue." James held up the leather journal. "Francisco de Orellana mentioned finding evidence of an unusual tribe in the lowlands. Their traditions and beliefs were foreign to what he had observed with other local Indian tribes. There's also mention of worshiping a sun god. Here, take a look for yourself." He handed Dr. Isling the journal.

"James, I can hardly believe the attention to detail. This document could have been written yesterday. It's extremely well preserved."

"Their basement has the perfect conditions," Aidan said. "The room's moderate humidity and cool temperature provide perfect storage. The Jesuits knew what they were doing: no dry rot, no cracked bindings, and no mildew. These leather-bound books wouldn't last five weeks in the dry atmosphere of a conventionally air-conditioned building nor could they have lasted if they were exposed to the hot and humid Amazon."

"I agree." Isling focused on one of the passages. "We've found similar quality documents preserved in ancient Maya tombs that had been sealed for centuries. In comparison, this is also one of the most concise records I've ever seen. Yellowing of the pages is minor. It's as though—"

"Dr. Isling." James held up another journal.

"We should bring portable lights during our next visit." The professor slid his glasses up onto his forehead and rubbed his eyes. "Yes, what do you have there?"

"Could be another reference to the Burbános. It says here," James pointed to the text, "a 1637 Portuguese explorer named Pedro Teixeira came across a tribe who worshiped a serpent." He handed Dr. Isling the record, almost dropping it in his excitement.

"Be careful, James!"

"Sorry, professor."

Isling frowned. "Can we correlate his sighting with Francisco de Orellana and pinpoint a location?" Aidan asked.

"This material is excellent," Dr. Isling said. "James, you're our cartography expert. What's your best estimate?"

"It's difficult to say." Grabbing a topographic map from a wooden storage shelf beside their worktable, James evaluated the ground references. "We have a few things going against us. Seasonal meanders in the Rio Negro and torrential floods have modified the terrain, not to mention a few vegetative eco-shifts. Teixeira mentioned he never found a permanent city." James scratched his cheek. "There's a solid reference to the Solimões, which would be the modern Amazon River. Based on these other descriptions, I would guess their contact with the Burbános was no more than 340 miles northeast of the confluence of the Negro and Amazon rivers. Or about 80 miles upriver from here, but I can't be sure."

"Excellent job. We have our starting point." Dr. Isling placed two fingers on the map. "James, mark the spot and bracket it with a twenty-five-mile search radius. Then contact Dr. Leland and tell him we want recent and historic satellite imagery for the region. He can download the data via our satellite link."

James rolled the map up and gave the chronicles to Aidan. "Do you want the standard photographic suite of color, black-and-white, and false-color infrared?"

"Sounds fine," Dr. Isling confirmed. "Get some low altitude pics; we'll need the detail. Orthographic photos would also be helpful for ground reference and topographic comparisons."

"While I'm at it, I'll contact the University of Washington. They're helping NASA on a remote sensing project targeting the lowlands north of Manaus. I'll also call the Institute of Geological Sciences at the University of Rio de Janeiro. Their Center of Natural and Mathematical Sciences is running a floral study program up this way. Did I miss anything?"

"Nothing comes to mind. Sounds like a great start to me. Aidan, do you have anything to add?"

"Not much, Henry. This stuff is all beyond me. I think I'll saunter over to the local clinic and talk diseases. Maybe their staff can give us an idea of what to expect. I'm hopeful that they'll have something more substantial than Father DeLeon's grisly message. Catch you two in awhile." He waved and left the basement.

No sooner had the door shut when the missionary pushed it open. "Excuse me, señor. The rest of your team has arrived."

7:23 a.m.—Malibu, California

Sally Brinkman slept deeply; the feared nightmares had not come. Was she finally home? Wind gusted outside her window and waves broke on the tiny beach below the house. Monstrous black cumulus clouds hid the morning sun. It was going to be an interesting day.

Tossing back her bedsheets, she swung her feet onto the hardwood floor. The touch was familiar; it brought on more memories, and she closed her eyes. Her brother stood in the doorway dressed in his wild-west pajamas, the morning of his eighth birthday. He laughed, then dashed from the room, yelling his famous war cry and stalking Daddy. Sally imagined the smell of bacon and eggs on the fryer. Fresh fruit would be on the table. Her mother had always insisted on fresh fruit. . . . Good times gone.

Sally put on her terry cloth bathrobe, tugging the belt tight, and left her room to look in on Wade. He was asleep in the adjacent bedroom. She pulled on the blanket and sheet and covered his shoulders, then touched his forehead. No fever. His skin color was normal and his breathing regular, a good sign. Sally returned to her bedroom, dressed, and passed a brush through her hair in front of a colonial armoire mirror.

The beach house had been vacant for too long. Her first order of business, if they planned to stay, was to buy groceries, and although the maintenance people had kept things in working shape, a quick cleaning would bring life to the place. She also had to manage BenaTex; a short call from a payphone at the supermarket should be safe enough. Sally placed a note on the nightstand next to Wade and left.

7:35 a.m.—San Francisco, California

Jolon Steele entered the boardroom and directed Ben

Singular to a seat. The animosity between them was intolerable. One way or another, their relationship would soon end. Maybe, he would take care of this one himself. The thought amused him. He crossed the room to the wet bar.

"Care for a morning cocktail, Dr. Singular?"

"Uh, no thank you."

"Are you sure?" Steele gave him a shrug and a little smirk.

"Yes, I'm fine."

"Then, what do you have for me?"

"As you requested, we now have enough statistical data to submit to Houston. Hard numbers are being validated and will be ready in a few days. The ECR is above the 92nd percentile and the thermal tolerance limitation has been corrected." Steele showed no reaction.

"Very well. My man will make the product transfer tomorrow afternoon." Steele lifted the lid on a cigar case behind the wet bar and removed a new Havana. He unscrewed the protective aluminum case and flung it into the trash, then fondled the cigar's sides, testing its firmness, checking for moisture between his fingertips. With a connoisseur's finesse, he clipped one end and lit the other, contemplating the swirls of smoke rising to the ceiling. He took a seat at the conference table. "Nothing like the aroma of a good cigar. Don't you agree, Dr. Singular?"

Singular gave Steele's left hand a curious look. "If you say so."

"I do." Steele adjusted the bandage protecting his palm. "So how is your personnel cleansing going?"

"Not as smoothly as I'd like, but we'll wrap it up by the end of the week."

"It seems you have been having a great many difficulties lately. I see Fields skipped through the net you set for him; must be smarter than you thought. Have you identified his contact? The one who was killed." Information of the boy's murder had reached Steele a few hours earlier, which, of course, would be unknown to Singular. The geneticist ducked his head to hide his surprise.

"No, the police arrived before we could remove the body. I assure you it won't happen again."

How easy it was to unbalance the good Doctor. Steele groomed the end of his cigar on an ashtray. "There will be no more mistakes." His tone had its desired effect. The fear was evident in Singular's eyes. "Do you have any idea who is protecting your spy?"

"We're not entirely certain." Singular squirmed. "Another employee helped him, and I'm assuming Giles is somehow providing support to them both. But I can't disregard the possibility of a competitor."

A sneer crossed Steele's face as he rose from the leather executive's chair and motioned toward the door. "Until we meet again, Dr. Singular."

10:36 a.m.—São Gabriel da Anjo, Brazil

Never before had James Monal seen him so upset.

"What on God's green earth!" Dr. Isling ranted.

Veins in the professor's forehead bulged, throbbing in time with his racing pulse and reddening face. If Dr. Isling did not calm down soon, James was afraid the professor would pass out, or at least burst a blood vessel. Regardless, someone was going to pay dearly for this intrusion.

"I don't care what Leland okayed. You're not coming with us. This is a scientific expedition, not a damn television sideshow!" Dr. Isling stomped his feet, kicking up a cloud of fresh road dust. "Lady, what experience do you have in tropical environments?"

"None."

"Damn! We're not going into a hostile jungle with

some prissy reporter and her cameraman. Is Leland crazy?"

"Dr. Isling," Kelly Karrie said. "Given a choice, I'd prefer to be in Los Angeles, where the hottest thing I have to worry about is the temperature of my Jacuzzi. However, like you, I didn't have a choice, and I reluctantly accepted my banishment to this hell hole. This letter will explain." She handed Dr. Isling a sealed envelope with Stanford's Archaeology Department logo printed on the front.

The professor ripped it open and perused the contents. His eyebrows curled downward as the strain to contain himself grew. "It appears your news station cut a deal with the school and I'm stuck with you if I want to continue." Dr. Isling shuffled in a tight arc. "You're on your own. Just stay out of my way. James, call me when the real team members arrive. I want a strategy meeting. This is great. Damn." He tromped away muttering to himself.

James waited for the Isling whirlwind to pass before assessing the cause of his stress. "Miss Karrie, you have to understand, Dr. Isling lost two close friends in the plane crash, and he expected to find their replacements, not a news crew. He's right to be cautious, considering the dangers we face. I'm sorry to say, I agree with him. You shouldn't be on this expedition." James hesitated, wondering how much he should tell her. "We've heard rumors of atrocities being committed by the Burbános Indians. If they're true, our lives are in grave danger."

Kelly Karrie's cool expression never wavered. "Then we should help each other." She picked up her bag, pivoted on one heel, and walked away with her cameraman.

"I didn't ask for this, Aidan," James said.

"Don't look at me. I'm just the hired help. Have cuts, will bandage, otherwise, I'll be in the mission's basement if anyone needs me." Shaking his head, Aidan strolled in the opposite direction of Ms. Karrie, leaving James alone to reflect on what had transpired.

8:34 a.m.—Malibu, California

Sally Brinkman unpacked the groceries while putting the finishing touches on breakfast. After adjusting the temperature of the stove's induction surface to low, she went into the living room and knelt in front of the black flagstone fireplace. She crinkled a bundle of outdated newspapers, pushing them beneath a rack of dried oak logs. Striking a long wooden match against the flagstone, she lit the paper and fanned the flame. Before long, a fire spread, radiating its warmth into the living room. Floorboards behind Sally creaked and she swung toward the sound, holding the fireplace poker in front of her.

"Oops, didn't mean to frighten you." Wade rested a gentle hand on her shoulder as she set the weapon down. "You seemed occupied. I hope you don't mind if I interrupt."

"Don't be silly." She jumped up and guided him to the futon couch beside the fireplace. "You shouldn't be out of bed."

"I look that bad?"

"I've seen ghosts with more color."

"Thanks."

"Only kidding. You're looking pretty good . . . I mean—"

"It's okay, I understood what you meant."

"Humph, this is awkward. How're you doing?"

"Much better. Have you given any thought to becoming a doctor?"

"The way things are going, I might need a career change."

He showed her a teasing grin. "I'd still think about getting help with your bedside manner."

"You should talk. Here, let me check that bandage." Sally removed the old dressing.

Wade winced. "Ouch."

"Baby." She smiled sympathetically.

"How is it, doctor?" He watched her out of the corner of his eye, maintaining a contorted grimace.

"Not bad, just slightly red and swollen. I think you'll live." She retrieved a first aid kit from the downstairs bathroom and replaced the compression bandage with a lighter gauze covering. "Now that we've taken care of your shoulder, I assume you have no other maladies I need to address?" He shook his head. "Good, then. Can your stomach handle breakfast?"

"Sounds great. I'm starved." Wade unconsciously straightened his posture and surveyed the surroundings. "This is a nice place. I'd have come here often, if it were mine."

"Thanks. I know it isn't much right now. It used to be beautiful, but it's been empty for too long. There's no television or radio. My father doesn't care for them." Sally shrugged." At least we were able to talk him into keeping the telephone."

"Who cares about TVs and radios? I think it's very nice. Do you give tours?"

Sally gave him a slight nod and a partial smile. "Sure, maybe later." She hesitated, biting her lower lip. "Right now we need to talk." She bent down and adjusted a pillow behind Wade's back. "On the way here, you mentioned someone. Sounded like Ruhpor. Is he a doctor? Can he examine your shoulder?"

"No, no." Wade gave her an uncomfortable laugh. "I . . . I was delirious. Ruhpor's a professor at Cal Poly in San Luis Obispo. An expert on viruses, he's been assigned to a special project by BenaTex. That's all. I came across his name while skimming through Singular's files."

"Jesus, Wade." She gasped, held her head with both

hands and calmed herself. "Amazing. No wonder you always seemed to know more than everyone else. I can see why someone's mad at you."

"Thanks for the vote of confidence."

She gave him a fixing gaze and his head shrank back into the pillow. "What did you think you were doing by going through Ben Singular's files?"

"Don't ask. I'll explain in a minute."

"Seems, you have a lot to explain."

"I know, and I will. Trust me. The truth is, I made some calls and checked him out; Dr. Ruhpor, I mean."

"Why?"

"Let's just say professional curiosity." Sally frowned. Wade cleared his throat. "Ruhpor's a soil microbiologist; one of the top three in the country."

"Is he someone who could help you now?"

"Possibly." Wade rubbed his chin as he considered her suggestion.

A buzzer went off in the other room, startling Wade. Sally glanced toward the sound. "Time to eat. Can you make it on your own?"

"I think—" He stumbled.

"Here, let me help you up." Sally showed him to the counter separating the dining room from the kitchen. After getting him situated, she picked up the telephone and dialed information, then Cal Poly's main number. She wrote a phone number on a scratch pad. "Thank you," she said before hanging up. "Here, it's up to you, Wade. But if it were me, I'd call him."

"Maybe later." Wade returned the receiver and pushed the telephone aside. "As you said, we need to talk. I have to tell you what you're getting into before we go any further."

"I'm listening." Sally tried to hide her uneasiness, but she knew Wade sensed how uncomfortable she had become. Her professional future, and maybe even her life, had merged with his.

"The other night you mentioned a change in my speech pattern. Right after you accidentally whacked me on the head with the lamp. Remember?"

"Yes." She adjusted her place setting, rearranging the alignment of her silverware.

"My southern boy-next-door persona was a simple ruse I used to disarm people."

"I don't understand." Sally stopped fidgeting and stared at him suspiciously. "Why?"

"When people assumed I was a harmless southern gentleman, they were more willing to talk openly. It's amazing what someone will say when they don't feel threatened or challenged. Besides, I'm a good old Texas boy at heart."

"Why did you need to deceive everyone?"

Seeing her frown, Wade shifted in his seat. This was more difficult than he had imagined. He struggled with telling her the truth ever since crawling onto the bank of the San Lorenzo River. Now he had no choice. She deserved to know everything. Supported against the kitchen counter, he saw the hurt in her eyes. "It was not my intent to deceive people. It was . . . I used to . . ." He took a breath. "I observe things for a group outside the company."

"What . . . things?"

"I don't know how much of this you've already guessed, but shortly after I started with BenaTex, I was asked to become involved with a certain group."

"What group?"

"I've never met them exactly, although I have my suspicions. A go-between handles our communications."

Sally placed a glass of orange juice on the counter and patiently waited while Wade took a large drink. "How can you trust these people if you've never met them?"

Wade set the glass down. "The man who contacted me, and who now acts as the go-between . . . he's my older brother, Timmy, Tim Fields. He hates it when I call him Timmy."

"You have a brother working for BenaTex?"

"I don't really. Tim's part of a specialized group that guides BenaTex and other genetics companies from behind the scenes."

"Guides?"

"Sort of." He shrugged. "They're a group who are concerned that genetic research might be pressured into obscurity, similar to the nuclear industry, if the wrong decisions are made and public perception turns hostile. Future success of our industry is too important to allow that to happen."

"Genetic cops?" Sally gave Wade a questioning glance. "This is difficult to believe."

"When Tim came to me, I was skeptical too. Then after days of soul searching, I began to empathize with what he was doing. Policing genetics research has to occur from within. Neither the government nor the public can ever comprehend the great things geneticists will achieve. Few outsiders appreciate the economic temptation facing many companies to push the ethical envelope." Wade wavered, nearly losing his balance.

"Are you okay?"

"Yes; a little weak I guess."

"Here, have something to eat." She took two warm plates off the stove and placed a ham-and-cheese omelet and a stack of toast in front of him. "Solid food will go a long way right now in getting your stamina back."

"And that's important?"

She frowned.

Wade blushed and covered his face while pretending to cough. "Excuse me, thank you."

He took a bite of the omelet as Sally pulled up a seat and sat next to him. "Where was I? Oh, yes. I collected tidbits of industry information for the group. They used what I provided to monitor various projects and keep everyone on the right track."

"How?" She dipped a corner of her toast in her juice.

"It all started in 1975 with the Asilomar Conference and the establishment of the NIH Recombinant DNA Advisory Committee. A renegade group believed the Committee hadn't gone far enough, so they went underground, forming their own watchdog collective. They are powerful people who use their connections to direct policy at various companies."

"Three decades . . . unbelievable." Sally shook her head. "How can they affect decisions within independent companies?"

"Simple. They get various Board positions and if the group comes across a project that it doesn't care for, the funding simply dries up."

"Who's to say they know what's best?"

"Someone has to make the determination."

"Oh Jesus, Wade, they sound like dictators."

"Anything but. Too often corporations base their decisions on profit margins and not on ethical considerations. Which would you prefer?"

"I may sympathize with your point, but I don't necessarily agree with the method."

"There's more." As they ate, Wade described everything that had happened up until the moment he had collapsed on her floor.

"Sally, these people are deadly serious, and now I've gotten you involved."

"Hush." She placed her hand and on his thigh, silencing him. "My decision was made the second you fell through my front door." Her expression changed into a determined scowl, warning him not to question her commitment. "I told you I was going to help, and frankly, you have no choice in the matter. And, Wade, one more thing . . ." Sally's stare held his eyes.

"Yes."

"I never did like the accent."

3:46 p.m.—São Gabriel da Anjo, Brazil

An isolated cantina on the west side of town allowed the archaeological team private moments to collect their thoughts and visit without being disturbed. But as the afternoon wore on, Dr. Henry Isling saw how solemn the group had become. They moped around the weather-beaten wooden table, masking their pain behind tequila shooters and warm beer chasers. Dear friends had been lost in the plane crash, and each person had taken that knowledge to heart.

To a degree, James and Aidan had come to grips with the tragedy. Dr. Saleman and Dr. Utesha, the two new people who had just arrived, were only now beginning to face the grimness of the situation. Isling quietly watched while the four of them conversed over another round of drinks. Archaeologists did love their alcohol.

Fenmar Saleman was a crusty UCLA professor of paleobotany in his late fifties who looked comfortable with the extreme hardships of field expeditions. Although he was slight, with thinning gray hair and unusually long legs, his unflagging energy could burn out a twenty-year-old track star. Saleman had the constant motion of a Colorado River rapid.

On the opposite side of the personality spectrum, Myrta Utesha was a heavyset no-nonsense archaeological investigator from Berkeley. Her unrestrained mannerisms, strong physical appearance, and pointed opinions intimidated those who didn't know her. She was especially forthright when it came to trudging through jungles or pushing her scientific theories. When Myrta found a road to discovery, she cut the shortest path possible. Next to a slug of Irish whiskey in a clean glass, chasing down lost artifacts was what she relished most.

Although Isling had known the new members for several years, he had underestimated the impact that the deaths of Ann and David would have on them. The academic world was a small place and its members a tight family. To lose a colleague felt the same as losing a brother or a sister—a personal tragedy.

"You've all had enough time to get acquainted. And I'm glad you folks arrived safe and sound, but enough of this sadness." Isling wanted to break the grim mood. Discussing the expedition's needs might clear their minds. "It helps me when I remember the great adventure we're about to embark on, one which requires us all to stay sharp. Don't forget, our colleagues were vested in our success and would want us to complete what they started. We'll get through this together." He measured the group, giving them a moment. "I assume everyone's ready to begin."

Seeing Fenmar nod in agreement, Isling continued, "Let's do it then. James, you set up transportation and check the quality of our support people. Myrta, you work with James and prepare our route. I suspect we can download the last of the photoreconnaissance data later this afternoon. Aidan, you put the final touches on the medical supplies."

Isling turned his attention to Dr. Saleman. "And Fenmar, your assistance is required in cataloging the last of the mission's archives. Their records describe a variety of plant species which could help us refine our search pattern." He appraised the group. "Does anyone have questions?" He was not looking for a response. Keeping them busy was his goal, and before anyone spoke up, he continued. "Good, let's get moving. We leave tomorrow morning."

As they filed toward the exit, Isling seized James by the arm. "I want you to do something for me." He handed him a note. "This man has been hired to go along with us. He has special talents; ones which could be useful if we run into trouble."

"Ernesto Rubelio?" James read aloud the name written on the paper. "I don't understand."

"Sit down, James." Isling moved his chair closer to his assistant. "Don't tell the others, but I've learned the airplane crash might not have been an accident. There's also the likelihood we're waltzing into a hornet's nest with the Burbános. Either way, I'm not going to risk anyone's life."

"The plane crash wasn't an accident?" James' eyes widened. He grabbed his beer and rolled the empty bottle between his hands.

"I'm not saying for certain, because I'm not sure yet. A friend with the Brazilian government contacted me." Isling scrutinized the cantina's patrons, then whispered. "He's searching for evidence that the plane was tampered with."

"Why?"

"The ground crewman who was supposed to do our preflight . . ." Isling scanned the room again. "He was found murdered the morning after the crash."

James took a deep breath, composing himself. "What do you want me to do, Dr. Isling?"

The professor tapped the paper with his fingertips. "Meet this man here at the cantina tonight and brief him on our plans. He's going to sign on tomorrow as our guide."

"Can we trust him?"

"I hope so. He's the cousin of Father DeLeon." Isling's eyes trailed through the open front doors and then to the jungle beyond. "I'm worried there's a dangerous secret hidden out there."

"I'll wait for him here tonight." James tucked the note into his shirt pocket.

2:30 p.m.—Shell Beach, Central California

Matt Wells rolled a pencil between his palms as Allyx stretched, straightened her jeans, and tied her hair into a loose ponytail.

"Do you want more coffee?" She reached across the

dining table for his cup.

"Yes, thanks." Matt nodded without looking up from his notes. "Do you agree the Doc gave us a preemptive clue?"

"You mean the note?"

"What else?" Matt massaged his temples, careful not to hit the knot on his forehead. For the last four hours, they had stayed in the small motel room, poring over BenaTex's financials, the laboratory's logbooks and graphs, the computer files and references collected at the Doc's office, and the original note. The mass of information made Matt's head spin, and so far, they had a lot of theories, but no solid leads—zilch.

"I'm not as sure as you are about the note," Allyx said. "Because of your work with Dr. Ruhpor, you might know him in ways that I don't. Explain again what you think he was trying to say."

"If I were to put myself in the Doc's shoes," Matt leaned back in his chair and surveyed the material spread across the table, "I'd say he was guiding us down a specific trail, starting when he cornered us on the class project. We assumed he intended for us to investigate viruses, but I'm not so sure anymore."

Allyx returned from the kitchenette carrying a fresh cup of coffee. She set it on the table in front of Matt, next to a chipped glass vase decorated with pink plastic roses.

"Thanks. When the Doc coerced us into teaming together, he insisted we do our paper on viruses that attack the human immune system."

"I don't get the connection." She took a seat next to him.

"You asked earlier why we were chosen to work on such an esoteric project."

"Big deal. That doesn't imply anything." Allyx wadded up a piece of note paper and tossed it onto the table. "Dr. Ruhpor is famous for his varied interests and creative teaching approaches. I have to keep moving, it helps me concentrate." She finished her coffee, then went into the kitchenette and rinsed the cup.

"Okay, maybe he was doing his regular thing. But as far as we know, no one else got a note from him. Why was I the fortunate one?"

"He was in a hurry and didn't have time to write friends and family. So what's your point, Matt?" Her last words dripped with sarcasm. She was frustrated with their lack of results and he couldn't blame her.

"My point is that it might have been intentional."

"You're saying, he anticipated the danger and covered himself and his students by telling only you?"

"Since I'm a nobody, why not? The Doc's a smart man. Contacting too many people might have sent the wrong signal. Remember Dr. Thiem's phone conversation."

"Yeah, that was a little weird."

Matt watched Allyx as she stretched onto her tiptoes and placed the plastic cup on the cupboard's top shelf. He admired her quick and questioning mind—not to mention her nice long legs. The more time he spent with her, the more aware he became of the intriguing facets to her complex nature. She caught him staring.

"Uh, where were we?"

Allyx wiped her hands with a kitchen towel, then returned to the dining area, where she paced around the table. "The note. You're suggesting it ties all the other loose ends together." She scrunched her lips into a thin frown and sneered. "It seems to me, it was a little slow in getting you up to speed."

"Hey, it's not my fault. But wait a second." Matt pointed to the message with a pencil. "If I've read the first two sentences correctly, then my guess is there's still an issue with his special project. Since he's already given us a clue to problems with the virus research, I find no advantage in him referencing nasty, ubiquitous creatures or good health in the later sentences. We've missed something."

"If nothing else, Dr. Ruhpor is a very meticulous man,"

Allyx said. "He wouldn't put those references in the note unless they were important."

"That's my contention too. However, there's a problem. Dr. Ruhpor could have meant a dozen different things."

"About the only one I'm convinced of was the reference to Tom. It was a lure to get you to the lab."

"Makes sense." Matt shrugged. "Which we agree is why I found certain documents. Their placement was designed to attract my attention."

Approaching the table, Allyx picked up the note. "I buy the beginning; however, there's a switch in the remainder of the message."

"What if it's a warning?" Matt flipped the pencil onto the table. "The introductory sentences sent us one direction, then he gave us the last as a warning to watch our rears."

"Explain," she said.

"His love of 'ubiquitous' has always seemed strange to me. During our class lectures, the Doc used that term when he highlighted how pervasively evil an organism was. You even used it when quoting him." Matt sipped his coffee.

"I see where you're going with this. He used it as a subliminal means to get our attention."

"Precisely. His reference to nasty creatures and health was intended to be a warning, and there's another aspect. Keep in mind, he disappeared right after I was jumped." Matt tapped the side of his cup with his fingers. "I believe he's cautioning us to watch for bad guys, while suggesting they're everywhere. This is big trouble."

"But why make the note so complicated?" Allyx readjusted her ponytail. "He could have told you all this in plain English."

"Cautious, possibly even a little paranoid. The Doc played it safe and hid the note's true content with doublespeak in case it was found by the wrong person."

"He didn't trust someone on the inside. Another professor maybe? The Dean?" Jogging to the front door, Allyx threw Matt his backpack, knocking over his empty coffee cup. "Get your stuff together. We're making another trip to the school's library."

"BenaTex?" Matt asked as he stuffed the financials and a notepad into his backpack.

"They're still our best lead and you said that we might have missed something. We have to establish a motive for them to subvert Dr. Ruhpor's work. A good search of the news periodicals might give us answers. BenaTex could have a history."

"I don't know. Showing up at school might be dangerous. Our friends are probably watching for us." Matt hoped Allyx might back down. Not likely, he concluded.

"We'll blend with the crowd. Besides, what other choice do we have?"

Matt shook his head. "I guess it's worth the risk."

"While we're at it, you can also use the laptop to see if your friend in San Diego replied to the e-mail on the financials you sent her."

"Your call."

She smiled and opened the door. "Of course it is."

2:41 p.m.—Malibu, California

Sally Brinkman tiptoed across the bedroom floor while watching the storm rip into the narrow beach below the house. Whitecaps hammered the unprotected shore as dark gray bulbous clouds unleashed their brutal downpour. A watery gust lashed the redwood sundeck, blowing over a potted palm. Sleeping like a newborn, oblivious to nature's fury, Wade had buried his head beneath the thick plaid comforter.

The sweet scent of the cedar paneling permeated the room, sending soothing sensations throughout Sally's body. Smells, sights, memories: it was good to be home. She sat on the side of the bed and shook him gently. "Wade . . . Wade, it's time to check your bandage."

He rolled onto his back and blinked the sleep away. "Whatever my doctor wants." Wind vibrated the bedroom window. "It's getting nasty outside."

Sally gave him a tender smile. "When it calms, I'll show you the sundeck's ocean view." She neglected to mention the strong weather warning that had flashed on the car radio during her shopping trip. It would only worry him.

"Let's look at that shoulder." Although Wade could have done it on his own, Sally helped him onto his stomach. "Not bad. One more day and you should have your strength back."

Wade glanced up at her. "Then everything will be fine?"

3:00 p.m.—San Jose, California

The dingy room was like any other and it should not have bothered him, but Osborne was tired, tired of Steele and his demands, tired of having to do everything himself, and tired of a lifestyle that required living in cheap motels. Seventeen years was enough; he had the money. Was it possible for him to quit?

Osborne punched numbers into his cell phone. "Lawyer, this is Osborne. Have you found them? . . . I realize sixteen thousand students attend Cal Poly. Did Barns and Spanks show up? . . . Tell them I'll be there by eight-thirty tonight. We have to wrap this one up with no loose ends. Meet me at your motel."

Setting down the receiver, Osborne wondered how he was going to find Wells and Katero. Did he want to find them? With Ruhpor and his student taken care of, the two kids were the only wild cards he had left. "Shit," he said. "Why me?"

He grabbed his coat and travel bag, stopping in the doorway on his way to the parking lot. "Just another motel." He frowned. Was it too late for him?

4:30 p.m.—Shell Beach, California

Matt Wells strummed his fingers on top of the motel room nightstand, waiting for Cindi to pick up her telephone. He and Allyx had struck out at the library, and he hoped, with the right prompting, Cindi might provide them with something they could use. But he worried. They had not spoken since Cabo. When she answered, his throat went dry. "Hi . . . uh . . . sorry to bother you, Cindi. This is, uh, Matt."

"I recognize your voice. It hasn't been that long since Cabo; though, a letter or card would have been nice. I assume you can still write?"

"Um, sorry. You know how I am." Matt hated talking on the telephone. Not seeing Cindi's body language fed his anxieties. On this one occasion, it didn't take a full-size color picture for him to clue in on her feelings. He cringed, hoping she had finished taking your chunks.

For what seemed like more than a minute neither of them spoke. Matt worried. Calling Cindi might have been a mistake. His affection for her had not dried up and blown away on the warm Cabo wind. Emotions were still alive, but he had accepted it was over between them. Had she?

"Not writing just to say hi must be a guy thing. What's on your mind, Matt?"

"Uh, yeah, I'm calling about your e-mail, but first, I'd also like to say I'm sorry for the way things ended between us." He covered the mouthpiece with his hand and took a deep breath.

"Go on. I'm listening."

"School changes began to move too quickly. When the decision came down, like always, I was unable to express myself without stumbling over my tongue."

"An understatement."

"I'm, uh well . . . I wish things had gone differently. You're uh, a special lady, and I should have discussed my decision with you. I care for you and uh, never wanted to hurt you."

She sighed. "Yes, Matt, I know you didn't. Our paths went a different direction, that's all. I was fully aware of what I was getting into when I dated you."

"What do you mean, 'getting into?' "

"Let's just say, you didn't have much of a reputation for long term relationships."

What reputation? Was he atoning for past sins? "But, I—"

"It's okay, Matt. I made the decision knowing there was no guarantee. I'm a big girl, so quit beating yourself up over this."

"Thanks, I think." He tried to relax and find common ground. "If you ever need me, Cindi, I'll be there. Putting my feelings into words is where I run into trouble."

"When you find the right woman, the words will come."

He rubbed the back of his neck, uncertain. She sounded so self-assured, confident. Women—they were so frustrating.

"Matt? Are you there?"

"Uh, yeah. Sorry. Got a little distracted."

"I bet. What about my return e-mail."

"Uh, right. The e-mail." Damn, Matt, get it together. It's not as if she ran you over or something. He composed himself and put things into perspective. "Let's see. Based on your comments, their financials are okay."

"That's correct. BenaTex's debt-to-equity ratio is within industry standards. Their price-to-earnings ratio and earnings per share are high, but the numbers aren't too unusual for an aggressive genetics company. Their growth rate has been stable, averaging fifteen percent per year for the last three. I'd say they're a solid company."

"Any reason to suspect their financials aren't accurate?"

"No, Matt. They're audited. Tell me what you're fishing for and maybe I can help." He didn't respond. "Okay, don't tell me. Besides, I anticipated your call and researched the school's business archives and the Web, where I found an article in the Wall Street Journal. The story was brief. It documented a shortcoming regarding the extent of BenaTex's existing and future contracts."

"If their financials are good, then why the problem?"

"It's simple. A company like BenaTex relies on its existing contracts to sustain current business and to develop future business. The casual term for this reliance is 'backlog.' "

"I'm still confused."

"Here, let me give you an example. Take Boeing and their airplane production. Even with two dozen planes left to build, those would be recorded as a current asset. A simple analysis of their long-term financial stability includes building the planes they have on the assembly line, the number of planes that remain to be built, and future sales. The second item is often referred to as backlog. When you consider—"

"I get it. Boeing and BenaTex can't grow if they don't acquire more orders than their current workforce can handle."

"Right. Keep in mind there's also a stock market aspect to this. If their backlog dips too low, market analysts will downgrade them to a short-term hold, or even worse, a sell. Any negative perception can push their stock value down and cut into their cash flow. Does that help you?"

"Cindi, you're my shining star. I'll write."

"Sure, you will."

"I promise."

"I'll believe it when I see it."

What could he say?

"At least try to do one thing for me.

"And what's that?"

"Stay out of trouble. Bye, Matt." She hung up.

Sweet girl. Too bad things hadn't worked between them. He visualized the financial scenario Cindi had painted as he flopped backward onto the bed. Damn, he had blown it badly with Cindi. What a disaster. Still, she had come through for him. She had provided a possible motive for BenaTex to risk traveling on the dark side of business. Too bad she hadn't found a sinister tie to Dr. Ruhpor.

Matt rolled over and grabbed the clock radio. Allyx had left over thirty minutes ago. Why she had to go out at that specific moment was beyond him. When he raised a word in opposition, she cursed something about "privacy and fresh air." The idea of her alone bothered him. She was out there, unprotected, where anything could happen. Allyx was too damn stubborn for her own good.

He grumbled. Why should he worry? Allyx could take care of herself.

No one had spotted them at the library, but that didn't mean they'd get lucky twice. Why take stupid chances? He wished Allyx were at the motel, safe, with him.

4:46 p.m.—San Francisco, California

"Thank you, Mr. Border. Your Malaysian flight 3423 leaves in 45 minutes from gate 52."

Latch put the one-way ticket into his inside jacket pocket, tipped his head to the agent, and picked up his travel bag. He studied the public mingling by the TWA counter before making his way into the crowd; his experienced eyes analyzed the faces nearest him. What a fucking mess. Singular never intended for him to bring Fields in, at least not alive. If he had only foreseen the world of crap he was walking into. Well, that was the past, and his immediate need was to fade into oblivion. The cash Singular had given him would help.

His ex-Special Forces compatriots were hanging in Sandakan, along the Sulu Sea, and it was a good day for a visit. A lot of money could be made while bouncing between islands of the South China Sea. With the right talent, a man could bankroll a few thousand into a tidy sum. Anyway, Latch didn't have much of a choice. His local contacts had warned him that his northern California meal ticket was gonna be severed, and before long, the players would burn him too. That bit of information was not to be taken lightly.

He stopped at a blue screen monitor and verified his departure status. "On time" was highlighted in the column to the right of his flight number. In ten minutes he would board, and in twenty more, he'd be feet wet on his way to the South Pacific. Thanks, Dr. Singular, pleasure doing business with you. Latch headed for the gate.

5:22 p.m.—Shell Beach, California

"Did you miss me?" Allyx Katero asked. "Hope you like granola." Matt grumbled and she laughed. "Don't worry; I picked up some standard meat-eater junk food too. I also grabbed a copy of the Telegram Tribune. Thought we might want to keep current on the local news."

"Thanks, I'll fix something." Matt peeked inside the grocery bag as he carried it to the kitchenette. "How do chicken sandwiches sound?"

"Delicious. How'd the San Diego call go?"

"Better than I'd hoped."

Allyx arched an eyebrow, imitating Matt's curious expression.

"Uhmm," he cleared his throat. "BenaTex has a potential long-term cash flow problem. Although they look good on paper, their existing workload isn't enough to sustain them over the long term."

"Interesting little discovery. Financial desperation is a motive to push the ethical envelope. It's too bad Dr. Ruhpor didn't give us more. It's also odd that they were so generous with their grant money if future finances were tight." Allyx sat on the bed and skimmed the newspaper. "Where do we look next?"

Matt placed a sandwich and a plate full of baked potato chips next to her. "There are two places we haven't considered: messages on my voice mail and the Doc's."

"Can you get into Dr. Ruhpor's voice mail?"

"No problem. He gave me the password. That way I could monitor his calls when he was busy."

"Then do it." Allyx rolled onto her side and read the newspaper.

Matt dialed his own voice mail and listened. "Not much on mine. Dr. Pembar wants me to stock his laboratory with deionized water. Could take a while. I hope he can wait." Matt punched in the Doc's mailbox number and entered his five-digit password, then pressed the number three on the touch pad and retrieved the messages.

"Here's one, Allyx. Someone at BenaTex contacted him."

She perked up, leaving the newspaper open on the bed. "Well?"

"A guy named Fields called. Said he's with Bena-Tex. He sounded shaky and was adamant about discussing a special project with the Doc."

"Did he give any details?"

"Only an unlisted phone number."

"Call him." She moved the newspaper. "Matt, wait! Oh my God." Allyx pointed, then covered her face with her hand.

The headline on page two read: *"Celebrated Cal Poly Professor and Student Die in Car Crash."* Matt looked up, and Allyx was gone. The motel room door slammed shut.

8:30 p.m.—South of Cal Poly, Central Coast, California

Osborne entered the motel room and two of the four men stood. They were all stocky, scarred, and deadly, in an ignorant muscle sort of way. "Pull the curtain and give me an update." He rested his hip against a round particle-board table and crossed his arms. "Status?" Everyone looked at Lawyer.

"Watchin' the college was a fuckin' waste," Lawyer said. "But we struck mama's sweet spot on the wire taps."

"And?" Osborne uncrossed his arms.

"Two calls were made to Ruhpor's phone today. We got 'em both on tape. The first was Wade Fields. Wasn't he the guy we're watchin' before?"

"Yes. And the second?"

"We don't know. He had the code to get into Ruhpor's voice mail."

"Wells."

"That's what we're figurin' too. He did work for Ruhpor. The Fields dude left an LA number. Our man at the phone company's on it."

"Call me on my cell when you get the address." Osborne handed a business card to Lawyer. "Don't keep me waiting. Maintain surveillance on the school until I tell you otherwise. Any questions?" They shook their heads and Osborne left the motel room without further comment.

Sitting in the driver's seat of his rented Ford Taurus, Osborne lit a cigarette and contemplated this change of events. A hit on Fields might lead them to Wells, but it could also bring on another complication. Fields was supposed to be someone else's problem. Osborne unlatched the car phone from its cradle and dialed.

"Mr. Steele, this is Osborne. . . ."

8:41 p.m.—Shell Beach, California

"Where did you go?" Matt Wells asked.

"I went for a run. I had to be alone." Allyx crossed the room and sat at the dining table. Matt had never seen her look so frail. Her hands shook as her fingers traced the sides of the flower vase. She had been crying.

Matt didn't know how to respond, nor how to comfort her. His instinct was to hold her, but his intellectual side told him to give her space. He would wait and be there if she needed him.

Allyx left the table and sat on the bed, clasping her hands together. Her eyes were red and puffy and she moved slowly, unsure of herself. When their gaze met, she could not hide the deep sorrow tormenting her. She wiped away a tear with her hand.

"I hadn't realized how close you two were," Matt said. "I'm sorry."

She hesitated. "He had a special side few ever saw."

A prolonged silence and Matt suppressed another impulse to hold her.

"When I was growing up in Atlanta, my grandfather was my best friend. He was my buddy, my confidant. Mom and Dad were okay, busy with jobs, education, meetings, the demands of everyone else." Her hand brushed the ribbed texture of the brown bedspread. "They were there when I really needed them, just not during the day when the little things happened, the day-to-day stuff I needed to share with someone. No matter what, my grandfather was always by my side." Her eyes reddened.

"You don't have to tell me this." Matt held perfectly still.

"Yes, I do." She rubbed her wet cheeks with the back of her hand. "We played cards, drank sun tea, and fantasized about secret adventures. He'd tell me of the past and his childhood in Greece, and I'd tell him my dreams for the future. When my grandmother died, I was all my grandfather had. Then less than a year after she died, I lost him too. It happened during my freshman year at Cal Poly."

Matt laid his hand on hers. "Are you okay?"

She pulled away. "I went home during a school break. The day was your typical hot and muggy Georgia afternoon." She slowed, taking her time, choosing her words carefully. "I found him lying on the floor, heaving and holding his chest. They had beaten him. The skin around his eyes was so swollen. Blood dripped from his nose and ears. I went to him. He tried to speak, straining to catch his breath. His expression overflowed with unbearable pain, and then, he drifted away. Lost to me forever." Tears streamed down her cheeks.

"I don't even remember calling the paramedics. They tried to save him, but nothing helped. His heart just stopped. He had given up. I held him in my arms until the end." She wiped her eyes and looked at Matt. "He loved me."

"I know."

Allyx stopped, bit her lip, then rose suddenly and walked to the bathroom, returning a few minutes later. "The police said they had caught two teenage boys, seventeen-years old. The assholes had broken into what they assumed was an empty house. When my grandfather confronted them, they attacked him. He was eighty. What sick shit of a mind would beat a defenseless elderly man to death?"

"I don't know." A frustrated rage burned inside Matt. He wanted to fix her hurt.

"When I got back to school, academics was the last thing on my mind. It didn't take long before I fell into the fraternity party scene. Everything began to unravel. I got embroiled in a bad relationship, things happened, and I was almost thrown out of school. That's when I met Dr. Ruhpor."

Matt was uncomfortable with hearing the rest, but he remained by Allyx's side, listening, accepting there was little else he could offer her.

"He helped me find my sorry self. After three months with him, I felt like I'd been enrolled in an emotional rehab program. It was one of the most agonizing times of my life." She raised her head and look at Matt. Her red tearful eyes squeezed his heart like a vise. "I survived and I owe everything that I am to him—to Dr. Ruhpor."

"But I assumed . . ." Matt did not continue and Allyx stared at him suspiciously.

"I protect myself," Allyx said. Determination hardened the look on her face as she set her hand on his. "Keeping my distance, holding my heart in check, I won't be hurt again by anyone."

"What can I do?"

"The people who killed Dr. Ruhpor and Tom Harden, I want them punished."

9:10 p.m.—Malibu, California

Sally Brinkman stood by the main floor-to-ceiling window overlooking the sundeck. A floodlight mounted above the porch pointed toward the ocean. Strong winds churned the sea into a frothy mess. Huge waves slammed the beach below. The rain had stopped and the skies remained cloudy and ominous. She had been through this once before, the storm of '79, the one where her dad had described the night as "black as the road to hell." That storm killed ten people.

She looked up as Wade entered the living room. He wore a cream-colored terry cloth robe and dried his hair with a thick towel.

"How was your shower?" she asked.

"I've been reborn. Thanks."

"You're welcome."

Wade stood next to her, quietly observing her momentary distraction with the storm. "How's the weather?"

"Wet and wild." Sally shied away from the window. "Your new accent, or lack there of, is going to take some getting used to."

He laughed. "For you, Miss Sally, I'll gladly speak the language of a Southern gentleman."

"Cute." She rolled her eyes. "While you were rejuvenating, the phone rang."

"I thought I heard something." Wade draped the towel over his good shoulder and ran a comb through his hair. "Anyone we know?"

"A call back on the message you left Dr. Ruhpor."

"Oh." He hesitated, then walked to the counter, where he folded the towel and set it on a stool. "What did the professor have to say?"

"That's the interesting part. It wasn't Dr. Ruhpor, but one of his students."

"I don't like that."

"Consider your options." Sally gave Wade a moment. She remained at the window, leaning against the heavy, brown anodized aluminum frame. Mottled black clouds rumbled behind her. "He didn't go into details. Apparently he wants to meet tomorrow."

"You didn't tell him where we were?" Wade shifted on his chair.

She frowned. "Of course not."

"Good."

"I set up a meeting in Marina Del Rey. It's far enough from here that he won't be able to pinpoint the beach house, although close enough that we can get there in forty-five minutes." Sally went into the kitchen and took a Perrier out of the refrigerator. "Do you want anything?"

"No thanks, maybe later. Will he be alone?"

"There'll be two of them. He's with a woman."

"Sounds familiar."

She grinned mischievously, a distracting smile. "Doesn't it." Wade feigned ignorance at the correlation.

"What time tomorrow?"

"The meeting is set for twelve at the Islands Restaurant. We'll blend in with the local lunch crowd. Is there anything we should do to prepare?"

"Clothes would help." He twisted his face and inspected her father's robe. "Nice, but—"

"I get the hint. I'll make a run to a department store. What are you, a size 40 regular?" Sally stood at the counter and assessed Wade's physique. "Shirt, slacks, something a little more professional. Um, that should fit fine."

"This is weird." He shied away from her probing eyes.

"Not like you're in any shape to go out in public."

"Yes, ma'am. But I don't want you out there by yourself."

"We don't have much choice. You'd attract more attention than a lone woman shopping for her man." Wade's ears seemed to perk up. "Don't get any ideas, buddy. You're beginning to have delusions of grandeur and I think bed rest is in order before you get in trouble. While you sleep, I'll shop for our rendezvous."

"If you insist, doctor." He pressed his lips together until they turned white, showing no effort to hide his unhappiness with her decision to travel alone.

"Sally, you know this could be a trap."

"I know."

October 12

7:33 a.m.—São Gabriel da Anjo, Brazil

Five motorized canoes beached next to São Gabriel da Anjo's aging wooden pier. Dockworkers had been packing the boats with supplies since before sunrise. Secure and uniform distribution of provisions was a critical charge when preparing for the trip upriver. Not all of the Rio Negro contained smooth water and if the team became careless, boats and equipment might be lost or damaged during an unfortunate accident. Nothing was taken for granted.

James and their new guide, Ernesto, followed the shoreline, approaching the canoes from the west. The team carried enough food and provisions for three weeks of isolation. They had limited each loaded craft to four passengers. James had discussed every aspect of the expedition with Ernesto.

Although James quickly concluded that the man possessed a unique understanding of the jungle, one that bordered on obsessive, his initial apprehension regarding hiring Ernesto had not eased until after spending most of the previous night and early morning getting to know him. Born in Brasília, Ernesto had been a guide since childhood, and his Amazon history traced back five generations. He was at home in the jungle, preferring its solitude to that of human company. When Ernesto spoke of the wonders he had seen, there was a stirring gleam in his black eyes, and his enthusiasm became contagious. James felt the respect, an almost religious awe, he held for this land and its people.

A relatively small man, James sensed in Ernesto the strength of someone twice his size. His features were dark and muted by a round face and a disproportionately wide nose. Fluency in English, Spanish, Portuguese, French, and many of the local Indian dialects had made him an invaluable interpreter and a sought-after guide. James surmised that Ernesto's professional traits fit in well with the archaeological team's needs. He could see why Dr. Isling had added him to the expedition.

When they approached the nearest boat, James noticed that it had been packed with sleeping and shelter provisions. The second boat held their GPS and digital satellite communications equipment—their only means of outside contact. The third and fourth canoes carried their gear for plant, soil, rock, and air sampling and analysis. Medical supplies were stored in the last. Food stocks had been distributed evenly among all five craft. Each had its own pilot, two native laborers, and one archaeological team member. James continued his inspection while Ernesto trailed along to the dock, tending to other details.

James stopped at the last boat, squatted on one knee and examined the canvas tarp covering the supplies. He yanked on the tie downs; they were secure. Glancing over the bow of the eighteen-foot canoe, he saw Dr. Isling wave as he made his way from the center of town.

"How's it going, James?" Two additional canoes pulled onto the muddy beach.

"Everything is going well. Ernesto is a crack organizer."

Confused by the other two canoes, Dr. Isling lifted the brim of his expedition hat and squinted. "Are these part of our group?"

James shook his head. "Not according to the manifest. I'll ask Ernesto."

Dr. Isling saw Dr. MacKiernan head their direction. "Hi, Aidan. How's the basement?"

"Dark and quiet, Henry. Things shaping up here okay?"

"Not bad. Was the mission clinic of any help?"

Aidan beamed. "As a matter of fact, they were. The medical supplies have been augmented quite nicely. They provided us with creams and ointments for contact rashes and indigenous insect bites. Oh, and by the way, Dr. Utesha finished her review of the aerial photographs and confirmed our study grid. She said James did a great job pinpointing the area. Sounds like we're on a roll."

"Excellent. Finally, favorable news. James estimates we can be on the river in a couple of hours." A slap on his back and Isling jumped.

"Hey, Henry. How are your primordial pebbles hanging?"

Dr. Isling grimaced. "For a second, Myrta, I was worried you'd lost some of your infamous enthusiasm."

"Silly, man, I only improve with age." She laughed and waved toward town. "You have to agree, though, this place is getting rather boring. I want to unearth some artifacts and frolic up to my ass in the dirt."

"Be patient, Myrta, not much longer."

She watched the dock for a movement. "Patience . . . humph. The archives have lost their glamour and the local beer doesn't rate very highly with me."

Sneaking into the conversation, James said, "You have my vote, professor. Warm beer is unnatural, and I'd do anything to get out of the mission basement." He whispered into Dr. Isling's ear. "The two extra canoes are for the television people."

A grimace formed on the professor's face, but he withheld comment. Everyone knew his position on the matter. "We're almost ready to leave, Myrta. Are you packed?"

"As of an hour ago, Henry."

"Good then. James, has Ernesto accounted for the additional travelers?"

"Doing it right now." James pointed at the boats. "It shouldn't be a problem. The news crew came equipped for everything from a monsoon to a drought."

"As long as they stay out of the way. I'll be in the basement if you need me." Dr. Isling grumbled and tromped into town, waving James off.

"He's going to have to accept them," James said, "or this is going to be a very long expedition. Dr. MacKiernan, Dr. Utesha, interested in taking a break and giving us a hand in auditing our loading procedures?" They gave him affirmative nods.

"Well then, let me show you our masterpiece in canoe preparation." He gestured down the muddy beach with a curt bow and wave. "It's already too hot and humid to sweat the news people. They're on their own."

8:04 a.m.—San Francisco, California

Ben Singular kicked the metal elevator door with the tip of his Roma patent leather shoe, leaving a smudge on the gleaming surface. "Who the hell gave that asshole the right to meddle in my family's business. Steele might have bought his way into my company, but that purchase didn't include my son. My son. Dear God, my son. What have I done?"

The elevator doors opened and Ben entered Steele's office.

"Dr. Singular."

"Mr. Steele." Ben stopped a few feet short of Steele.

"You called this meeting."

"That's correct."

"Can I get you anything?"

"No thank you. This won't take long."

"Very well." Steele took a seat behind his desk, lacing

his fingers across his chest. "Proceed."

Ben stepped up to the desk. His neck muscles twisted into knots, and he ignored the pain. Steele had gone too far. "One of my field reps informed me that Dr. Ruhpor brought a new student into the program a few days ago. His name's Matt Wells."

"Your point?"

"My point is, nothing happens on this project without your blessing. Why was my son recruited?" Steele's yellowish eyes hardened. Ben stood his ground.

"He was looking to make a change and Dr. Ruhpor needed assistance." Steele smiled as he stroked the top of his cigar case. "There was no collusion. I just facilitated the meeting."

"I don't buy it." Ben caught the taunting tone. Steele assumed he had the upper hand; Ben knew otherwise. A miscalculation on Steele's part. How rare.

"It was simply an innocent academic recruitment."

"Nothing with you is ever innocent or simple." Ben's resolve deepened as he reached toward Steele. "Here are the final numbers on the retrovirus and I've delivered the specimen sample to your man. Now, leave my son alone."

"Do not worry, Dr. Singular, he's a bright boy and I am sure he will do just fine."

"Yes, he will be fine. Because as of this moment, our business relationship is permanently severed."

Steele stood. "As you wish, Dr. Singular."

8:22 a.m.—101 Highway, South of Santa Barbara, California

The drizzle had increased in its intensity after they passed through Santa Barbara and Allyx Katero adjusted the speed of the windshield wipers to compensate. Gloomy weather contributed to her uneasiness. How they could expect to take on a corporation and win was beyond her. Yet, they raced toward Los Angeles, chasing a chance meeting with a man named Fields, another piece taking up space on BenaTex's complex game board. Events moved too fast, decisions happened too quickly; she felt manipulated by an unknown foe.

With all that had happened, Allyx could barely comprehend the senseless deaths of Dr. Ruhpor and his graduate student, Tom Harden. The newspaper called it an accident. They just happened to be out at night driving at high speed on Corbett Canyon's one lane road, with a pinhole in their brake line no less. Like Matt had said, too many coincidences pointed to murder.

"Are you sure I can't drive?" Matt asked.

"If you don't stop babying me, I'm going to scream." Her strength was in her independence, and Matt's paternal reflex had become too confining. Deep down, she sympathized. There had been occasions when she too felt the need to protect someone.

"Do you want to talk?"

"No." Allyx squeezed the steering wheel. Hatred, fear, anger: she agonized with her feelings over the death of Dr. Ruhpor. She had been through it all before with her grandfather. The vision of him dying in her arms remained as vivid as ever. "Not again. I won't let it happen—"

"What did you say?"

"Nothing. Just thinking. You know that he was one of the nicest, kindest, people I'd ever met." She took a moment. "I learned more from him in one quarter than I had in an entire school year with anyone else."

"I understand. He's the reason I left San Diego State for Cal Poly."

"You agree then, he'd never hurt anyone."

"Of course."

"Then why kill him?"

Matt took his time answering her. "I haven't a clue. But I promise, they'll pay for what they've done."

"How can you be sure?" She saw him hesitate as the

rain splattered the windshield. It seemed crazy to put her trust in a guy she hardly knew. Matt was an obvious babe-scammer. Still, there had to be more to him than an insecure libido. Then again, would his past get in the way? Their very survival depended on the depth of his character and the strength of his conviction. She watched him closely. Was Matt Wells worth the gamble?

Their conversation wavered and the silence between them grew. What was he thinking? Allyx hoped he had what it took to see this through. She listened to the wiper blades slap across the windshield as they sped south along the 101 Freeway.

"In my heart," Matt said, "I believe we'll help catch and punish whoever killed Dr. Ruhpor." He shrugged. "It's one of those things you can't explain."

"I wish I had your confidence."

"It's not confidence. We haven't finished yet. I see a future with things left to do and I can't picture it ending here."

"Hmm." With a slight nod, she referenced the dashboard's digital clock. "In less than four hours, we'll get a glimpse of what that future holds."

9:43 a.m.—Central Coast, California

Osborne sat at the motel room's simulated wood table, facing Spanks and Lewis. The other two men, Barns and Parks, were outside loading the car. Rob Spanks handed the Malibu address to Osborne. "Got this a few minutes ago." He considered the location, his intuition telling him Wells was on his way to meet Fields. Events were coming to a head.

During their last conversation, Steele had directed Osborne to kill Wells and Fields, and anyone else who got in the way. Their goal was simple; however, the logistics were complicated. Additional targets required more manpower, detailed planning, and precision timing. He looked around the table. Not this group.

"Lawyer, you contact LA and get someone on the location. Put the beach house under 24-hour surveillance. I want to know who's inside. We have to verify the targets."

"It's gonna take some doin'." Lawyer Lewis shook his head. "Our LA people are busy with a bunch of ignorant truckers."

Spanks snarled a chuckle. "Yeah, they want more of everythin'. What they're gonna get is broken bones."

Lawyer ignored Spanks, while he watched him fish a booger dangling from his nose with his finger and casually flip it onto the floor—human trash.

"I'll call Marty Lithbaine. He's got a couple of cannons sittin' 'round with nothin' to do but dig lint outta their butts."

Disgusting bunch of scum, Osborne thought. "Whoever you find reports to you, Lawyer. No one else is to know what's going down. We pay cash for the job and no questions." He turned his attention to Spanks, who was excavating for leftover breakfast between his teeth with a soggy toothpick. "Did you locate the additional guns?"

"Yeah, I got two East LA shooters. No brains, all balls."

"Gangbangers?"

"What else?"

"They're unstable punks." Osborne stared into Spanks' baggy eyes, catching him flinch. "You're responsible for keeping them in line. Hold them at the safe house until they're needed. We don't want them bragging to their gangbanger buddies."

"Got it handled." Spanks blinked and looked away.

"Are six of us gonna be enough?" Lawyer asked.

"We'll make a determination when the surveillance team reports in."

"A couple of college babies and two nerd scientists gotcha worried, Lawyer?"

"Fuck you, Spanks. I ain't worried about nothin' but your sorry ass-lickin' face gettin' in my way."

Osborne eyed both men and they shut up. Coiled snakes, spoiling for a fight; they were poetic arguments for restricted procreation. "Have our equipment sent to the safe house. We'll meet there tomorrow morning by seven-thirty. Don't be late. Any questions?" He didn't trust these two alone, but other business had to be taken care of before joining them in Los Angeles. "None? Good, then get moving."

11:51 a.m.—Houston, Texas

The viral data's spreadsheets stood in five neat stacks on Greg Gunder's wraparound workstation. Greg tapped his blue highlighter on the top sheet of one stack. He had been with the ZenLab Group for thirty-nine months, and his peers considered him to be the best numerical modeler in the business. Was that why he was given the more esoteric projects? Twirling the highlighter between his fingers, he studied his new challenge while listening to the rain beat against his office window and the Stones on his stereo.

Actually, rain was a poor description for the liquid deluge; a cloud burst would have been more accurate. Though at least two inches would fall in the next hour, this was Houston and southeastern Texans called these downpours sprinkles. When this storm ended, the indoor mold count would go up another percentage point, but Greg didn't care. He had grown accustomed to the Gulf's soaking showers and the inevitable high humidity.

Being from the drylands of southeastern Washington, his introduction to a Texas drizzle was, to say the least, a shock. The day Greg arrived in Houston, he was on the Beltway, a mile southwest of Intercontinental Airport, when a sudden shower drowned his rental car's windshield. He had never seen that much water fall out of the sky; a fire hose could not have been more powerful. Individual rain droplets were the size of swollen green peas, Nature's way of welcoming him to Houston.

Strange as the storm was, it hit on the same day he had decided to accept ZenLab's job offer and work amongst the tall evergreens of northern Houston. That was two months after graduating from the University of Washington with a Master's degree in computer programming. In many ways, his new home reminded him of his college days in Seattle; both places had continual rain. Northern Houston just came with hotter summers, colder winters, and an unbroken horizon. He looked toward his window . . . what a place . . . then down at his desk.

The modeling approach would be kept simple. Greg dropped the highlighter on the desk and with his skeptical eye for detail scanned the viral data. His assignment was to isolate a small percentage of the population with specific social characteristics. The model would predict how long it would take the virus to pervade his control group, then move on and mature to endemic proportions within the general population. Within modern disease analyses, this was a commonly applied case scenario.

He rocked back in his chair and took a bite of a sugar donut. As Greg set the carbo-loaded junk food on a napkin next to the computer, he grimaced at the bulge extending over his belt. No longer that lean intramurals athlete, he had put on a hefty thirty-four pounds since being with ZenLab. Face it, he was on his way to becoming a pudgy middle-aged adult, and the thought of joining a gym terrified him. A spattering of white powder stuck to his upper lip. He licked it off with his tongue.

Greg suppressed thoughts of his sagging waistline by scrawling notes in a daily logbook. He wrote everything down; a habit developed during graduate school. In this way, he rarely missed anything. Seemingly insignificant issues always became more important as a project progressed. Details, quality analysis was always in the details.

To start, he'd glean data chunks from the CDC archives, then develop a viable analytical model. That should kill the afternoon. By morning, he'd be ready to smooth the fluctuation of selected sensitivity parameters, which included virus transmission, host dormancy, and the influence of any restrictive natural genetic barriers. A sensitivity analysis such as this was essential to verify boundary limits for the primary factors influencing the virus' movement within his virtual human population. These limits were the most difficult modeling criteria to ascertain, and he would derive his adjustment protocols from published research papers and personal experience on other projects.

He had run associated exercises on two previous occasions for the Hanta and Lassa viruses. Except, unlike his current modeling assignment, those earlier projects did not have a specific carrier group. This project was similar to his cancer scenarios, where he had used target groups. With those studies, he had been able to demonstrate statistically that people were more prone to certain diseases based on their genetic characteristics and specific lifestyles. His groundbreaking analyses had won him a nomination for the Nobel Prize. That was more than two years ago. He had been twenty-seven at the time.

Greg highlighted his e-mail icon button, waited for the dialog box to appear, then typed a message to his absentee boss.

"Tell the client I can finish the job within a week. Final certainty will be above the ninety-fifth percentile. I have all I need and will stay in touch. Greg."

Sending the message and then switching screens, he reserved four large blocks on the Cray II Super Computer starting in three days. That should give him enough flexibility to develop the analytical model and time to rough out the numerical model. Greg smiled. He often took for granted the cost of the technology he had at his disposal. But then, as he had always said, "The elite don't come cheap."

11:55 a.m.—Marina Del Rey, California

"She gave instructions to ask for Sally at the hostess counter," Matt Wells said while casually spying about the interior. The Islands restaurant had a South Pacific motif mixed with a subtle splash of Spanish flavor. Tile counters and tabletops were color coordinated with pastel blues and greens and beige wood trimmings. In the center of the room was a large bar surrounded by highback booths—an open setting.

Allyx approached the hostess. "Excuse me; we're here to meet a friend. Her name is Sally."

"Welcome to the Islands. Your friend left instructions that she'll be running a few minutes late. This way, please." The hostess led them to a vacant booth in the rear of the restaurant. "Your server will be with you in a minute."

"Thank you," Matt said and took a seat next to Allyx. He maintained watch over the front entrance. "Interesting place. She must be more comfortable meeting in public."

"Can you blame her?"

"Not really. I'm just glad she agreed to this."

"She's not here yet."

"Always the optimist."

Fifteen minutes and a Corona later, a woman approached the table. "Are you Matt Wells?" she asked.

"Yes."

"I'm . . . It's you! What, what is this?" Sally hesitated, looked over her shoulder, then scooted into the booth, facing Matt and Allyx.

"We had no idea," Matt defended, seeing Allyx's startled look. "Your name never registered."

"Are you Berkeley reporters, or Cal Poly students? Which is it?" Sally squirmed. "I don't like this."

Allyx leaned forward, closing the distance between Sally and herself. "We didn't mean to surprise you. If we had known it was you, we would have said something over the phone. I swear." She gave Matt a confirming nod.

"That's right, Sally. We used the guise of reporters to gain entrance into BenaTex. All we wanted was information."

"I don't . . ." Sally shook her head. "I just don't want any trouble—"

"Sally, we're the good guys, honest."

"What the heck am I doing, this is all too weird."

"Please trust us." Matt sat forward, doing his best not to appear intimidating. "You're our only hope."

"Why am I doing this?" Sally whispered to herself as she pressed both hands against her forehead. "Okay, we're in too far already. What are your real names?"

"This is Allyx Katero, and I'm Matt Wells."

"It's good to meet you once again, Sally."

"You too, Allyx . . . I think." She scanned them quizzically; a disarming frown formed. "Why didn't Dr. Ruhpor come?"

Matt glanced toward Allyx. "Uh, before we go there, where's Mr. Fields?"

"In a minute. Let me see your Cal Poly ID's. I feel a little trust verification is in order."

"We understand." Matt and Allyx handed her their student identification cards.

Sally studied the photographs, comparing them to Matt and Allyx. She inspected the green and gold Cal

Poly seals, then gestured to a man standing at the bar. He walked over and sat next to her without saying a word.

"Mr. Fields, I presume." Matt extended his hand.

"Mr. Wells." Wade returned the handshake, and greeted Allyx with a slight bow. "Sorry for the intrigue."

"You can't guess the half of it."

Wade gave Sally a questioning look and an awkward silence followed. "I suppose we all have to be careful."

Impatient, and a little groggy after the long road trip, Matt got to the point. "In your message to Dr. Ruhpor, you mentioned BenaTex."

"Yes I did. By the way, where is Dr. Ruhpor?"

Matt and Allyx exchanged another glance. "We're sorry, but he was unable to make the trip."

"Nothing serious I hope."

"We can talk about that later. Mr. Fields, you were about to explain your relationship with BenaTex?" Wade grimaced, obviously uncomfortable with being put off, but for now, Matt felt it prudent to keep the Doc's death a secret.

"Uhmm, yes I suppose." Wade viewed them suspiciously, but continued anyway. "We both work . . . worked for BenaTex." Sally folded and unfolded a napkin while Wade spoke. Unsettled by her nervousness, Allyx moved closer to Matt. Their meeting was becoming very awkward.

"So what's your connection with Dr. Ruhpor?" Allyx asked.

"We contacted him for an exchange of information." Wade's eyes panned the room. "But this isn't the place to go into those kinds of details. Let's order and maybe afterward we can go somewhere more secluded."

A lump grew in Matt's throat as Allyx squeezed his hand under the table.

3:20 p.m.—Rio Negro, Brazil

The river flowed deep and wide. More than two hundred yards of water stretched between its banks, shimmering smooth as black onyx, reflecting brilliant shoreline images. Colorful birds swooped through the sky, diving on insects skating above the surface. Somehow, even the foliage growing along the reach seemed richer and more vibrant than what James Monal had seen near Manaus.

Glad to be finally on the acidic waters of the Rio Negro, and free of the bothersome mosquitoes that plagued most of the Amazon Basin, James relaxed and absorbed the lush jungle features with all his senses. Rich organic jungle scents lingered in the moist tropical air as the canoes cut a path through the water. Searing heat and soaking humidity constantly reminded him that this was not a place to be underestimated. Nature's energy seemed to have affected everyone. He noticed that even the native laborers had become uncharacteristically awestruck. They all had embarked on a Jules Verne adventure, traveling deep into an unexplored world.

The subtle hint of unknown danger added to the mystical lore. Legends of ancient warrior women to the reality of deadly piranhas; this was truly one of the last frontiers. How raw and untamed the Amazon must have appeared when the Spanish conquistadors arrived during the seventeenth century. James shielded his eyes with his hat, listening to the hum of the outboard motors and thinking of the events that had led them to this point. He had a visceral urge to pay homage to the gods of the Rio Negro for safe passage.

They all had different reasons for joining the expedition. Adventure and recognition drove some; for most, insatiable curiosity incited them to explore history for answers to the human condition. James was convinced that by interpreting the past, he would gain insight into humanity's future. People were creatures of habit, destined to repeat mistakes while striving for new levels of mental awareness and comfort.

Was that what brought him to the Amazon? Could the Burbános unlock the secrets of the ancient Maya and provide answers to many of archaeology's haunting mysteries? But then, there was the darker side of the Maya, both brutal and pagan. Was he ready for either possibility? Had the others considered the potential danger?

In a canoe on his right, Myrta removed an orthographic photograph from her rucksack. She had marked crucial ground references on its topographic overlay. As they moved along, she verified the accuracy of her computations to actual ground and river features. That was Dr. Utesha, always busy.

Aidan used a duffel bag for a pillow and reclined against the side of his canoe, allowing his Red Sox baseball cap to cover his eyes. The rhythmic slosh of the river on the sides of the boat lulled him to sleep.

Dr. Isling made full use of his 35mm camera, taking shot after shot of the spectacular scenery. A constant array of rich vegetation and flamboyant birds fed his lense.

Fenmar satisfied his curiosity by studying the flora and fauna blossoming along the shore. He glowed with the look of a paleobotanist lost in a tropical flower shop, exhausting a notepad with labeled sketches of exotic plants.

Ernesto sat in the stern of James' boat, next to the outboard motor. He watched the river, reading the currents, anticipating changes in the hydraulics, always searching for hidden dangers. James saw by the way Ernesto's eyes picked out details, and the minor adjustments he made to their path, that he was as comfortable on the water as he was on land.

Then there was Kelly, sitting in a canoe to James' left. Her arms were crossed and she frowned beneath sweat-drenched hair, showing no enthusiasm for the wondrous environment they were passing through. All day, Kelly had clenched her teeth in a perpetual grind while she conceived of ways to torture those who had dumped her in the Amazon's bug-infested swamp. James smiled. She wouldn't last much longer.

Glynn, her cameraman, followed the group in the last boat. Once his craft had made smooth water, he recorded twenty minutes of background footage and then fell fast asleep, snoring in tune with the rumble of the canoe's outboard motor.

A noisy splash and James turned, as did the others, to see a crocodile, a black caiman, flail violently within the shallows. The caiman thrashed about in desperate thrusts, flinging its leathery hide left and right as an undulating dark olive green and black-spotted anaconda snake encircled the beast. Twenty or more feet of slithering snake squeezed, wriggled and rolled with each movement, always tightening its grasp on the caiman. As the croc slowly lost its fight, James experienced a sympathy pang for the hideous black reptile, then they rounded another bend in the Rio Negro and the gruesome scene disappeared.

James leaned against the canvas tarp protecting their provisions. He stared into the deep blue Brazilian sky. The team had entered a place unblemished by western culture. How small he felt in this dangerous, yet beautiful land. Seven small canoes traveled up the Rio Negro. Seven small canoes on a journey into the past.

1:25 p.m.—Malibu, California

Wade Fields heard what Matt had said, yet it seemed impossible. Dr. Ruhpor and a student dead? His mind struggled to accept the information, as though all hope would be lost if he did. The color had faded from Sally's face. The implication of murder had hit them hard, re-inforcing their fears. One-by-one, they would be found. One-by-one, they would be killed.

"The poor man." Sally poured herself a glass of wine with a shaky hand. "You . . . you said the newspaper called it an accident."

"Was my shoulder an accident?" The words came out harsher than Wade had intended. He studied her re-action. This ordeal had been difficult for her. Sally had spent her entire professional career with BenaTex. They were supposed to be the white knights of the genetics industry, and by helping him, she had given it all up, put her life on the line. If they were going to prevail, much less survive, Sally had to forget her loyalty to the com-pany. Wade vowed to be her strength.

"My God, what's going on?" Sally sat next to the fireplace and stoked the coals, refusing to make eye con-tact with anyone.

"That's what we're here to find out." Matt stood next to Allyx by a window overlooking the ocean. "We'll do it together," he said.

"Sally, I wouldn't have believed this of BenaTex a few days ago." Wade flinched and rotated his stiff shoulder. "Now, I'm convinced they're capable of anything." He saw she was sinking fast. "But don't worry, we'll get through this. I promise."

Had doubts crept in now that Sally had more time to consider what she was giving up? What about Matt and Allyx? What was their true motivation? He watched the young couple as they looked out over the ocean, preoc-cupied with their own worries. Were they having second thoughts too? Wade caught himself. What the hell was he thinking? His uncertainties were dangerous, possibly contagious. He had to keep his fear under control. Wells was right. If they were to have any hope at all, they had to pull together. They had no other choice.

"BenaTex was a leader, a pioneer," Allyx said without turning around. "Everyone in the genetics field admired them. My only wish was to be part of such an inspired company when I graduated. How did they go wrong?"

"Money?" Matt suggested. "Greed."

"Is it enough to commit murder?" Sally asked.

"We can't answer that yet." Matt crossed the room and sat on the couch near Wade. "Earlier, you mentioned that the voice of the man who shot you sounded familiar."

"I'm certain it was Latch's deep all-business grumble. He's head of BenaTex's security."

"If so, that confirms they're the power behind the gun," Allyx said.

"What if someone's pulling their strings?" Sally's questioning eyes explored Wade's, searching for answers he didn't have. "Donner and Singular aren't the types who shoot people. They're dedicated scientists." Wade remained silent.

"Let's hope so, Sally," Matt said. "But there's something we didn't tell you. We discovered BenaTex's financial future might not be too bright." He told them what Cindi had found.

"Oh my God. You're saying they did this to secure the company?"

Wade stood and went into the kitchen, where he poured a glass of Burgundy and then returned to the conversation.

"I'm only saying it's possible, Sally. Where do you draw the line when a company and its people are hanging in the balance?"

Sally left the fireplace unattended to sit on the couch by Wade. She sipped her wine. "Regardless, you and Allyx don't know them. I'm convinced an outsider is running the show. It can't be Ben or Nathan. I'll never believe that of them." She looked to Wade for reassurance and he tried to give her an encouraging smile, but knew he wasn't very convincing.

"They can't be involved." Sally shook her head.

"People change," Allyx said. "Money, power, desperation: these are the essential ingredients for breaking even the strongest, and BenaTex faced them all."

"You don't understand. Ben and Nathan are good people. I can't see them ever crossing the line without being pushed."

Matt moved to the window and stood by Allyx. "Okay, Sally. Say someone else does exist. Unless we suddenly get more help, we won't ever know who."

"A depressing prospect," Wade acknowledged their point. Noticing how protective Matt was of Allyx, he moved closer to Sally. "Matt, you and Allyx said Dr. Ruhpor's testing focused on a limited range of conditions. If I consider your information in light of what I collected at BenaTex, I'd say the virus is related to medical genetics." Wade pondered potential applications for a new retrovirus, keeping his military theories to himself. He swirled his wine and sniffed the air above the glass, inhaling the subtle woodsy aroma while watching the thick liquid legs flow down the sides. A brief distraction. Still, he needed to know who had contracted the work.

Perplexed looks passed between Matt and Allyx. "Medical genetics," Matt repeated. "Why does that strike a chord with me?"

"Damn it, Matt. Dr. Ruhpor wanted us to research naturally occurring viruses capable of attacking the human immune system. Is BenaTex researching such a virus?"

"Or creating one." Wade cocked his head, and Matt looked questioningly at him, but kept his opinions to himself. For the longest two minutes Wade had ever experienced, the room remained quiet. No one spoke as they sorted through their own theories.

"I'll have that wine now," Allyx said, breaking the silence.

Wade started to get up and Sally placed a hand on his forearm. "You sit. I'll get it." She went to the kitchen and grabbed an open bottle from a wine rack next to the refrigerator and another glass off the counter. "If the three of you are right, what pharmaceutical value is there in creating a virus that attacks the immune system?"

"Another good question," Wade said. "I have a contact and she might have answers." He reached for the telephone.

"It's probably not safe to call from here." Matt gave him a questioning glance.

"I see your point."

"Matt, would you care for some?" Sally poured the wine and handed a glass to Allyx.

"No, thank you."

She set the bottle on the coffee table. "The grocery store has a phone. I've used it before."

"Sound okay to everyone?" Wade asked. They looked at each other and nodded. "Then it's settled, I'll call from the store."

"Do it now. We don't have long." Sally cradled her wine glass with both hands. "Cooper said the project was almost finished."

2:14 p.m.—A Bluff Overlooking Malibu, California

Kendall Jones wiped clean a circular patch on the fogged front windshield and peered over the bluff at the street below. Twenty minutes earlier, it had been impossible to see the road much less the house through the heavy rain. "Nothin' much happening. Still a wet-ass mutha." He reclined on the wraparound leather bucket seat and took a chug of his lukewarm Heineken.

"This rain sucks." Tony Lister glanced through his side window. "Can't see shit. Whatta you say we—"

"Ah, shut up and chill, man. They're paying us heavy bucks to sit here and do nothin' but watch the house. Look what we got, man. We're hangin' in a sleek Mercedes sluggin' high dollar beer. Beats suckin' down buck-fifty wine in your old Buick any night."

"Yeah, up yours." Tony unzipped his black leather jacket. "I like my ride, and I'm still friggin' bored."

"Check that thermal sensor thing. It'll give you somethin' to do." Kendall took another drink of his beer. "Do all the floors."

"Off my case, asshole. It's not like I haven't done this before. 'Bout twenty times in the last hour." Tony flipped his Raider's baseball cap on backwards and rolled down the window. He aimed the electronic device at the beach house, then punched the read button. "We've got four warm bodies. All of 'em downstairs."

Beer foam clung to Kendall's bushy mustache. He swiped it away with his flannel shirtsleeve. "I'm hungry. Give me the chips. Anythin' on the sound mike?"

"Crap, man, all the rain's still messing with it." Kendall shoved a handful of chips into his mouth. "And if you keep eating like that, you'll be a fat-ass mutha before this job's done."

"You keep dissin' me, Tony the weenie, and we're gonna have trouble."

"In your dreams."

"Just shut up and watch the house. It could be worse."

"How?"

"Least we won't be bangin' soggy, street whores tonight." Kendall hit the electric switch and the leather bucket seat tilted back. "That's betta'." He reached over and increased the bass volume on the car stereo while listening to his favorite Gangsta Rapper, Master P, tapping to the beat with one hand against the dashboard.

"You're just a lazy mutha', Kendall. Smokin' a little bud and bangin' a horny whore sounds more fun than this shit."

Kendall set his beer in the center console's drink holder. "Don't show me attitude, man." He rubbed the side of his cheek and smiled. "Tell you what. We can do some cards. Got any loose green?"

"None you can get." Tony showed him a bundle of crumpled bills that had been buried in his baggies' front pocket.

"Bring it on, brotha'." The whites of Kendall's eyes grew wider at the sight of Tony's wad of cash. "I'd love to lift a chunk of your green leaf."

"Not the way you play."

5:18 p.m.—Amazon Lowlands, Brazil

Before the first canoe had stopped moving, James Monal and the natives jumped onto the narrow, mud beach and began blazing a trail into the jungle. They hacked a path with their razor-sharp machetes through the thick green stalks of the *Gleicheniaceae* ferns blanketing the overgrown shoreline. Behind them, the boats were hauled from the water and unloaded by the rest of the archaeological team.

The Amazon sun set a half-hour into their activities, and James took a brief respite to inspect the progress. Their efforts had begun to show the signs of a real base camp. The location Ernesto had chosen was a safe distance away from the river and downwind of any game trails. He had organized the camp to provide distinct functional areas. Their communications equipment was set up in a corner with a view of the Amazon's equatorial sky. Food provisions were placed in a remote spot and stored inside animal-proof containers. Sleeping quarters were aligned in a half circle around the main conference tent. Laboratory supplies were housed in an open-air shelter at the far end of the camp. INN's news crew had their own domain nestled closest to the river.

James was pleased to see how efficiently things were coming together.

Like James, the others had also been engrossed in the camp's organization. Dr. MacKiernan readied his tent to double as a field hospital equipped to handle minor accidents. Though severe injuries on these trips were rare, it was still always wise to be cautious. If necessary, he could stabilize and prep serious trauma cases, then evacuate them via a helicopter summoned from Manaus. A downscaled mobile version of the base camp's hospital would be used on trips into the interior.

Dr. Isling finalized the sample collection and tracking system with Dr. Saleman. The success of the expedition depended on maintaining well-documented physical archaeological evidence. Dr. Isling was a stickler for detailed records, requiring all samples to be photographed, catalogued, and preserved. The professor's fastidiousness had evolved the hard way, through experience with inadequate procedures on previous archaeological expeditions.

Urban legends and hallway rumors aside, an indoctrination into the archaeological sciences via Dr. Isling's tender care was always an eye-opener. James remembered his initial taste of Stanford's Archaeology Field Procedures, and the subsequent pounding he had received during his first expedition with Dr. Isling.

The professor drilled him, requiring meticulous notes on even the smallest of details—in duplicate wherever possible. Only when James had acquired the skills to adequately record his own work, based on the professor's stringent standards, did the lessons covering storage and preservation begin. At the time, James hated the experience. More recently, he appreciated his ability to catalog irrefutable evidence in support of his archaeological theories. Dr. Isling had given him a gift that would last a professional lifetime. A gift he hoped to someday repay.

James basked in the enthusiasm of the camp's activities while on his way to join Dr. Utesha outside her tent. He found her mulling over a pile of aerial photographs and topographic maps. "See here, James." She pointed to a photograph's northwest quadrant. "The vegetation shows signs of new growth."

"Are those bamboo plants?" he asked.

"Good eyes. Bamboo isn't very competitive in this environment, which makes it a reliable indicator of a stage change within the indigenous plant species. The only thing that could cause this drastic of a vegetative shift would be rapid defoliation of the native plants by humans. Thermal imaging also shows unusual temperature shifts at that location. I'm confident we have our first Burbános contact site."

"Based on what you've found, Dr. Utesha, I suggest we start our probe here in the southeast and then move northeast." He pointed and drug his fingertip across the photo showing her the route.

"Will that fit the pattern you and Dr. Isling developed?"

"I don't see why not. If we move inland from our current location," James pointed, "for about three miles, that should put us in the center of the search grid. We can set up a temporary camp there. The second site will support us on extended treks into the rain forest. As the search for the Burbános widens, the interior camp will be relocated to provide whatever aid is necessary, a kind of mobile supply station."

"Works for me." Dr. Utesha pointed to a rock outcrop identified in the southeast quadrant of the photograph. "Using this ground reference gives us a familiar origin for each trip inland. We can sweep the region using 500-yard arcs radiating outwardly from this central point. Do you concur? And, James, shed the formalities. My name is Myrta."

He held up each photograph in succession, using the light of a gas lantern to see specific details. "Okay, Myrta.

The infrareds show a tract where the vegetation was impacted. When the same section's viewed in black-and-white, unnatural angular shadow-lines appear among the foliage. Could be manmade."

"Good eye, again. Agreed."

"The color photographs document a high percentage of new growth, which I'd guess was a shift in the ecosystem's stage development. With all of these clues, I suggest we start—" A video camera appeared out of nowhere, jarring James. "Uh, uh . . ."

"I'm not disturbing you, am I?" Kelly asked. "We're collecting more background footage. Life in the campsite stuff."

"Uh, yes, I mean no," James said. "We're reviewing our search pattern for tomorrow—"

"James, over here," Dr. Isling called.

"Oh, too bad, Kelly, I've been summoned. I'm sure Myrta, Dr. Utesha, would love to be photographed."

Myrta's eyes widened and her lips scrunched together.

"Sorry, guys. Gotta go, a higher duty calls." James smiled sheepishly, suppressing a smirk, and trotted over to Dr. Isling. "Yes, sir."

"Hope I didn't interrupt anything." He eyed his assistant.

"Of course not. No, sir."

"Good, then. I need you to take care of the communications gear. Ernesto has everything ready." Dr. Isling spun around and left before James could answer.

Seemingly no longer angry, the professor was still growing moodier by the day. James had hoped once they were deep into the fieldwork, Dr. Isling would get back to his old self, but as of yet, that hadn't been the case. One minute he barked orders and took charge, then an imperceptible switch occurred and his actions became almost irrational. James decided to speak with Aidan, maybe he had noticed the professor's unusual behavior.

"Ernesto." James waved and met the guide in the center of the camp. "Dr. Isling wants me to try the communications equipment. Why don't you show me how far you've gotten?"

"Yes, señor. I will show you." Ernesto tuned their portable 18-inch satellite dish to track along an equatorial arc. He had already cut down the vegetation, giving the device a full 90-degree view of the sky.

"Excellent job." James patted Ernesto on the back. He then put the electronics through an operational precheck. The system was designed to leave messages that could be picked up on the receiving end whenever convenient. As a favor before leaving school, an electronics hacker friend of James' modified the device and gave them an option for interactive communications. The equipment was state-of-the-art and conditioned to handle the tropics. It performed with the smoothness of a vintage Rolls Royce on a flat stretch of road.

Within minutes, James had Dr. Leland piped into the camp. How ironic, the enticement that drew many archaeologists to their work was the solitude, and thanks to satellite technology, that same privacy was becoming a lost luxury. With a strong battery and the flip of a switch, James could harass someone from the heart of the Amazon. Pretty cool when he thought about it.

"Hi, Dr. Leland. I hope North America is running smoothly without us."

"As well as could be expected. It's good to see you in the flesh, James, so to speak."

"Thanks, you too. I'll get Dr. Isling and tell him the SATCOM is—"

"I'm right here, James." Dr. Isling stepped in front of the video monitor. "Hello, George. It's nice to see you're in."

"Your tone says it all, Henry, you're not pleased. Let me guess; the news crew?"

"What gave you the right to saddle this expedition with them? I am a scientist, not a tabloid wet nurse!"

"Calm down, Henry. A little positive publicity will help both you and the department. I know you'll do your best to get along. Be nice, INN is footing the bill for the expedition."

Dr. Isling removed his glasses and wiped them with his shirttail. "All right, George, I'll be the congenial host. But I'm telling you, don't ever pull a stunt like this again." He abruptly left without further comment.

"He's not very happy, Dr. Leland."

"That's his problem, James, not yours. Just help him where you can and stay in touch."

"I will, sir. I'll update you in a couple of days." James switched the transmitter to standby. "Ernesto."

"Yes, señor."

"You did a great job." James surveyed the camp. "Will we be ready to hit the trail by first light tomorrow?"

Their guide removed his hat and rubbed his forehead with a red bandana. "Si, everything will be ready."

James looked in the vicinity of Myrta's tent. "I'll get the maps and we can review the logistics."

"That will be fine, señor. I will speak to my men, then meet you in a few minutes." Ernesto disappeared among the tents and supplies.

As James stood alone on the edge of the campsite, he hoped Dr. Isling would come to terms with the news crew once they were on the move—unlikely, he concluded. When the professor made up his mind, he rarely reconsiders his position. That same stubbornness made him a top-notch investigator, and it also contributed to his reclusive tendencies. He looked toward Kelly and her cameraman. If nothing else, James surmised, this expedition might become one of the most entertaining.

4:23 p.m.—Houston, Texas

For numerical modeling purposes, Greg Gunder had

fine-tuned his virtual human population to be theoretically disassociated from mainstream society. He manipulated physical, chemical, and biological boundaries, thereby narrowing potentially available transport pathways. Creating, then exploiting these theoretical factors slowed and controlled the spread of the virus.

His client-directed requirements were another twist that shifted Greg's efforts in a direction opposite from standard virus promulgation analysis. The project related specifics explicitly stated that the carrier had to be human, and the transmission pathway was limited to casual contact. Which begs the question, how do the infected humans get the disease in the first place? There was also an ethnicity component, similar to that of the SARS virus. A possible animal source?

Down through history, major plagues and communicable diseases had often been transported by living organisms—animals. Rats and mice have always been common carriers. In many cases, their fecal droppings and bodily parasites proved more deadly to humans than a direct bite or scratch. Other animals such as monkeys, birds, and, to an extent, domesticated pets have also served as disease vectors. The eventual eradication of these biological vectors required blocking their proliferation using natural barriers—interesting that there were no such criteria on this project.

Considering his client's viral transmission-specific criteria, Greg chose single males in their early thirties and forties, successful businessmen who wanted their sexual activities kept private. Their choices of intimate encounters were discreet and limited. In addition to being small, in relative numbers, when compared to the mainstream population, their special lifestyle slowed the initial spread of a blood-borne disease.

The difficulty Greg faced wasn't with the functionality of his control group, it was with the sensitivity calibration of the model. He had to statistically relate virility to cell function, then propagate that relationship using the probability of a random encounter. Easier said than done, he suspected. One advantage Greg had, was the data describing the virus' physical properties were extremely detailed—unusually so.

Previous projects had relied upon esoteric assumptions, essentially educated guesses, since data were scarce for many viruses. Besides, he mused, if medical science knew everything relating to a particular disease, no one would need his unique services. With that novel thought in mind, it again struck him as odd that this particular virus came so well documented.

Those portions of data he had already modeled showed this retrovirus took less than twenty-four months before it moved into the general population. It started slow, having an average host dormancy of roughly six months. Once it became pervasive within his target community, it made the jump to the mainstream. From then on, the proliferation of the virus accelerated, as it was no longer restricted by the host's lifestyle.

Not a bad beginning, Greg concluded while reviewing the modeling results on his computer screen and folding his arms across his chest. He would finish the analysis of his last run and do the writeup in a day or two. This was easier than he had calculated, primarily because the unknowns were few. Someone, it seems, had tailored this project with a goal in mind.

Greg shut down the computer and swiveled side-to-side in his executive-tucked leather chair, pondering the most recent modeling results. Something didn't feel right. After doing this type of programming for so many years, six in college and almost four as a paid professional, he had gained an intuitive sense for these things. He closed his eyes and visualized the virus making its way through his hypothetical world, marveling at how well adapted it was for its mission—maybe too much so. What was its real purpose? A casual check into the origin of this assignment seemed appropriate.

He opened his eyes and grabbed his electronic Rolodex. A quick search and Greg found the name he sought, then dialed long distance.

A woman answered, "Yes."

"This is Gunder. I have a project with anomalous characteristics."

"I'm listening."

5:34 p.m.—New York, New York

Claire Brown sat alone in her third floor corner office, cynically reviewing the day's action on Wall Street. The pharmaceuticals had been the most prolific bull market gainer of the previous six months. Next to municipal solid waste and insurance, pharmaceuticals were the third largest service provider—a hard cash moneymaker, in the United States.

Prescription health medication raked in one hundred and five-billion dollars over the last decade and had maintained an impressive annual growth rate of eighteen percent. In today's fast moving marketplace, a single medical breakthrough could generate millions of dollars in sales, and even the hint of such an opportunity made financial strategists dance on their toes. A new drug discovery could send a pharmaceutical company's stock value skyrocketing; even the possibility of such an occurrence fueled fierce competition for advanced drug technology. Claire remembered the frenzied buying on the Street when Viagra hit the news; that was one hell of a ride. And then there was always the murkier side of medical profiteering, like the time, shortly after the September 11, 2001, terrorist attack on the Twin Towers when the anthrax scare prompted a massive increase in the production of Cipro—another monetary boon for the industry.

As Janstone Pharmaceuticals' main liaison with Wall Street, Claire worked the financial community to maintain the company's aboveboard image and mediate unwanted shifts in their stock value. Too often, the Street's perception directed a company's fiscal value, and it was her job to ensure they had the proper view of things. If the world's financial gurus assumed her company had a solid management team, stock values could rise significantly—despite earnings and roller-coaster rides such as during the Viagra scramble.

A few powerful companies swayed Wall Street's judgment with financial sleight-of-hand and lots of well-placed dollars. These corporate giants held millions in unidentified reserves. They funneled those funds into the market using umbrella accounts, where they acquired and liquidated stock holdings at will. Powerful executives orchestrated each maneuver to create artificial opportunities to expand their portfolios and increase their interests in emergent companies. Many of these same professionals occupied Board seats on multiple corporations, helping them sway the actions of their elusive competitors.

Even in this game of mega-deals and financial treachery, Claire knew the subtle difference between the actual and inferred rules. The stakes were high and the downside deadly. Jail, suicide, even murder was a distinct possibility; just look what happened at Enron. The thought of Enron and Global Crossing chilled her to the bone.

Company representatives should not intentionally lie to the Street and only a certain percentage of their stock could be bought or sold at any time. All senior executive transactions, which could affect stock value, had to be completed no later than two weeks prior to circulating company news. These rules provided the public with a certain level of comfort, suggesting everyone operated on an even field. Of course, things were not always what they seemed.

Claire flipped through a stack of business cards. Her network of confidants included critical contacts within the pharmaceutical industry and the financial world. This intricate web placed her in the pleasurable position of identifying critical stock trades before anyone else. Claire's high profile and profitable business success also made her vulnerable to government scrutiny and management oversight, both of which kept her very busy.

A devious thought materialized. Whom would she rescue from a sinking ship: a stockbroker, an insurance salesman, a lawyer, or a convicted felon? A tough decision. Even if she altered their identities, once a rat always a rat. Her private e-mail flashed—no major life saving decisions today. She clicked the icon and opened the encrypted file.

"Hi, dearest. I wanted to tell you the big guy is going to make a move. He's got some scheme in the mill, and no one's talking. Nothing definite as of yet on the timing. I'd say he'll solidify his position within the month. He's under stockholder pressure to meet the current budget and will have to pull a miracle out of his sock. Or knowing him, as I do, somewhere else. He's going to bump the company's new rising, corporate stars—it's a control thing—and replace them with his own. When this happens, the Street will experience a fiscal burp. Take care. We'll do lunch."

"Thanks. I owe you one." Claire fired off a reply, then closed and deleted the message as she considered possible financial manipulations. If a new treatment was made public, strategic stock movements might maximize profits, both hers and the company's. Janstone's retirement plan was widely distributed between blue chips and mutual funds. With the correct timing, those investments could be redistributed, but there were other things to consider. Steele's first action would drive the value of Janstone's stock down, and before he did, Claire had to measure the prevailing winds with her sources.

She pressed the rapid-dial memory button on her phone. A woman answered. "This is Claire. You were right. He's reshaping the company's mid-level managers with his own people to make a power move. . . . No, I'm not sure what he's after. My contact said he was consolidating his troops for a big move. This could be a major cash deal when it all washes out. . . . Yes, I've known her for years and I trust her judgment completely. . . . You take care too, and I'll stay in touch."

Claire set the telephone receiver down. She had just gone outside the company with sensitive corporate information. Besides being fired, a jail term was a definite possibility. Her single consolation was that her contact was a good person, and good people did good things. If this went bad, that last sentiment would make a nice epitaph for the walls of her cell. But she didn't care for Jolon Steele and his power plays. In her opinion, he had trampled on too many people during his presidential tenure with Janstone Pharmaceuticals. The time had come to put him down.

8:21 p.m.—Amazon Lowlands, Brazil

They finished the base camp and the team settled in for the night. James Monal sensed the group's eager anticipation of tomorrow's trek inland. He too felt the excitement and sleep was impossible. During his work with Myrta, she had pinpointed a promising spot for a first contact with the Burbános, which he took as a mixed blessing. No one knew what to expect. His imagination ran on adrenalin as he crossed the camp, casually reviewing the final preparations and appearing very businesslike.

He stopped at a solitary tent. Diffused light of a gas lantern radiated above a small folding table.

The night air had cooled to a comfortable temperature, and the irritating bugs that thrived within the jungle during the day had secreted themselves away.

"Hi," he said. "A 'welcome to the team' gift."

Apparently unsurprised by his visit, Kelly smiled and remained seated in her folding chair. "For me?"

"An orchid." Kelly Karrie had recently bathed using their portable shower bag, and James smelled the fresh aroma of soap lingering on her creamy white skin. She seemed to glow in the light of the lantern.

"James, it's a velvety yellow angel."

A blush overcame him; luckily, the poor light hid his awkwardness. "Fenmar said, *Oncidium concolor* to be precise." How sensitive, James thought. What other words of romance would soon dribble from his eloquent tongue? If she were an ancient Maya, he'd know what to say. Too bad he wasn't his brother; Matt would know what to do with a beautiful woman.

"Academics. They're all the same. Well, I think it's lovely."

"Thank you, I think?"

"Please sit." Kelly pointed to a second folding chair, then tucked the delicate orchid behind her right ear, in the age-old Hawaiian fashion.

James took the folding chair and opened it. "Dr. Isling's been tough on you, and he . . . I wanted you to understand we weren't all that bad. I . . . he doesn't—"

"It's not your fault we started on rough ground. I was just in a mood. I call it travel PMS. Once you get to know me, it passes quickly."

He squirmed stiffly on the small chair; his long legs seemed to get in the way. Being an introverted field rat made it difficult for him to relax around women, especially one so beautiful, and so forward. The advantage of digging up fossils was he did not have to be particularly debonair or talkative, and Kelly's celebrity status just added to his awkwardness. She sat too close. His heart began to palpitate. "Dr. Isling's a good man. He has a lot riding on this expedition."

"I understand and I'll support him wherever I can. Besides, I'm looking forward to our Mayan adventure."

"Ouch, don't let Dr. Isling hear you say that."

"What? I thought—"

"I'm . . . sorry." His eyes glanced down at the ground. "What I meant was, don't use the term 'Mayan' around him."

"Why?"

"It, uh, well . . . it's an irritant. Kind of derogatory." James shuffled his feet in front of the chair, almost tipping himself over. He glanced up. She hadn't noticed. "There's no such thing as a Mayan. Just like there's no such people as the Apachans, only the Apaches. The proper use of Mayan is applicable when referring to their language. Everything else is Maya. Dr. Isling considers the term Mayan to be an insult to the Maya and a sign of ignorance. Not that you're—"

"Don't worry." She showed him a sensitive smile. "Thanks for the advice and I'll be more careful of what I say in the future. I still have a lot to learn."

"I'll help."

She smiled again, her lips full and sensual. "Thank you, James."

Her eyes were seductive blue pools, and James found himself drowning in their translucent current. "My pleasure . . . I meant, I'm glad I could be of . . ."

"It's okay, James. Relax a little."

"Miss Karrie—"

"Call me Kelly."

James hesitated. "Kelly, the jungle's a rough place and if there's anything else I can do for you, please ask."

"You'll be the first one I'll think of."

"Uh, well, yes, uh, thanks. We'll be up early. You

should get some rest."

"I will." Kelly stood and paused at the entrance to her tent. Her shapely figure was backlit by the gas lantern. The warm glow made its way through her shirt, silhouetting her full breasts and tiny waist. Embarrassed, James looked away.

"I'll see you in the morning, James."

His heart sputtered. "Goo . . . Good night." He stood, almost tripped over the chair, spun and bumped into Aidan, who was wearing a devilish grin.

"She likes you."

"Miss Karrie was only being polite." James reflected on their conversation.

"Sure, right, whatever."

"Aidan, you're a dirty old man."

"I know."

"I can't talk to you." James stomped away, stopping when he reached his own quarters. Before he ducked in, his gaze swept the encampment, including a lingering assessment of Kelly's tent. Was Aidan right? Was she interested?

5:23 p.m.—A Bluff Overlooking Malibu, California

Kendall Jones scooped up the cards and grabbed his leather jacket off the backseat. "Poker's over, man."

"Whatta sayin'?" Tony complained. "You got fifty bucks of mine."

As Kendall slipped into his jacket, he pointed. "Our squirrels are on the move."

"Damn. Right when I get a good hand. Figures." Tony threw on his matching jacket. The one with their neighborhood logo, a hawk with blood dripping from its talons, embroidered on the back.

"Quit bitchin' or you'll miss 'em."

"I want a shot at getting my money back." Tony stuffed what was left of his cash into his pocket.

"If you're lucky. Here're the keys to the other car."

Tony poked his head outside. Raindrops showered his face. He slammed the door closed. "Rain, rain, more fucking rain." He looked again. "Shit, it's pouring."

"Get goin'." Kendall shoved Tony into the side door.

"Cool it, man. I hate the damn rain. I always have to go. Why don't you? Shit, man, I can watch the house."

"Ya wimp ass mutha. We don't have time for this whiny crap. I'll go this time, but you'd betta' watch the house close like or Osborne's gonna be pissed."

Kendall grabbed the keys and pushed the car door open. His new Air Bud high-tops landed in a puddle on the roadway. He slammed the door shut and grumbled. Pulling his jacket up above his ears, he climbed into their backup vehicle—a '96 Chevy Lumina. He felt like a soccer mom.

"That shit Tony owes me big time. This is degradin'."

5:25 p.m.—Sausalito, California

Ben Singular slapped Nathan Donner on the back, then inhaled the crisp evening air, savoring its salty taste. In the waning light of dusk, the surface of the San Francisco Bay looked calm and reflected a turquoise sheen he had never noticed before. Ben accepted the view as a sign of good things to come. "Nathan, if nothing else, it's great to be out from under Steele's thumb. He has what he wants and we're free to pursue our own research."

Nathan grimaced. "I've aged ten years on this project."

"I know how you feel, buddy. Are you up for a good dinner? We can swing by the Tempura Palace and unwind."

"Sounds cool to me. I know how you like Japanese. A

fitting feast for the victorious genetic warriors."

"A philosopher you're not, Nathan. I'll drive. That beat-up corvette of yours isn't fit for human transport."

"Hey, my car has style, unlike your imported piece of yuppie junk." Nathan stuck his nose into the air in mock snobbery.

"You're just jealous."

"Hardly."

They sauntered along the sidewalk in front of the parking garage.

"It's been a long eighteen months," Nathan said. "For a while, I was certain we weren't going to make it."

"Things did get wild." Ben gave Nathan a skeptical frown. "But the viral secrets we uncovered made the trip worth the pain. Come on, Nathan, you enjoyed the challenge."

"Maybe."

"Come on." Ben smirked. "The truth—a puzzle you couldn't resist."

"All right, I admit I was intrigued. The design scenario was an unusual mental exercise." Nathan slowed by a planter, reached up and tore a yellowing leaf off a Ficus tree. He appraised its symmetry. "God's creations are ours to manipulate." He laughed. "You and I are the only ones in the world to have recoded a retrovirus. It's bloody amazing." Nathan seemed to grow taller. "At least now we can apply the data to our medical projects."

Ben grabbed Nathan by the arm, leading him into the parking garage. "This way my exuberant friend, or you'll be hitchhiking to the restaurant." They rounded the corner and followed the entrance ramp, laughing and jabbing at each other like college kids.

"It's gonna be a richly raw night, beaming with costly spirits." Ben smiled and climbed into his car. "I'll medicate my ulcer tomorrow. Who knows, I might even get home early enough to hug the kids and make love to my wife."

"Careful, they might not recognize you."

"Huh, very funny." Ben nestled into the formfitted bucket seat. "I love this car. Nothing like the smell of quality leather upholstery."

"Stinks like gasoline to me."

"Knew it." He laughed. "You're jealous, Mr. Donner." Ben inserted the key into the ignition, cocked his head and faced his partner. "Nathan, thanks for your help. I never could have pulled this project off without you."

"No problem."

"Just like the old days, huh, buddy."

"You bet."

"Oh, and Nathan."

"Yeah."

"I have some news for you. Something I've wanted to tell you for a long time."

"What's that?"

"I have a son."

"What do you mean? 'You have a son.' "

"It's a long story. One that will soon have a happy ending." Ben held the BMW's steering wheel with his left hand and twisted the ignition key with his right. He stopped when he heard a click. "No!"

6:26 p.m.—Malibu, California

Wade Fields sank into the padded wicker chair. Resting comfortably on the thick cushions, he released an exhausted sigh as Sally handed him a cup of hot tea. "The call to my contact's been made," Wade said. "I had to leave a message. I'll check in tomorrow at one forty-five, but don't worry, the wheels have been put into motion. She'll take care of us."

Matt and Allyx sat next to the stone fireplace, opposite Wade. Oak logs crackled as the fire spread. "Run into any problems?" Matt asked.

"No, it went smoothly." Wade shrugged. "I didn't see anyone suspicious lurking in the shadows, if that's what you mean."

"These people are pros. Odds are we'll never see them."

Wade assumed Matt hadn't intended on sounding negative, just cautious. Los Angeles was a big place, and they were safely hidden away at the beach house. "Have a positive attitude, Matt. We were careful. Sally kept watch and I made the call."

"Sorry, Wade." Matt shrugged. "After all that's happened, we're a little paranoid."

"You don't have to explain." Wade massaged his shoulder. "I can relate."

Sally left the kitchen carrying an armful of white containers. "Excuse me, gentlemen. Worrying isn't going to help, but eating will. We got takeout. I hope everyone likes Chinese."

Allyx stood and helped Sally with the food. "Leave it to an intelligent woman to know what's really important. It smells delicious. Thanks."

Matt grimaced at her offhanded gender dig while he helped set plates and utensils on the living room's wicker coffee table.

"Sally, how long have you been with BenaTex?" Allyx passed her a container heaped with rice.

"Six years."

"With all you've been through, it must be difficult." Allyx placed her hand on Sally's arm and watched her form a weak smile.

"Haven't faced it yet. Things happened too quickly."

"I know how you feel. If there's anything we can do, we're here to help." Allyx caught a glimpse of Matt staring at Sally, and then her.

"Uhm," Wade interrupted. "The food is great." He watched Sally rearrange her Mongolian beef, in the same way she had her potato salad that day they talked in the

BenaTex lunchroom. This ordeal had been a heart-rending ride, sending a demoralizing signal of how fragile their lives were. Wade prayed that somehow they'd get out of this mess.

"Matt and Allyx, whenever you're tired, you'll find two bedrooms upstairs on the second floor." Sally set a log onto the fire. "They're yours for the choosing. The second room at the top of the stairs on your left has a beautiful balcony overlooking the Pacific. You'll find linens in the hall closet next to the bathroom." She motioned toward the stairs with a wave of her hand.

"Thanks for everything," Matt said. He stretched, yawned, and looked toward the stairs. "It's been a long few days, and I'm beat."

Allyx scrunched her lips together.

October 13

6:58 a.m.—Amazon Lowlands, Brazil

A machete sliced through the air, dropping another chunk of green overgrowth to the wet ground. The native guides worked as an alternating team, hacking a path for the others. Each person in the scattered line toted a daypack and flailed a machete, helping clear the way.

The expedition had departed the base camp when sufficient light penetrated the jungle canopy, a half-hour after sunrise and James Monal didn't expect to set any distance records their first day out. Spectacular sights and grueling temperatures made it easy for the team to get mentally distracted, which in turn, slowed their progress. He slapped a multi-legged insect, squishing the bug against his hip pocket. The morning air was moist and heavy.

Sunlight struggled through the thick overhead foliage. A trail of leaf-cutter ants crossed the narrow footpath carrying green chips and moss scrapings. A troop of black-faced Howler monkeys screamed their threatening roars in the trees above, sending a shudder down his spine. James listened to warbling finches sing their flutelike squeals, only to be drowned by the rumbling cry of a Hyacinthine Macaw. The jungle was alive, thriving beyond its restrictive primeval tree barrier, entangled vines, and bloodthirsty insects—a sensory extravaganza.

Everyone seemed overwhelmed by the saturated colors and rich plant fragrances. As strange new organisms bloomed around the team, their movements became more animated and playful. A fascinating change, considering the introspective mood James had observed while on the river. The heavily oxygenated air had obviously raised the group's consciousness, gaining them a new appreciation for the vast world they had entered.

The more distance they put between themselves and the base camp, the denser the overhead foliage became as it fragmented the sun's rays into individual beams of light. Nearly eight yards above the ground, the green layer was composed of medium-sized trees and broadleaf shrubs. An intermediate canopy, ten yards taller, dwarfed the first with its towering hardwoods. James knew a third and final canopy existed more than forty yards above the second, fifty-eight yards above the floor, and he wished he could catch a glimpse of it through the other two; undoubtedly a magnificent sight.

Barely an hour into their journey, the rains began. The torrential downpour lasted only a few minutes, drenching everything in sight. Soaking wet clothes stuck to their bodies tighter than an outer skin. Steam rose into the air, forming an ethereal shroud above the vegetation. Complete silence followed the rain, and then in a sudden flurry, the animal screams and hoots returned.

Taking advantage of a rare break in the forest canopy, James switched on his handheld GPS and locked onto four satellites. He read the triangulated ground coordinates and marked their respective location with a blue dot on his map. Orienting themselves without the aid of his satellite positioning equipment would be nearly impossible, and it was important to be accurate. They had to arrive at the interior camp before nightfall. The Amazon was even less hospitable after sunset. Based on this latest reading, James was confident they would reach their destination within plenty of time.

Aidan nudged James on the shoulder. "How's it feel to be on the move?"

"Good. I'd have gone nuts if we spent another day at the mission."

"Me too." Aidan laughed. "It's also helping Henry. He's in a much better mood. Even the news people aren't irritating him."

"Personally," James laughed, "he's getting a kick out of watching Kelly struggle without her curling iron. But I'm glad he's not riding her anymore. I was getting worried about them. Besides, she's okay, once you get to know her."

"Why, James, you like the girl."

He fought a blush. "I'm just being nice."

"If you say so." Aidan pushed on before James could refute the accusation.

James shook his head and continued down the trail. A hopeful smile formed as he thought of Kelly.

7:22 a.m.—Los Angeles, California

Naomi Giles lounged on her favorite Elisabetta Bagliani easy chair tucked away in her private study and watched the business report with a dispassionate stare. An electronic ticker rolled the latest Wall Street numbers in the background above Connie Cox's head. Ms. Cox faced the camera and described the latest market action.

"This morning Janstone Pharmaceuticals announced their earnings fell short of analysts' predictions. The news stalled an early Wall Street rally. Janstone's Corporate President, Jolon Steele, stated increased competition within the global pharmaceutical market has cut into their profit margin, causing the company to shift its business focus. When questioned regarding restructuring, Steele confirmed it was a possibility."

The screen view split as a new window appeared above Ms. Cox. A man in a light gray suit stood at the foot of the New York Stock exchange's stone steps. The field correspondent placed a hand on his earpiece. "Yes, Connie, the mood on the Street is apprehensive. Janstone has been a leading indicator stock for the last decade. If they don't meet expectations, the rest of the pharmaceuticals could follow suit. Currently, they're trading down five points, or about three percent."

"Thank you, Michael." Connie Cox shifted her view to straight ahead. "On to other business issues, the Dow Industrials . . ."

Giles pressed the channel button on the remote and the television screen switched to the INN world health report.

"A killer virus is again making news today," John Bonner announced. "Emergency health services have been powerless to stop its spread and lessen its deadly human toll." The newscaster adjusted his position as the view of a dry African prairie appeared in the upper right corner. "Eight days after a chilling outbreak of Ebola was first detected, zombie-like people can still be seen wandering aimlessly in portions of southern Zaire. Hundreds have already perished from the dreaded disease, and experts estimate that the death toll could reach the thousands before the medical community can contain the situation. For an on-location update, we now take you to Paul Hoaglare in Zaire. Hello, Paul, can you give us the latest?"

In the center of a desolate, native African village stood a thin man, wearing khaki bush clothing. "Yes, John. The Red Cross and the Centers for Disease Control consider this a new strain of the Ebola filovirus. Symptoms are classic, including skin lesions and bleeding from the mouth and eyes."

The scene behind Hoaglare panned to a rudimentary field hospital set up beneath a brown canvas tent. "Facilities in this part of Zaire are very limited and the Red Cross is finding it difficult to assess the extent of the impact. A group sent in by the CDC is providing technical assistance." The camera zoomed in on a stretchered body being carried into the hospital tent. A hand, covered with red lesions, dangled over the edge.

"Paul, what is being done to combat the outbreak?"

"Right now, a re-engineered batch of convalescent plasma serum is being administered to the afflicted people. This serum is a major breakthrough, effectively treating the disease at any stage. The most serious limitation the Red Cross has had is the serum's availability."

The correspondent motioned toward the hospital tent. "In the interim, and since one o'clock local time this morning, military patrols have been scouring the countryside for victims. Ambulatory patients are taken to the field hospital, while the dead are collected and burned. The government of Zaire hopes to identify the extent of the impact, then implement a total isolation of the outbreak within the next twelve hours. The current quarantine radius extends fifty miles beyond the village behind me."

A map of Zaire with a red dot and a circle showing the village and quarantine location appeared to the right of the newscaster. "Thank you, Paul, for that report. We now take you to our in-house virology expert, Dr. Stephano Hermani, in Los Angeles, California." A split-screen, live video of a tanned man in his early fifties was positioned next to the newscaster and opposite the map of Zaire. "Dr. Hermani."

"Good morning, John."

"Good morning, doctor. Is it true that Ebola Zaire is fast acting?"

"Relative to other such viruses, that is correct. Death commonly occurs between fifteen and twenty days after contracting the disease. Although, this recent outbreak may be a new variant."

"What is this plasma serum Paul mentioned?"

"Less than a week ago, the FDA gave approval to Janstone Pharmaceuticals to treat Ebola with this medication. They're the developer of the plasma. Since that action, Janstone has accelerated its production."

"Tell me, Doctor. If this drug treatment is as effective as they predict, Janstone's going to have a gold mine on their hands."

"Ah, I suppose that is an accurate appraisal."

Giles switched the television off and pondered the changing events. Could this tragedy in Zaire have been a deliberate act? If so, her worst fears had been set into motion.

A door opened, light danced across the hardwood floor and a tall man dressed in a business suit entered the library. "Excuse me, ma'am."

"Yes."

"Our insider is alive after all. He phoned in yesterday evening, but we had a mix-up and I wasn't notified until an hour ago. We're to call this number at one forty-five today."

"I'll take care of it." Giles tapped her fingernails on the table next to her chair. The world was never what she expected, always changing, always dynamic. Maybe circumstances had shifted in their favor.

10:33 a.m.—Amazon Lowlands, Brazil

James Monal squatted down on the side of the trail next to Dr. Saleman. "What do you have there?" James asked.

"It's a baby monstera plant, *Monstera deliciosa*, to be precise." Fenmar stroked a tiny, pinkish red bud. "This is the first opportunity I've had to sheath my machete and put on my botanical hat. Now that we're out of the jungle and into the rain forest I can hardly believe my eyes. Look, James, there's a Brazilian example of an

Australian tree fern, *Cyathea australia*. A few yards behind us was a prime specimen of a cat's claw vine, *Uncaria tomentosa*, and before that—"

"Okay, okay, I get the idea." James chuckled at Fenmar's enthusiasm. "Ernesto said from here on the going will be easier. Enjoy your greenery, and I'll see how the others are coming along."

Kelly and her cameraman were shooting scenery when James approached. He appraised the thick canopy, remembering less than fifteen percent of the sunlight ever made it to the floor. Even with the insects swarming everywhere, the muted light gave the rain forest an eerie beauty. "Is there enough natural light?" James asked Glynn.

"No prob. We're cool." Glynn hoisted the video camera down from his shoulder. "This new film's super sensitive. If you can see it, I can capture it."

From the corner of his eye, James watched Kelly take notes. The sweat staining the back and sides of her khaki shirt was erotic. James chided himself for his lusty thoughts. He had definitely been chasing the dead for too long. "If you need anything, just ask." James politely dipped his head, then strolled away in search of Dr. Isling.

Halfway along their trodden trail, Aidan pulled James aside. "You should show this to Fenmar. It's a prime specimen of mamperikipini. *Fittonia acanthaceae*, I think is the scientific name. Kofan and Siona-Secoya tribes of Ecuador use it for headache treatments. Supposedly, when administered in large enough quantities, it's a fair hallucinogen. You know, James, we haven't even come close to discovering a fraction of the potential medicinal resources hidden within the Amazon."

"Amazing, Aidan. I'll tell Dr. Isling the first chance I get." James hurried along the path. "Jeez, everybody's a plant guru today."

"Over here, James." Dr. Isling called to him while

standing alone at the head of the caravan. "I see Aidan and Fenmar are having a good time."

"Yes, sir."

"There's a change of plans. We're going to leave the native workers and make our way to Myrta's first potential point of contact."

"But . . . ?" With a fleeting glance, James probed the thick undergrowth. Father DeLeon's warning came hurtling back. Splitting up the group was a bad idea. "Who will take care of the interim campsite?"

"Ernesto and the laborers can handle it. Besides, if our timing's good, we'll finish up and meet them a few hours after they get there. This will give us a jump on things."

James removed his outback hat and wiped his forehead with his shirtsleeve. "This doesn't sound . . ." His gaze wandered along the trail to the rest of the team. Visions of the plane crash were fresh in his memory. Dr. Isling's decision was a mistake. James surveyed the towering trees. The Amazon appeared exceptionally foreign at that moment.

"Is there a problem?" Dr. Isling crossed his arms. His mind was set.

"I guess not."

"Then tell the team we'll separate here." He patted James on the back. "You'll see. Once we get there, it'll all be fine."

Probably the overwhelming aura of the Amazon had unsettled him, but James still wished he could change the professor's mind. What was it about this place? He had never felt this uneasy in the Yucatán.

On past expeditions, everything had been methodically plotted and planned until they had a complete blueprint. Nothing happened before a detailed analysis was performed—the way of the archaeologist. This was especially true of the nitpicking Dr. Isling, who usually insisted on a preplanned approach. They were racing in without assessing the Burbános' cultural complexities;

a dangerous decision. Why run the risk? Was there something James had missed?

"What did Ernesto say when you told him?"

"He sees no problem with going on ahead, even suggested it."

"I'll divide the maps up with him and grab the extra GPS." James smoothed back his hair and put on his outback hat. "It shouldn't take more than twenty minutes to get everyone else ready."

7:34 a.m.—Venice Beach, California

Standing on the street next to his Taurus, Osborne assessed the surroundings and conceded Lawyer had chosen a good location for the safe house. A barefooted teenager, carrying a surfboard and wearing a torn pair of swim trunks, headed for the beach two houses away. Venice Beach's culturally mixed rental house neighborhoods were accustomed to strangers wandering the streets at odd hours of the day and night. His band of misfits and muggers fit in well with the local weirdos.

Osborne entered the safe house, unchallenged. Security was a little too lax for his liking, but it was at the level he expected from street thugs. Six men sat around the kitchen table. He searched their eyes, detecting no fear, simply the thirst for a brawl. They had the loathsome facial glaze of urban animals, ready and eager to kill and maim. It took a certain type of individual to take a life without flinching, and these men were that type.

When a person possessed the slightest hint of moral consciousness, they often experience a split-second of indecision before committing cold-blooded murder. A lot can happen during a split second. Osborne considered the motives of each man, accepting he was not in a position to be too choosy. With any luck, he'd dump them and the rental before long; only the time it took to fulfill the contract and then fade from sight for at most thirty days.

"You go tonight," Osborne said.

"How do we hit the place?" Lawyer asked, leaning on his elbows, bored with the proceedings.

"The front door." Osborne laid a sketch of the exterior of the Malibu house on the table. "Our surveillance team made this. You can see here," he pointed, "weather makes the side and rear entrances too difficult." A trained team could handle it, but not this band of rabble. This bunch, with their diminished mental capacity, required a simple and direct approach.

Lawyer Lewis was the only one with at least half a brain. He had been charged with various felonious activities on eleven occasions, with no convictions, thereby earning the nickname Lawyer. Osborne had heard his real name was Theodore.

"Who's gonna run the show?" Spanks asked.

"When you're inside, Lawyer calls the shots." Spanks rolled his eyes. "Do you have a problem?" Osborne asked.

"No man." Spanks shook his head. "Not me."

"Sweep each room. Three men downstairs and three upstairs. Lawyer will decide the teams."

The thugs became more animated now that they had the scent of blood. Even Spanks was smiling. Osborne assumed that was what to call his crooked-tooth scowl.

"What time do we hit the place?" Lawyer studied the map.

"Between ten and midnight. It depends a lot on the weather." Osborne watched their expressions. "Any questions?"

"Does we kill 'em all?" Spanks asked.

"Eventually. Lawyer knows the details."

3:34 p.m.—Amazon Lowlands, Brazil

James Monal bent down and picked up a feather. He caressed its ribbed texture. The team had been on the site for about forty minutes and the group had scattered across the open space, knee-deep in thick groundcover. Each person collected samples, took pictures, and marveled at their individual findings. Documenting this as an active Burbános location had brought everyone a surge of nervous anticipation, that is, everyone except James. He would have preferred a village, anything other than this location. The place was just too damn eerie for him.

The rain forest loomed high, creating the illusion of being inside an open sky amphitheater. From across the clearing, about two hundred feet away, he heard Aidan and Myrta's private conversation. The sound of their voices carried so well they could have been standing right next to him. Their words had a crisp tone, as if hyperbolized through a concrete tunnel. It made him think of the tinny music produced on an antique gramophone.

On the opposite side of the clearing, facing Aidan and Myrta, Fenmar grumbled an "ouch" after pricking his finger. James laughed. With a simple turn of his head, he could hear anyone within his line-of-sight. He had experienced a similar sound phenomenon while standing in the center of the Pelota Court at Chichén Itzá.

"It's unbelievable," Dr. Isling said.

"What?"

"Pay attention, James."

"Sorry, professor."

"The preserved detail is remarkable. I never anticipated finding anything like this." He frowned, twisting his lips together. "James, are you taking adequate notes?"

"Yes, sir. I see it too. Incredible." James ripped a piece of paper from his pad and placed it against the stone petroglyph. He traced the image with a pencil and smeared the graphite outline with his fingers to create a rubbing. "Weathering is minimal. I'd expect much more in this climate."

Dr. Isling scratched a corner of the carved rock with his pocketknife. "Even more fantastic is to find an altar in the middle of the Amazon made of limestone."

"Yucatán source rock?" James' eyes widened as he visualized a quarry buried deep within Maya land.

"Quite possible. Gather photographic evidence for comparative petrographic analysis. When Aidan finishes picking plant specimens, have him collect scrapings of those stains for DNA analysis." Dr. Isling pointed at six sampling spots.

"The sacrifice must have been recent," James said.

"I am aware of that possibility," Dr. Isling chided.

"What is that thing?" Kelly asked, eyeing James for a response.

The two scientists hesitated, then turned quickly. "But, uh . . . ," James stammered.

"An altar stone," Dr. Isling explained while James groped for words and Glynn zoomed in for a closeup

"Okay . . . is that blood?" Kelly pointed to the mottled discolorations on the top and sides of the altar. The same places Dr. Isling wanted sampled. "Looks fresh."

"A ritual animal killing," James said.

Her eyebrows dipped as she squinted, staring at the marks. A frown formed. "How can you tell?"

James took a breath before answering her. "This is a sacred meeting ground. The way the vegetation has been deforested is a good indication of human impact. An emergence of bamboo plants further confirms the occurrence of some unnatural process. There are also signs that gifts had been placed at the foot of the altar. See those markings at the base?" He pointed. "Not long ago the stone was raised above the ground. I'd say—"

"You're babbling James, and that's not what I asked." Kelly scowled at both men, especially James. "How can you be certain those aren't human blood stains?"

Myrta interrupted their conversation by laying two satellite photographs on the altar. "This is the place all right. Stressed veggies were a dead giveaway."

Great choice of words, James grimaced. Even before they had entered the site, he was aware of the negative sensations emanating from the sacred ground. They were different from those he had experienced at the female ruler's tomb. She wanted to be found; these people did not.

The rest of the team was unaware of the danger, or at least not experiencing the same dread as James. To the complete opposite, Dr. Isling and the others seemed captivated with their surroundings; overaged kids romping through an Amazonian amusement park. Watching them, James began to question the misgivings of his vivid imagination. It had been a long trek to the site and he was tired.

Frustrated with not getting her questions answered, Kelly switched subjects. "How can you be certain this is a Burbános location?" She replaced her notebook with a small tape-recorder.

Dr. Isling motioned with his walking stick, gently tapping the petroglyphs etched on the sides of the altar stone. "These cuttings are definitively Maya. Graphic images of a humanoid face emerging between the jaws of a serpent are a classic theme in their art. The Toltec influence expanded the importance of the feathered serpent, which suggests this piece is no older than the twelfth century."

James squatted on one knee, giving the carvings a detailed examination. "A Toltec association places the origin of this stone beyond the suspected Maya migration date of the Late Classic Period. The arrival of the Burbános could correspond with the later decline of the Yucatán Maya during the Post Classic."

"Good theory, James. It fits well with the increased

occurrence of the Maya's reliance on blood sacrifice and the timing also implies an exodus of sorts from the Yucatán."

Removing his hat, James ran his fingers through his hair. "They might have come by sea and not over land as we had presumed." He stuffed the hat in his rucksack.

Dr. Isling considered James' hypothesis as he circled the altar. "Another possibility, which would corroborate the Toltec influence, would place the Burbános in the Post Classic period when commerce via sea travel was more aggressive. Migration across the Caribbean Sea, then down the South American coast and up the Amazon makes sense to me. I like it." Dr. Isling rested his hand on James' shoulder. "All we have to do is find evidence other than a single altar stone and a few questionable blood stains."

"That's all," James grumbled.

"Don't worry, son. It's nothing."

"Wait, Dr. Isling. This effigy?" James pointed to a sculpted head, running his fingers along the rough surface. "Is it . . . ?"

"By God, the pendant from the mission. Now I remember where I've seen its likeness before." Dr. Isling dug through his vest and pants pockets. "Damn, I must have left it at the campsite. I'll have to take care of that later." The professor scratched his chin, a look of confusion on his face. "Hmm, like I was saying. An expedition exploring Chichén Itzá's Cenote Sagrado during the 1960s found skulls of what they assumed to be children deformed in a similar manner. The investigators attributed the cranial abnormalities to an unknown Maya ritual. Damn, I can't recall the members of the team. My memory's starting to fade."

"Yeah, right. If I only had half your memory." James smirked in mock disgust. "When we get to camp, I'll use the SATCOM and contact Dr. Leland. He can pull the references and shed light on the Cenote team. Seeing the same depiction on the third to the last ascension gives it a chilling significance."

"I agree, James. Why deform the head of a living child unless the Maya were creating a lifelike image of a familiar deity? The practice suggests a specific emulation versus the more abstract art forms they typically employed."

"What disturbs me more is why you found the pendant in the mission's basement?"

"Slow down," Kelly said, butting into their conversation. "You guys are going ninety miles an hour. Now explain this stuff using words that us non-archaeological types can comprehend."

James glanced at the ground, unable to meet her inquisitive stare. He felt embarrassed. It had not been his intention to ignore or dazzle her with techno jargon, but he didn't know what else to say. Just how was he supposed to casually converse with such a beautiful woman, especially about such mundane matters as a recent ritual Maya sacrifice? Oh yes, he mused, this is where our lost tribe hacked some poor animal to death. What do you think Ms. Karrie?

"Humgh." James cleared his throat. "See here, Kelly. The stone is banded with thirteen inscribed layers." He laid his hand on each successive layer and explained. "They signify the Maya's belief that the heavens have thirteen levels of ascension, each represented by a different deity. The levels also correspond to the thirteen cycles of their Sacred Round calendar, which some researchers have correlated to the annual occurrence of thirteen full moons. Simply, the cycles of the Sacred Round are similar to our twelve months. The Maya were astronomically advanced, even compared to modern standards. They had a 365¼-day calendar and had identified the 584-day orbit of Venus around the sun. The Dresden Codex goes into the Venusian cycles in great detail."

"Why are the calendar and Venus' cycle so important?" she asked.

"In their context as Maya, they're not," Dr. Isling said. "Simply, the glyphs provide further documentation that this is not an indigenous Amazonian Indian site. You see, the local tribespeople have no concept of a future or a past. They live in what's called the 'Great Present,' and even the simplest of astronomical revelations are foreign to them."

"Incredible. Thank you for the clarification."

While James blushed a shade redder, Dr. Isling's smile broadened, and he continued the lecture. "Ms. Karrie, the accuracy of the Maya calendar system might also intrigue you. They projected the end of the known world to be in 2012 A.D. Our analysis has established—"

"Dr. Isling," Aidan yelled and waved, "over here."

"Do you mind, Ms. Karrie?"

"Not at all, professor."

"Marvelous then, shall we join them?"

"It would be my pleasure. Glynn, you coming?"

"Naw. You go ahead. I want some more footage of this altar thing."

James eyed the duo. Apparently, Dr. Isling and Ms. Karrie had found some common ground, as they now seemed to be old buddies. This damn expedition was getting weirder all the time.

Dr. Isling grimaced. "Is there something wrong, my boy?"

"Uh, no, sir."

"Then get a move on, lad, and let's see what Aidan wants."

They jogged over and joined Dr. MacKiernan. "What have you found there, Aidan?" Dr. Isling asked.

"Myrta and I have come across dozens of these burned spots." He pointed to a small patch of blackish ground. "The charring pattern suggests they're recent."

"All right, everyone," Dr. Isling said, his arms gesturing in a circular pattern, "spread out and stand on a burn mark. I want to see how large an area we're talking about."

The team dispersed, and within moments, they faced each other, outlining the perimeter of an optically perfect circle. James had paced slightly over one hundred and eighty-two feet from the altar to the first burn mark, making the open ground approximately three hundred and sixty-five feet in diameter. The distribution of burned locations created a visual representation of the Sacred Round, and the distance across was numerically proportional to the number of days in the Vague Year calendar. The altar was in the exact center of the clearing, a symbolic placement of the sun. During a ceremony, hundreds of Indians could fit within the open ground. James had a dark sense of graphic violence as he surveyed the view from his position on the fringe. The same bewildered uneasiness was evident on the faces of the others.

Dr. Isling waved them to the center. "Let's get everything together. We'll come back early tomorrow when we can spend more time and document our findings." A series of uncertain nods supported his decision and the group began collecting their gear.

While everyone prepared to leave, James stuffed maps into his rucksack and took a GPS reading, trying to forget the team's unsettled looks. The handheld computer locked onto five satellites, providing a location accuracy of two feet. Under the rain forest canopy, he would be lucky to link with the minimum of three satellites. The coordinates showed they were almost a mile from Ernesto and the intermediate camp. If they pushed on, a solid two-hour hike might get them there.

James surveyed the site as he battled with his conflicting feelings. His scientific side wanted to stay and continue; his emotional side said, get far away. He sensed the same mixed feelings burdening everyone; their carefree attitudes had suddenly vanished. James shook his head and slung his rucksack over his shoulder, then headed off to meet the rest of the group. The Amazon was ruled by a set of laws not governed by western ideals and being here alone was a mistake. They should have never left Ernesto and the others.

"James," Dr. Isling said. "You take the lead. Everyone else, fall-in behind. We'll have to move quickly, it'll be dark—"

The professor staggered; everything slowed for James. His mentor's mouth froze in mid-sentence; his eyes wide and shocked. An arrow had gone all the way through his neck. Its sharp wooden point protruded below his right earlobe. Blood trickled beneath the puncture made by the hideous brown shaft. His friend stood still, staring, no pain on his face, only the regret of a man not finished with discovering life. A tear formed in the corner of his eye, and he slumped to his knees.

Henry Isling stared, vacant, groping for words, "You . . . My son . . . Tell the world. . . . Run!" His eyelids fluttered, and he landed face first on the muddy ground.

Stunned, confused, James searched for the rest of the team. Myrta's body sprawled beneath two thick bushes. Glynn had doubled over next to her. Fenmar was nowhere to be found. The Burbános were shadows, hidden among the trees, ghosts of the forest, killing with a wicked bloodlust. Someone grabbed James' arm, giving it a powerful yank.

"Snap out of it!" Aidan raced into the forest, dragging James along, but he stumbled on a tree root and jerked them both to a stop.

"The others?"

"Dead!"

"Kelly?"

"I'm here, James."

The sound of her voice abated his paralysis. He took her hand, squeezed her tiny palm against his, and ran.

2:16 p.m.—Malibu Beach, California

Matt Wells looked beyond Allyx toward the crashing waves. Three diehard surfers floated outside the breakers, a hundred yards to the southwest. As far as Matt could see, except for the surfers, they were alone on the beach. The sky had opened up and the wind had died down to a whisper. If not for the danger they were in, it would have been another enchanted Southern California afternoon. "I'm glad you suggested a walk." He watched Allyx stand along the water's edge, hardly aware of his presence, consumed with her thoughts. "We needed to get out, breathe a little fresh air."

"Matt, do you get the sense it's all coming to an end?"

"Yes and no, I guess."

Allyx picked up a rounded half of a mussel shell. She brushed away the crusted sand and let her fingertips glide over the swirled blue and white inner surface before returning it to the surf. "Sally and Wade are nice people." She smiled and strolled along the foamy surge.

"They are. And even with all that's happened, I can't believe he was shot." Allyx let his comment go, and Matt wondered what she was thinking. He had noticed she seemed preoccupied ever since speaking of her grandfather and Dr. Ruhpor. It must have been difficult for her to share those feelings, exposing painful memories. How could he ever—

"It's beautiful here," she said.

"Uh, it sure is." He noticed the worry had etched tiny lines below her otherwise strikingly brown eyes. She was tired, pushed to the brink. "Too bad the storm didn't leave us a whole lot of beachfront." Less than ten feet to his left, a blackened redwood balcony belonging to a multistory house hung suspended above the ground. Greenish blue surf hit the shore within twenty feet to their right. With the storm's hiatus, the tide had receded, but soon both would resume and engulf the narrow strip of sand.

She nudged him toward the ocean. "Surfers don't seem to mind."

Matt chuckled as he sidestepped the watery ripples. He watched an insane teenager wearing a black Body Glove® half-wetsuit jet across the face of a shimmering wave. Water sprayed behind the surfboard as he cut back into the curl. "Locals probably pray for days like this, where strong winds kick up the swells. They'd ride a gutter wave if the water was deep enough."

"I'd love to have nothing else to do right now."

"When this is over," Matt arched an eyebrow, "I'll take you to a spot south of Santa Barbara called Rincon. I used to hang there when I was in high school. We'd drive up early, sleep in our cars, and be on the water before the sun peeked above the horizon." A small swell enveloped their bare feet, overflowing their footprints. The pull of the receding tide gave Matt a philosophical sensation. The sea was trying to reclaim one of its own.

"Rincon sounds wonderful. You still owe me a Highway 1 cruise and a classical music concert."

"My debts are accumulating."

"And I intend on collecting. We'll put you on a payment schedule." Allyx's tanned skin gleamed in the sunlight as she surveyed the horizon. More footprints were lost to the surf behind them. "I love the ocean, Matt. My grandfather and I walked along the beach for hours. He'd say, all you have to do is treat her with respect and you'll be fine." She looked deep into Matt's eyes searching for answers. "Why can't everything be that simple?"

"Sometimes it can be." Matt flashed her an empathetic smile, then skipped a flat rock along the water's surface. " 'Knowing nature never did betray, the heart that loved her.' "

"That's beautiful." Allyx stopped him from skipping another rock. "Did you make that up?"

He saw a sensitive twinkle in her eyes. "No. It's from

William Wordsworth."

She bit her lower lip. "Do you know any more?"

" 'Let those love now who never loved before. Let those who always loved, now love the more.' " Matt surprised even himself. He had grown up with poetry books in one hand and sports magazines in the other. His mom said it made for a good balance. She had been determined not to raise an air-headed surf junky. Dad didn't have time for such nonsense, and Matt's friends quickly learned not to tease him. But it had been years since he had quoted Wordsworth or Parnell. Why had they come to him now?

"Hmm, a poet." She looped her arm under his. "A week ago, we argued academic semantics. A couple of days ago, we battled faceless thugs to stay alive. Now, we're barefoot on a secluded beach. Does it all seem a little surreal to you, or is it just me?" She snuggled closer to him.

Surprised by her sudden intimate behavior, his mouth had gone dry. "Kind of." Smooth Matt, from poet to imbecile all in one move. Did she feel his uncertainty? God, emotional stupidity ran deep in his family. Why couldn't he talk to this woman?

"Matt . . . do you really believe they're going to let us walk away from this?"

He didn't answer. Her wavy golden brown hair streamed in the gentle breeze. His natural carnal instincts had been replaced with a protective urge, a desire to hold her in his arms. "We should head back. Wade and Sally will be worried."

Allyx snuggled next to him. "I suppose you're right." She sighed.

2:23 p.m.—A Bluff Overlooking Malibu, California

"Crap, local PD. What're they doin' here?" Tony Lister yanked the car phone out of its holder. He strummed his fingers on the steering wheel. "Hurry up and answer."

"Yeah?"

"Damn, Kendall. This is Tony. What took yuh?" He peeked above the dashboard at the cops, hoping they didn't glance his way.

"I'm busy here. My two are gettin' off the phone. Whatta yuh want?"

"PD's at the house. What's going down? Anything on your end?"

"Chill, man. Where's the other two?"

"Doin' the dirty on the beach." Tony spied the coastline through the windshield with his binoculars.

"Cool youself. Cops are goin' door-to-door evacuatin' everyone. A big storm or somethin's gonna hit some time tonight. If they don't find no one at the house, they'll move on."

"I don't like this." Tony stretched his cramped legs and pushed back against the Mercedes' leather seat.

"Osborne said watch the place. He don't care what you like. Now, leave me alone. I've gotta keep an eye on the other two." Kendall hung up.

"Shit-crap." Tony threw the car phone on the passenger seat and banged the steering wheel with the side of his fist. "This job sucks."

A rap on the side of the car. Tony rolled down the window and craned his neck around to see. "Yeah, what do you want?"

Partially concealed by a large overcoat, the stranger bent down. "Can I get directions to 15056 PCH?"

"Man, what do I look like? Try a gas station."

"Thank you anyway." He said no more and left.

Tony rolled the window up. "Friggin' tourists."

5:32 p.m.—Amazon Lowlands, Brazil

James Monal raced on, too scared to stop, charging deeper into the cover of the rain forest. Tripping over bushes and smashing into trees, he pushed harder and harder, but never let go of Kelly's hand. At times, he was dragging her, then there were moments when she had the weight of a feather. Shrubs snarled their legs, and vines dangled above their heads. He experienced the same helpless dread while slogging his way through the cabin of the downed airplane.

Visions of Dr. Isling and the others chased him, their cruel murders replayed in his mind. "Please, no more." James couldn't handle any more death: the emptiness, the loss. They were not simply friends, mentors, or teachers, they were family; the only one he had known for the past three years. Now they were gone, and he was alive. Why? A tug on his hand jarred him.

"Need to rest, James." Kelly crumpled to the ground. "Not," she inhaled, "not another step."

They were all exhausted. Sweat poured down James' face and his sides ached. "We can't stop."

"Have to." Kelly gasped for air between words. "Where are we?"

The limited light slicing its way among the trees was diminishing fast. They'd be in total blackness within the next few minutes. This place was dangerous enough during the day. At night, they didn't stand a chance. He ducked away from Aidan and Kelly, not wanting them to detect his fear. Were they going to die like the others? He knew too well the Maya's mania for sacrifice.

"We lost ground by running in the opposite direction of where Ernesto and the others are. My last GPS reading indicated we're a few miles southwest of the camp. All we have to do is follow the compass northeast and we'll be there before long."

"It was hideous, James."

"I know. Don't think about it." She was shaking: fear, fatigue, adrenalin? Maybe all three. He swept back a strand of Kelly's sweaty auburn hair and stroked her pale, soft cheek with his hand. "We're going to make it."

"Your words help. Don't let go of me."

"I won't, and they're not mere words. They're a promise."

"Thanks, James. I . . ." Kelly stared at the trees behind them. "Do you think they're alive?"

"For their sakes, it might be better if . . ." James couldn't finish, he knew the alternative. "It doesn't matter, we must push on."

"But, James?"

"Now's not the time, Kelly." He placed his hand under Aidan's arm and helped him to his feet. "Are you okay?"

"Leg hurts." Aidan winced. "I can make it."

"It's not far. We can do it together." James pointed in the direction, then began a slow jog while towing the others. They had to stay together, to keep moving, to stay alive.

2:35 p.m.—Malibu Beach, California

Wade Fields leaned on the bar counter while Sally poured two glasses of water. "I talked with my contact and told her everything." Wade tilted his head to the side, stretched tired muscles, and wished it was already over. They had been thrown in front of an out-of-control steamroller and it was only a matter of time until they were trapped under its merciless bone-crushing drum—a pleasant thought. "You want the good news or the bad news?"

"I hate this," Allyx said. "How can it get any worse?"

"We also made a call to BenaTex." Wade took one glass from Sally. "Thank you."

"Was that a good idea?" Matt arched an eyebrow at

Allyx. She shrugged her shoulders.

"It's my fault," Sally said. "I had to see how things were going."

"And?"

"My supervisor." She looked away, unable to meet anyone's eyes. "My supervisor, Ed Cooper, committed suicide a few days ago." Sally's paused, stared at the group; words had become impossible. Her hands trembled as she set her glass on the counter. "He saved us, Wade."

"It's okay." He placed his hand on her arm, then faced Matt and Allyx. "In addition to Sally losing her boss, the founding partners, Donner and Singular, were killed in a car explosion."

"When?" Allyx sat on the couch next to Matt.

"Yesterday evening."

"While we were having dinner," Sally added.

Matt shook his head. "So, someone else is pulling the strings."

"Cold, but accurate. And they're getting rid of everyone." Wade's comment popped out before he realized what impact it would have.

Sally reacted first. She sat on the barstool next to him, trembling. Her eyes reached deep inside, stirring his emotions, the way only his wife had before she . . . If Sally were ever hurt because of her involvement with him, it would be too much to bear. He would not let it happen.

"Is it ever going to end?" Sally asked.

No one answered. Wade was caught speechless. If his contact didn't show, they were lost, or even worse—dead. What other option did they have? BenaTex was not the real enemy, and now they had no way of knowing whom to fight. They had become victims, waiting to be slaughtered.

"We're all that's left," Allyx mumbled.

"We'll handle it." Matt set his hand on her thigh. "What's the good news?"

"My contact's going to send a team to pick us up."

"When?"

"Soon, I hope," Allyx said.

"Tonight, or at the latest, by morning." He read the doubt on their faces. "They'll come. It takes time to put these things together. That's all." Wade had his own misgivings and didn't mention the call to his daughter. She was fine, and it had given him a lift to hear her sweet voice—so innocent. Thank God they had not found her.

The decision to involve his family had been wrought with turmoil. At first, Wade had hesitated to put his daughter and sister in danger, and considered contacting his brother. But then, Tim could have been compromised because of his industry association. Wade had no choice. The lives of millions might be at stake. In a desperate move, he sent his sister and brother copies of everything, accompanied with instructions to protect the documents until contacted by a friend.

His sister was an ace in Wade's hand; the one he hoped no one suspected. While sitting next to Sally, watching Allyx and Matt, he questioned his actions. Was this conspiracy more important than personal considerations? Someone seemed to think it was worth the loss of innocent lives. He assessed the mood of his three companions. "We can hold on that long, can't we?"

"Sure we can," Matt said, rising from the couch. "We have to."

"Oh, yeah," Wade continued. "I'm almost embarrassed to mention it, but adding to our fun, Mother Nature is going to take a nasty shift. A major storm system's threatening to shake up our little hideaway. Beach communities south of us have been evacuated. The police passed by when we were out, and although it's not likely, they could return."

"What next?" Allyx asked. "A tsunami? Why don't we go to the police and tell them everything?"

Wade shook his head. "We have nothing. No proof. No hard evidence of any kind. We don't even know whom to accuse. The technical data and circumstantial evidence we've compiled aren't enough. We need more before they'd even listen to us."

Matt crossed the room to the window, pulled back the curtain. Black clouds swamped the last section of blue sky. "One way or another, we'll have to leave."

Allyx stood beside him and whispered. "Let's hope it's not too soon. I feel safe here."

4:23 p.m.—San Francisco, California

A brass lantern clock sat next to his cigar case. The timepiece's tempered hands moved with crafted precision, passing another minute with ease. The ornament was a gift from his personal assistant, another finely tuned accessory in Jolon Steele's collection. He loved to admire his possessions.

The telephone rang and Steele picked up the receiver, anticipating the call. "Yes."

For a long period, there was silence, then a scratchy voice asked, "Have you completed the arrangements?"

Steele experienced an uncharacteristic chill. He would soon sever this relationship also. "Everything is going as planned. The final annoyance is being taken care of tonight."

"The virus is viable?"

"Completely."

The man hacked a thick wet cough. "Houston was a risky choice."

"He is brilliant, and that is all that matters." How dare he question his decisions? Jolon Steele was the genius behind the plan, not this sickly toad on the other end of the phone. The Ambassador was simply a puppet supplying arms to the highest bidder, another immoral scum sucker taking advantage of the oppressed.

They all thought they were so clever. Well, the world would soon see. One more task to complete. Steele smiled, gloating in the glory of his growing power base. Ah, what a great feeling; nothing else like it. The only thing more pleasurable would be to end this ridiculous conversation, and with his own hands, squelch the breath from the mucusy pig; a primeval act reminiscent of his ancestors.

"Keep an eye on Gunder. He's smart and well connected."

"He will be handled." And so will you, Steele neglected to add.

"He'd better be." The man hung up.

Steele considered the call. Was there more to the conversation than had been said? He was prepared for any possibility, always a step ahead.

10:11 p.m.—Amazon Lowlands, Brazil

"I don't see anybody." James Monal said as he pushed aside a twisted vine. "The camp should have someone on watch."

"James, I'm scared." Kelly peeked over his shoulder. "We won't survive much longer. We have to take a chance."

Aidan leaned against the side of a tree. He had not spoken for more than forty minutes. His face flushed with fever. James worried he had been bitten or scratched by something poisonous. At the rate Aidan was fading, and without adequate medical treatment, he was going to die.

"This isn't good. Ernesto should be watching for us."

"But there's a fire going in the center of the camp."

"Doesn't mean anything."

"Someone had to start it."

Uncertain, James felt Aidan's forehead. He was burning up. "Okay, you stay here with Aidan. Don't make a sound or move until I get back." He took a deep breath, then stepped into the light of the fire.

The tents had been unpacked, and two were set up. Supplies were stacked to one side, still crated. Where was everyone? Ernesto was too smart a guide to mount a search at night, even if the archaeological team was hours overdue. Why abandon the campsite and leave the fire? James yanked open the canvas flap on the first tent. A flickering glow danced across the breach. He leaned his head inside, one hand holding the center post for support. His fingers touched something sticky, like sap on green wood, and he tore his hand away.

Jerking his head back from the empty tent, James glared at his fingers and his body began to shake. An icy cold struck him, tiny pins piercing his skin. Staggering to the middle of the camp, he stalled next to the fire, watching the flames jump into the air, listening to the wood crackle as it burned. The camp was deserted, yet there were signs. It had been sudden and silent, the same as at the sacred site. His sticky fingers flexed and he rubbed them against his pants. Slowly, then faster, and faster, but the blood from the tent pole remained, becoming a permanent stain. He had been marked for death, the same as those before him, the ancient ones of the Yucatán.

James panned the perimeter of the campsite, worried about Kelly and Aidan. They could not get away—why even try? His head throbbed as he visually probed the fringe of the light, straining to pick out details. Were they being watched? The Burbános were out there, somewhere, everywhere.

They would come and nothing could change that fact. James and Aidan would die in a brutal fashion—the warrior's way. Yet in comparison to Kelly's torture, their pain would be nothing. The greater her torment, the closer would be the bond between the Burbános and their gods. Burbános men would wear her teeth as a sign of strength and consume her heart for spiritual unity. During the ceremony, she would be humiliated then disfigured. A thorny branch would be ripped through a hole in her freshly pierced tongue. Sections of her skin would be peeled, layer-by-layer. Her female organs . . . James' knees weakened, and he staggered away from the fire, weeping. He had to stop them, to protect her.

Summoning his strength, James made for the supplies, ripping apart boxes and crates. He had to find the communications equipment. Frustrated, he knocked over a folding chair, then raced to another tent, but it too was empty. Then he saw the box, at the farthest reach of the fire's light. He approached apprehensively. Nothing made sense to him anymore.

The container was tipped over, the top ripped open. James picked it up and peered inside. With a defeated sigh, he fell to the ground, cradling the medium sized reinforced box. He began to laugh. They weren't going to make this easy, were they? The box tipped, spilling the mangled electronics onto the ground. How did they know?

James rose and dusted himself off. His face became devoid of expression; his thoughts focused. He returned to the supplies, grabbed three canteens, a medical kit, and a package of dried beef. They had to make it to the Rio Negro. The camp, the jungle, neither was safe.

7:54 p.m.—Malibu Beach, California

Matt Wells lifted his head and the shower spray hit him in the face. Pulsating jets beat against his temples, relieving the tiredness above his eyes. Hot, steamy water cascaded across his shoulders and down his back. His spent emotions streamed through the perforated drain cover, lost forever in a vortex of soapy water.

Helplessly waiting was not an action he understood. What if Field's contact never showed? Then what? He no longer knew who the enemy was. Had he ever? They were targets, trapped in a house, on their own. He had to assume there were no constants, no givens; anything could happen.

Even his relationship with Allyx remained volatile. At times Matt perceived he felt a genuine caring for her, a rare sentiment for him, but as was the case more often, she maintained her distance, adding to his confusion. After she spoke of her grandfather, a window to her soul had opened, and for the briefest moment, they shared the same emotions, the same sense of need and belonging. Then, just as quickly, her protective shell returned and he was more alone than before. Maybe she was still in love with Dr. Ruhpor. He had been there for her, sharing an intimacy Matt might never know.

He slapped both hands on the shower's ceramic tile wall. How was a man supposed to know what action to take, what path to choose? Cindi had said, when his feelings were true, he would find the words. She made it sound simple. Bullshit!

Past relationships had been easy for Matt. Unsolicited, beautiful women came to him. He never questioned why nor did he put much thought into their motives. They sought him out, and he let it happen. On occasion, he'd laugh with friends about his effortless good fortune. Then there were the other times, when he lamented how easy it was to fall into a meaningless relationship. He eventually began to look upon his womanizing as a curse. His male friends said not to question whatever natural force governed the attraction of women to him. Don't mess with a good thing they'd warn. But they didn't understand, something was missing. And then Dr. Ruhpor changed everything by throwing him together with

Allyx. Is that what he had planned?

She gave Matt a completeness he had not known before, unlocking his inner thoughts, while exposing the shallowness of his past desires. With a single word, Allyx drove him to such intense highs, only to change direction and send him into a spiraling dive. Was she the missing piece in his life that he sought? He wanted to go to her room, speak his heart and take her. Instead, he succumbed to his lack of confidence. Indecision ruled his heart. . . . Why hadn't his dad prepared him for this, for any of it? Only once before had Matt gotten this close to a woman. . . . He should have stopped Jody from killing herself. Would the same thing happen again?

"Shit, I'm losing it."

This was neither the place nor the time to have these thoughts. Survival ranked higher than impulsive needs, desires. He turned the shower off and shook his head, sending water spattering down the walls. Smoothing his hair back, Matt swung open the glass door and grabbed a white towel on the counter.

He wrapped the towel around his waist and stopped at the bathroom sink, where he unzipped a borrowed shaving kit. After running a comb through his hair, he cleared a spot on the steamy mirror with a swirl of his hand and patted shaving cream over his scruffy cheeks and neck. The menthol spice made his skin tingle.

One smooth pass of a double-edged razorblade down the side of his face and Matt rinsed the blade in streaming hot tap water, musing on how much he hated to shave. Slicing your face was an unnatural act and a waste of energy. He took another swipe below his chin. How to handle Allyx? The question persisted. He had to—

A gentle hand touched his forearm; another cupped the razor. Matt did not resist. Allyx took the gleaming blade and dipped it under the hot water. With a delicate stroke, she ran the instrument up his neck. Placing her fingers on his chin, she raised his head, straightening his neck and smoothing his face, then she guided the razor along his jaw line. She rinsed. Two more delicate passes and she had finished.

Allyx admired her workmanship with an approving expression, gently dabbing his face with a steamy towel. She moved to his back, never allowing her touch to leave his body. Her fingertips radiated an electrifying warmth as they moved across the muscles framing his shoulders and sides.

Like so often before, Allyx had trapped him in uncertain territory. To let go of his protective inhibitions, was that the answer he had been searching for? Strange the muddled meanderings that filled his mind during times of self-doubt. He turned and faced her. She wore a short, black silk bathrobe that flowed along her sensual curves, drawing his eyes to her tan features. Matt swallowed hard. "I—"

She placed two fingers on his lips and silenced him, then traced the muscles of his chest with her hands. Her caress sent vibrating chills deep beneath his skin. He forgot the danger lurking outside and the confusion haunting him only minutes earlier.

Matt scooped Allyx into his arms and carried her into the bedroom. She had become part of him. His towel dropped to the floor as he gently lowered her onto the mattress of the mahogany four-poster bed. Her silky hair fanned across the pillowcase, and the lavender comforter formed to her body.

Allyx's almond-shaped eyes were magical magnets, drawing him closer. Her passion coursed through him, and he took his time, moving gently, getting to know her, welcoming her sensual intensity. A candle floated inside a blue bowl atop an oak dresser behind them; flickering, it cast dancing shadows on the bedroom walls.

His hands explored her firm sultry body under the robe. Her skin tightened, then relaxed, responding to his touch.

The silk garment slipped from her shoulders onto the bed. She moaned, softly and sensually. He caressed the outline of her body with his eyes—how beautiful she was. Allyx raised her head and their lips met.

10:56 p.m.—Amazon Lowlands, Brazil

"Can't rest," James Monal said. "Gotta keep moving."

"Please, James, no more." Kelly's voice sounded light, dreamy, far away as she caved against the trunk of a slick mossy tree. Shock and exhaustion were pushing her over the brink, and James didn't know how to help her. Their only doctor had already lost touch with reality. Aidan mumbled incoherently while James helped him to the ground next to Kelly. The poor man had been delirious for over an hour, and he worsened by the minute.

"Here, drink some water and have another bite of meat." James handed the canteen and food to Kelly. Not Aidan; he was too far gone.

"Thank . . . you." She gulped the liquid, oblivious to the water spilling down her torn shirt.

"Go slow. Not too much. I have no idea how long it has to last." James wiped Aidan's face with a damp handkerchief, then peered into the darkness surrounding them. The quiet emptiness of a black night had replaced the daylight noises.

He was grateful for no signs of the Burbános since fleeing the clearing and the abandoned campsite, but he remained worried. They had not seen the rest of their team for hours, and in their haste to escape, they had traveled in circles. With night upon them, their troubles now included hungry animals, stalking their movements. Time was not on their side. At best, they had three more hours before reaching the Rio Negro.

Even though James realized their odds of seeing another sunrise were slim, he presented a confident facade. It was all he could do to stay busy, collecting another GPS reading and appearing to be in control. He probed the jungle with what little night vision he had, saving the batteries in his flashlight. The river and base camp were the only remaining threads of life support, and James vowed to find them. Even if it cost him his last breath, he would not let Kelly lose whatever glimmer of hope she had left.

"James, will we get there soon?"

"Not long." Hearing his name on her lips still made his heart skip a beat. "We're going to be all right. I promise."

"I believe you." She took his hand and he helped her up.

Kelly had worn jasmine perfume the day they met in São Gabriel da Anjo; its soft scent lingered in his memory. She was the most incredible woman he had ever met. "We're going to make it." He squeezed her delicate hand in his. Kelly gave him a weak smile as she helped lift Aidan to his feet. James clicked on his flashlight and thought he saw her blush in the dim glow. His imagination or not, the vision helped him believe they had hope.

"This way." He led them into the darkness.

10:02 p.m.—Malibu, California

The couch was extra long and wide, and Wade Fields took full advantage of its spaciousness. While his eyelids drooped shut, Sally cuddled next to him. Her breathing was soft, and he knew she was not asleep. The closeness of their bodies created a soothing familiarity. They had not spoken for nearly an hour, simply enjoying the intimacy.

Wade's cares drifted to more relaxing memories, ones not so hectic or threatening. He longed for peaceful days with his daughter, where his single largest worry was helping her finish a homework assignment. She was a good, if not gifted, student, and he missed those challenging evenings experiencing new things with her. Adrienne's youthful mind eagerly absorbed information, all the time seeking answers to solve nature's mysteries. She would someday make a good scientist.

Although his daughter might have been in the forefront of his mind, his more recent mental family picture included images of Sally, which was strange. He had not considered letting anyone else into their world since his wife's death. Admittedly, his time with Sally reminded him what it was like to have a woman at his side; a special person, capable of drawing him out. Experiencing emotions that had been suppressed for years was a bit scary. Wade worried, questioning whether he was ready to gamble with his love again. To let his feelings run their natural course would expose him to past hurt. Snuggled next to Sally, his thoughts seemed petty compared to the danger outside; he didn't care.

The storm had worsened. Wind and rain vibrated the downstairs windows. Wade ignored nature's onslaught and pulled Sally closer. She nestled within his hold, resting her head on his good shoulder. He smiled and eased into a contented sleep.

11:42 p.m.—A Bluff Overlooking Malibu, California

Tony Lister banged the headset against the dashboard. "Piece of junk. How're we supposed to be lookouts if we can't talk to anyone? These radios are garbage."

"Careful man," Kendall said. "You'll fuck it up."

"Stuff's cheap crap. The damn thing's never worked right." Tony rubbed his shirtsleeve over the car's side window. "Can't see shit through these foggy windows. And

I'm tired of sittin' in this stupid car."

"You on the rag or somethin'?"

"Up yours. It's Lawyer. He gives me the creeps. You never know what he's thinkin'."

"So what. In a few minutes, Lawyer's gonna take down the house. Then we get paid the rest of the money and lay low for a month—slam dunk. Nothin' to it, man."

"Sounds too easy."

"Quit whinin' and see if you can get that thermal imager thing to work."

Tony watched rainwater pour down his side window. "Yeah, right. In this rain? You lost your right nut or somethin'? It won't do its thing until the rain lightens' up, and there ain't nothin' I can do 'bout that."

"Then tell Lawyer, as far as we can see, it's cool to go."

"Yeah, right. It's your ass if this job goes in the shitter." Tony put the headset on and adjusted the microphone with another whack. "Looks good," he said into the walkie-talkie.

Lawyer responded, "We're on our way."

11:49 p.m.—Malibu, California

Matt Wells yawned and switched off the bathroom light. He passed the empty bed. Allyx was awake and standing by the window. She had dressed in one of his flannel shirts, giving the garment shape in places where there had been none before. Matt climbed into a pair of blue jeans, then crossed the room and gently maneuvered his arms around her waist; neither of them spoke. The storm beat on the window and the ocean's treacherous waves carved up the beach. Rain swept the sundeck in surging torrents.

"It's gotten worse." Allyx hugged his arms.

"A little." Matt held her, not wanting the experience to

end. He kissed her neck, tasted a hint of salt, detected the faint smell of sweat . . . the unique touch and smells of a sensual woman.

Something both wonderful and terrifying had happened to him. During their lovemaking, Matt had let go. He was overcome by the experience and a lifetime of self-protection crumbled in the blink of Allyx's eye.

He had never before felt so light, so free. Could he tell this woman his deepest thoughts, those hidden secrets he had never shared? What would he give to be with her? In his heart, Matt had committed to sacrifice everything for Allyx, realizing he might not ever be certain she had the same feelings for him. Making a commitment with no guarantee, was that true love? In some ways, he was more confused than ever.

* * *

The deadbolt was a Westlock, difficult, but not impossible. Lawyer inserted his picks and massaged the top and bottom plungers, then twisted the lock to his right. The metal shaft disengaged and the door eased open. He nudged his hired guns, "We're in."

They extended their weapons and entered the house. Lawyer pointed and whispered, "You two upstairs. You three take the downstairs with me."

"Osborne said three upstairs," Spanks argued.

"I don't give a crap what Osborne wants. I'm running this show." He raised his handgun. "Move it."

"Yeah, whatever." Spanks grabbed Barns and they took to the stairs.

11:51 p.m.—A Bluff Overlooking Malibu, California

Tony Lister rubbed the side of his jaw. Sittin' inside the

car might have been dry, but it wasn't much better than standing in the middle of the downpour outside. Rain hammered the roof of the Mercedes, nature's version of a Chinese water torture. To make his day even grosser, Kendall stunk worse than a grease pit at an all-night truck stop. Between Kendall's smelly body and rotten breath, Tony swore the guy never bathed or brushed. The yellow gunk festering below his gums looked like dried wood glue. "An East LA grunge," Tony grumped. "Raper and mugger of skanky old ladies."

"What'd you say?" Kendall asked.

"Nothin'."

"Uhmph." Kendall eyed Tony.

"How 'bout another game of cards?" Tony asked. Fleecing Kendall for his fifty bucks might mellow the stink.

"Oh, yeah. Let Osborne catch us doin' cards when we're supposed to be watchin' the house for Lawyer."

"You still got a bunch of my money."

"Yeah, and I'm gonna keep it."

Tony pointed to the window. "Crap, it's not like we can see anythin' anyway."

"Quit your—"

The front two side windows of the Mercedes exploded inward, showering glass over Tony and Kendall. Stunned, and before they could react, they were tagged in the necks by small, feathered darts. Tony lurched sideways and Kendall drooped over the steering wheel, causing the horn to blare continuously.

*   *   *

Two figures wearing black jumpsuits and matching balaclava hoods reached past the shattered windows. Their hand motions were precise and professional, no movement wasted. One of the two men pulled the driver away from the steering wheel and switched off the reading lights while his partner examined the passenger. Rain pelted the car; the intensity increased. The hooded figure on the driver's side raised his AN-PVS-9 night vision goggles when a third man stepped forward. He had been standing behind the Mercedes, observing, partially shielded by a large black umbrella.

"Both contacts are neutralized, sir."

The man responded with a subtle dip of his umbrella. He turned his back to the wind and spoke into a cellular phone. "Two targets are down, but alive. We'll wrap them up nice and tight and deposit the entire bundle in front of the West Los Angeles Police Department. . . . Yes, ma'am. Should give someone an early Christmas bonus. I'll contact you when we've secured the situation."

He signaled his men with a second nod and they opened the car doors.

11:52 p.m.—Malibu, California

Wade Fields felt something bang his leg. He snubbed the annoyance and nestled closer to Sally. Her shape fit his perfectly, and her warmth healed his damaged body better than a heating pad. Jostled again, Wade rolled onto his side and rubbed his eyes. "What?"

"I said, get up, sleepy."

An ugly brute stood above Wade waving a gun in his face. "Who are you?" Wade shifted his position, moving between the gunman and Sally.

"Name's Lawyer, and I'm the man who's gonna help you see heaven if you don't get your ass off that couch." Two thugs yanked Wade into the air and he staggered to his feet, letting them hold his weight. When Lawyer grabbed Sally, she winced.

"Sally!" Wade sprang straight up, catching one of the intruders in the ear with an elbow and kneeing the other in the side. He lunged for Sally.

"We've had 'nough of that." Lawyer pistol-whipped Wade to the back of the head and laughed as he floundered onto the floor. "Much better. No more trouble outta you." Lawyer pointed the gun at Sally's face. "Or you."

She looked away and knelt beside Wade. "Are you okay?"

"Yes." He watched Lawyer out of the corner of his eye. "Why do people insist on hitting and shooting me?"

"Must be your bubbly personality." She whispered into his ear and helped him to his feet. Wade staggered, trusting in Sally's strength for support, then he squared his shoulders and stood tall in front of Lawyer and his thugs. They would see no fear; he would not give them the pleasure. His confidence waned as he worried about Sally's safety. Escape scenarios ran through his mind, none of them too hopeful. A stupid mistake would cost them their lives. If they were going to have any chance, Sally had to stay tough, and he had to be careful.

"Thinkin' 'bout gettin' away?" Lawyer rubbed the bruise forming on the side of Wade's cheek with the metal barrel of his chrome-plated Colt 45 automatic. "That's what I'd be doin' right now." He rested the weapon's muzzle between Wade's eyebrows. "It ain't gonna do you any good. You're both gonna die." Lawyer swung his head toward the French doors. "It's a nice night. You could use the fresh air." He waved to his men. "Take 'em."

The four hoods escorted Wade and Sally onto the sundeck. A wind gust knocked them sideways. Blinding rain came down in sheets. Waves crashed on the beach below, sending rumbling vibrations through the redwood planks under Wade's feet. The deck swayed in the storm's torrent and the group bunched together.

Wade reacted to the confusion and swung one man into the other, swooping their legs with one of his own. The thugs collided and sprawled into a pile. When Wade shifted, he found Lawyer ready. Wade swung. Lawyer ducked and moved to the side, where he slammed Wade on the bridge of the nose with the heel of his hand. The blow knocked Wade backwards across the redwood deck. He stumbled, tripped over a potted palm, and landed flat on his back.

Just before Wade hit the deck, Sally dove for Lawyer's throat. He parried her lunge and caught her on the temple with a back fist. She tumbled sideways onto the wet redwood. Wade jumped to his feet, fighting the elements for another charge. A bullet exploded a clay pot next to his leg.

"If we're done screwin' 'round." Lawyer gave Wade an evil grin, spitting rainwater as he spoke. "I want the both of you," he waved the gun, "against the railing. Now!" His three goons crawled to their feet and Lawyer grunted. "Shit for brains. Do somethin' useful and get out of my face."

Wade lifted Sally's limp, wet body into his arms, supporting her head against his chest, protecting her from the slashing rain. She trembled, and he knew she was terrified. Regardless of her fear, she had thrown herself into harm's way. What a woman, incredible.

He watched the gunman's shifty black eyes and it became apparent the crud was not in a hurry to kill them. To tell the truth, Wade was surprised they weren't already dead. Lawyer's sadistic persona was dragging it out, and that, Wade decided, was a mistake. With a little timing, and a strong prayer, he could turn the scum's morbid fascination with torture against him.

* * *

Matt Wells heard thunder rumble outside, and then the door to the bedroom creaked open. He expected to see Wade or Sally, but instead, a hooded figure entered the room. A bad situation carrying a gun had just arrived. Matt tensed.

The intruder stepped left. "Wrong!" Matt let go of Allyx

and vaulted the bed, slamming the killer into the wall.
Grabbing a handful of thick dirty hair, he rammed a
cheekbone into the oak dresser. The candle snuffed out.
As his head rebounded, Matt quickly twisted and slung
an elbow into the thug's jaw. Bone cracked and blood
spewed down his attacker's mouth. The thug doubled-
over unconscious. A second intruder burst through the
doorway, shoving a handgun into Matt's face.

"Don't move, man!"

The gun barrel grazed his forehead and Matt's eyes widened. A shadow blurred by the bed. He ignored it, staying
fixated on the weapon, watching for the slightest twitch.
Then he saw Allyx, on the edge of his peripheral vision.
She grabbed the bedpost and swung by him high and
fast, whacking the gunman in the temple with a round-
house kick. The pistol spiraled into the air and Matt dove
left. A shot fired. A bullet embedded in the wall above
his shoulder.

When Matt looked up, Allyx had landed on both feet,
still moving. She raised her right foot with catlike reflexes
and sidekicked the man in the knee. Cartilage snapped and
his leg buckled.

Matt sat stunned, an observer. "Now that had to hurt."

The gunman dropped onto his other knee as Allyx spun
around to his right. She raised her leg at the last minute
and hooked him with her heel across the bridge of the
nose. His eyes glazed over. He wobbled and fell to the
floor next to his partner. The entire skirmish lasted less
than half a minute; he hadn't stood a chance. Matt shook
his head, eyeing the two bodies, and then Allyx.

She frowned. "What?"

"Just glad you put on some underwear."

Allyx smirked and slugged him in the shoulder.

Matt shrugged her off and squatted next to the first
hood. "Help me get their weapons and tie them up."

*   *   *

A gunshot's discharge exploded above the noise of the hammering waves. Sally recoiled as Wade's head twisted toward a second story window. Rain pelted his unprotected face. He suddenly lost hope for Matt and Allyx. "God, please help them."

"What the hell?" Lawyer yelled, and shook his finger at his men. "You two, check it." Wade caught sight of a grimace on their faces. Where had the gunshot come from? Apparently, Lawyer wasn't entirely certain. Maybe they weren't supposed to kill Matt and Allyx, at least not yet.

"You stay with me," Lawyer said to his remaining thug.

The rampaging storm and gunshot had created additional confusion among the thugs, providing Wade and Sally a sudden window of opportunity. Wade studied Lawyer's rain-soaked features for any indication of what he suspected, then eased forward. Patience, Wade repeated. Wait for an opening. When the two thugs went into the house, the odds would be cut in half. Take the chance; rush them then.

"Sorry to disappoint you." Lawyer raised his gun. "This is where we part company. But before we do the fun stuff, I've gotta ask you about a briefcase. You've got something that doesn't belong to you."

"I'm not giving you shit," Wade grunted. "You're going to kill us anyway."

"True, but I can make it less painful."

"Go to hell."

"Your choice." Lawyer pointed the gun at Sally's kneecap and cocked the hammer. "Trust me, this is gonna hurt."

*   *   *

"I'll go first." Matt scanned the hallway.

"Why do you always go first? Some sort of macho

thing?"

"All right, you go first . . . but keep your pretty head down."

Allyx crept into the hallway. Matt moved up behind her. She stopped next to the stairwell, motioning with a wave of her hand for him to stay close to the wall. As if he needed the encouragement.

"Did you see something?"

"Women's intuition."

Matt arched an eyebrow.

"I heard voices. Does that make you feel better?"

"Yes. Do you know how to use that?" Matt pointed to the pistol she held in her right hand, one of the two weapons they had removed from the unconscious hoods.

She ejected the clip from the Russian-made 9mm Markov, counted eight rounds, and shoved it inside the handle butt. With a quick movement, she pulled on the slide and released it, then nudged the safety into the firing position with her thumb. "Action's a little stiff."

Matt gave her an approving smile while holding his borrowed 9mm, Ruger P94 auto pistol with both hands, pointing it down the hallway. The weapon of a criminal, light to his touch. He had noted the high capacity magazine had twelve rounds left. One had been fired during their scuffle. Had the other two missing bullets been used in a crime, even a murder? Matt mumbled a quiet prayer that when this went down, he'd fire fast and shoot straight.

"Are you ready?"

Her tone had such casual confidence it made Matt's skin crawl. "As ready as I'll ever be. You take the right. I'll go left." She moved into place without question.

"Count three," Allyx said as she raised her weapon, "and we take the stairs."

"On three," Matt acknowledged. He detected a fighter's will to succeed in her expression. This woman knew no limits. Matt sucked in a chest full of oxygen and sprinted to the other side of the stairwell where he pressed his back into the wall.

Allyx held up three fingers. Matt's heart pounded in his ears. She dropped one. His pulse raced; he smelled his own sweat. The second finger went down and he squeezed the pistol's handgrip. He could do this. The third finger rolled into a fist. Matt held his breath and inched around the corner, crouching in the stairway alongside Allyx.

* * *

"Stop!" Wade yelled. "Don't shoot!"

"Give me the case."

"I can't."

"Then she dies slowly, painfully."

Wade looked down at Sally. As she recovered her senses, the physical weight of holding her might have lightened, but the emotional weight of her life in his hands had become very heavy. Still dazed by Lawyer's vicious blow to her head, she appeared so fragile in his arms. He could not let her die, nor could he dare take another crack at Lawyer. What choice did he have but to give in to the crud's demands?

"I'll make it go quick if you tell me where the briefcase is."

Holding Sally close, Wade stumbled backward and banged into the waist-high redwood railing. He peeked over. Spray from the huge waves flared into the air as the sea crashed against the pilings supporting the house. With or without the information, Lawyer would kill them and dump their dead bodies into the ocean. Wade gazed into Sally's eyes. "I'm sorry. There's nothing I can do."

She held him by the waist. Rainwater streamed down her face and her eyes carried no bitterness. He shook his head, it can't end like this.

*   *   *

It happened so fast Matt thought the living room shadows had tricked him. Then he saw it, a very subtle change. Allyx crouched to his right—still as stone. Had she caught the movement? Using his peripheral vision, he tried to penetrate the darkness at the bottom of the stairs. Someone was hidden beyond his view, waiting.

Matt took a slow, calculated step. A shadow shifted. "Shit!" He fired and dove for Allyx, grabbing her arm and cartwheeling into the upstairs hallway.

Two gun blasts lit the stairwell behind him while bullets zinged overhead. One hit a bookcase to the right of Matt's face. He ducked reflexively and crawled to Allyx, where he propped himself against the wall, breathing deeply.

"I'd say we have more company. Are you okay?"

"Yeah," she said. "Thanks."

"My pleasure."

She stared deep into the darkened stairwell. "What the hell do we do now? The bedroom telephone was dead when I tried it and we're trapped up here."

He calmed his breathing, listening to the sounds of the ocean, and the creaks of the house. "You have an uncanny ability to paint the blackest picture."

"And you don't? Come on, Matt. For all we know, they've already killed Sally and Wade."

*   *   *

Wade heard a strong rumbling noise. A vibration shook his legs. He glared at Lawyer. "Do it if you've got the balls." He was tired of being someone's target. "We're not telling you anything."

Lawyer laughed. "Man, if my balls got any bigger, I'd have to hire help to carry 'em. Lights out, honky." More gunshots rang out from inside the house. Lawyer squeezed the trigger as the deck began to shift. His feet slipped and he dove for the French doors.

A bullet creased Wade above the left ear at the same instant the redwood floor came apart under his feet. He twisted and fell, surrounded by broken timbers. Sally hugged his waist as they plummeted toward the thrashing ocean. Wade slammed into the water with Sally and half the sundeck landing on top of him. The frigid sea swamped his head; total darkness engulfed his mind.

*   *   *

"Matt!" Allyx yelled.

The beach house shook and dipped toward the sea. "Oh, crap!" Matt lost the pistol and dug his fingers into the short shag carpet. Pictures fell to the floor. A bookcase crashed at the end of the hallway. The shaking subsided; leaving the house tilted at a precarious angle.

Rain pounded the broken windows. Walls creaked under the pressure of the wind. "Allyx, are you okay?"

"Yes, I think so. Was that an earthquake?"

"No. Wrong kind of shaking. Waves must have undercut the foundation. This house isn't going to be able to take a whole lot more. We've got to get out."

She stood, holding the wall for support. "Maybe now we can sneak by those thugs downstairs."

Matt rose to his knees. "It's worth a—"

"I don't like being called a thug, bitch," a man said, holding the barrel of his pistol against the small of Matt's neck, just below his skull. "Dump the gun, before I cap you and your boyfriend."

"Damn, this night's taken a turn for the worse." Matt caught a glimpse of Allyx. She had moved ever so slightly, taking a better angle.

"You ain't seen nothin' yet, man. Now do it, asshole!"

The cold steel barrel rubbed Matt's skin and he searched Allyx's face while his fists flexed. Her only chance was to

keep the weapon; take the shot. These guys had no intent of ever letting either of them live. Could she do it?
He didn't speak, imploring her with his eyes to take the
hood down. She knew what he wanted. The gun rose.

"I can't, Matt." Allyx set the pistol on the carpet
and pushed it across the hallway with her bare toe. She
held out her empty hands.

"Smart girl. Now get your tight little ass downstairs."
Matt tensed, his eyes burned. "Don't try anything cute,
stud. Move." He shoved Matt toward the stairwell.

October 14

"Don't worry, it'll be light soon. We'll be all right then." James Monal curled up against the braided stalk of a strangler fig tree as he caressed Kelly's cheek, holding her in his arms, slowly rocking. She felt frail, no longer that tough newswoman who had gone toe-to-toe with Dr. Isling.

What a sight they were that day on São Gabriel da Anjo's dusty street: Dr. Isling's foot stomping and gruff voice echoing off the buildings, Kelly's auburn hair blowing in the breeze and her cool professional, businesslike manner. The professor's floppy expedition hat hung on the side of his head and the sweat stains grew under his arms and along his back. Heat radiated above Kelly's starched gray two-piece suit as she stood strong, defiant in the burning sun. James laughed at the image of the two. His eyes began to sting and he wiped them with the back of his hand. The man who had introduced him to the wonders of the ancient world was gone. In one brutal instant, James had lost everything he held dear. He was alone, lost.

Kelly wiggled and buried herself deeper into his shirt. Her skin was cold to his touch and when she shivered, James pulled her closer. Why had she come to him now? Where could they go? Why was Dr. Henry Isling killed?

Confusion, loss, remorse, James' head spun. What if Dr. Isling wasn't dead? He could be calling for him. James: the scared little boy who abandoned his friends. "Please, no!"

"What, James?" Her voice was soft and shallow. "What did you say?"

"Nothing, Kelly. Don't worry—rest."

The rustle of a bush startled him. In his mind, he pictured predators lurking in the darkness, positioning to pounce. Then there were the Burbános, trailing the three of them, prolonging their agony, pushing their sanity to the limit. Their evil eyes peered through the creeping foliage, thirsting for sacrifice. Their expressionless tattooed faces, traceable to over four thousand years of Maya history, worn as a symbol of honor to their brutal gods of war. He smelled the fresh blood on their hands and smeared over their bodies. With a quick and almost imperceptible movement, their poison tipped arrows would fly, and the killing would begin again.

They had to get up, make it to the river. Aidan and Kelly depended on him. Where had everyone gone? "Dr. Isling! Ann! I'm sorry!" They beckoned for him to end their pain, to stop their suffering. Tears streamed down his cheeks.

12:48 a.m.—Malibu, California

Matt Wells held Allyx's hand, keeping her at his side. Downstairs was a shambles, reminiscent of his townhouse. The sudden shift in the beach house's foundation had tweaked everything. Paintings had been knocked off the walls and shelves packed with mementos had fallen to the floor. With all the damage, it was surprising the double-pane glass windows overlooking the Pacific were still intact. However, the view through the main window was dismal; the sundeck was gone. Wind and rain vibrated the glass, and for the first time in his life, the sight of the ocean gave Matt a dark and ominous feeling.

He panned the room, hoping to find Wade and Sally. Allyx shrugged her shoulders and gave him an almost imperceptible shake of her head. The strain in her expression was obvious; she too was worried about their friends.

"If you're wonderin'," a burly man draped in drenched clothing said, "your two buds and one of my men decided to take a swim."

"No!" Allyx yelled, but the apparent leader just smiled as another thug took up his position, putting one on each side of Matt and Allyx.

Matt laid his arm across Allyx's shoulders. A forlorn sense of hopelessness sank its teeth into his will to fight. He should have grasped the situation long ago; they couldn't win. Money, power: their adversary had too much of each. Just like the others, Wade and Sally were dead too. If he and Allyx hadn't come to Malibu, they might still be alive. Allyx reached up and pressed her hand into his, lacing their fingers, and squeezing. She must have sensed his doubts, his feeling of responsibility and loss. When Matt explored her eyes, those deep brown pools, he saw she had not given up, and neither would he. There had to be a way.

"Sit!" The man pointed to the couch.

Moving slowly and cautiously, Matt watched the gunman's actions for a glimmer of empathy or a sign of weakness, anything to suggest they had a chance. Instead, all he found was cold and sadistic emptiness. Even facing the obvious odds, their best option was to fight. Allyx was a match for any man. He nudged her leg. She had to be ready and react quickly when he made his move.

As Allyx prepared, the subtle change in her demeanor was hardly noticeable. Her body tensed ever so slightly, assessing the men, measuring their capabilities. Matt hooked the edge of the couch with his fingertips, positioning his legs to propel him onto the closest man, waiting for an opening.

Their leader took one man aside and whispered, pointing at the stairs. They were going to find the two thugs that he and Allyx had whacked in the bedroom. The situation was changing, becoming dynamic. He watched and waited.

When the third man, the one they called Parks, left the room, one of the remaining two men flanked the couch, keeping his distance. Their repositioning made a direct assault difficult and dangerous. Matt noticed the frustration on Allyx's face, and before things became even more desperate, he decided to act. A light tap on Allyx's hand with his finger signaled her to get ready. Matt slowly inhaled as he looked—

The window to the left of the French doors disintegrated. A spherical black rock bounced into the center of the living room. Everyone stared. Rain poured past the broken glass. An expanding flood spread across the hardwood floor. Wind gusts swirled and the thunder of breaking waves reverberated between the walls. The downstairs had become a maelstrom of confusion.

No longer so cocky, the two remaining men moved farther away from the couch. Their mood said something had gone wrong. Matt shifted to one side, keeping them in view, primed to take advantage of their indecision. When his gaze passed over the rock, he suddenly dove for Allyx—a instinctive move.

An eardrum-ripping explosion knocked him backward followed by a flash of bright light. Completely disoriented, his ears pounded, and his vision had turned into a white-and-black speckled blur. Of his remaining senses, smell and touch were the only ones that functioned.

Matt groped his way along the couch and found Allyx lying on her side. He pulled her toward him, using his body as a shield. At first she put up a weak fight, then calmed when she realized it was him. He held her in his arms, uncertain what came next.

Fighting the ringing in his ears, Matt felt heavy footsteps hit the hardwood floor, then he discerned angry voices and scuffling. Rain splattered on the windows and floor. Shots echoed. Silence.

Someone pressed down on his shoulder, holding him still.

6:29 a.m.—Rio Negro, Brazil

James Monal observed a bright light through his blurred vision and it struck him as odd. An evil black jungle was the last thing that he remembered. He tried to concentrate, focusing his mind to summon details since he had fled the Burbános site. Trees, vines, and fear were all that he could recall. Since his jungle nightmare remained sketchy, James concentrated on the present.

The sides of whatever he was lying on chaffed his wrists. Its surface felt familiar, and he grabbed hold of the rough canvas material, running his fingers along the support poles. Was he on a cot? They must have made it to the base camp.

"Don't move," was all he heard before a large pair of hands held him down. He fought to get loose, jerking sideways, but wasn't strong enough to break free and slumped onto his back.

"Where . . . where, am I?"

"You're on the trawler, James. It's me, Brian, and Dr. Thorne's here also." The hands loosened their grip on his shoulders.

James propped himself onto his elbows and the room swirled, tilting a different direction with each movement of his head. His vision worsened. He fought the nausea. The sweet odor of fresh paint and gear oil hit him. He flopped onto his back. "I can't remember . . . Kelly!"

"I'm right here, James." She grabbed his hand.

Her voice calmed him, and the tension in his muscles evaporated. His eyes began to adapt to the cabin's fluorescent light as he looked into the faces of the Biodiversity Team, then he saw Kelly on a cot next to him.

"How did you find us?"

Brian glanced uncomfortably toward Dr. Thorne. "Just before sunrise this morning, we stopped at your base camp to see how things were going. We found it in shambles. A search of the jungle turned up you and Kelly."

Air escaped from James' lungs as though someone had sucked them dry. The clearing, the jungle, the campsite: it all hit him.

"No. That's not right. Aidan was with us."

Silence followed as Brian looked away. "James, you need rest. Cuts on your arms and legs are infected, and you might have other injuries that require more serious attention. We can talk later."

James grabbed Brian's arm, pulling himself up. "Where is he?"

"We didn't find him. Just you and Kelly." James gave Brian a blank stare. "We were lucky to find the two of you."

"That means . . . they're all gone." James let go of Brian's arm and collapsed onto the cot. "Everyone's gone." His heart pounded. Kelly squeezed his hand. They had to live to tell the story. They had no other choice. Those were Dr. Isling's last instructions.

"Rest now," Dr. Thorne said as he guided Brian and his team to the door. "We'll arrive at the mission clinic soon. They will take good care of you there."

"But . . ." Brian frowned. "We can have a helicopter meet us and send them on to Manaus."

"It'll be okay," Dr. Thorne assured. "Missionaries in these remote places are equipped to handle the sick and injured. Brazil averages one trained doctor for every ten thousand people, and in these rural areas, professional physicians are all but nonexistent. Normally, not the best of odds if you get injured." He ushered Brian out. "You two get some rest. You'll soon be in the capable hands of Father DeLeon."

The door closed and Kelly leaned over and kissed James. "You saved me."

He didn't know how to respond. No words existed that could express his feelings. Her pale face, scratched and bruised, held his heart and love. In her blue eyes, James saw the strength and beauty he had beheld that first day on the street outside the cantina.

Kelly sensed his turmoil, as she gave him a warm and sympathetic smile. "We'll be home soon, James."

"I guess."

She reached over and caressed his cheek. "What are you thinking about?"

"Oh nothing, just my brother. I was wondering what he was doing right now."

"Are you two close?"

"Very."

"Tell me about him."

"Matt, yeah. He's really my half brother; only a year older than me. We had different dads." James laughed. "He got the wild genes; you'd like him. He's a Mechanical Engineer at San Diego State."

"I look forward to meeting him soon."

When James didn't say anything more, Kelly rolled onto her side. "It hurts. I know."

"It's just . . . when we get to the States, you'll head south and I'll return to Stanford."

"Oh." Kelly let his hand go and gave him an introspective smirk. "When I last checked, INN had affiliates up that way. I'm tired of LA anyway." She leaned over his cot and kissed him again, this time on the forehead. "Sorry I lost your orchid."

He took her hand into both of his. "I'll get you another."

"And I'll hold you to that." She flopped onto her back. "But right now, James, all I want is a chicken fajita from the Hollywood Hard Rock® Café."

"Hmm," he laughed, then coughed. "A plate heaped full of spicy fries."

She closed her eyes. "Two overflowing glasses of draft beer."

"I'll buy you one of those 'save the planet' hats," he said.

"I'll get you a polo shirt embroidered with Hollywood Hard Rock®, and then we can . . ."

James watched Kelly drift off to sleep as he dreamed of a life spent with her. The smooth outline of her jaw, the upturned shape of her tiny nose: Kelly Karrie was a beautiful woman. She appeared so content. Her chest rose and fell with each small breath. Was this how it was to end? The Maya believed every death created a new beginning.

3:29 a.m.—Malibu, California

A woman with smooth ebony skin and a full head of graying curly hair flicked a penlight in both of Matt Well's eyes. "No more bright lights. Please." Matt held his hands up.

"Sure." She switched it off.

The woman sat on the coffee table in front of him. She wore a black pullover sweater and charcoal gray slacks. Her expression was calm and reassuring, but her dark eyes probed Matt's consciousness. "How do you feel?" she asked.

"I'd be doing better if my head quit pounding." Matt rubbed his aching temples with his fingertips.

"That will pass."

"What the hell happened?"

"Sorry, we used flash-bangs to mask our entry."

"Who are you?"

"Name's Naomi Giles and this is my team." She pointed to the men scattered around the room, and then she held out her hand. "I'm a friend of Wade Fields."

"He never mentioned you." First Matt then Allyx shook Naomi's hand.

"That's because, officially, we never met. Wade's brother, Tim, handled our assorted business arrangements."

"So, Ms. Giles, you're the mysterious contact."

"Call me Naomi. And you must be Matt and Allyx?"

She knew their names. Matt was taken back, but he assumed Wade had told her. Naomi was obviously well informed. "That's correct."

Allyx adjusted her shirt and swept back her hair. "What happened? Where is everyone?"

"If you're referring to your unwanted guests, they've been bundled up and are on their way to the police."

Matt appraised the room. "What a mess. Naomi, can you tell us what happened to Wade and Sally?" A man carrying a black leather briefcase moved in behind Naomi.

"Give me a minute please, Matt."

"We found this upstairs as reported, ma'am."

"Thank you." Naomi motioned and the man set the case down. "Get the team together and prepare to leave."

"Yes, ma'am."

The two interacted with military precision. Matt wondered if there was more to this woman than Wade had suspected.

Naomi popped open the case and nodded with satisfaction. She rifled through the papers, cassette tapes, and computer disks, then closed the lid and spun the locks.

"Now, where were we?"

Her smile was disarming; yet, her serious expression hinted at hidden truths. "Wade and Sally?" Matt watched Naomi suspiciously. He hoped his doubts about the woman were the residual affects of a bad night rather than another one of those apocalyptic feelings.

Naomi stood and walked to the French doors. Leaning her shoulder on the wall, she studied the gloom outside. One of her men had covered the broken window to her left with a walnut bookcase, shutting out the storm. "Best we can tell, they went into the water with the redwood deck."

"That's terrible," Allyx placed her hand over her mouth.

"I wish I'd gotten here sooner," Naomi said. "Maybe things would have been different. I just didn't have enough of the pieces."

Matt put his arm around Allyx. "How did they find us?"

"Based on our intelligence gathering, BenaTex's management suspected something was amiss and wired the offices and homes of certain employees, ones that might not support the company line."

"Was that legal?" Allyx asked.

"Not really. They used the pretext of protecting themselves from corporate espionage. I suspect they also hired an outside private firm to do their dirty work. The information they collected enabled them to zero in on Wade right away." Naomi returned to the coffee table and set the briefcase on her lap. "A transmitter was placed in his briefcase. They used it to track his movements." She pointed to a small metallic object wedged in the corner seam of the case's leather cover.

"It's so tiny." Matt peered at the device, running his hand along the seam. "This is right out of some spy flick. Was that how they were able to ambush him in Santa Cruz?"

"I assume so. The unit was damaged after the attack, when he fell into the San Lorenzo River. That's why they lost him."

"Then how did they follow him to Sally Brinkman's place in Half Moon Bay? She must have been on their list."

"Correct, Matt. That's how I see it."

"But Sally got away after the call from her boss and brought Wade here," Allyx added. "Too bad their escape was short lived."

"Wish it had been different," Naomi said.

"She gave up everything for him." Allyx's attention wandered toward the ocean.

When Matt reached for her hand, she pulled away and stood, then walked to the French doors. A moment later, she retreated to the kitchen.

"How did they find this place?" Matt asked.

"We're not certain." Naomi handed the briefcase to one of her men. "Please put this in the car. Thank you." The man left, and Naomi turned back to Matt. "My guess is the same way you did."

"The call to Dr. Ruhpor's office."

"Precisely."

"I don't understand. Why was Dr. Ruhpor targeted?"

"BenaTex had subcontracted him to isolate a natural viral strain with specific characteristics, one which they could genetically fine-tune. His project knowledge and curious nature proved meddlesome to the company. To protect themselves, they had him removed along with his principal graduate student."

Allyx returned from the kitchen. "What would drive someone to hurt innocent people over a stupid virus?"

No matter how tough Matt thought she was, her eyes told the truth. Allyx's pain tore at his emotions. He wanted to erase the hurt and punish those responsible.

"How does genetic terrorism sound?" Naomi asked. "The virus is—was—intended to be used as a weapon. The world is intimately familiar with the ravages of new 'tough' viruses, ones with immunity to conventional treatment technologies. Their mutation has set the groundwork for a catastrophe. Few events are more chilling than full-color photographs of a virus-ravaged village or historical accounts of burning bodies during the Black Plague of medieval England, especially when those events strike in our own backyard. In this country, we have the Hanta virus, Africa has Ebola, Asia has Dengue Hemorrhagic Fever, and so on. New viruses are springing up every day. Just look at the outcry when a few elderly people died from anthrax after September 11th."

"I don't get it." Matt shook his head.

"It's not so difficult. Imagine wielding a lethal virus at will? One that could be discreetly introduced into any community, flourishing undetected, spreading geometrically among its unsuspecting victims? Then when the dormancy period ends, death reigns as the virus attacks the human immune system with impunity. And think, if there was an ethnicity based target group, the medical community would be stumped, rendered irrelevant. The symptoms would resemble a multitude of common illnesses. Later mutations of the original strain would lead to more aggressive outbreaks. Billions of dollars could be extorted from governments based on the terror factor alone. Then there's the monetary value of researching and developing an actual cure. And those are only the financial angles."

"This is monstrous," Allyx said. "It's inhuman."

"Perhaps. But not everyone values life as highly as you or me. During the peak of South Africa's apartheid, the ruling party's military experimented with diseases that attacked black Africans: a modern and subliminal form of genocide. Consider the biological experiments conducted by the Nazis and the Japanese during World War II. And, until its repeal in 1997, our government granted the military the right to test biological agents on unsuspecting human subjects. Based on our information, there's no denying, BenaTex's retrovirus was developed to attack specific human characteristics."

"This is disgusting." Allyx shook her head. "Genetics is supposed to benefit humanity, not tear it down."

"I fully agree with you."

Matt wasn't convinced. The whole thing seemed a far

stretch to him, a sort of twilight zone reality. "Only way this genetic terrorism scenario works is if you've already developed the cure. Otherwise, it could get out of control."

"Correct again. Mapping the virus' genetic structure and mode of transmission is key to its exploitation. Based on recent events, we even suspect that someone might be experimenting with disease introduction right now. There's an unexplained and suspicious outbreak of a variant of the Ebola virus in Zaire."

"Just seems to get more disgusting by the minute," Allyx moaned.

"I know it all sounds shocking, but it's not that uncommon. As we speak, the Australian government has imported a strain of Myxomis to contain their wild rabbit population. Unfortunately for the Australians, shortly after its initial introduction the virus coevolved and lost its virility, requiring a reintroduction of the original strain. The rabbit's adaptation is a form of natural selection, a typical response when a biological entity is impacted by a nonindigenous disease. The same sort of genetic drift happens with humans, just a little slower."

Allyx gave her an incredulous grimace. "How many people would have to die to achieve this evolutionary immunity?"

"That's the problem, isn't it?"

The implication was lost on Matt. He was more concerned with their immediate troubles. "The top guys at BenaTex are dead, who's running the show?" Naomi paused and Matt interpreted uncertainty in her expression.

"For your own safety, it's better if we don't discuss every detail. Let me assure you, the responsible man will be taken care of." One of Naomi's men whispered into her ear. "Right now, the most important thing is to get clear of this house. If that storm has its way, we're all going to need rescuing."

"Where can we go?" Allyx gave Matt an insecure frown as her attention bounced between him and Naomi.

"I've taken care of that. You're spending the night at the Hotel Sofitel, uptown on Beverly Boulevard. It'll get you out of the way of this storm. And tomorrow, one of my people will drive you to Cal Poly."

"Where life is calm and gunmen are few," Matt quipped.

Allyx chewed on her lower lip.

Naomi pointed at the door. "We have to leave now. The road won't be passable much longer."

Matt and Allyx glanced at each other.

"I can see you're hesitant." Naomi gave them a warm smile. "You have to trust someone." She waved her hand toward the door. "Shall we go?"

4:42 a.m.—Wilshire Boulevard, West Los Angeles, California

Naomi Giles pressed a black button on the right side, console panel and the limousine's opaque window divider rose, isolating the spacious backseat. She reclined against the padded leather, listening to the rain hit the roof and the wind whip alongside the car. The first phase of her mission was complete. Matt and Allyx were safely on their way to the hotel.

Naomi took the moment to relax. How she ever got sucked into such a solitary existence was beyond her comprehension. She never imagined it would go this far, and even though her mission was necessary, the constant vigilance had worn her down. All too often, her job was a thankless effort to protect a science she had begun to question. Then there were the people she had helped. Were they what kept her going, or was it pride?

"You didn't tell them everything?" the man sitting across from Naomi asked; his face barely visible in the limo's weak interior light.

"No." Rainwater streamed down the tinted side window. "For their own safety, I deemed it best to omit a few details."

"What will happen to them now?"

"We'll soon cut the head off the lead dog, and hopefully, their lives will return to normal."

"Normalcy after losing their professor and almost being killed themselves?"

"They've experienced an extraordinary ordeal, I agree, but we've made arrangements."

"Oh?"

"When they arrive at school, they'll find a few improvements, ones intended to soften the blow." Naomi frowned, saddened by the events. "Dr. Ruhpor appears to have been a special man. His death is very unfortunate. Some things are beyond even our control."

The man sitting opposite Naomi slouched along the spacious seat, and the exhausted woman with him slept in his arms. "They're young," the man said. "They have plenty of time to recover."

"I wish I was so young," Naomi responded.

"You'll outlive us all. Oh, and by the way, thanks."

"My pleasure. Besides, you did all the hard stuff. All I had to do was show up." Naomi patted him on the knee. "The doctor said you need rest. It's been a long night."

"We owe you everything." He closed his eyes and dozed off.

Naomi watched them sleep. "No, I owe you."

The limo veered onto the southbound 405 Freeway. In a couple of miles they'd take 10 east to Ontario. LAX and Burbank airports had canceled their flights due to the bad weather, narrowing her window of opportunity. Naomi had a private jet to catch, and one more thing to finish.

9:53 a.m.—Mission São Gabriel da Anjo, Brazil

The side of the trawler banged the pier, and before the vessel had completely stopped, Father DeLeon, accompanied by four native workers, hurried onboard. Dr. Thorne and Brian met them on the lower deck. Cordialities were brief and the men followed the biologists to where James and Kelly rested. When they entered the cabin, they found the young man and woman sound asleep.

"Please leave them on the cots," Father DeLeon requested. "My people will carry them to the mission clinic."

"Are you sure you don't want our help?" Thorne asked, staring at the young couple the way an attentive parent watched over his children. No one could imagine the horrendous nightmare they must have experienced. Soon, they would tell their story, and he would learn what happened to his friend Henry Isling and the others.

"Your assistance will not be necessary. We will be quite all right."

"I'd be happy to go along," Brian said.

"No, thank you." The priest glanced sadly toward James. "The symptoms you described suggest complications. If they worsen, we will have to send them on to Manaus." The missionary gestured for the natives to take the cots away.

"I hope that's not the case, Father," Thorne said. "It's imperative we talk with them. We have to know what happened to the others. The authorities are also going to have questions."

"I will do all in my power. We must go."

"They're going to be all right, aren't they?" Brian repositioned his massive body in front of the doorway.

The missionary's eyes narrowed as he approached Brian. "We have their best interests in mind. You may come and see them after they have received proper rest and care."

"But—"

Thorne placed his hand on Brian's shoulder. "If you say so, Father. We'll be upriver until the end of the week. Please notify us if their condition worsens."

"I will do so, my son." The workers carried the cots onto the deck as the missionary led the way. The door swung shut.

Brian shook his head. "I don't like this. He seemed defensive to me."

"He feels the pressure, Brian. The failure of the Stanford expedition and the investigation that's going to follow puts his mission in the center of attention."

"I'm not comfortable leaving them."

"Neither am I. To settle both our minds, I'll cut our trip upriver short and we can see how they're doing in a day or two. We can also stop by the campsite and see if the authorities have found anything."

Brian frowned. "I sound like a whiner."

"Don't worry about it." Thorne led him out of the cabin. "Now get to work. We have things to do."

With Brian gone to the upper deck, Thorne stood alone, trying to shake free of his own worries. He walked to the railing and watched the native laborers carry the cots along the shabby pier. Sunlight reflected off glassy ripples shimmering on the surface of the black river. The morning seemed hotter than usual and he wiped his forehead with the back of his hand. "Good luck, my friends. May God be with you." He didn't know why he had said that, but it seemed appropriate.

9:33 a.m—San Francisco, California

Jolon Steele sat comfortably in his studded leather executive's chair, puffing a cigar and watching smoke billow into the air. He ran the cigar beneath his nose, appreciating its sweet smell, thinking about his personal assistant. World events were moving toward their foregone conclusion, as it had been laid down in the ancient prophecy. His objective would soon be completed. The Maya would reign again in the year 2012, with him as their political leader. He grinned; the future was his. The main double doors to his office parted and three men and one woman entered.

"Who let you into my office?" Steele set his cigar in the ashtray and sat up straight.

"We all have our connections, Mr. Steele."

"What do you want?" He pressed the intercom button, summoning his secretary. She didn't answer.

The intruders closed the door.

"Do I know you?"

"Possibly—the name's Naomi Giles." They closed on Steele and two of the beefier men next to Giles flanked the desk. Steele remained seated. "Mr. Steele, I don't have patience for pleasantries, nor do these gentlemen, so if you'd please come with us?"

"I will not!" He sprang to his feet. "How dare you enter my office and put demands on me? I will call security and have you thrown out of here."

"Highly doubtful," Naomi said. "I've had a long night with no sleep, and I'd appreciate it if you'd come quietly."

Steele felt his resolve falter, then he regained his confidence. They had nothing on him. Obviously, these morons had no idea whom they faced. "You have nerve coming here."

She approached the desk and stared at Steele, eye-to-eye. "No, you're the one with the nerve."

"I will break you for this, bitch." Steele swung his head to the side in a show of disdain.

"Not today." One corner of her mouth curled upward. "You're on your way to a career digging graves in some third-world country. Maybe even Zaire."

"What are you talking about?" Steele sneered, but hesitated when Giles held up a VHS videotape. "Is that supposed to intimidate me?"

"It should. It's a special selection, direct from your office video library if I'm not mistaken. Oh, and it's the first of a three-part collection that also includes computer documentation and laboratory research data."

"Bullshit. I have never seen that before." No wonder he had not heard from that fucking Osborne. Steele's hands balled into fists.

A large man wearing a dark suit entered the room. Giles handed him the tape and watched as he placed it inside a briefcase, then left. "Consider it a gift from an anonymous patron of our business." A subtle hand gesture from Giles and the two men by the desk stepped toward Steele. "You have a choice. You can come with us or go to the police. Either way, these men are prepared to remove you."

"You cannot do this. I have powerful friends."

"Don't count on them. Genocide and murder tend to upset people." Giles motioned to the office door. "This way, please. We have a helicopter waiting."

"Can I at least take a few cigars with me for the trip?"

Giles shrugged, then motioned for her men to move closer. "If you wish."

Steele reached into his cigar case. He felt the knife, hidden under the ragged cloth. His fingers wrapped around the hilt. With one swipe, he could end this charade. Giles eyed him, as if she knew. The two bodyguards stiffened.

"Mr. Steele." Giles gestured to the door with an empty hand. "Judgment day is here."

The top to the cigar case clapped shut and Steele dropped it on the desk. "You will see, Ms. Giles. My time has just begun." He lit a cigar.

"Never assume." She smiled, then frowned. "Get him out of my sight." The two men grabbed Steele by the arms and escorted him from the office. Naomi let them pass, then hit the light switch and closed the doors.

2:23 p.m.—Mission São Gabriel da Anjo, Brazil

James Monal's eyes were open, although his body had not yet responded. His mind drifted in a murky fog, clearing the remnants of a hazy dream. He examined his surroundings using his peripheral vision. The room had a vague familiarity and he tried to remember.

He recalled the sensation of floating in the air, the hot sun beating down on his face, and the sound of water slapping the shore. They must have picked him up on the boat. Brian had mentioned the mission. James inhaled a stale musty odor. Had they arrived at the Mission São Gabriel da Anjo? Why couldn't he move? He heard a voice.

"Do not struggle." Someone stood in the shadows to his right. Why was he hidden? James felt his panic grow.

"The drug I gave you is similar to *Succinylcholine*, a common muscle relaxant used by medical doctors during surgery. Unlike your people's modern version, our drug has been refined over the centuries and does not affect the lungs. You will be able to breathe during the entire procedure, awake and aware, with all your senses alive and sharp, however, I am afraid, unable to physically respond."

What procedure? James strained to move his body. What happened to Kelly? Where's Brian and the others?

"There is confusion in your expression. Understandable. You see, my ancestry dates back four and a half centuries, to the era of the great scholars. Those who first ruled this land."

A man in a white robe came into view. Thank God, Father DeLeon. He'll know what to do. "Help me, Father." James called, but no sound escaped his mouth. He was a paralyzed mute.

"You still do not fully understand, my son. It is important you do."

The missionary lingered above James' head, his black eyes wild and glassy, and his hot, herb-tainted breath beat down on James' face. A horrified chill coursed through his body. He had been listening to Father DeLeon all along.

"I am the reincarnated Feather Serpent man-god, Quetzalcóatl. I will guide my people to glory."

Oh my Jesus, he's crazy. Two Indians moved into positions by James. One resembled the man he had seen the day they arrived at the dock. The other was . . . Ernesto! You son-of-a-bitch! Where are my friends? He had set them up. It had been a trap all along.

Through his helpless rage, he caught something strange. Ernesto wore the sparse clothing and jade jewelry of a Maya. The vision awakened something in James and he understood. They had recreated a ceremonial atmosphere. Garlic, maybe curry, and other even more aromatic scents were in the air. The smell, the lighting, the basement: he was hidden away in one of the rooms the archaeological team had not been allowed to enter. Then he remembered the clearing and the fresh blood on the altar stone.

"Ah, you see a humble Jesuit missionary." Father DeLeon began to disrobe. "Although many of my people have embraced Catholicism, we have not forgotten the true origin of our past." He disappeared from view. When the missionary returned, he was dressed in little more than a brown loincloth. His face was painted and his bare chest had the tattooed scars of a Maya high priest.

James realized the danger, yet he was entranced by the sensations permeating the room, the energy was strong and vibrant. Images of temples and thousands of undulating naked bodies swirled though his mind. He stood atop a great pyramid looking down upon the masses. They had come to see him, to see the sacrifice.

The vision disappeared as James thought of Kelly. What had they done with her? He prayed they had left her on the trawler. Men—warriors—were a more valuable sacrifice to the Maya gods. Women had other uses, but she had auburn hair, which to the Maya was a sign of spiritual power. He had to know. Father DeLeon continued, oblivious to James' fears and thoughts. The priest was zoning, transitioning into a religious epiphany, losing touch with the humanity on the table before him.

"I did warn you. Now it is too late. You desecrated our sacred ground and the gods demand the blood ritual."

Father DeLeon looked deep into James' frozen eyes. "In a way, by experiencing an authentic ritual of an ancient culture, you are achieving the ultimate aspiration of an archaeologist. This is the greatest gift I can give you. Soon, your spirits will be liberated by the pain, and you will abandon your Christian way to be with the one true god."

He said, "your." Who was in here with him? No, not Kelly!

"Your mercenaries considered us laboratory mice for their evil genocide experiments. They are now dead, and we will survive, as we always have. For our time is here. Yours has run out. You will join the others in death and my people will once again vanish beyond the prying eyes of your technology. I can see by your stare, you do not comprehend all I say. It no longer matters. The moment has come to take you to the next level of enlightenment. Through pain you will understand."

The missionary had transformed himself into the man-god, placing a feather-laden crocodile headdress over his head and shoulders. James' stomach wrenched into a massive knot. Apparently, those muscles were not affected by the priest's concoction. A glimmer of hope formed and his mind began to race. Was the drug's influence wearing thin?

"Before long, as it was foretold, my people will break the bonds of Western tyranny. On the dawn of the next Spring Solstice we will leave the protection of our mountains, and from that day forth, Maya from Brazil to Mexico will stand up for their rights. All they need is their god, and he is here, in me!"

Ernesto leaned forward and James recognized the sound of tearing fabric as his shirt was ripped away. Cool air swept across his naked skin. He felt light, suspended in the air, no longer restricted by the confines of his body. Kelly was in the room. First, he perceived her presence in his mind, then he saw her lying next to him on a large steel table. How strange that he was able to physically see her. He could not explain the experience, the sensation; it felt so real.

She was horrified. The clothes had been torn from her body. Effigies were marked in blood on her creamy skin. The face of a deformed human skull had been drawn between her parted breasts. The more she fought the drug, the more terrified she became. If James could hold her, speak to her, he could ease her fear. He visualized the ritual sacrifice and imagined the excruciating pain she would have to endure. His own sadness slowly began to consume him. Death would be her only salvation. He had to stop them.

James begged his body to rebel against the drug. A tingling started in his fingertips and he concentrated to sustain it, but quickly lost the sensation. He blocked the distractions, trying to repeat the movement. Nothing happened.

As James surrendered to despair, Father DeLeon— Quetzalcóatl—recited an ancient Maya chant. His words echoed against the barren walls. He circled the table, facing four different directions with each pass. The ceremony had begun. A finger on James' left hand flinched, then another.

Father DeLeon stopped and raised his head. Chanting in Mayan, he asked the gods to accept these meager sacrifices. The missionary stretched his arms to the ceiling, holding a ceremonial scepter high into the air. Its blunted end was shaped into a gray oblong sphere and the carved handle showed the thirteen levels of the Maya ascension. Dried blood stained the wicked weapon. James sensed muscle control returning in his other hand—a twitch. He had to hurry.

The chanting hushed and Father DeLeon met James' gaze. At that instant, he conceded there was no escape. His love for Kelly would not be allowed to grow. He would neither experience her touch nor hear her voice again. What they had . . .

The scepter came crashing down.

October 15

Dr. Leland's hands gripped the sides of the podium. His heart beat deep and irregular as he struggled to maintain his composure, to make it through the next forty-five minutes. This was his last official act before his retirement took effect.

He looked above the crowd, intentionally not focusing on anyone in particular, and began. "Deeply disturbing news reached our office at seven-thirty yesterday morning. We received notification from the Brazilian government that our archaeological team had met with disaster. The information was initially kept confidential in the hope that two of the surviving members, James Monal of Stanford and Kelly Karrie of Independent News Network would recover and shed light upon the whereabouts of the rest of our team." He paused, regaining his self-control. "However, James and Kelly's nightmare had rendered them delirious and while under medical care at the local mission, they wandered into the jungle. Their remains were discovered this morning by native workers during an exhaustive search of the region surrounding São Gabriel da Anjo."

Shocked silence followed his announcement, then a reporter raised his hand. "Dr. Leland, will there be an investigation?"

"Yes, the Brazilian government is conducting one, but we don't hold much hope. It's their belief that our team befell to the inherent dangers of the Amazon jungle and they don't expect any survivors."

"Who rescued Ms. Karrie and Mr. Monal and took them to the mission?"

"By a stroke of good fortune, a research team from the University of Arizona was in the area. They found James and Kelly unconscious a few yards from the team's jungle base camp."

"Dr. Leland, who identified the bodies of Ms. Karrie and Mr. Monal?" Joe Lines with the Oakland Tribune asked.

"Father DeLeon. He's the same missionary who was helping them. I'm sorry. I can't continue. Thank you for coming. We'll have a written statement available later today."

Stevie Walton of the San Francisco Times waved her hand. "I'm sorry to hear about your colleagues, Dr. Leland. Does this conclude the expedition?"

He turned back around, his head dipped low. "I'm afraid so. We have no indication the team was onto anything and the original records vanished with them."

A young woman wearing a baseball cap over her short black hair stood at the back of the room, away from the crowd, avoiding their whispers. Her features appeared Native American, possibly even Spanish; few knew the truth. She listened intently, watching the reactions of the correspondents and Professor Leland. What fools they were.

She had warned them. Her people would not fall victim to their deceit again. The last phase of the true calendar was upon the white devils and judgment was on its way. She smiled; the world had evolved to the next ascension of humankind. The age of Christianity had ended.

5:22 p.m.—The Mosel River, Wincheringen, Germany

A young girl hung onto the top of a black iron railing, part of a stone bridge that crossed westerly above the Mosel River. Her shoulder-length brown hair blew in the breeze as she stood on her tiptoes. The girl leaned over the railing and plucked a flower growing in a planter next to a sandstone pillar. In the center of the pillar was a plaque with Wincheringen stenciled in gold and blue letters above a small road map. She referenced the map, her eyebrows scrunched down, then she pointed. "Luxembourg, Daddy?"

Wade Fields gave her a pleased smile. "Yes, sweetheart. We'll cross the bridge tomorrow morning and tour the Grand Duchy."

"Cool." Lost in her daydreams, the girl's gaze trailed off in the direction of Luxembourg's green rolling hills. A sweet-smelling breeze blew leaves into the air around her ankles. Behind her, at the base of a small foothill, was the center of Wincheringen, an old-world German village located in the wine country southwest of Trier. She held onto the railing and pointed to a sleek, white motor yacht traveling the Mosel toward Rehlingen. She waved energetically when the vessel passed under the bridge, delighted by simple things, the way only an innocent child could be.

It had been too long since Wade had taken simple joy in Adrienne's innocent expression, full of love and laughter.

"She's beautiful," Sally said.

"She sure is." He stretched his legs beneath the café's wrought iron table, sipped his wine, and eyed Sally lustfully.

"Stop it, Wade. You know what I mean."

"Yes, I do." He took another sip and relaxed.

"Is this truly what you want?" Sally asked, placing

her hand on his.

Wade set his wine glass on the table. "When I lost my wife, my daughter, Adrienne, became everything to me. I was convinced there'd never be anyone else to share my life with again." His daughter climbed along the top of the railing. "When we met, I knew right away that I'd be a fool if I ever lost a chance with you."

"All I want is for you and Adrienne to be happy." Sally held his hand.

He gave her a serious expression. "I will be if you say yes."

She kissed him on the cheek. "You have my answer. What about Adrienne?"

"When I mentioned it to her, the response was something like, 'Gee, Dad, took you long enough.' "

Sally laughed, and Wade detected the stress in her voice. Her beliefs had been trashed; her trust shattered. BenaTex was her catalyst for a better world. He hoped with his help, her nightmares would fade and the healing would begin.

Wade looked into her eyes, remembering when they had first met. She was stuffy and thought he was a jerk. He chuckled, she was right.

"I'll never understand. Donner and Singular were good men. What happened to them?"

He cradled her hand in both of his. "They lost sight of what we're about and broke our most intimate trust. As geneticists, we shall never subvert nature's gifts."

Sally sighed. "If not for Giles and her men in that pontoon boat, we'd have died, drowned in the ocean that night." She watched swells form along the river, their wavelets slapping the rock supports beneath the bridge. "Someday, we'll have to go back."

"Don't worry so much. No one can find us, and with the money we retrieved from my safe, we can make a new future for ourselves."

"Please hold me, Wade."

His arms encircled her shoulders. "I love you."

"I know."

11:29 a.m.—Spring, Texas

Naomi Giles and Greg Gunder sat on the open-air patio of a secluded saloon north of Houston. Their table choice was more a function of avoiding construction debris than preference. The bar's interior was being renovated, at least that was what the owner called his interesting work-manship with random sheets of knotty white pine.

The other patrons did not appear to mind climbing over two-by-fours and bellying up to an unfinished bar—they were Texans. Nonexistent seating and substantial chaos did not bother the business at the four active pool tables either. Boisterous couples smacked balls and flirted over beers. Naomi watched the inside activities with a degree of detachment. Here's to you," she said, holding up her beer and drinking.

"Ah, you were the one to bring it together," Gunder replied.

"I wouldn't say that. Timely calls from you, Claire, and a few of the others helped. And Fields' information was pivotal. He and the kid led us to Ruhpor's data."

Gunder bowed his head as a salute. "Modest to the end."

Cajun spices streamed beneath Naomi's nostrils as a plate heaped full of boiled crawfish was set in the middle of the table. Their bite-sized, appendage ridden, seasoned red bodies made her throat constrict. How any vaguely normal person could swallow the tiny mudsuckers was beyond her comprehension.

Greg expertly pinched and pulled one in half, then gobbled down the exposed morsel of whitish meat. Naomi had just witnessed the barbaric act of a demented mind and a strong stomach. "Barbaric. How can you eat those things?"

"With enough beer in me, they become kind of seductive." Gunder consumed the innards of another crustacean. "Sure you don't want some?"

"They don't make a beer stout enough."

"Since I've been in Houston, I've developed a fondness for Cajun food. It grows on you."

"So I see." Naomi pointed to a small bit of meat on the corner of Gunder's mouth, then watched her associate swoop it up with his tongue. "This is gross."

"Come on, Naomi, dive in." Gunder laughed when she grimaced. "Oh well, your loss. If you're not gonna eat, then you must drink." He raised his glass. "To those who have gone before us."

Naomi tapped his glass with her beer bottle. "To our friends, may they rest comfortably wherever they may be."

The show on the television above the bar switched to an INN station broadcast and they shifted their attention to the wide screen. Naomi read in the announcer's expression that she was genuinely moved by the story.

"Today, INN received a confirming report from a high-placed Brazilian government source that Kelly Karrie died while on assignment in the Amazon Jungle. Miss Karrie died while in the company of James Monal, a member of the Stanford archaeological team. They were the sole survivors of an ill-fated expedition into the Amazon Lowlands. A preliminary finding showed they died as a result of injuries received during an attack by wild leopards. At seven-thirty Eastern time on October 29, INN will run a special feature documenting Kelly's career."

A low altitude aerial view of downtown Long Beach opened to the left of the news correspondent. The changing image showed downed trees and damaged buildings. "In Southern California this morning, Governor Rothman assessed the aftermath of Tropical Storm Lisa. His private helicopter flew over the ravaged coastline and the hard hit inland locations of Orange County. At the peak of the storm, three embedded tornadoes touched down in southeastern Long Beach and massive waves wreaked havoc on the harbor. Damage estimates for Lisa have reached 2.3 billion and are still rising. During his news conference, the governor 'thanked God' that the storm had lost some of her momentum before coming onshore. In an emotional moment, he emphasized 'Californians were going to remember the impact of Lisa for many years to come.' "

The view of Long Beach was replaced with a green and yellow line graph depicting the latest activity for the Dow Jones Industrial Average. The chart showed a fluctuating slide of two hundred and sixty-seven points. "Business news today took a negative dip when the president of Janstone Pharmaceuticals announced his resignation. Jolon Steele had risen to his position within the company during the mid 1990s. He was considered by his peers to be the American pharmaceutical industry's single most influential person, spending the last two decades as an acclaimed advisor to three US presidents. He was regarded as a visionary of alternative medicines. Although Mr. Steele was unavailable for questions, on his behalf, Janstone's vice president Al Garver cited medical reasons for his sudden and unexpected departure."

Naomi watched Gunder's reaction. "Well?"

"Things worked out."

"Yes, as good as we could have hoped. We have Dr. Ruhpor's research data, a sample of the retrovirus, and most of the BenaTex stuff."

"Too bad we didn't get everything."

"But an analysis of the altered and unaltered retrovirus should tell us something."

"Yeah, I guess. But that will take time." Gunder scratched his chin with his hand. "You know, we'll never be sure if there aren't other samples of the retrovirus out there. Basically, we still don't know the why's and where's about Steele and his pet project."

"And he'll never talk," Naomi added. "The Republic of Zaire will see to that.

"True. It's a shame so many answers went to the grave with Singular and Donner. What a waste of good talent." Gunder drank his beer, then wiped his mouth with a napkin. "I still say someone ran Steele."

"We do what we can."

"You're so philosophical." Gunder's expression took on an unusual seriousness. "Will we ever discover who sent you the tapes?"

"Doubtful. Most likely a sudden change of conscience brought it about."

"We might not have nailed Steele without them."

"I don't believe that. We'd have found a way."

"We always seem to." Gunder rolled his beer glass between his hands. "This time was different though. Steele, he was different."

"Be glad, he's Zaire's problem now."

"A little of his own medicine."

"True enough." Naomi pictured Steele striped naked, huddled in the corner of a dirty, stoned-wall cell, lesions covering his body . . . A woman inside the bar squealed with delight.

Gunder smirked. "Someone's in a good mood. Why do you think Steele did it?"

"What drives anyone? Greed? Power? Who's to say?"

"The guy didn't seem like the type who could be seduced by the normal human weaknesses. He had a certain air about him. I'm just glad this one's over. He was scary." Gunder gulped his beer.

"It's never really over." Naomi swirled her beer in the bottle, watching the foam stick to the sides. "Someone's always in the background, ready to take their place. Whether it's another company or another egomaniac, the game's still the same."

"You're a lot of fun." Gunder raised his glass. "Then until the next one comes along."

"The next one." Naomi sipped her beer and gazed across the table at the plate piled high with steamy crawfish. "Yes, always a next one."

9:31 a.m.—Central Coast, California

Matt Wells and Allyx Katero parted company once reaching Cal Poly, the day after Tropical Storm Lisa devastated the Southern California coast. They had things to do, lives to reclaim. Dear friends were gone, and the realization of how little control they had over their own destiny was hard to accept. For Matt, that was only part of the story. That night in Malibu had altered his reality. He was not the same nearsighted man who viewed women as sports toys while holding his emotions in check.

Matt stopped outside the Science building and took his time to savor the serene Central Coast sky and a mild easterly breeze. The sun warmed his face as vivid memories tugged at his heart. A vision of Allyx strolling barefoot on the damp Malibu sand made him smile. Of all the women he had been with, Allyx was the most remarkable. She provided him a wholeness he had never known before. He had also found a passion within her, a passion that shed light upon himself and his past, helping him to see the walls he had built and the future he wanted. With all that had happened to them, how could Allyx be gone forever?

He wrestled with his desire to chase after her. If she saw the new Matt Wells, would that make the difference? But then, there were his self-doubts. He had never pursued a woman before. Maybe such an impulsive emotional reaction was not wise. She needed time to sort through things. Any feelings Allyx had for him, had to come at her own pace, on her own terms. If Fate deemed that he'd never see her . . . No, that wasn't right. That's the old Matt's way of thinking. He had found the woman he wanted.

"Damn, this is getting—"

"You could get trampled stopping in front of a doorway like that."

Matt spun around. "Huh, what?"

"I see your astute wit's at it again."

"Allyx!" Uncertainties masked his ability to speak. Did she seek him out, or was this meeting merely by chance?

"Don't give me that lost puppy-dog pout. What? Did you think I had forgotten you?"

"The possibility crossed my mind." Reddish highlights in Allyx's hair shimmered, reminding him of the splintered light of a morning sun as it rose high above the Pacific horizon. Matt savored the vision but kept his distance, afraid to make the first move.

He recalled his intimate revelations that night in Malibu. Risking everything for someone special was what life was about. Gambling with his emotions was the one thing he had never been willing, or able, to do. Matt crossed his fingers. The time to take a chance was now.

"You did it to me again."

Her eyebrows arched upward, imitating Matt. "Did what?"

"What you do."

"What I do what?"

"Unbalance me. Mess with my head."

"Don't blame me for your head problems."

"There you go."

"It's not intentional."

"Sure it is." Matt grabbed Allyx and pulled her close, sliding his hands into the back pockets of her jeans.

"But—"

He kissed her.

Allyx slipped her arms under his. "Humm. Guess you did miss me."

"You could say that."

"Sorry I disappeared. I had to deal with stuff. Which of course, also included you."

He understood. Not enough time had passed to help him organize his own feelings about her and cope with the deaths of so many good people. Yet, as they stood outside the Science building, he realized being near Allyx made all the difference. He felt free. His shoulders relaxed—a dozen or so years of doubt suddenly evaporated.

"Allyx, I know that, well, uh . . . , you and the Doc had a, uh, personal relationship, and . . . but . . . ah, crap, Allyx, I'll just say it. You touched my heart in ways that no one ever has, and I—"

She placed her fingers on his mouth. "Sometimes, Matt Wells, you're awfully dense. Trust me when I tell you, I've worked out all my emotional questions. Dr. Ruhpor was simply a good friend, and you're the one I want more from."

"You're not going to tell me—?"

"Nope."

He arched an eyebrow. "Where do we go from here?"

"Oh I don't know. Seems that you owe me a laundry list of commitments."

"And I always pay my debts." Matt scrunched his lips together and gave her a warm smile. "A week ago my goals were simple: make it to class and get myself. Well . . . you know, a guy thing." He hesitated. "Now, those same desires seem strangely foreign to me, like it was another person who had them."

"What can I say, Mr. Wells? Emotional maturity is inevitable, even for you. But don't lose hope. I'm sure a few strands of childishness still linger inside you somewhere."

"Thanks." He ogled her with a devilish grin.

"You're so weird, Matt." Allyx gave him a playful kiss on the cheek. "By the way, a lot has happened during your time of self-discovery." She tilted her head toward the blue sky and ran her fingers through her hair. Her tan cheekbones glowed with a faint blush. "Did you see the proposal for the new science wing in the Mustang Daily?" she asked.

"Sure did. Apparently, Janstone Pharmaceuticals thought highly of the Doc. Sounds like guilt to me."

"Guilty enough to donate twenty-three million to the university in the professor's name. I also heard your dean, what's his name?"

"Dr. Theim."

"That his departure was tied to the donation."

"One of those no-return sabbaticals I assume. A one-way trip into academic oblivion."

"Coincidence if you ask me, and I know how much you believe in them."

"To name one of many." Matt pulled her even closer. He could feel her heart beat against his chest.

"Was there something else?" she asked, catching the playful gleam in his eyes.

"It seems BenaTex left me a gift: an irrevocable, full-ride scholarship. They also sent a letter requesting that I go to Sausalito and discuss stock options. Something to do with an endowment. I didn't quite get it."

"Pretty cool," she smirked. "As it happens, a financial aid award letter was waiting when I arrived at my apartment. Apparently, some anonymous contributor just paved my academic future, which also tied me up since we got back."

"Will wonders never cease?"

"Maybe not, Mr. Wells. Our rental car tab was paid by another anonymous friend."

"So was my credit card bill. Are we being bought off or what?"

"You think?"

"Sure feels like it."

A man leaving the Science building bumped into Matt. They made eye contact. He was near six feet tall and medium build, but strange as it seemed, Matt wasn't certain. The man's physical characteristics seemed to morph with his movements. If not for the cold stare of his greenish eyes, he would have passed unnoticed.

"Excuse me," the man said, and tipped his head. "Glad to see you're doing well; happy holidays." He moved on, whistling a melodic Irish tune.

"Interesting," Matt said.

"Holidays?" Allyx shook her head. "Do you know that guy?"

"Nope, and right now, I don't care either way." He gave her a long slow kiss. "The heck with finances and school. You're all I want to think about."

"Hmm, I can tell. What do you say we start on your list?" She smiled mischievously.

"I say . . ." Matt watched Allyx as a light gust swirled into the air. Her white tank top softly fluttered while the peaceful sounds of leaves rustled on a bush next to her. "What we need is a real vacation."

"Oh," she said. "I'm seeing a warm sun and an expansive beach."

Matt laughed. "Skimpy bathing suits, and funny colored drinks."

Her eyes rolled in mock exasperation. "Bathing suits?"

"Sunburn protection?" He blushed.

She laughed.

"This term's garbage anyway, and my meeting with BenaTex can wait. Can you be ready by noon?"

"Already packed."

"Amazing. I can't wait to introduce you to my brother, James."

"If he's anything like you, that'll be interesting."

"He's nothing like me." Matt laughed. "Then it's on to new adventures."

Allyx gave him a nod. "No looking back."

The shadows along Cal Poly's main road wavered. He placed his arm around her small waist and she rested her head on his shoulder. The rustling leaves hushed. "No looking back."

She reached up and kissed him.

*   *   *

Osborne entered a large grassy expanse overshadowed by a Spanish-style clock tower. The entire lawn was packed with students and the sight reassured him that he had made the correct decision by involving Naomi Giles. Pleased with himself, he walked with an uncharacteristic skip in his step. Who could have imagined this was how things would end?

Covering his ass against Steele had been a huge gamble, an act of self-preservation more than anything else. In Osborne's unique line of business, considering all the angles was a necessity, except the process did not usually include crossing your client. However, Steele was a special case, requiring a more proactive approach and minor adjustments to Osborne's standard operational practices. Swiping high-tech secrets was one thing, killing innocent people was another. Still, client crossing made referrals a tad difficult to come by. If Osborne was serious about staying in his current occupation, he had to remove that last sliver of nagging bothersome moral fiber—it was bad for business.

In the final analysis, the call had not been that difficult. Osborne had intuitively known the Malibu job might crater and had assumed he would have more trouble with Steele. Successful or not, Jolon Steele would have gotten rid of anyone even remotely associated with his private project. So Osborne bought life insurance when he sent Giles—who happened to have been a previous client—an anonymous gift.

Interesting how things always seemed to find their natural balance. The kids lived and Steele had been sequestered to his new calling. Evidence in hand, Osborne remained skeptical that Steele was gone forever. The man wielded a great deal of power and many connected people owed him favors. Seldom did men like that disappear for long. If Steele ever did surface again, the kids had more to worry about than Osborne; he was used to looking over his shoulder.

Although Osborne would never admit to it, his concern for the two students had prompted this unscheduled visit to Cal Poly, which was another interesting twist of moral consciousness for him, especially after planning their deaths a few days earlier. The calmness he felt when he saw Matt Wells and Allyx Katero together was an interesting experience. They were going to be all right. And if nothing else, this meeting with Wells was less exciting than their previous encounter outside Dr. Ruhpor's office.

Osborne looked up, admiring the simplicity of the striated clouds streaking across the powder blue sky. It seemed, lately, that the only thing he could count on was change. Maybe there was hope for him after all.

10:33 p.m.—Chicago, Illinois

The metal security door locked behind him and the Ambassador listened to the hum of the air conditioner, which he guessed was actually a white noise transmitter; another of the devices employed by the Twelve to block eavesdropping. These were the most powerful men in the world, a society so secret only a handful of people even suspected they existed, and the Ambassador assumed they took every precaution to protect their interest.

The group was formed in 1946 when an assortment of industrialists and financiers came together to rebuild a fragmented global economy. World War II was a direct result of incompetent leadership. The ruling elite had become weak and could neither direct international markets nor manage rogue dictators. In a desperate move, two clandestine agencies, one from England and the other from the United States, made an alliance with what would evolve into the *Group of Twelve*, an off-shoot to the *Order of the Skull and Bones*.

The Allies sought the Twelve's assistance in restoring world stability, but they declined the invitation, preferring to implement their own master plan. Aligned with no specific country, the Group of Twelve wielded their unchecked power by covertly implementing their policies. Financial domination was their mission. Assassinations, market manipulations, strategic police actions: these became their essential tools. The world was simply a three-dimensional Chessboard, and giving-and-taking were all part of the game.

To the Twelve's credit, they had successfully manipulated global affairs for over half of a century. Unlike those wannabee political hacks and pocket dictators who make their pitiful presence known on INN's nightly news, the Twelve took direct and decisive action. And the Ambassador was one of their knights, executing their directives without question.

After associating with the Twelve for more years than he cared to count, the thought of who they were and what they had accomplished still gave him an excited chill. He pulled his cardigan tightly around his neck and then assessed the meeting room—always cautious.

Ceiling lights were on low, the dark gray walls barren, and the air temperature barely in the sixties. The starkness of the rectangular space was unsettling. Twelve large screen monitors supported on molded aluminum stands formed a half circle encompassing the center of the room; the rest of the concrete floor space had been left vacant. The Ambassador approached a center monitor. When he closed within three feet, an image appeared. His contact—the only one he had ever met in person.

The sharply dressed man was relatively young, no

older than his late forties, an Italian-born Swiss banker, who obviously was not one of the original Twelve. A descendant, thought the Ambassador. He had often wondered how they handled attrition. Most likely they still recruited from the cream of Harvard's elite.

"Steele?" the man inquired, getting right to the point.

"Terminated." Another chess piece sacrificed to further a pending play by the Twelve.

"Location?"

"A holding cell in Zaire."

"Did he suspect?

"Our connection? No." The deluded son-of-a-bitch never had a clue.

"Did he talk?"

The Ambassador hacked back a wet raspy cough. Years of skulking in-and-around disease-ridden Third World countries had mutilated his left lung. "Excuse me, sir." He turned away and wiped the corner of his mouth before facing the screen again. "We have found no indication that he shared his knowledge or suspicions with anyone else."

"What of the man who gave him up?"

"Osborne?" His boss gave him an angled nod. "Disappeared." The Ambassador wondered, why did Osborne turn on Steele? Osborne was a pro and his betrayal had been unexpected, even uncharacteristic. Had the Ambassador missed something?

"Unfortunate. And Naomi Giles."

"Too high of a profile right now, and too well protected."

"You'll have to contend with them both soon."

"Understood." The Ambassador smiled. He lived for a challenging quarry; there were so few left.

"The others?"

"Ignorant pawns. Not worth the trouble."

"The virus?"

"Handled."

"You've done well."

"Will that be all?"

"Yes."

The monitor went blank.

11:53 p.m.—Washington, District of Columbia

"If you want to live long and stay healthy, do nothing to endanger yourself while in the room." Darren Michaels repeated their instructions, over-and-over. He checked his SCBA for a third time, relieved to find the air pressure numbers had held steady. When he had asked his employers what would happen if he had an accident, they just stared and said, "Don't."

They called him when they had a job no one else wanted, and despite his better judgment, he always said yes. The money was good and paid in cash. While standing in front of a polished vault-like titanium door, his decision seemed rather impulsive.

He punched a seven-digit alphanumeric code into an electronic pad, then held his hand on a holographic palm-reader. He replaced and resealed his glove when a green light above his head switched on. The vault door swung aside with an audible hiss as the negative pressure inside the sealed room sucked air past him. Standing in the opening, Darren verified that the VELCRO™ wrist and ankle straps on his powder blue biosuit were sealed, and he was clear of any sharp objects—keeping with his employer's instructions.

Hesitantly, he plodded through the doorway, then entered a second code into another keypad and watched the door close behind him. His ears popped as the filtration system vacuumed all the oxygen out of the room. They warned him about the claustrophobia, but he had no idea how intense it would be. The sensation increased as he became more uncomfortable with his artificial imprisonment within the blue biosuit. He closed his eyes and chanted a personal mantra, ignoring the fact that only two things prevented him from having an unpleasant death: three millimeters of thin plastic and an airpack on his back. Even though the supplied air inside his positive pressure suit was extremely dry, sweat had soaked through his undershirt.

When Darren opened his eyes again, he stood in a very long and narrow room, forty feet in length, and at most, fifteen feet wide. The wall in front of him contained hundreds of stainless steel doors, jamming the space from the floor to the extra high ceiling. Each of the ten-inch doors was numbered according to their row and column position. He read the engraved, nonreactive brass labels until he found number 6-24.

Darren approached the wall and entered a code into a third keypad. The small door opened and a shelf extended from the wall. He held down a yellow button on the pad and rotated the stainless steel carousel inside the compartment. An empty slot appeared and he stopped the rotation. This part of the procedure was the most dangerous.

He placed the stainless steel cylinder he had been carrying on the shelf, removed the lid and extracted a narrow glass vial. The green liquid swirled with a metallic glow, like it was alive. His skin crawled as goose bumps formed on his flesh. He inserted the vial into the open slot and locked it down, only then did he breathe again.

Once Darren secured the door, he scowled at the other enclosures. What did they contain? Their glistening, barren steel facades gave him the creeps. He turned his back to the wall and walked away, swearing, big money or not, he would never return.

Trust, but verify.
—President Ronald Reagan (1911 -)